continued . . .

BUBBLES
ALL THE WAY

Sarah Strohmeyer

AN ONYX BOOK

ONYX
Published by New American Library, a division of
Penguin Group (USA) Inc., 375 Hudson Street,
New York, New York 10014, USA
Penguin Group (Canada), 90 Eglinton Avenue East, Suite 700, Toronto,
Ontario M4P 2Y3, Canada (a division of Pearson Penguin Canada Inc.)
Penguin Books Ltd., 80 Strand, London WC2R 0RL, England
Penguin Ireland, 25 St. Stephen's Green, Dublin 2,
Ireland (a division of Penguin Books Ltd.)
Penguin Group (Australia), 250 Camberwell Road, Camberwell, Victoria 3124,
Australia (a division of Pearson Australia Group Pty. Ltd.)
Penguin Books India Pvt. Ltd., 11 Community Centre, Panchsheel Park,
New Delhi - 110 017, India
Penguin Group (NZ), cnr Airborne and Rosedale Roads, Albany,
Auckland 1310, New Zealand (a division of Pearson New Zealand Ltd.)
Penguin Books (South Africa) (Pty.) Ltd., 24 Sturdee Avenue,
Rosebank, Johannesburg 2196, South Africa

Penguin Books Ltd., Registered Offices:
80 Strand, London WC2R 0RL, England

First published by Onyx, an imprint of New American Library,
a division of Penguin Group (USA) Inc.

First Printing, November 2006
10 9 8 7 6 5 4 3 2 1

ACKNOWLEDGMENTS

This book could not have been written without the assistance of Luci Zahray, the "Poison Lady," Gun Tart Nancie Hayes, who gives new meaning to the term "going ballistic," and Stephanie Cotterman, a Bubbleshead who has on more than one occasion come to my aid. Nancy Martin, author of the sizzling Blackbird Sisters mysteries, held my hand through most of this, as did Ellen Edwards, one of the few remaining editors who still meticulously go over each manuscript. Plus, Ellen did a bang-up job in record time. Thank you! It was Charlaine Harris, author of so many engrossing books, including the bestselling Sookie Stackhouse vampire series, who suggested trying Bubbles as a paperback original. And Kathy Sweeney encouraged a radical twist to Bubbles's life. Finally, thank you, Charlie, Anna, and Sam, for cheerfully and willingly tolerating what turned out to be one hellish year.

Chapter One

Debbie Shatsky was the kind of woman that I, Bubbles Yablonsky, loved to loathe.

Just the way she entered a room was obnoxious, pounding her superhigh heels and blinking her big, overdone eyes as though she expected everyone to admire her expensive, genuine leather department store shoes. Or her LOUD VOICE and high-pitched giggle that forced you to pay attention even if you were trying your best not to.

But nothing aggravated me as much as her constant and incessant bragging.

Debbie showed no reservation when it came to boasting about how perfect her life was, how well decorated her house, what unbelievable sales she got at Hess's the rest of us had missed, and how her travel business allowed her to visit the most exotic locations free of charge. Blah, blah, blah, blah, blah.

But the thing—or, rather, the man—she bragged about most was her husband, plumber Phil Shatsky. A colorless, weak-chinned doughboy who could install a whirlpool tub in the bathroom while whipping up a mean crème brûlée in the kitchen. It was enough to make a middle-aged woman go all crazy, thinking about

Phil with an apron on, scrubbing the stove and—pant—matching socks from the laundry.

And those weren't the only devastatingly sexy stunts in Phil's repertoire. He also took out the garbage without being asked, vacuumed the house twice a week, swirled Ti-Dee Bowl in the toilets, scraped leaves from the gutters and did all the grocery shopping—with coupons!

Plus, he never, ever watched televised sports.

On this the female population in our steel town of Lehigh, Pennsylvania, agreed: you could keep your George Clooney; give us a Phil Shatsky any day. Phil Shatsky was a Swiffer-bearing god above all men.

Unfortunately, Deb's favorite place to brag about Phil happened to be in our little pink-walled salon, the House of Beauty, where innocent clients were forced to listen to Phil's feats of greatness, held captive, as they were, by their noble pursuit of beautiful hair and all the strenuous sitting that is required.

"I feel kind of sorry for everyone else, not having husbands who dote on them like Phil does me," Debbie prattled as Sandy and I slaved over her complicated up do. "I mean, I married the perfect guy. You have to admit, I'm the luckiest woman alive."

"You're the luckiest woman alive," Sandy had to admit.

"I just know other women hate me for it."

"I'm sure no one hates you." Sandy smeared on some glue and affixed another champagne blond hair extension to Debbie's scalp so Debbie could have the biggest hair at the Plumbers and Pipe Fitters Local #10 annual Christmas ball that evening. "Right, Bubbles?"

I was pretty sure people hated Debbie, so I didn't say anything. If you can't say something nice about a person, then sit next to me, was the way my mother's favorite saying went.

Besides, Debbie wasn't my client, so I wasn't obligated to suck up. I no longer worked at the House of Beauty, now that I was a full-time reporter at the *News-*

Times. The only reason I was there was because my former boss and forever best friend, Sandy, was swamped. It was the Christmas season, her busiest time of the year. Also, the nuttiest.

This was when Sandy lost all control and turned the House of Beauty into Santa's crack house. Blinking lights were strung everywhere. Tinsel dangled from every mirror. Mistletoe hung over every doorway. There was not just one normal-sized Christmas tree, but three, including a miniature one covered in red-and-green-foil Hershey Kisses that Sandy kept by her register. Not to mention the maniacal plastic Kris Kringles smiling from every window.

And if that weren't enough to cause permanent brain damage, consider that the standard House of Beauty smog of Final Net and nail polish fumes was mixed with Lysol Holiday Pine Breeze. Don't even get me started on the music. If I never again hear Karen Carpenter whine "Merry Christmas, Darling," it won't be too soon.

Sandy gave me one of her meaningful stares, an ocular order to play along with Debbie's need for reassurance. My best friend was under a lot of pressure these days to keep customers happy now that a competing salon—Jeffrey Andre—had opened up in our newly revitalized "warehouse" district. I understood what she needed me to say.

"Of course no one hates you, Debbie. Sandy's right."

Sandy mouthed, *Thank you.*

"You're only saying that because you don't know Marguerite," Debbie said.

"Marguerite?"

"This desperate housewife who's trying to get her claws into my husband, though as far as I'm concerned, she doesn't stand a chance of spit in a windstorm. I mean, Phil choose someone over me? *Puhleese.* Marguerite would have to step over my dead body first."

I tried not to strangle her as she smiled approvingly at her reflection in the mirror.

Debbie took a sip of bottled water and continued chattering. "Have I ever told you Phil does the laundry? He does. Folds and puts away. Pretreats, too. Plus, he even watches Lifetime with me. I can't tell you how many nights we've spent in front of the TV, Phil and I, crying our eyes out over some Victoria Principal movie. And the next thing I know, there we are making the kind of passionate, toe-curling love you only see in those videos. He even lets me sleep on the dry side of the bed afterward."

Was it hot in here? I shifted my feet. Sandy's pupils were dilated, imagining a night of masculine laundry folding, Lifetime viewing and dry-sheet sleeping.

"Yessirree, Phil and I are bound to one another till death do us part."

Sandy's eyes met mine. She didn't have to speak, I knew what she was thinking: *Till death do us part, Bubbles.*

Sandy had been on my case lately because I'd ruined all chances of marrying my own soul mate, the devastatingly sexy Associated Press photographer Steve Stiletto. He of the flashing blue eyes and the tight, creased jeans. The one man who could make my heart stop with a knowing look, the brush of his hand, the suggestive twitch of his lips.

The first time I met Stiletto we were thrown together on an assignment to cover a "jumper" from the Philip J. Fahy Bridge. I knew it was trouble when Stiletto not only violated police orders by climbing onto the bridge, but also positioned himself on a precipice fifty feet above the Lehigh River—just so he could get a great shot of my legs. Also of me falling over the edge.

Of course, any man like that is full of himself, an egotist, overconfident and infamous for having brief, fiery relationships with foolish women. Of course, I was madly in love with him.

What Sandy couldn't understand was why I'd turned

down Stiletto's marriage proposal (and returned his three-carat Harry Winston ring) so I could remarry my ex-husband, Dan, aka "Chip," Ritter.

What Sandy didn't know was that Dan was black-mailing me.

How to describe Dan. He's a lawyer, though not what you'd call high caliber, seeing as he has already been disbarred once and kicked out of his firm with a court order never to return. Plus, he advertises on urinals. How classy is that?

These days he's a personal-injury attorney who habitually leaves his business card on icy parking lots, on grocery aisle floors where Tide's been spilled (by him, no doubt) or any place where a slip and a fall could mean bucks in his pocket.

I had to remarry Dan for one reason and one reason only. I got pregnant—eighteen years ago.

And now our seventeen-year-old daughter, Jane, was going through a serious crisis from being kidnapped last month. After much analysis, the family counselor we'd been seeing, Dr. Lori Caswell, decided the blame for Jane's trauma lay with me and me only. I am, in her professional opinion, an unfit mother, a selfish career woman who through negligence and risk exposed Jane to an extraordinarily nasty crime.

According to Dr. Caswell, I lack even the basic skills of mothering since I let Jane live on A-Treat and Tastykakes and allowed her to pierce several body parts and wear ripped jeans to school. Add to that my licentious relationship with Stiletto, our many nights in his mansion achieving sexual heights that in some parts of Georgia are grounds for imprisonment, and it was a wonder the division of family services hadn't knocked on my door sooner.

Should a judge ask, Dr. Lori Caswell informed me, she was fully prepared to report that Jane should be barred from any and all contact with me and she should move in with Dan. Unless Dan and I remarried. Then Jane could live with both of us—provided Dan kept vigilant watch over my erratic behavior.

Dan had already asked me to remarry him, but I had wavered. Now, with Dr. Caswell's declaration, he held the trump card. I needed to either say yes to his proposal once and for all or lose my daughter. If I turned him down, he vowed to seek an emergency custody revocation order and have Jane removed from my home by Christmas.

So as much as I despised him, as much as I could not bear to sit across the table in view of his puffy face or even hold his fat hand, I said yes. But I agreed only because Jane wanted Dan and me together as parents. She told me she felt safer in a home with a father and a mother under the same roof, more secure, more *normal*. And I would have done anything, *anything,* for Jane to feel normal again.

Next I knew, Dan had started divorce proceedings against his socialite wife, Wendy, in the highly respected jurisdiction of Guam. I had no idea where Guam was. I'd flunked that course: "Seven Foreign Countries Where You Can Get a Quickie Divorce" at my alma mater, Two Guys Community College. Apparently Guam is not a foreign country, but part of America, according to information I later received. (Damn Two Guys and its used 1949 textbooks.)

With the divorce almost final, Dan had arranged for us to get rehitched on Saturday. In fact, as soon as I was done with Debbie, he was picking me up to apply for the license at city hall.

Sandy had no idea what a terrible dagger Dan was holding over me. I was too embarrassed to confide even to her that a psychologist had ruled me an unfit mother. Of all my failures in life—and, trust me, I've failed more than most—this was the absolute worst.

Nor had I been able to tell Stiletto. I mean, what would he think if he knew that I was too much of a screw-up to raise a kid? He'd find me revolting, that's what. Better he remain under the misimpression I was remarrying Dan simply for the sake of Jane and leave it at that.

Though, God, I did miss him. Missed the way his capable hands would slide over my bare hips, how he pressed his hard naked body against me, purposeful, unrelenting, determined ...

"Hey!" Debbie gave me a dirty look. I realized I'd been yanking her hair.

"Sorry," I apologized. It was true what they said in magazines. Sexual frustration can lead to baldness, but only if it's your hairdresser who's frustrated.

Debbie returned to her cell call. I stopped thinking about Stiletto and concentrated on the up do. And then, just as we were finishing her hair extensions and I was applying the last coat of shellac, uh, Final Net, the most awful, devastating, horrific event ever to befall the House of Beauty befell.

Debbie blinked and rubbed her eyes. "Is it getting warmer in here? I feel dizzy."

That was when I noticed the red blotches. First on her neck. *Hickey,* I thought, immediately reconsidering when another red blotch appeared under her ear.

I motioned for Sandy to take a look.

Sandy's very practical and not easily flustered. She wears peach polyester uniforms and keeps her curly brown hair tied up neatly in a matching peach bow. She padded over to inspect.

"Debbie?" she inquired. "Do you feel okay?"

Debbie was clutching her stomach, the cell phone shaking in her hand. "What's wrong with me? I feel so dizzy. I feel like something bad is going to happen." She began to scratch maniacally. Little red welts were popping up all over her arms. Her nose was running like a dripping faucet.

The welts. The dizziness. The running nose. This was an allergic reaction.

"Debbie, are you allergic to anything?" I asked.

"Latex," Sandy said, adding quickly, "but I didn't use it."

"Not that." Debbie wheezed. "Remember? Wheat ... fatal. Shouldn't forget."

A fatal wheat allergy? Holy crap!

Suddenly, Debbie brought her hand to her throat. "Ugh" was all she could manage. "Ugh." Her tongue was swelling and she was breathing funny.

Sandy's eyes widened. "Oh, no. I'm calling 911."

Completely panicked now, I leaned over and slapped Debbie's cheeks. She was going. She was going fast. This was a code blue. Whatever that was.

Sudafed, I thought, grabbing my purse and searching for Benadryl or any antihistamine I could find through the mess of lipsticks, pens, paper, bank receipts and assorted tampons. So much makeup. All my Maybelline for a single EpiPen.

"Does anyone have any Benadryl?" I hollered across the salon.

Sissy Dolan and Trula Kramer, octogenarians in hearing aids, lifted their hair dryers. "What?" they both hollered. "There's a fire drill?"

Oscar, Sandy's miniature poodle, hopped off his plaid doggy bed and began yipping madly just to add to the commotion. I wanted to slap some sense into all of them.

Sandy was on the phone describing the scene to the dispatcher. Before I knew it, sirens were blaring across the South Side. Alerted by their uncanny sixth sense for incoming tragedy, a crowd of babushkas gathered outside, equipped with aluminum lawn chairs and bags of popcorn for the free show. Then an ambulance pulled up and emergency crews rushed through the door. They were so fast, they must have been next door at Manny's Bar and Grille having a beer when the call came in.

Wouldn't be the first time.

Sandy directed them to Debbie, whose face was now

a queer shade of purple. I stepped back and looked away while they did their jobs.

"Where's the fire?" Tula Kramer said, rollers stuck all over her gray hair. "I don't smell no smoke."

Sandy gathered Oscar into her arms and began petting madly as the medics pounded on Debbie's chest and applied oxygen. Finally, after zapping her a couple times with portable defibrillators, they lifted Debbie onto a stretcher, tucked a white sheet around her and carried her to the ambulance.

They left behind Lehigh detective Monica Wilson, otherwise known as "Vavavavoom" or "Vava," for short.

Vava used to be a knockout before she became a cop, starting out as a lowly meter maid and working her way up to the rank of detective. She was busty and tall and gorgeous with high cheekbones and the kind of figure that made men forget their first names.

Vava brought out a tablet and began asking Sandy and me questions: who was Debbie, how old was she, who was her next of kin.

"Next of kin!" Sandy screeched.

"It doesn't look good. They weren't able to resuscitate her. I'm assuming they'll pronounce her DOA at the hospital."

"Oh, no," Sandy wailed, petting Oscar so hard he was getting static cling. "This is horrible. Just horrible."

I thought of Phil. What would he do without his soul mate? Scrap that, what would the single women in my neighborhood do once they found out the most ideal husband in Lehigh had been widowered? There'd be so many casseroles he could open a restaurant.

"Who called in that it was poison?" Vava asked.

"Poison?" Sandy said. "I called 911, but I didn't say anything about poison."

"Well, someone did because at 13:05 an anonymous call came across dispatch that one Debbie Shatsky, age thirty-eight, was in the process of being poisoned at the House of Beauty."

Stunned, Sandy and I looked at each other. I felt an odd sensation at the back of my neck—the one you get when you realize that the due date on your Visa bill changes each month so Visa can collect more late fees.

The feeling you get when you realize you've been set up.

Chapter Two

"That's outrageous," Sandy said. "What kind of creep would make a disgusting crank call like that to the police?"

A handsome, red-haired man in a navy jumpsuit and rubber gloves carrying a kit of test tubes and swabs and other alarming scientific stuff walked through the door. I recognized him as Eric Wachowski, a nice enough guy who went to St. Anne's Catholic Church and was putting himself through med school by working as a tech in the medical examiner's.

I knew all this because he happened to be Sissy Dolan's grandson, which meant as soon as Sissy saw him she would announce to the world that Debbie was dead.

"Crime lab," Vava said flatly. "Mind if he takes a few samples?"

"I have nothing to hide. Go ahead." Sandy tossed him the keys to her office.

Sandy may have had nothing to hide, but as a crime reporter myself—as well as the ex-wife/fiancée of the sleaziest lawyer in town—I wasn't so sure letting the crime lab have free range without a search warrant was such a hot idea. I mean, when a girl's got rights, she needs to protect them.

"Oh, look, it's Eric!" Sissy squealed. "That must mean Debbie didn't make it. That must mean she kicked the bucket."

Tula Kramer gasped.

Sissy waved crazily. "Hi, sweetie! Is wittle Ewwic woowking hawwd?"

Eric waved hi to his grandmother, bowed his head out of mortification from being addressed in baby talk and headed to Sandy's office.

"Why does he have to take samples from there?" Sandy asked, her voice reaching a new level of panic.

"Just following the tip," Vava said.

"Must have been some tip," I observed, "what with all the excruciating detail."

Vava nodded. "It was very thorough, yes. By the way, you know anyone who might have wanted to harm Mrs. Shatsky?"

That was when I remembered the mysterious Marguerite. Right before she broke out in hives, Debbie had been yapping about how this desperate housewife was out to claim Phil and how Marguerite would have to step over her dead body first.

Like they say, be careful what you wish for.

I decided to keep the Marguerite info to myself. This could be a blockbuster news story and I wanted to get to the main suspect before the cops did and ruined all my fun.

"Not really," I answered. "Everyone liked Debbie. Say, Sandy?"

Sandy furrowed her brows.

Vava bent down and picked up the hair extension Sandy had been applying when Debbie suddenly went berserk.

"What's this?" Vava asked, sniffing the glue end of the hair extension.

"A hair extension," Sandy said nervously. "Debbie gets them here all the time."

Vava looked doubtful. "All the time?"

"Whenever she and her husband go out to dinner or a special occasion. She likes to have her hair piled up high."

Had to have the highest hair in the room, that was our Debbie.

"It smells weird," Vava said.

"That's because of the special hypoallergenic glue I have to use. Debbie mixes it herself at home and brings it in." Sandy bit her lip. "That's what I'm afraid of, Officer. Debbie's allergic to latex. Superallergic. She told me once that a pair of false eyelashes could kill her. Or even a condom."

"No kidding," Vava said. "A lethal condom."

And here I'd assumed that was an urban myth boys used to spread in high school.

"It's true," Sandy insisted. "That's why Debbie brings her own glue. She brought a fresh batch today. It's right there. On the vanity."

Vava leaned over and sniffed the small Tupperware container of white stuff. "And is that the glue you used?"

"Oh, absolutely. It's the glue I always use."

Vava snapped on a pair of rubber gloves, pulled out a plastic bag and dropped in the hair extension. Then she got another bag, capped the Tupperware and threw that in.

Sandy's eyes were bugging. She was used to living a normal life, running a respectable salon where nothing dramatic happened except maybe a dryer overheated or the washing machine overfilled. She paid her taxes quarterly, kept her premises litter-free, got a Pap smear every year and invested regularly in her IRA.

She'd been married to the same boring man for twenty boring years, going to bed at eight and waking up at four because he was a baker. She was not used to the police holding hairpieces she owned as evidence or the crime lab going through her back office.

"Are you sure you didn't accidentally confuse Debbie's glue with a latex-based glue?" Vava asked.

"I'm positive." Sandy held up her hand, Girl Scout–like. "I'm always careful."

I came to her defense. "It's true. Sandy is the most conscientious hairdresser I know. If Debbie's dead, it must have been by natural causes or murder."

"Murder?" Vava wrote this down.

Sandy poked me. "Thanks a bunch, Bubbles."

I rushed to clarify. "What I mean is that Sandy would never cause a client's death, at least not through negligence."

"Negligence? Did I just hear my favorite word?"

Dan was pushing his way through the crowd. As usual his black hair was slicked back and he wore a black wool coat. I didn't know what look Dan was going for. Maybe Vampire *GQ*.

His fat white fingers were adorned with garish gold pinky rings, including one for Lehigh University, where we met at a fraternity party and—after five minutes of conversation, one glass of rubbing-alcohol punch and two minutes on a sticky, beer-soaked fraternity floor—conceived our daughter.

I'd forgotten that he was supposed to pick me up so we could get our marriage license today. Funny how that slipped my mind.

"What's all the commotion?" he asked, glancing at Vava, trying to place her.

"We had an accident," I explained. I knew Sandy would be worried that Dan might misconstrue or, worse, might claim to be Phil Shatsky's lawyer and file a lawsuit on the spot. "A client suffered an allergic reaction."

Dan raised an eyebrow. "Is the client okay?"

"Not really," I said. "She's kind of dead."

"That sucks," he said.

Vava pointed her pencil at him. "Aren't you Chip Ritter, the lawyer? You must have broken every speed limit to catch up to that ambulance."

Dan smiled, as if chasing ambulances were a special

talent. "Actually, I was on my way to pick up this little lady." He wrapped his arm around me. "How's about a kiss, foxy mama?" He pursed his bluish, wet lips. They were like two slugs fresh out of the garden.

I fought back a gag.

"You two know each other?" Vava asked.

"He's my ex-husband," I said.

"She's my fiancée," Dan answered.

Vava seemed confused.

"It's complicated," Sandy explained. "Honestly, you don't want to know. It's sordid. Let's get back to Debbie."

A bright light flashed. Over Sandy's shoulder I could see Travis Miner with his omnipresent TV camera. Travis Miner was a patrolling shark, just like Dan, though instead of searching for victims to exploit through litigation, he searched for victims to exploit through grainy cable TV news.

Not that Travis worked for a television station. He was a freelancer—or mercenary, depending on your perspective—who kept two police scanners on his belt and cruised the town, trolling for that mother of all news stories: the five-car pileup, the full-blown house fire or, if lucky, a homicide in a beauty salon.

"What's *he* doing here?" Sandy hissed.

"Don't you worry, Sandy. Let me handle this." Never one to miss an opportunity to grandstand before a television audience, no matter how small or how housebound, Dan brushed off his coat sleeves and marched toward Travis.

"Perhaps I can help you. I'm Chip Ritter of the law firm of Ritter, Ryjeski and Gold. We'll sue when others won't." Dan then molded his eyebrows into his "serious squint," which he always did at the end of his introduction. "What're your concerns, son?"

"Um," said Travis intelligently. "I don't know if you'd exactly call them concerns. I'm looking for the owner. A Sandy something. I got a tip that a murder just took place here."

A murder? I looked to Sandy, who had petted Oscar so his head was a smooth ball while the rest of his fur stood on end.

"There was no murder!" Sandy corrected. "And it wasn't poison."

Travis swung his camera onto her. "Poison, you say. Do you often go around poisoning your clients? And I happened to notice that your license on the wall has expired."

Damn. I'd reminded her about that just yesterday.

Vava went over to check the license and took it off the wall, dropping it in yet another plastic bag.

Sandy burst into fresh tears.

Travis said, "We had a tip this joint was behind code."

"Hmm-mm." Detective Vava Wilson shook her head. "All these tips. There is something fishy going on here."

I checked my watch to see if school was out yet. That might explain the bogus murder tips. Kids.

"Excuse me, Detective Wilson." Eric the lab guy was back, holding another Ziploc bag with something white in it. I noticed that Travis had swung his camera off Sandy and was now focused on the bag.

"Yes, Wachowski?" Vava said.

"Just want you to know that we found this in the locked bathroom in the office. It appears as if someone might have been trying to flush it down the toilet."

Sandy wiped her tears. "But I'm the only one with keys to the bathroom. I didn't put anything down the toilet."

"What is it?" Vava asked.

"It's a type of adhesive," Wachowski said. "It appears to be homemade."

Debbie's hair glue. But why would someone have tried to flush it down the toilet?

"And this?" Vava asked, handing him the bag with the glue Sandy had been using. "Is this latex?"

Wachowski opened the bag and sniffed. There certainly was a heck of a lot of sniffing going on. I mean, how scientific was it to just sniff?

"Well, I haven't run any tests, obviously, but it smells latex-based to me. Pretty strong odor, like a brand-new car."

Thunk! Sandy was on the floor, having fainted. Oscar leaped out of her arms and yipped hysterically.

"Hold on," Dan said to me, stepping over Sandy as if she were driftwood. "Are they saying this client died from an allergic reaction to glue Sandy applied?"

I nodded.

"Well, then, that's a whole different story. Sandy's in a heap of trouble if that's the case." He kicked off Oscar, who was leaping and snapping at his pants leg. "I hope she has good insurance, Sandy, 'cause she's looking at a multimillion-dollar lawsuit. Dang, I'd bring it myself if I wasn't getting married to you, Bubbles. A settlement like that could pay for the entire wedding and then some."

He actually rubbed his hands in greedy glee.

I don't remember what happened next. There was a flash of red, which could have been either my bloodlust or the brand-new press-on nails I'd applied that morning. And then my hands were around Dan's flabby white neck.

Fortunately—or unfortunately, depending on whether you're me—Travis Miner was there to film it all.

Chapter Three

On a good day, a day when he hits four under par, when Hess's takes out two more pages of full-page lingerie ads and First National doesn't call to inquire about his wife's overdrawn checking account, *News-Times* editor in chief Dix Notch is *still* in a bad mood.

But this afternoon, as I stood in the newsroom with him and every other reporter watching the extremely local news on Channel 93, public-access cable, Mr. Notch wore an eerily benign smile.

It was the kind of smile you used to find on mental patients after successful lobotomies. The kind you see on the faces of rich women still sweaty from yoga class when they're shopping for organic quinoa down at the co-op and privately congratulating themselves for being so healthy.

Dix Notch's smile made me feel nostalgic for the good old days, when he would blow his stack and hit things.

"Johnson," he said calmly. "Please play that part again, the part where our beloved Bubbles lunges for Mr. Ritter's throat."

Beloved Bubbles?

Justin Johnson, our high school intern, pressed the rewind button on the remote.

Playing the tape backward, it seemed like Detective Vava Wilson was bringing Dan and me together instead of separating us. It was humorous in a *Funniest Home Videos* kind of way. Mama and her best friend, Genevieve, would have found it knee-slapping, wet-your-pants hysterical.

Johnson freeze-framed the point where I was strangling Dan. At the risk of sounding vain, I have to admit I looked pretty good, considering a woman had just died in front of me, my best friend was being wrongly implicated in her murder and I was running on all sorts of crazed emotions. My roots weren't too black, my sunshine blond hair wasn't too brassy and my legs looked terrific. I've said it before and I'll say it again: leopard-print leotards are a girl's best friend.

Dix Notch cocked his head, as if Dan and I on the screen were monkeys and he was simply curious about our primitive social rituals. "Mind explaining what happened here?"

I stopped to think, forming my words carefully since Mr. Notch tended to so easily misconstrue them.

"Dan was rubbing his hands with glee over the prospect of my best friend getting sued for all she was worth because Debbie Shatsky happened to drop dead in her salon. It was really nasty of him and I just couldn't help myself. I saw his neck and I went for it."

"Okay. I hear your anger. And I'm validating that." He tented his fingers. This was a gesture he did a lot lately. I think it was Buddhist. Or maybe he was showing off his new male manicure. "But let me ask this, if I might. Do you always go about strangling your ex-husband?"

"He isn't my ex," I said. "He's my fiancé."

Notch's eyelids fluttered. "I apologize. Perhaps I don't have my listening ears on."

Okay. What the heck were listening ears? Were they somehow different from regular ears? Maybe there were such things as "eating" ears or "seeing" ears.

"Do you mean to tell me, Bubbles," he went on, "that the person you attacked today on the news, the man you've declared is an inveterate liar and . . . what was that you called him again?"

"Greasy, scum-sucking leech."

"Yes. Hmm. Interesting choice of words. Anyway, this greasy, scum-sucking leech is going to be your husband?"

I tried to put a positive spin on it. "For our daughter's sake. Our family counselor thinks she could do with the stability of a nuclear family."

Notch pointed to the freeze-framed image of me with my hands around Dan's neck. "I'd say that looks less like the foundation for a nuclear family and more like the foundation for a nuclear war, wouldn't you?"

Nuclear war. If I had a nickel for every time someone had cracked that line since Dan and I got engaged, I'd have, oh, at least eighty-five cents.

An impossibly trim and healthy young woman stepped forward. She had long brown hair and flawless golden skin, and she wore stylish black pants that flared slightly at the bottoms. She couldn't have been much older than Jane.

Notch turned to her and spread his arms wide. "Alison! I'm so glad you joined us. Have you met Bubbles Yablonsky?"

"Oh, my." Alison reached out and gave my hand a bone-breaking squeeze. "I've read all your stories and heard so much about you."

Aww, that was very sweet. My first fan. "Is she the intern replacing Justin?" I asked Notch.

"I should hope not. Alison Roach is a Columbia University Journalism School graduate, the kind of caliber I've been trying to recruit for some time."

Alison the Columbia University journalism student beamed.

"She's not Justin's replacement," he said, adding, "I hope someday she'll be *yours*!"

I blinked once and resolved not to convey my shock. *Never let 'em see you sweat* is my personal motto, second only to *Underwear is good*.

"Really? That's nice." I couldn't have sounded more blasé.

"Isn't that awesome?" Alison gushed, sliding a strand of hair behind her ear. "I mean, I wasn't even looking for a job. Here I'd spent all summer hiking around Portugal and Spain with my girlfriends, and when I came back, I was so exhausted and, like, not really into the clock-punching trap. You know how that is."

"Oh, sure." In my dreams. At my house, not really into punching the clock means not really into eating food.

"Then one day when I was online, I saw this ad for a reporter at the *News-Times* and, well, I was getting pretty bored just sleeping late at home and I did need mad money to pay off the old Saks card. So here I am."

She slapped the sides of her pants as though finding a job was, gee, as easy as making friends at Brownie camp.

Whereas I—not that I'm complaining—had had to bust my ass to get so much as an opportunity to write an obit for this rag. Working days shampooing down at the House of Beauty, attending eight years of night school at Two Guys Community College while playing single mother and raising Jane. And still Mr. Notch had been loath to bring me on full-time.

As for calling my salary "mad money"—don't even get me started.

"That's swell," I said, wishing someone would explain what would be happening to me when Alison of the illustrious Columbia Journalism School took over my beat.

Then I had a revelation. Maybe Alison would be covering Mahoken Township. Hallelujah, because I was getting darned sick and tired of those Mahoken sewage council meetings. A girl can take only so much talk about hookups and flows.

"Listen," Alison said, "I'd love to stick around, but I have an interview in two seconds and I have to rush. I just wanted to bring you up to speed on what I found out about latex allergies on the Internet."

Now that was strange. It sounded like Alison was covering the Debbie Shatsky homicide.

"Ah, a reporter who actually researches. What a refreshing concept." Mr. Notch touched Alison's back in his new new age, touchy-feely way. "Why don't we discuss this in my office? I have a pot of lemongrass herbal tea warming. We could sit on my yoga mat while you fill me in."

Yes, good idea. I could tell them Debbie's revelation that a woman named Marguerite, a client of her husband's, was trying to get her claws in him. This was the kind of information that they call an "exclusive" in our business, though, being bighearted, I might let Alison work on the story with me. You know, to allow her some hands-on experience.

I was trotting after them when Notch held out his hand to stop me. "I meant Alison and me. You don't have to join us, Bubbles. It's not really necessary."

Not necessary? That was ridiculous. Alison didn't have the exclusive. I did. What exactly was going on?

"But I know all about her latex allergy," I blurted.

Notch raised an eyebrow. "Oh?"

"And Debbie's last words, about how a woman was after her husband."

Instead of exclaiming, *Why didn't you say so? Step into my office right away,* he said, "Really, Bubbles? Then let me read your notes."

Damn Notch and his stupid hang-up about notes. Who remembers to carry around a little pad and pen, anyway? You think leopard-print leotards have pockets? "I don't have notes, not technically," I bluffed. "Besides, I wasn't reporting anything. I'd been doing hair extensions." What a pathetically lame excuse!

Mr. Notch did not seem persuaded. He did that odd

thing he'd been doing lately, closed his eyes and murmured some prayer for "strength" and "serenity." And then he inhaled and exhaled several times.

"I believe I've warned you," he said with exaggerated patience, "about the need to take notes—in any situation. My word, Alison probably learned that while reporting for the newspaper at her elementary school."

What, five years ago?

"It's true," Alison chirped. "I did."

"Now why don't you stick to your regular beat, Bubbles? I haven't decided who will write this story, you or Lawless, but when I do, you'll be either the first or the second to know."

He took Alison by the arm like a true gentleman and was about to lead her into his office when I couldn't stand it anymore. I had to know.

"If Alison's supposed to replace me, does that mean I'm being promoted to courts like you promised?"

Notch turned and cleared his throat. "Actually, I've had to put off your promotion, Bubbles, what with you going on your honeymoon next week and the holidays and all."

Honeymoon. I didn't know if you could call an overnight in the Hotel Lehigh a honeymoon. When I think of honeymoons, I think high class. I think of the Poconos. Champagne bubble baths. Heart-shaped beds. Sex. And though Dan refused to believe me, we wouldn't be having any of that.

As I had made quite clear to him, if he wanted sex, he'd have to visit the hookers on Fourth Street like all the other lawyers in town. After I'd rolled around on the sheets with Stiletto, no other man would do for me.

Sex with Stiletto. All reality suspended as I recalled the way Stiletto liked to come up behind me, slipping his strong arms around my waist, pushing aside my hair and kissing the part of my neck right under my ear. There was no stopping us once that started. He'd spin me around and, at first, kiss me gently on the lips and then, his hands roving where they damned well pleased, pull me to him harder, his kisses more intense, his jeans straining in a certain alluring way.

That reminded me of that night in Amish country when he cornered me in the parking lot and lifted me onto the hood of a car in the rain and ... Why, it was like yesterday. I could still hear him saying my name as if he were whispering it in my ear at this very moment.

"Bubbles?"

There was a tap on my shoulder.

I opened my eyes and found I was staring straight into his blue ones. There he was in his leather bomber jacket over a black T-shirt. His face was a little leaner, more tan. There was a slight bit of stubble over his strikingly square jaw and a few strands of gray in his blackish-brown hair. But it couldn't be. Stiletto was in England. He'd left weeks ago to take over the London bureau for the Associated Press.

His lips parted in a cocky grin. "Surprised you, didn't I?"

Oh my God. It *was* him.

"Sti—" I was about to throw my arms around his gorgeous neck when I spied my news editor, Mr. Salvo, standing off to the right, shaking his head ever so slightly.

Right. Stiletto wasn't mine anymore. We were over. I bit my lip and stuck out my hand. "Hi, Steve."

He furrowed his brows. "Hi, Steve? What kind of crap is that?" Then he bent down and kissed me smack on the lips in front of the whole newsroom.

That was Stiletto for you.

"God, you taste good," he murmured, reaching behind to pull me to him for what I suspected would be another, deeper foray.

"Ahem." Mr. Salvo parted us like a referee. "This is a place of business."

"Your point being?" Stiletto said.

"No making out in the newsroom."

Stiletto frowned. "We weren't making out. I was simply being friendly, greeting a colleague with whom I'd worked on many tough and rewarding stories, right, Bubbles?"

I tried not to smile. "Right. I mean, two people who survive a mine explosion have this kind of relationship, Mr. Salvo." I didn't feel it necessary to explain *how* Stiletto and I had ended up in the mine to begin with or what we'd been doing and why the word "shaft" had more than one meaning in this context, not to mention explosion.

"That wasn't the only tunnel." Stiletto's eyes twinkled. "Remember the night we explored the cave off the Monocacy?"

The cave that led to the Sun Inn, I thought dreamily. My legs got that warm, liquid sensation as I recalled Stiletto taking me to bed for the first time, carrying me to the four-poster and laying me down before slowly unbuttoning his white shirt.

"That was one of our more, uh, *rigorous* assignments," he said.

"Okay, cut it out, you two." Mr. Salvo pushed us farther apart. "You're making me blush and I've been a news editor for over twenty years. Besides, aren't you getting married this weekend, Bubbles?"

"Details," Stiletto said.

But Mr. Salvo was right and I knew it. I had to stick with the game plan for Jane. I took a deep breath, cooled off and said, "What are you doing here anyway, Stiletto?"

Mr. Salvo answered for him. "Stiletto flew back from London to attend the Help the Poor Children fundraiser at the Masonic temple tonight."

"All the way from England for a rubber-chicken dinner?"

Stiletto shrugged. "What can I say? I'm a generous guy."

"Help the Poor Children is the pet project of his new

girlfriend," Mr. Salvo said, unable to hide the hint of victory in his voice.

Mr. Salvo and Stiletto were old friends who went way back. Mr. Salvo had always been the ugly duckling to Stiletto's swan, and so it had been Mr. Salvo who first advised me against dating Stiletto on the theory that I'd get my heart broken.

My heart hadn't been broken. It had been delicately placed between two pieces of waxed paper and pounded into a quarter of an inch.

"Yes, *girlfriend*." Mr. Salvo stressed. "An actress, no less. From Allentown."

I looked to Stiletto for confirmation. Was this true? Could Stiletto have actually stooped so low as to date a woman from—spare me—Allentown?

"Her name is Sabina Towne," Stiletto said calmly. "We met in London, introduced by mutual friends. She was in *The Cherry Orchard*. She's a lovely person. And yes, Tony's correct. She's originally from Allentown."

"Oh, Stiletto," I said, emphasizing my disappointment. How could Stiletto date a girl from Allentown? Allentown is Lehigh's rival city. Lehigh is to steel as Allentown is to pork products. Nothing in common. For a Lehigh boy to date an Allentown girl was like a Shark dating a Jet. A Hatfield a McCoy. A McDonald dating a Burger King. It was unnatural. It defied the laws of the universe.

"You should meet her. If you came to the fund-raiser tonight, you could." Stiletto kept his gaze on me. I had the feeling he wasn't interested one little bit in me meeting Sabina.

"No can do, old boy," Mr. Salvo said. "Bubbles has to cover the Mahoken council meeting tonight. They got a proposed development going up with a pretty tricky sewage issue, yes, sirree. Screams B1 all the way."

Stiletto chuckled. "Yeah. I love it when Bubbles goes all the way."

I swallowed. Awful, naughty schemes popped into my

mind. Okay. I was going to that stupid fund-raiser, come
Mahoken hell or its dirty high water. "Who is covering
the Help the Poor Children fund-raiser, anyway?" I
asked.

"Flossie Foreman for 'Talk of the Town.' " Mr. Salvo
nodded to Flossie, a joweled old lady who wore so much
pancake that she left powdery stains on her chair.

Flossie had been writing "Talk of the Town"—what
passed for the *News-Times* local gossip column—since
William Penn had ripped off the Indians. People in this
town loved Flossie. She was once voted "Lehigh's Dear-
est Treasure." Her desk was always covered with flowers
and teddy bears, cute gifts people sent her in thanks for
mentioning their bridal showers or retirement parties in
her column.

"You think you can make it?" Stiletto asked.

"I'll find a way," I said. "Somehow."

Stiletto stuck his hands in his pockets and smiled as
though he knew that of course I would.

But how?

And then I heard my solution. Or rather, solutions.

One tall, one short, both round and shapeless and
reeking of Ben-Gay and potato perogies, pestering our
poor receptionist, Veronica.

They might be old. They might be gray. They might be
totally whacked from consuming grapefruit with their
blood pressure medicine, but they'd know how to handle a fellow battle-ax like Flossie Foreman.

Chapter Four

"**L**ooks like you're wanted," Stiletto said. "You better go."

"Yes," I said, partly grateful for the interruption. I didn't know how much more of Stiletto I could stand. I wasn't exactly famous for my self-restraint.

He and Mr. Salvo went off, judiciously avoiding the receptionist's desk, where all hell was breaking loose.

"I don't need no stinking appointment to see my daughter. BUBBLES! Help me, Bubbles!"

Mama was being yanked back by our gatekeeper, Veronica, who at one hundred pounds was no match for Mama's meatloaf-and-potato heft. Mama broke away, sending Veronica flying into her swivel chair.

Veronica swore a blue streak, prompting Mama to make a quip about young girls these days driving like Mario Andretti with a NASCAR potty mouth.

I knew what Mama and Genevieve were after. Free publicity. A few weeks before, they'd hit on a get-rich-quick scheme to turn our decrepit steel town into—voilà!—the *discount* Christmas City.

All their lives they'd watched with sadness when, every season, busloads and busloads of otherwise loyal senior Lehighites saddled up and did their shopping in nearby Bethlehem, the *historic* Christmas city. There they snapped up every last Moravian star, snow globe, Bach music CD and jigsaw puzzle featuring Bethlehem's famous "putz." You name it, they bought it like their money was made out of paper. And to top it off, they took the "Christmas City by Night" tour before heading home to Lehigh.

Meanwhile, all anyone bought in Lehigh was wrapping paper and tape.

Enough with Bethlehem already, was Mama's attitude. The Moravians were so over. Plus, Bethlehem's Christmas fix was further ruining Lehigh's already ruined economy. Something had to be done to stop the hemorrhaging.

Which was how Mama and Genevieve came up with a scheme to turn Lehigh into a destination discount stop for all your holiday needs. Same snow globes, same Moravian stars—albeit maybe not so sturdy—same music. (Okay, so the Bach was recorded off the senior center's Wurlitzer. Still, it was Bach.) And similar jigsaw puzzles, though the first round of "putz" puzzles had been unfortunately misinterpreted by Mama's distributor in Brooklyn.

(You wouldn't believe what putz means in some parts of the country. Let me just say this: piecing together a picture of this male anatomy would be enough to send Grandma running for the eggnog.)

Anyway, the big news was that all the tchotchkes would be for sale at forty percent off Bethlehem's prices at Mama and Genevieve's Christmas Fair and Mega–Garage Sale on Friday.

In addition, Mama and Genevieve promised everyone a real, live Christmas pageant with real, live senior citizens—though, as Mama said, with some of them that's not so guaranteed. The pageant was turning out to be a huge hit with her geriatric crowd. As of last count, there were eight angels over the age of seventy-three, including two with walkers.

And there'd been at least one diva disaster. Mrs. Zuma and Mrs. Moriarity had had a falling out after Mrs. Moriarity was passed over for the role of Mary because Mrs. Zuma was allegedly sleeping with Joseph, who also happened to be the director.

That was what you got with the Lehigh Senior Center. The scandals never stopped.

I headed Mama and Genevieve off at Veronica's desk and adroitly steered them toward our one conference room so they wouldn't disturb the newsroom, since they tended to talk at full volume about the most intimate of bodily functions and the miracle of whole bran.

Before I could say, *Don't sit. I don't have time,* they sat across from me, purses in laps, ready to pitch their scam. Mama was wearing a red sweater, light-up Christmas-ball earrings and a reindeer pin. Two bright pink spots of rouge on her cheeks were practically aflame.

Genevieve, a good foot taller, was extremely ill at ease. Newspapers, in her mind, were elitist institutions bent on withholding real news from the working class. She kept stealing cautious glances through the conference room windows and awkwardly pulling her dress, which she'd sewn herself out of material with a Christmas-tree pattern. I knew for a fact that the Christmas-tree material was supposed to be used for table cloths and runners and not women's apparel, as I'd been at JoAnn Fabrics the week before and seen it on sale in the home-decorating department for $1.99 a yard.

Mama reached in her purse and pulled out a plastic bag of brown candies, tied with a red-and-green grosgrain ribbon. "Look what we're going to sell at the flea market."

I stared at the bag. "Molasses sponge candy?"

"Doesn't that bring back memories? Everyone's going to be so excited."

Molasses sponge candy was a unique, um, treat in the

Lehigh Valley. The church ladies made it every Christmas. It was hard and somewhat bitter and tasted faintly of baking soda. When it was made well, it melted in your mouth and disappeared. I have never seen it sold in a store and there might very well be a good reason for that.

"Listen, Mama, I can't go over your discount Christmas scam today. There was a crisis—"

"This ain't about that, so cool your jets." Mama snapped open the clip on her purse. "I just want to go over the wedding plans once more and then we'll be out of your big hair."

Wedding plans. *Groan.* Every day Mama went over wedding plans. "I don't want to go over wedding plans."

"Just a few photos to keep you up to speed."

Mama was laying out magazine clips of wedding dresses—which I had yet to buy—and samples of the white matchbooks that said DAN AND BUBBLES? (the ? was a typo, but I had voted to keep it in).

Next from her bag she produced Polaroid photos of the smoky union hall where our reception was supposed to be held. I could see from the pictures that already it was festooned with white tissue streamers and white tissue wedding bells.

Seeing the decorations pushed me over the edge. It was happening. It was really, really happening. I was going to be married—remarried—to Dan at the end of the week. Now I knew what prisoners on death row felt like when the lights flickered during dry runs of the electric chair.

"You looking mighty pale there, Sally," said Genevieve, who called all girls Sally and all boys Butch.

"What do you expect?" Mama said. "She's a bride."

"A bride without a wedding dress." Genevieve stuck out her chin. "When are you gonna get one of them things?"

I shrugged. "I dunno. I got other stuff on my mind."

Mama looked up from her display. "Like what? What

could be more important to a woman than her wedding dress?"

"How about Debbie Shatsky's murder at the House of Beauty today?"

Mama and Genevieve eagerly pulled up their chairs. I wondered if they were really here to talk veils or if the Polaroids had been just an excuse to get me alone.

"You don't seem so surprised by that," I observed.

"We heard it was an accident." Mama shoved the Polaroids back in her purse. "Not murder."

"Sandy screwed up and used the wrong glue 'cause she was rushed and disorganized—that's what Tula told us," Genevieve added, licking her lips.

"Sandy did not screw up," I said firmly. "Someone murdered Debbie. I'm sure of it. She was intentionally poisoned with latex."

Mama sat back as if it was a relief to hear Debbie had been murdered and not accidentally killed. "Good thing because one big screwup can close a salon forever."

"Remember Mario?" Genevieve asked.

"Like yesterday. One day you couldn't get an appointment there if you were Mario's mother herself. Next day the place was empty and Mario was offering a 'get two cuts, get the third cut free.' Bad perm, was what he did. Seared Ellie Merkel's hair right off."

A chill came over me. I'd heard of such hairdressing horror stories.

It was true what Mama and Genevieve were saying. Rumors that Sandy had been slipshod could ruin her. And even if she closed down the House of Beauty and tried to reopen under a different name, there'd be no hope. Lehigh was a tight steel town that didn't forget bad perms or deadly hair extensions. If Debbie's death wasn't revealed as a murder and soon, Sandy would be finished.

I tapped my press-on nails and thought about this. I needed to talk to Phil Shatsky. I needed to find Marguerite. Most important, I needed to figure out who switched Debbie's hair glue and dumped it in Sandy's private bathroom.

"You do know," Mama said slyly, "that Debbie was married before."

I stopped tapping.

"His name is Ernie Bender, better known as Ern. Maybe you remember him. He used to make the cherry Cokes down at the Save-T Drugs. He was a pharmacist there."

I thought back to the many cherry Cokes I had at the Save-T Drugstore, but I couldn't recall a pharmacist except for the grumpy dinosaur in a lab coat.

"You mean the old guy?" I asked.

Swat! I expertly ducked as Mama tried to hit me with her purse.

"He wasn't old. That's Clarence. He's our age. And he's not Ern. Ern's a kid. Longish brown hair. Wears it in a ponytail."

"Oh," I said, reemerging from under the conference table. "My mistake."

"His mother lives in the senior high-rise three floors up from me," Mama said.

"She shoots skeet," Genevieve said, thereby imprinting Mrs. Bender with her stamp of approval. Anybody who shot anything—a musket, pistols, gun, squirrels—was A-okay by her.

"She's also mighty ticked at her former daughter-in-law," Mama said. "Debbie up and divorced Ern when he was at his lowest." She paused. "In jail."

That was a twist I hadn't expected. "In jail? For what?"

"For nothing. Doped up on a few of those Cokes, was all. Heck, in our day, that's what Coke was. Dope. You got it at the druggist's counter, too."

I studied Mama and Genevieve, the doped-up coke addicts, with new eyes. Those two were very squishy about what constituted crime, especially Genevieve. It was best not to ask how she had managed to outlive her many husbands.

"Then I don't blame Debbie for divorcing him," I said. "I wouldn't stay married to a pharmacist who drank doped-up cherry Cokes, either."

"You should get his side of the story before you go around, high and mighty, making snap judgments," Genevieve said. "Ern works down at the Christmas tree farm at the corner of Union and Third, if you're looking for a scoop."

"He's out of jail?"

"Got out last week. We threw a party for him up in his mother's apartment. Debbie wasn't there, of course."

"Of course," Mama said. "He hates her."

"Or did," Genevieve corrected. "You can't hate the dead."

I wasn't so sure about that.

This new information raised a whole slew of new questions. A felonious pharmacist who despises his ex-wife gets out of jail and one week later she's dead? Not only is she dead, but she is dead from a latex allergy. And who would have known that she had a latex allergy? Her ex, thank you very much. And wouldn't he, as a pharmacist, also have known how to get hold of latex?

I got that prickly feeling, that startling electric surge of my innate journalistic instinct signaling me that I was on to something big.

There was a knock on the conference room door and Veronica poked her head in, regarding Mama warily before informing me that there was "some crying woman on the phone who refuses to call back."

Geesh. There were always crying women on my phone refusing to call back. Usually they were the clerks from Mahoken, sobbing about how poorly I'd written a story.

"Guess that's our cue to go," Mama said.

"Hold on." I grabbed Genevieve. "See that woman out there—the one with the little hat and the flowered dress?" I pointed through the conference room window to Flossie Foreman, who was on the phone and eating a Christmas cookie some fan had undoubtedly sent her.

"Oh, sure."

"That's Flossie Foreman."

"*The* Flossie Foreman," Mama gushed. "We love her."

"We sure do," Genevieve added. "First thing we read, straight after the obits, of course."

"Terrific. Then I wonder if you could take her out tonight. You know, use your connections in the senior circuit to preoccupy her. I need to cover something she's assigned to do."

Mama squinted. "This wouldn't have anything to do with that no-good Italian gigolo Stiletto, would it?"

"Where would you get an idea like that?"

"You were just talking to him. I saw with my own peepers."

I had to throw her off the scent. "If you treat her right, Flossie might be swayed to mention your Christmas City scam—I mean, Christmas City *project*—in her column. Might even give your perogie store a plug, Mama."

Mama brightened, Stiletto all but forgotten with the prospect of being featured in "Talk of the Town."

"So you just want us to take out Flossie," Genevieve said. "For the night. Not longer?"

"No. A night will be fine."

"Okay." Genevieve sighed, straining to heave herself out of the chair. "The things I do for you kids."

I watched them waddle through the conference room door and down the stairs. When they had waddled themselves out of the building, I took the phone, fully expecting that the dismayed caller had given up.

She hadn't.

"Oh, thank God, Bubbles. You've got to come down

right away. You wouldn't believe what I've found. This might solve everything!"

It was Sandy.

I was out the door in a flash.

Chapter Five

It was a disconcerting thing to see images of Santa Claus, apple cheeked and jolly, surrounded by yellow plastic DO NOT CROSS police tape. It was worse to see the tape hanging on the metal storm door of my favorite hangout in the world—my best friend's warm and homey salon.

I'd always considered the House of Beauty a safety zone—a place where you could kick off your pinching high-heeled sandals, lean back into warm, soapy water and talk freely among close friends and trusted neighbors. Here you could trade recipes for pot roast in a crock pot one minute and just as easily express your disgust for certain local politicians the next. Most of all you could gossip freely.

Who was sleeping with whom. Whose kid had disappeared for days. Who was so desperate to remarry that she was hanging on to a boyfriend who treated her poorly. Who was out of cash and running up her credit card with disastrous abandon. Who had killed the cheerleader with Slim-Fast.

I had dug some of my best dirt at the House of Beauty. Now the House of Beauty *was* the dirt.

I parked the Camaro out front, applied a bright sheen

of Raspberry Riot lip gloss to my slightly chapped lips and practiced smiling in my rearview. I didn't want to greet Sandy frowning or, worse, unglossed. There simply is no excuse for being unglossed, no matter what the circumstances.

The babushkas had gone, taking their aluminum folding chairs with them. Only pieces of popcorn remained behind. The front door was locked, so I went around back. A few days until Christmas and the HOB was empty. I'd taken a gander at today's appointment book before Debbie keeled over. It had been full up. The salon should have been packed.

I tried not to think of Mario and the bad perm.

"Come in," Sandy called feebly. Her voice sounded hoarse, as if she'd been shouting. Or crying.

Turned out it was all those, plus smoking. Sandy was lower than I'd ever seen her. Gone was her peach polyester uniform and carefully contained hair. It was all frizz now, as if she'd been pulling it out by the roots. Her dingy yellow sweat suit—I didn't know Sandy even owned a sweat suit—was stained with coffee and littered with flecks of gray cigarette ashes. It was all very depressing.

"Sandy!" I plunked down my purse and went to the sink, pouring her a glass of water, which happened to be the only thing I could think of to do.

She was at her desk, hunched over and staring at something in her hand. "I shouldn't have called you down here. I don't know what I was thinking. Sorry."

I handed her the Dixie cup and ordered her to sip. She was shaking so violently she had to grip the cup hard to bring it to her mouth.

"I was hoping . . ." she started, as if getting out the whole sentence was too, too much work. "I was hoping this would have the answer. Now . . . I don't know what I'm doing." Wincing as if in pain, she clutched her stomach and bent over. "Cramps. Damn cramps."

This was bad. It meant Sandy was having her period,

which meant she wasn't pregnant. She and Martin had been trying for years to have a baby, unbeknownst to me—until recently.

I'd always assumed she was happy without kids. I mean, those two were such neat freaks. And cloggers. Cloggers who liked complete quiet when they weren't clogging. Also, they were into early bedtimes and sleeping late on the weekends. Not exactly little-kid material.

But then, after the thing with Jane last month, Sandy let it slip that getting pregnant didn't come as easy to her as it did to me. Or at least as it had eighteen years ago. She and Martin were actually desperate to have a child.

"I'm sorry," I whispered.

"It's the stress." She cringed again. "I was positive this was the month. Guess not. I think this is the worst day of my life. All I want is to go home and lie down, let Martin take care of me."

I rubbed her back, feeling bad that I couldn't do more for her. The muscles were bunched and twisted between her shoulder blades. I'd intended to ask her more about how someone could possibly have gotten into her locked, private bathroom, but decided now was not an ideal moment. "What can I do to help?"

She held something out to me, the thing she'd been staring at. It was small and metallic, and as soon as I understood what it was, my heart fell. I was no good with these. In fact, one might call me a disaster.

"It's a cell phone," Sandy said.

"I know."

"Debbie's cell phone."

The words hung in the air. My first thought was *Take this to the cops,* which was not a very good thought for a crime reporter, especially a graduate of the Two Guys Community College School of Journalism, where Mr. Salvo had encouraged us to be resourceful.

Woodward and Bernstein wouldn't have taken this cell phone to the cops. Then again, cell phones hit the market long after Woodward and Bernstein. Probably Woodward and Bernstein wouldn't have known to press SEND or END. They'd be staring at it stupidly, as I was, banging it against their heads or something, like monkeys.

"Wasn't Debbie talking on her cell when she . . . you know?" Sandy asked. "I think she was. There's a way to find out what calls she received and what calls she made." Sandy started pushing buttons.

Why did I have the feeling that Sandy had already checked what calls Debbie had received and made?

"See. You just press this button and then this one and, whoops, well now I've gone and done it."

She was prattling faster than a runaway express train, her prior depression taking a backseat to a burst of hysterical energy. "Hmmm. Look at all these numbers. They're the same ones. In and out. Look, Bubbles. You're not looking."

I was looking. It was just that the number repeated over and over had no meaning. Was it Debbie's home? Get Together Now! Travel, where she worked?

"Hey." Sandy tapped her chin. "I wonder if this number is the number for Jeffrey Andre of Jeffrey Andre's Salon. Let's look it up."

The phonebook on Sandy's desk was already open to ANDERSON–ARONSON. Sandy's finger ran right down the list of names to a greasy spot by ANDRE, J.

Sure enough. The same number.

"What do you think it means?" she asked.

"That she was calling Jeffrey Andre at his home and Jeffrey Andre was calling her." I didn't want to hurt Sandy's feelings by observing that maybe Debbie was arranging a hair appointment. "He could be a client. Maybe he wanted to book a trip through Get Together Now!?"

"No, I don't think so," Sandy said. "I think it means something else. But I can't go down to his salon and find out because, well, because I'm not sure my legs work anymore. I'm not sure I could face him in my . . . my disgrace."

And with that, Sandy covered her face with her hands and burst into tears.

Clearly, I had no other option.

Five minutes later I was at the door of Jeffrey Andre's swanky salon.

The "warehouse district" was on Third Street, precariously close to Lehigh Steel. To the workers slogging in and out of the Steel, as it was called, the collection of shops, restaurants and boutiques in their factory's old warehouses must have loomed like a vulture waiting to pick apart their dying carcasses.

What was the wimpy fate that awaited the once mighty industry that constructed our nation's bridges, its skyscrapers, the ships that carried our soldiers overseas to defeat Hitler?

Williams Sonoma. Starbucks. Jeffrey Andre.

The thing is, we fear change in Lehigh. We don't like eating dinner after six. It's too late, too European. And if we eat ravioli, it should be filled with meat or cheese, not pumpkin. If something's been blackened, it's been burned. As for coffee, it should be served in thick ceramic mugs with plenty of creamer and, no matter what, it shouldn't cost four bucks.

Which might explain why Jeffrey Andre was not as busy as I might have expected.

"Do you halfff an appointment?" A young man with short, short black hair sat on a high stool before a podium like a maître d', instead of at a regular desk as God intended.

"Umm," I said, still taking in my surroundings. Wide blond oak floors. Super-high ceilings and the pervasive smell of cappuccino. It was so big and . . . bare. Not a Christmas decoration in sight. Not even one of those fruity white-and-gold trees. It didn't even smell like a normal salon. It smelled like grapefruit . . . and cappuccino.

"We're verrrrry busy," Mr. Receptionist said. "We are all booked up."

Actually, as far as I could see, there was no one here. Only . . . was that G?

G was Jane's old boyfriend who went by one letter for a name. G, as he was fond of saying, stood for God or Genius, depending. He used to be a slacker with an incurable addiction to SpongeBob SquarePants until his true, amazing talent as a stylist emerged quite by accident.

Now G was all in demand, except by Jane, who had dropped him after "the incident." Jane had dropped a lot of stuff after "the incident," including her courage and ambition to become a world-renowned physicist.

"Hi, G!" I called out.

G was foiling a businessman's hair. Seeing me, he gulped and concentrated on his foiling, as if I were a total stranger.

That wasn't like him at all.

"If you came here to socialize . . ." Mr. Receptionist was saying.

"I'd like to talk to Jeffrey Andre," I said firmly. "It's important."

The man raised one—was that a plucked?—eyebrow. "I ham sooo sorry. Mr. Andre is verrry busy."

"I'm Bubbles Yablonsky from the *News-Times*. I'd like to know why his home phone number appears repeatedly on the cell phone of a woman who was just murdered." And then, in a stroke of brilliance, I remembered Mr. Notch's constant admonition, reached into my purse and pulled out my Reporter's Notebook.

The receptionist raised his other eyebrow at the notebook. "Oooohkay." He tossed a pencil on the podium, slid out of his high stool and shuffled off, I assumed to find Jeffrey Andre.

I clutched my notebook and waited, feeling unreasonably nervous. I was suddenly seized by a mad wish for Stiletto to be here and was massaging my temples to make my wish go away when G popped up next to me.

"I just want you to know that even though I work here, I am totally heterosexual."

G was holding the box of foil he'd been using a minute ago when he pretended not to know who I was. He was blonder than when I last saw him and there might have been biceps under the black sleeves of his supertight T-shirt. He looked pretty darn good.

"Okay? 'Cause if Jane hears I'm working for Jeffrey Andre, it's gonna get all over town that I've gone, you know, to the other side."

"No, it won't."

"I can't take that risk. My studly quotient is everything."

This was a total lie. Sleeping until two was everything to G.

It surprised me how happy I was to see him, though. I missed the boy. I missed the way he raided my Cap'n Crunch and left bowls of moldy cereal around the house. I even missed his smelly socks balled up on the floor.

"What're you doing?" he cried, flinching as I held out my arms.

"Nothing. I wanted to give you a hug."

"Ick. You're my ex-girlfriend's mother, Mrs. Y. That's like incest or something. Let's stick to Jane, okay? How is she? She still dating that jerk?"

It was my unfortunate duty to report that, indeed, Jane was still dating that jerk Jason. Jason who wore a pink buttoned-down shirt and was the high school "liaison" to the Lehigh Valley Rotarians. Jason who sported a buzz cut and wore a chastity ring and never let his jeans ride so low that you could see his underwear—unlike G.

G was obviously crestfallen.

"But don't worry," I said. "I have a plan. I'm inviting you to my wedding on Saturday."

"Awesome." G high-fived me. "You're finally marrying that old dude."

"What old dude?"

"Stalagmite."

"Stiletto?"

"Yeah, him."

"No," I said, bristling. "And Stiletto's not old. He's my age." I caught myself. I'd sounded exactly like Mama defending Clarence the pharmacist. "Actually, I'm remarrying Jane's father."

G jumped back. "Not the human oil slick?"

That was a pretty apt description, I had to admit.

"Our hope is that it will help Jane recover. Dr. Lori Caswell, our family therapist, is of the opinion that a nuclear family will do wonders." No need to confess what else Dr. Caswell said about my maternal inadequacies, especially after G had just accused me of "incest."

G shook his head. "I'm not buying it. I didn't grow up in no nuclear family and it didn't hurt me none."

That statement said oh so much.

"What're you doing here anyway? Heard you had some action down at the old HOB today. Seems Sandy really fu—messed up, say?"

There was muffled conversation at the far end of the salon. I suspected Jeffrey Andre was putting up some resistance to meeting me.

In a lowered voice, I gave G the quick rundown, making sure to stress that Sandy had not fu—messed up, but that Debbie Shatsky had been murdered.

"Sandy . . . a murderer?" G shouted.

I slapped my hand over the nimrod's mouth. "Shhh. Sandy didn't murder anyone. But it seems as if someone is eager to pin the blame on her." I dropped my hand and explained about the two hair glues and how one was found in her private toilet. Odd, confusing thoughts were running around G's mind. I could tell he wanted to delve further, but couldn't bring himself to question how hair glue ended up in a toilet.

"What I want to know is why Debbie was calling Jeffrey Andre repeatedly," I said.

G glanced over his shoulder and pulled me aside. "I don't know what this dead babe looked like, but some chick's been here bugging Jeffrey. Every time she shows up, he goes all crazy, starts demanding valium and bottled water with lime. Don't ever call him Jeff, by the way. He totally freaks."

There were footsteps echoing across the hard oak floor. I didn't want to get G in trouble, though I was dying to hear more.

"And I heard Jeffrey tell Paul—that's his assistant guy—that this client dying at the HOB might bring us business. He's offering HOB clients a ten percent discount on cuts, fifteen percent on cuts and color."

I was appalled. That was outrageous. That was worse than dogs picking over road kill. Fifteen percent! "Why . . ."

All of a sudden, G's eyes turned to saucers. He slinked away from me as if I was repellant. Jeffrey Andre was right behind me. I couldn't see him, but I could smell him. He reeked of syrupy aftershave that reminded me, vaguely, of my high school math teacher Mr. Zelko.

"Isss dis a friend of yours, Gerald?"

Gerald? I let out a snigger. So that was his real name. G darted me a nasty look.

"Mother of my ex-girlfriend." He curled his lip. "Glad that's behind me."

I was tempted to kick him, the little brat.

"Ah, girlfriends. Not exaccctly one of my problems. May I halp you, Ms. . . . uh . . ."

"Yablonsky." I spun around to face the mythic Jeffrey Andre, he who was enriching himself off Sandy's misfortune.

Jeffrey Andre was shorter than I with long silver hair and a huge piece of bling in his left lobe. Like Paul, his assistant, and G, he wore all black, including an all-black suit that seemed too loose for him. His pants were baggy and made of a thin material that undulated as he stood, giving him the impression of being fluid.

"How nice to meet you, Ms. Yablonsky." He shook my

hand tightly and made killer eye contact. Was he trying to read my thoughts? Or was this a sophisticated European thing I'd somehow missed during my Two Guys Community College course: Making A Good First Impression with Excellent European Eye Contact and Firm Handshakes.

"I am sooo sorry to hear about what happened to you at the House of Beauty," he said.

Okay. I hadn't said anything to Paul about being at the House of Beauty when Debbie died. All I'd told him was that I was a reporter for the *News-Times*.

Out of the corner of my eye, I caught G slipping behind a door to get rid of his foil.

"What may I do for you, Miss Yablonsky? I haff sent flowers, of course. And my condolencesss. I'm sure you will pass them on to the appropriate peoplesss."

"Actually, I came here in my capacity as a newspaper reporter. I have only one question."

"Of course. Anything!" Jeffrey threw up his arms, showing he had nothing up *his* sleeves.

"Why was Debbie Shatsky calling you repeatedly at your salon and your home minutes before she died?"

Jeffrey turned to Paul as if Paul could translate this. "Debbie?" he said. "I know no Debbie . . . uh . . . Shitsky, is it?"

"Shatsky. That is the name of the woman who died today in the House of Beauty. And you must know her because you called her, too. Your home number is on her cell."

"I do not know what you are talking about. I'm so sorry. I would like to help, but I am afraid I cannot. Let's see." He undulated over to a laptop on the podium. "Here are all the appointments. Paul. See if you can find a Debbie Shitsky."

"Shatsky."

Jeffrey stood aside, hands clasped, waiting for Paul to do his thing on the laptop. I wondered if Jeffrey's hands were so skilled at hairstyling that they could not be forced to perform menial labor, like typing on a keyboard. Maybe they were insured by Lloyds of London. Or maybe, like Debbie, he suffered from some rare allergy, in his case to letters on plastic.

"Nope," Paul said, tapping the down arrow repeatedly. "No Shatsky or Shitsky."

These boys were being difficult. "She might have used her previous name. Bender."

At the mention of Bender, Jeffrey Andre's insipid smile snapped into a tight line. Paul stopped tapping, his fingers petrified over the UP and DOWN keys.

"Did you say, Bender?" Jeffrey Andre's accent, like G, had also disappeared. "As in Ern Bender?"

"You know him?"

Jeffrey stared at me dully. This was not the meaningful French eye contact of minutes before. He was not connecting. He was remembering. Recalling.

He was seething.

"Let me give you a piece of advice," he said. "Sometimes it is best to let sleeping dogs lie, you know? As my grandmother in the old country used to say, the more you stir the shit, the more it smells."

Okay, that was the grossest line ever. I hate that line. What kind of grandmother talks about stirring shit?

"Are you telling me to stop asking questions?"

Jeffrey ran his finger under his lip, thinking. "What I am telling you is that you are a little hairdresser who works for a little newspaper in a little town. I have been around the world. I have lived in Paris, Milan, London and New York, though actually in Montclair, New Jersey, but close enough."

Paul put a hand on his shoulder, encouragingly because Jeffrey was getting quite agitated, perspiring and confessing about Jersey and all.

"I have learned from being worldly that sometimes the truth one finds is not always the truth, you know?"

"No." That made no sense whatsoever, in fact.

"Of course not. You are American. You can see only

black and white. You cannot see all the other colors in between."

That was completely untrue. Yes, I wore a lot of black and white, but also, pink, purple, hot red and the occasional silver sequins. I could see them just fine.

"So my advice to you is to leave this be," he said firmly. "What has happened was for the best. You do not understand that now, perhaps. You may not understand it soon. But someday you will come to accept that what I have said is right and that is what you Americans love—to be right."

"I'm not going to quit here," I warned him, ignoring his anti-American prejudice. "I have no intention of backing down just because you've told me to." I did not add that coming from a Frenchman, his threats sounded more like menu recitations than scary intimidations.

He stepped closer. His pores were very large, too large for a man in the business of beautifying skin. "Drop this investigation for your own safety, Miss Yablonsky. I don't know how I can be more clear. No one wants there to be, how you say"—he glanced at the ceiling—"more killings."

Then he abruptly clapped his hands three times, a signal to Paul, who snapped to his side.

"This interview is being concluded. I am bored with you now." And he and Paul undulated away, like snakes.

It was definitely time to meet this dreaded Ern Bender.

Chapter Six

The Christmas tree lot at the corner of Broad and Union was the sorriest Christmas tree lot ever. It was creepier than Jeffrey Andre's penetrating eye contact and about as depressing as Sandy's coffee-stained dingy yellow sweats. My first instinct was to get the heck out of there.

So was my second instinct. In fact, all my instincts were screaming at me to turn around or, at least, wait until daylight to hunt down Ern Bender. Although it was only four thirty, it was already dark, aside from the string of broken multicolored lights that illuminated the lot. And it was cold.

I positioned the Camaro in the driveway of a neighboring pizza joint, which had been closed years ago for health issues. Snow was falling. Not real snow. Flurries. This was the kind of evening meant to be spent inside eating tomato soup and grilled cheese sandwiches, maybe writing a few Christmas cards and wrapping presents.

This was not the kind of evening to be out picking up a Christmas tree or hunting down a paroled drug-pushing pharmacist.

The commuter traffic was heavy but no one seemed

interested in stopping by CHRISTMAS TREES—CHEEP! Then again, it was kind of difficult to read the misspelled sign, seeing as it was one side of a cardboard box propped up against a telephone pole.

I'd never questioned before how the enterprising arborist claimed Christmas tree lots. I mean, one day the abandoned lot is home to used Chevys or outdoor-grilled barbeque. The next day it's sporting Christmas trees. How does that happen?

And in this day and age of high unemployment, in a town where laid-off steelworkers roamed the streets and packed the unemployment offices hungrier than the undead in search of flesh, who in his right mind would hire a felonious pharmacist to sell trees?

I got my answer as soon as I stepped out of the car, heard the bell ringing and saw the lanky elf in a red suit and white beard waving at cars, hoping to solicit their Christmas tree business.

Ern Bender: Anorexic Santa Claus.

"Christmas trees," he droned, clanging the bell in a funereal rhythm. "Ho . . . ho . . . ho. Christmas trees. Cheap."

A few cars honked. Most sped up. No one stopped.

Somewhere a boom box blared Bing Crosby, in case the scene of an emaciated Santa on parole hocking trees at a used car lot wasn't depressing enough. I pulled my faux rabbit fur coat tighter and bent my head to the biting wind. I remembered that I hadn't bought a tree yet. If I were a nice person, I would buy one from Ern.

Or not.

"Mr. Bender?" I said.

A car zipped by, splashing me with December grime. Ern continued ringing, oblivious. He sported the hollow cheeks and sallow complexion of a person who doesn't take those admonitions to eat five vegetables a day seriously. A fake beard did little to hide the tattoo on his neck. If I had a little kid, I'd no more let him sit on Ern's lap than let him play blindman's buff with the Crips.

"Mr. Bender!" I yelled.

You'd think he'd be thrilled to see a customer so entranced by his bell skills that she'd rushed right up to introduce herself. But Ern was far from thrilled.

Ern was drunk. Or, at least, that's the way he smelled.

He drove his thumb over his shoulder. "Get your tree back there. I don't sell 'em. I bring 'em in."

I covered my nose to dilute the whiskey fumes wafting my way. "I don't want a tree. I need to talk to you, Mr. Bender. About Debbie."

He didn't miss a beat with the bell, not a ding or a dong. "I don't know a Debbie."

"Yes, you do. Debbie your wife."

"Ex."

"Okay, ex."

"Ho . . . ho . . . ho." He rang the bell. "Christmas trees. Get your Christmas trees. Cheap."

Another car swerved and splashed frigid black water onto my leopard-print tights, making my legs officially soaked with black muck. Cripes. The Mahoken Sewage Council was a trip to Disneyworld compared to this. I vowed that if I stuck with Ern for ten more minutes, I could treat myself to a long, hot bubble bath tonight along with a juicy Nancy Martin Blackbird Sisters mystery and a cup of hot chocolate.

Sidestepping another splashing car, I hollered, "Mr. Bender, I believe your wife has been murdered."

Finally, the ringing stopped. Ern tossed the bell aside so that it landed in the gutter with one last clang, and swaying slightly, he regarded me with rheumy eyes. "Who the hell are you?"

"My name is Bubbles Yablonsky. I'm a"—I thought twice about introducing myself as a reporter—"I'm a hairdresser down at the House of Beauty. I was there when your former wife had an allergic reaction and died."

Ern reached into his pocket and pulled out a small dark brown bottle. It looked more like cough syrup than liquor, probably an addiction leftover from his pharmacist days. "They told me it was an accident."

"Who?"

"Cops." He took a quick swig, closed his eyes and savored before recapping the bottle. "They didn't say nothing about a murder."

"Yes, well." I wasn't about to launch into a dissertation on the qualifications of Lehigh's finest. (It was the *Keystone* State, after all.) "I have a different opinion. I think she was intentionally, well, poisoned, for lack of a better word."

He pondered this. "Was it strychnine? Is that what they used?"

"No," I said, thinking, *What the hell was he talking about?* "Not strychnine."

" 'Cause that's an awful death. Thirty minutes of muscle convulsions, painful muscle convulsions. Off. On. Off. On. Until the heart gives up. Instant rigor mortis, though, so that's helpful. If you need to dispose of a body, that is."

"Right." I moved a few steps away, extending my escape hatch. "Actually, it was more along the lines of latex. She had a pretty severe allergy, I guess." I narrowed my eyes. "Were you aware of that?"

"Yeah, yeah, yeah. Claimed she couldn't clean a house because she'd have to wear rubber gloves. Wouldn't use a diaphragm, either." He shook his head sloppily. "I never believed it. Not for a minute."

"Maybe you should have. She died a few minutes after latex glue was applied to her scalp."

Ern shrugged. "Yeah? What were her last words?"

I hesitated. What an odd question.

"I . . . I don't know. I don't remember." What had been her last words, anyway? "I think she said she felt as if something bad was going to happen."

"No kidding." He looked off, toward the string of red brake lights on Union. I couldn't tell if he was crying or surprised or sad. "That might have been a reaction to the latex. You feel as if something bad is about to happen."

I would remember to write this down.

"Then again, she was probably thinking, Shit, I've been murdered. Not like she wasn't concerned. Debbie was paranoid—that's for sure."

All my senses were on edge. "Oh?"

"Though, the way I look at it, it was just a matter of time before someone got to her. Lord knows she deserved it."

This was it. This was the big exclusive experienced reporters always go on and on about. I took a second to mentally compliment myself for taking the initiative and tracking down Ern. "You don't mean that," I said, egging him on.

"Like hell I don't. If I told you what the real Debbie was about, you wouldn't believe it."

"Try me. I'm very gullible. Everyone says so."

"First of all, get this straight. It was my idea." He stabbed his thumb into his chest. "I was the one with the information. Debbie stole it from me and took over everything. It wasn't her scam. It was mine. She got too greedy."

I repeated the words in my mind so I could write them down later. I didn't dare bring out my notebook now. No telling how Ern might react seeing me with pen and paper. Not many hairdressers take notes.

"What kind of scam?" I took a step closer.

Ern was very tall with the wiry frame you often see on righteous dudes who prefer to hang out at NASCAR races or on death row. "Why should I tell you?"

I thought fast. "Because what you know might clear an innocent woman. My boss and best friend who owns the House of Beauty is watching her life fall down around her. Everyone thinks she is at fault in Debbie's death, and I know in my heart she wasn't. She's going to be punished unfairly, either with a civil suit that'll close her salon or worse. Possibly"—I took a breath—"criminal negligence charges."

"You think that gets to me? That doesn't get to me. I know all about being innocent in prison. I just spent the last five years being innocent in prison." He held on to the bottle so precariously I worried he'd toss it like he had the bell and that it would land on some commuter's windshield. Then there'd be trouble. "And do you know why I went to prison even though I was innocent?"

I stopped myself from answering. This might have been what they call a rhetorical question. I wasn't really sure what a rhetorical question was. It was like irony, I figured. Indefinable, yet beloved by English teachers everywhere. As part of my self-improvement program, I had set a goal to be able to identify rhetorical questions with ease by the new year. So far, I wasn't doing so well.

"Is that a rhetorical question?" I asked.

Ern didn't answer. Maybe he didn't know either?

"Debbie. She was the one who put me in prison. Wanted me out of the way so she could run our scam without giving me a cut. The bitch. Though it was good she was stopped. That scam of hers could've turned this town upside down."

We were silent, watching the cars zip by, Ern probably thinking about the unfettered scam, me trying to analyze what made that a rhetorical question. Why did they call it a question if you weren't supposed to answer it? I couldn't see the point.

Also, I thought about Debbie. She was certainly shaping up to be a far cry from the self-satisfied, perfect wife and travel agent I'd known for years as my neighbor and client. Yet Ern, being drunk, a criminal and dressed in a slim-fitting Santa suit, wasn't what one called a "reliable source." Plus, he smelled really, really bad.

"I'm confused," I said. "What, exactly, was this scam? Did it have something to do with her travel agency?"

He jerked his chin to a car across the street. "There's something you don't see every day."

He was right. Though it was dusk and traffic was whizzing by, it wasn't hard to miss the shiny black late model Mercedes. Foreign cars are cars you don't see much in Lehigh. We don't like them, nor do we trust them. We don't have mechanics to service them because buying one is right out of the question. Foreign cars push local people out of jobs. That was why the Mercedes kind of stood out.

Along with the fact that behind the wheel was a hulking man dressed in a Santa suit, a pair of what might have been either binoculars or night-vision goggles held up to his eyes.

"He's Santa Claus," I said, under my breath. "Just like you!"

" 'Tis the season."

The Santa Claus dropped his binoculars to take a cell phone call. Still, he kept his gaze on Ern.

Or was it me?

"If I were you," Ern said, sounding surprisingly sober, "I'd get real interested in buying a Christmas tree before that guy gets a bead on your head." Ern retrieved the bell from the gutter, gave it a shake and returned to his clanging. "Christmas trees. Get your Christmas trees here. Ho . . . ho . . . ho. Cheap."

My pulse was now racing. I stole another quick peek at the Mercedes. Santa was still on his cell phone, and I observed as I walked away, his gaze was focused one hundred percent on me.

Shit! What was going on? Why would I be followed for asking questions about what a few hours ago had appeared, by all accounts, to have been an accidental death from a latex allergy?

I zigzagged crazily to the lot entrance, where a man in blue overalls sat on a metal folding chair, smoking and tapping his foot to Elvis Presley's bluesy "Merry Christmas, Baby."

"I'd like to buy a Christmas tree. Fast."

"Saw you talking to my mascot over there," the Christmas tree salesman said, the cigarette dangling from his lips. "What were you up to?"

Panic. He might be in cahoots with the Mercedes. All this talk about Debbie's paranoia had rubbed off on me. "Oh, nothing." Crap. My voice was shaking. "Just asking for tree advice. You know, which ones smell good, which ones hold their needles, which ones last the longest."

"He don't know squat about trees. What were you really talking about?"

"Honest. Trees. He said I should get that blue spruce." I pointed to a mangy one—well, they were all pretty mangy—propped up against the fence. "That's the one he suggested."

"That's not a blue spruce. That's a pine."

How could he tell with his sunglasses on? And wasn't a spruce a pine anyway? "I don't care. That's the one I want, please. And could you tie it to the top of my car?"

I glanced over my shoulder. The Mercedes was gone. I didn't know whether to be relieved or more worried.

"That'll be twenty bucks, plus a buck for rope."

Rip-off! At the prospect of being swindled, I momentarily forgot my stalker.

"That's not worth twenty bucks. The bottom branches are brown and it's almost bare of needles. You should be thanking me for taking it off your hands. That thing's a fire hazard." I was not Lulu Yablonsky's daughter for nothing. Just because some fancy Santa was tracking me in the midst of a murder investigation was no reason to pay retail for a discount Christmas tree.

"Why do you want it then, if it's so lousy?"

"Because I'm banking on it being cheap—like your sign says."

"Eighteen."

"Ten," I said, "and you throw in the rope for free."

"Okay. But only because I'm filled with holiday cheer. Ho ho."

"Yes. That's obvious."

I pulled out my wallet and handed him the cash. Elvis had signed off and now Eartha Kitt purred "Santa Baby." The Christmas tree guy counted my money, cut off a line of rope and said, "While you were haggling over your tree, looks like my star attraction took a powder."

I checked the sidewalk. Ern had fled, too.

And then my not so cheerful tree salesman grabbed me and shoved me to the ground. Hard. Covering my body with his.

Chapter Seven

The boom that rang out echoed off the pizzeria joint where my Camaro was parked. Even with my savior on top of me, muffling the noise, protecting me from the needles and splintered wood that rained down on us, I could tell that it had been the unmistakable blast of a .22.

That's what happens when you hang around gun nuts like Genevieve.

We lay there, the two of us, cold pebbles digging into my cheek as we waited breathlessly for a follow-up. I could hardly breathe under his weight. The smells of pine sap and dirt filled my nose and I calculated that between this and the black water that had splashed on me from the gutter, my outfit was ruined.

"Stay down," he ordered with clear-cut authority.

His massive hand missed my nose by an inch as he hoisted himself off me. My chest ached, I realized, from being squished.

He crouched, unsure, listening. I rolled over and lay on my side, looking up at the trees under the street-lights, large snowflakes seemingly increasing in size the closer they got. I thought, *My ass Debbie was killed by an allergic reaction. This is what Jeffrey Andre was talk-*

ing about when he said he hoped there would be no more, how you say, killings.

"I'll tell you what it was," he said with a slight chuckle. "It was that violent wing of the anti-Christmas lobby, that's who."

I sat up. "What violent wing of the anti-Christmas lobby?"

"You know, the people who are trying to ruin Christmas. The ones who won't let you play 'Hark the Herald Angels' in Almart or mention Jesus's birthday in public schools. Now they're shooting up Christmas trees. Damn them."

I studied him carefully. He didn't seem that convinced of his own theory.

"How'd you know to get me down?"

He answered by pushing up his sleeve and revealing an impressive tattoo on his forearm. It was of a pair of green Army boots and a bulldog against a golden sunset. In bold black letters it said MIKE. "Marine. Served three tours of duty in Iraq. I can sense when a bullet's coming before the trigger's even pulled."

"Impressive."

"I came home. Mike didn't."

I smiled sympathetically. There wasn't much to say. Whoever this guy was, he wasn't an ordinary Christmas tree salesman—that much I could figure out on my own. He'd acted with rapid reaction and protected me as if I were the president of the United States.

He was a goddamn pro.

Once again I couldn't help but be confused. "Do you think he's gone? The shooter, I mean."

"Probably. That was a twenty-two long-rifle hollow point, sounded like to me, probably shot out of a modified KGB one-shot sniper no bigger than a lipstick you got in your purse."

A lipstick gun! That could be dangerous. I mean, what if you were late to work, applying your makeup in the rearview and you accidentally reached for the wrong tube?

"You know a lot about guns," I said. "Guess that comes from being stationed in Iraq, say?"

He didn't respond. Instead, he rose and brushed himself off.

"How about you lay low until I get this tree on," he said, wrapping the rope around his fist. "Just in case."

The way he said it, there was no room for me to argue. I lay there in the dark, thinking as he tied the tree to the top of my car.

Ern Bender had said Debbie deserved to die. He'd said she'd been running a scam that could have turned this town upside down if she hadn't been murdered and then he disappeared and then some jerk shot at me. A warning shot from a tube of lipstick.

I'd like to see Alison Roach, Columbia University Journalism School graduate, top that.

"The powers that be are in the nightly edit meeting. You can't disturb them," Veronica said, closing down her computer for the evening as I rushed in, breathless and excited, demanding to meet Notch. "And your mother owes me a new manicure. Look, I broke a nail." She held out her hand to display the chipped nail.

Welcome to my world, I wanted to tell her. "Lookit, Veronica, I will pay for a new manicure. Heck, I'll give you a new manicure myself, if you'll just buzz Notch and tell him that what I have to say can't wait."

Veronica did a quick check of my own nails for reference. They were slightly messy from digging into the dirt. "You do those yourself?"

"I nearly strangled my ex-husband/fiancé today and I got pushed to the ground when someone tried to shoot my head off and they still held up."

"You do French?"

"Pink and natural."

"Pink will do. With acrylic tips."

"With tips," I agreed.

She buzzed Mr. Notch, and one minute later, I was in

his office facing him at his large mahogany desk, Mr. Salvo sitting off to the side looking particularly weary, various other editors also gathered for the five p.m. edit meeting, including JoBeth Marquard, the lifestyle editor.

I had developed an instinctive aversion to this room, to its institutional green walls, the American flag drooping in the corner, the lone rubber plant and stacks and stacks of newspapers. However, I still liked the red leather couch. Stiletto and I had fooled around on it once. It brought back fond memories.

"This better be worth it," Notch said, eyeing my dirty leggings with repulsion. "I have a six thirty dinner date at the Union Club with the mayor and I'm not in the mood to be toyed with."

I swallowed. Notch's Xanax prescription must have worn off because he was no longer in his new age, touchy-feely mood.

"Debbie Shatsky did not die by accident today. It was murder. I have proof."

Notch tossed his pencil. "Here we go. Let me guess, you heard it from the girls at the salon."

"Better. I interviewed two key sources. Then, during one of the interviews just now, I was shot at, possibly by a representative of the violent wing of the anti-Christmas lobby."

Water off a duck's back. Mr. Notch rolled his hand. "And . . . ?"

Right. Notes. "And I have notes." Okay, I might have taken them in my car afterward, writing from memory, but notes were notes. And I should know because recently I was threatened with jail for not turning over my notes to the prosecution.

"Let's see them." Notch held out his hand and I gave him my notebook. He flipped through a few pages and said, "They're awfully neat."

"Stenography 101 at Two Guys, Dictation for Dummies." I winked at Mr. Salvo, my editor and former Two

Guys journalism instructor, the one who first convinced me I was a natural reporter, if not a natural blonde.

"Who's this Andre guy?" Notch asked.

"He runs a competing salon. He has some connection with Debbie, though I don't know what. She was on the phone to him when she dropped dead. I obtained her cell and counted over twenty-six incoming and outgoing calls to his salon and home within twenty-four hours of her death."

Notch continued reading. And then something miraculous happened. He said with absolutely no sarcasm whatsoever: "Interesting."

I was stunned. Notch never says my stuff is "interesting."

Mr. Salvo flashed me a thumbs-up underneath his clipboard.

"You think you can run this past the cops and write up a story tonight?" Notch asked. "If you can get police confirmation, this is page-one material above the fold."

Unreal! This was too good to be true! Page one above the fold. "Absolutely, I—"

"Actually, Dix, I'm afraid Bubbles has to work for me tonight." It was JoBeth, the editor of lifestyle, a department Notch passed off as "women's stuff," like panty hose and menstrual cycles. "She has to cover the Help the Poor Children fund-raiser."

What? What was this? Since when was I covering the Help the Poor Children fund-raiser?

"She can't do the fund-raiser. She's got to cover the Mahoken Sewage Council," Mr. Salvo countered. "The planned unit development is on the agenda for approval and they don't even have the leach field designed. I budgeted that for B1."

Leach field versus hooking up with Stiletto. Hmmm. How ever could I choose?

JoBeth fiddled nervously with her pen. JoBeth was always nervous. She had a long, thin nose that tended to drip moisture and a grotesquely long neck, which she tried to minimize—unsuccessfully, I'm afraid—with mock turtlenecks. She resembled one of those rescued greyhounds that are never quite right, still chasing the mechanical bunnies in their minds.

It didn't help that she was known for having "meltdowns" in the newsroom when art fell through or a correspondent didn't meet the deadline for a feature on how to bake the best peach pie.

But tonight JoBeth found her mettle. "I'm sorry, Tony. Bubbles has to cover that fund-raiser. She just has to. Flossie demanded it. From her bed in the St. Luke's emergency room. Poor woman, somehow she ended up with a smashed kneecap."

I was overcome with a sickening feeling. My own kneecap throbbed in sympathy. The pain must have been horrific. Though now, with Flossie being in the hospital, Mama and Genevieve wouldn't have to take her out. . . .

Take her out. I slapped my forehead. I'd actually said to Genevieve that she should take her out. And, of course, Genevieve had interpreted this the way any average person would—provided the average person was Tony Soprano.

"I don't know." Mr. Salvo hemmed. "This could be big stuff. If that sewage proposal passes, it could be an increase of .05 cents in the Mahoken millage."

Stop the presses.

"The fund-raiser raises fifty thousand dollars in one night!" JoBeth exclaimed. "And everyone who's anyone will be there. It's being run by Sabina Towne."

Sabina Towne. That name was so not Allentown. Only girls from swanky places like Stroudsburg could pull off a name like Sabina Towne.

"You know?" JoBeth was saying. "The actress? She is incredibly hot right now."

"So's her new boyfriend, from what I hear." Mr. Salvo gave me a knowing look.

I ignored him. "I can do it all, JoBeth. I can stop by the

fund-raiser and get some color." Okay, meet Stiletto. "Then I can zip over to the Mahoken meeting and, in between, write up the piece about Debbie and Ern Bender."

"Ern who?" Notch snapped to attention.

"Ern Bender. That's what E. B. stands for in my notes. He was a pharmacist at Save-T Drugs who was busted a few years back for selling drug-laced Cokes. He got out of jail last week and he told me tonight that Debbie deserved to die. Said he had a scam going and Debbie took it over."

"What kind of scam?" JoBeth asked.

I threw up my hands. "I don't know. All Ern said was that it was his idea, he had the information—whatever that meant—and Debbie stole it from him. Then she framed him and got him sent to jail. In Ern's words, it was good she was murdered because if she hadn't been, her scam could have turned the whole town upside down."

"My!" JoBeth exclaimed, her eyes glittering. "That's intriguing."

"That does sound like a lead. If it's true," Mr. Salvo said. "Whaddya think, Dix?"

But Dix Notch had turned to stone. He was pale. Paler than I'd ever seen him before. It was as if he'd just witnessed a dump truck crushing his priceless Old Tom Morris putter.

"Bender," he muttered.

"Pardon?" JoBeth said.

"Bender." Notch's eyelids fluttered. "Ern Bender the pharmacist."

Mr. Salvo jotted this down on his clipboard. "Lawless has written a few stories on Bender already. We ran them inside. You want me to call him in? He can help Bubbles on this."

I didn't need any help. Definitely not from Lawless, whose idea of assistance was fetching peanut M&Ms from the vending machine. Anyway, I was more concerned about Notch at the moment. He didn't look right. He might have been in the early stages of a heart attack.

"Not Lawless," Notch said, zombie-like. "She doesn't need Lawless."

Amen to that. "Thank you, Mr. Notch."

"Shut up, Yablinko," he snapped harshly, calling me by the old nickname. "Find Alison. Get me Alison Roach."

"The rookie?" Mr. Salvo shook his head. "She can't handle this."

Notch began quivering as if an earthquake were erupting within his muscled body. "Don't argue with me, damn it. Get her."

Mr. Salvo knew better than to protest further. He hopped up and popped his head out the door. "Roach! Get in here."

Faster than mercury, Alison was standing next to me and I felt an odd—not to mention disturbing—shift in the atmospheric pressure. Somehow I'd managed to get on Notch's bad side—again.

"Alison." Notch's jaw was clenched so tightly he could barely get out the words. "Tell me what you've found out about the Shatsky homicide today."

Alison didn't even peek at the notebook in her hand. "Seems it's nothing more than an accidental poisoning. I just got off the phone with Detective Burge. He's convinced the lab reports will show that there was nothing but latex in the hair glue. According to my research on the Internet, latex allergies are rare, but they can be deadly. Debbie Shatsky displayed all the symptoms. Hives. Difficulty breathing."

Yes, yes, yes, I wanted to say. *I knowww that.* The question was who switched the glue.

"What about the glue in the toilet?" Mr. Salvo asked.

"That was found in the private bathroom of the House of Beauty owner." Alison checked her notes. "Detective Burge said she was probably trying to hide the fact that she'd accidentally mistaken the two glues by dumping the latex-free one down the toilet."

I gasped in shock. "That is such a lie. Anyone could have been in Sandy's bathroom."

Alison pursed her lips as if she found this amusing. "I don't think so. Only the House of Beauty owner had the key."

"That's not true. Lots of people had a key. Like me, for instance."

Alison wrote this down. "I'll have to mention that to Detective Burge. Thank you."

"Hold on. *I* didn't dump the glue."

Alison tossed her hair. "So you're flip-flopping again. Now you're saying Sandy really did do it."

"No. Not Sandy, either."

"Then who did?"

"The murderer."

"Murderer?" Alison snorted and glanced at the editors in the room, seeking confirmation that I was a fool. "I guess you're totally out of it because the police have already ruled this a negligent homicide. Manslaughter at most. There's no murder."

"Try telling that to Ern Bender."

"Enough!" Notch pointed his pencil at me. "I don't want to hear the words 'murder' or 'Bender' out of your mouth again, Yablinko. You've got a serious and clear-cut conflict of interest here. It's obvious to everyone in the room."

He glared at JoBeth and Mr. Salvo and Alison, the only one who was nodding vigorously in agreement.

"After listening to you and Alison, there is no doubt in my mind, Yablinko, that you want to skew the facts to protect your friend, Sandy, to keep her from being sued. That's an abhorrent misuse of your power as a journalist and I find it disgusting."

Bullshit! I was not misusing my "power" as a journalist and Notch knew it. I'd simply been doing my job.

But Notch wouldn't let me interrupt his rant.

"Therefore, I'm imposing a ban. From now on you may not make one phone call, you may not ask one question regarding this Shatsky homicide. If I find out you've been digging into this case behind my back, I'll have you canned on the spot. That's the beauty of probation. I can fire you without explanation."

I brought my hand to my chest. "But . . . but two minutes ago you were asking me if I could write it up for page one."

"That was before I read all your notes. If you can call them notes. Hardly. They are the most pathetic bunch of lies I've read in my thirty years of being an editor. Total fiction." He closed the notebook and discarded it into a wastebasket. Then he leaned on the buzzer and called in Justin, our high school intern, to dump the trash.

I watched helplessly as Justin snatched the mesh wastebasket and confusedly asked Mr. Notch what he wanted him to do with it.

"The incinerator in the basement. I can't take the chance of them falling into the wrong hands."

"Those are my notes!" I begged. "You can't burn my notes."

"I can do whatever I damn well please, including ordering you out of my office. See that she leaves with you, Justin."

This was devastating humiliation. Justin was Jane's age. He was a kid and I was an adult. And I was being ordered to follow him. I turned to Mr. Salvo for support, but his head was bent over his clipboard.

Only JoBeth said, "I hope this means Bubbles is free to cover the Help the Poor Children fund-raiser, Dix. Flossie is insistent."

"Just as long as she doesn't come within ten feet of this story."

The room was silent. There was no point in filing my objections. Everyone felt uncomfortable. Everyone just wanted me to go. Everyone except Alison, who was smug with victory.

"Come on, Justin," I said. "I'll walk you out."

Justin politely opened the door and I stepped

through. As soon as the door closed, I reached in the basket and took back my notebook.

"I was going to give it to you, anyway," Justin said.

"I know." I gave him a peck on the cheek. "You're a good boy."

His baby face turned pink. "What happened in there?"

"Notch. Who knows what sets him off?"

But I knew what had set him off.

Ern Bender.

The question was why.

Chapter Eight

Parking was hard to find on West Goepp, even in my own driveway, where two strange cars sat uninvited. But that wasn't the worst of it.

The worst of it was the dozens of housewives clutching casseroles and shivering in the December chill on Phil Shatsky's covered porch across the street, waiting their turn to be allowed an audience with the widower so they could offer their sympathies—and maybe more.

Dressed to the nines in furs, high heels and likely not much else, Phil's most loyal clients were not so willing to let me pass when I asked to speak with him for just a minute.

"Not so fast." A woman in a soft gray chinchilla threw out her arm to block me. "You have to wait out here like the rest of us. Also, you need a covered dish." She held out a foil-covered casserole that smelled of corn tortillas and chili.

It was amazing what access a covered dish could provide. Through the plate-glass window at the front of the house I could discern tons of women crowding Phil's living room, sitting on Debbie's custom upholstered couches, passing around pieces of her Hummel figurine collection. None of them would have been allowed inside if Debbie had been alive. Seven-layer lasagna or no seven-layer lasagna.

"This is business," I tried to explain. "It has to do with Debbie's death. It's really very important." I reached for the doorknob but Chinchilla elbowed me aside.

"Even if I wanted to let you in, which I don't, you couldn't go. Over capacity. Besides, Phil's not seeing anyone now." She crimped the foil edges of her casserole. "He's with Marguerite."

Marguerite. That was the name of the desperate housewife Debbie claimed was after her husband. A buzz erupted as soon as Marguerite's name was mentioned. Clearly, she'd already been the topic of much speculation among the wannabes in line.

"Who is this Marguerite?" I asked.

Chinchilla shrugged. "It's a mystery. Whoever she is, she has a very high opinion of herself. Arrived in a fancy Lincoln Town Car with vanity plates that said BRIK-HOUS."

"She must be mighty, mighty . . ." I said.

"She was certainly letting it all hang out." Chinchilla sniffed. "She got out of the car and marched right past us as though we were nothing. Cut in line and entered like royalty. We were shocked. I swear, there was nothing on underneath her coat."

"What did she look like?"

"Built. Definitely implants. Big blond hair and expensive sunglasses, the kind you buy at Sunglass Hut in the mall. Though I don't know who wears sunglasses on a snowy December night. Someone who has something to hide, that's who."

I thought of the Iraq war veteran who had saved me. He'd worn sunglasses.

"After she showed, Phil didn't want to see anyone else. Here I'd made my famous chicken tortilla, waxed my legs and rushed right over to console him, only to find I was thirty-sixth in line. Then she arrives, without so much as a cupcake, and gets to see him like that. I'll

be damned if I lose my place to another interloper arriving empty-handed." Chinchilla gestured to my empty
hands.

I couldn't hang around waiting for Phil to finish up
with his mistress, either. So I wrote him a short note that
wouldn't give away much in case the housewives read it,
which of course they would. I handed it to Chinchilla,
politely asked her to give it to him and crossed the
street to my own house.

Unlike every other house on West Goepp, which had
been decorated with at least a plastic candy cane or two
since Halloween, mine was devoid of any Christmas
decorations. This was the first year that I was so not on
the ball and my bare door was fast becoming a neighborhood scandal.

Jane and I lived in one half of a brick-and-aluminum-
sided double with green Astroturf on the porch and, in
the summer, a red geranium. The other half was tidily
occupied by the Hamels, who, following the unwritten
Lehigh ordinance mandating Christmas decorations on
October 31, had strung icicles from the porch overhang
and colored lights on the bushes out front months ago.
Mrs. Hamel felt so bad for me that she had tacked a
cardboard snowman on my mailbox.

Mama was devastated that I wasn't keeping up with
the neighbors. In her mind, not having Christmas decorations was bad for Jane, bad for the neighborhood, bad
for America and, most of all, bad for her campaign to
turn Lehigh into the heretofore unknown Discount
Christmas City.

Which might explain why, on returning from Phil
Shatsky's, I found my mother industriously sawing at
the ropes affixing the Christmas tree to the top of my
Camaro.

"It's about time. How long were you gonna wait to
get a tree? December twenty-fourth?"

I'll be married by then, I thought sadly. "What are you
doing here?"

"You're going out tonight to that fund-raiser. Can't leave Jane alone."

This was true. Ever since "the incident," Jane hated being alone. After years of learning to cook herself dinner while I went to community college at night or stayed late at the House of Beauty earning extra tips or, more recently, covered meetings for the *News-Times,* she could not bear one minute by herself once the sun set. And, these days, it set pretty early.

"Hey, everyone. I jerry-rigged us a tree stand!" Genevieve appeared on my porch holding, ominously, a hubcap with the center cut out. It looked like it belonged to the Salabskys' Ford Windstar, which it probably did. "Jeezum. That's a sorry-looking specimen of an evergreen if I ever did see."

"Help me, will you, Genny?" Mama dragged the tree off my car.

I caught one end, feeling guilty that a little old lady— okay, she wasn't that old and not that little and, now that I thought of it, not much of a lady—was hauling my Christmas tree.

Genevieve heaved it onto her shoulder with ease. "Dangy, that's dry. This thing's going to catch fire faster than a lit match in a fart."

Who needed Shakespeare when there was such sweet prose from Genevieve's lips?

"Say, Genevieve," I said as we carried the tree up the steps, "what exactly did you do to Flossie Foreman?"

"Took her out, like you said."

"I was thinking maybe taking her out to a nice restaurant, to the movies. You know, some ice cream. I wasn't talking about taking out her kneecaps."

Genevieve let the tree down in my living room with a grunt. "Taking out is taking out. She should be glad I quit at one. I was itching to pop off the right but your mother wouldn't let me."

I winced. I would have to send Flossie a huuuuge bouquet in the morning.

"Mom? Is that you?"

Jane appeared on the stairs. She looked the same: grungy low-riding jeans, royal blue hair, a supertight Green Day T-shirt and studs all around. But she was clinging to the doorjamb and staring at us with almost palpable anxiety.

"Buffy the fun slayer," Genevieve grumbled.

My loopy daughter skipped down the stairs clutching the cell phone Dan had purchased for her. She never went anywhere without that stupid cell phone—in case the phenomenal Jason should call.

"Finally. A Christmas tree. I wondered if you were ever going to get around to buying one."

I gave her a dirty look.

"Are we going to decorate it?"

"Soon, hon," Mama said. "First, there's chicken you made today. And it's already six o'clock. Late."

Disappointed, Jane turned her attention to today's latest delivery of wedding gifts.

"You've got to open them, Mom. It's not polite to let them sit there. People will be expecting thank-you notes."

Mama was plunking on the table a lemon-roasted chicken with rosemary, a bowl of canned green beans and a tub of mashed potatoes. Genevieve lined a plastic basket with waxed paper and tossed in slices of Wonderbread. It was nutrition galore at the Yablonsky household.

"Maybe tomorrow I'll open the gifts. I have to go on assignment tonight."

"Again? You just can't wait to leave me, can you? Guess I'm not worth being around."

In the old days, I would have laughed off that kind of snotty teenage line. Not now. Thanks to Dr. Caswell's report, I was supersensitive to any allegations of maternal inadequacy. Jane's quip opened up a nice, fresh wound.

Ignore her, Genevieve mouthed.

"I can't wait until you and Dad get married. Then maybe you'll be at home more and I can have a real family for once instead of a television, Grandma and . . . *that*." She cocked her head at Genevieve, who, having distributed the Wonderbread, was spying out the window with her military-issue infrared binoculars, looking for Commies or whatever it was that got her so excited.

"Gotcha," I said.

"Dinner's ready!" Mama barked.

"Where are you going?" Jane asked as I headed toward the stairs.

"I have to get dressed for this fund-raiser I'm covering." It was hard to get out the words. My mouth had gone dry, realizing that Stiletto probably had some plan to get us alone so we could be together with no one else for the last time ever.

"You seem stressed," Jane said, pulling out her chair at the table. "Everything go all right at work today?"

"Um, okay."

"Nothing exciting happen?"

I was forbidden by Dr. Caswell from mentioning anything disturbing that might cause Jane to suffer a flashback. So even though there were a couple dozen housewives outside waiting to comfort a man whose wife had dropped dead right before my eyes, murdered by hair extensions, even though I'd been shot at by the violent wing of the anti-Christmas lobby, all I could say was "Not really, sweetie. Everything is hunky-dory."

"Good." Jane joined Mama and Genevieve, who were already engaged in passing, buttering, cutting and scooping.

There was a knock at the door. I stopped with one foot on the bottom step. Immediately, a shadow fell across Jane's face. "Should I get it?" she asked.

"No, Jane." I reached the door first. "It's okay. I'll get it."

Jane ran from the table and pushed me aside. "No, Mom. Let me. It's part of my therapy, learning not to be afraid to open my own front door. That's what Dr. Caswell wants me to do. Besides, you're here and Grandma and Genevieve and there's a peephole. Perfectly safe."

She pressed her eye against the peephole and sighed with relief. "Oh. I'm such an idiot. It's nothing."

"Who is it?"

She unlocked the door. "Nobody. Just Santa Claus."

Chapter Nine

"**N**OOO!" I threw my body against the door and flipped the latch.

Jane stepped back. "What's wrong? It's only some guy dressed as Santa Claus. Probably from the Salvation Army."

"It's a Santagram." Mama wiped her lips and pushed back from the table. "Let him in, Bubbles. Don't be so queer."

Genevieve waved a slice of Wonder. "My musket's right there by the door, Sally, if you're hankering."

I grabbed the rusted musket, surprised by how heavy it was. I had no idea how to fire this thing or if it was already "tamped and loaded," whatever that meant.

Knock. Knock. Knock.

My heart was pounding at breakneck speed. What to do? It might be Ern Bender or my stalker in the Mercedes. I simply couldn't take the risk.

Jane was regarding me quizzically. "Mom? Is something going on that you're not telling me?"

Knock. Knock.

Dampness spread into my underarms. "Noooo. I'm just being careful, sweetie. That's how mothers are."

"Careful about Santa Claus?" Jane scrunched her

mouth, as if such a thing weren't possible. "Maybe I'm not the only one who needs to see Dr. Caswell on Tuesdays and Thursdays, hmm?"

"Miss Yablonsky?" It was a man's voice. He might have been the stalker, but he was more sober sounding than Ern Bender. "Do you have a minute? It's me, Phil."

Phil Shatsky. Debbie's husband. Whew! Feeling like an idiot, I unlatched the door and let him in.

Phil was, indeed, dressed like Santa Claus and he appeared more frightened than any of us. "You always answer the door with a gun?"

I dropped my gaze to the rusted musket in my hand. "Sorry. Precaution." Then I pointed to his duds. "You always dress like an elf?"

"I do when there are customers filling my house with tuna noodle casseroles and I need to escape." He smiled a broad, sad smile.

Okay, so he wasn't textbook handsome or particularly built. Still, Phil Shatsky had a kind face and a swollen nose, probably from crying.

"I'm sorry about the note," I said, leading him to the couch. "I should have waited. I mean, this must be so confusing right now."

"What's so confusing?" Jane asked. She was standing over us with her arms folded and eyebrows raised.

"Nothing's confusing, honey," I said. "This is a personal matter. Maybe you should go to your room."

"My room! I haven't been sent to my room since I was nine."

Mama got the message. "Come on, Jane. Let's go out for dessert." She grabbed her coat off the hook by the door. "Your mother has work to do."

Jane stamped her foot. "No. Something's going on and no one's telling me. There are all these women outside and our neighbor shows up in a Santa suit and Mom's throwing around a musket. What happened?"

"My wife . . ." Phil started, before I could put up a hand to stop him.

"What happened to your wife?" Jane wanted to know.

"Jane!" Mama frowned the frown that still terrorizes me in my nightmares.

Mama's glower did the trick. It got my pesky daughter to back off, but not willingly. She was suspicious and for good reason. A woman across the street had been murdered, had died in front of her mother. This was not the kind of crisis we were used to in our neighborhood. This was way worse than untrimmed front doors and no Christmas trees.

This was the kind of crisis that even marrying Dan might not be able to set right.

"How can I help?" I asked, after Mama, Jane and Genevieve had hustled out to the Lehigh Diner for their famous peppermint stick ice-cream pie.

Phil took off his Santa cap and fingered the pom-pom between his thick, grease-stained fingers. "Tell me what happened. I want to know everything."

I couldn't see how describing Debbie's death would hurt anyone or hamper an investigation, so I started at the beginning, making sure to play up that Debbie had been singing his praises right until the end.

"Really? She said all that stuff about me?"

"You should have seen her, Phil, how proud she was to have a husband who watched the Lifetime Channel and folded laundry." I nudged him. "Said you made terrific love afterward, too."

A big tear rolled down Phil's flaccid cheek. He brushed it away and sniffed. "My grandmother taught me that real men cry. That's a lesson that kinda came in handy today."

"She's a good woman, your grandma. A good woman."

"Debbie is"—he paused and closed his eyes—"*was* a lot like my grandma. Too bad they never got to know each other."

My chest tightened. I would have given him a hug then and there if I wasn't afraid it would lump me in with the other desperate housewives outside. I could definitely see the attraction to Phil Shatsky. Under different circumstances, I, too, might have been tempted to pour some celery soup over chicken pieces for him.

"Look at it this way, Phil. Maybe they're getting to know each other right now." I patted his hand. "Now that your wife and grandma are together in you know where."

"Boca Raton?"

"Excuse me?"

"That's where Grandma is. In Boca Raton, Florida. She doesn't like to fly or drive long distances, so she didn't make it to our wedding. And Debbie never had a chance to get to Florida, what with all the other traveling she had to do for business."

Bells went off. A granddaughter-in-law in the travel business who didn't make time to visit her husband's elderly grandmother. A woman with enough frequent-flier miles to start her own airline? That wasn't right.

I added it to my growing list of facts that made Debbie weird, including once being married to a sallow pharmacist who went to jail, harassing by phone a self-absorbed hair stylist with two first names and running an alleged scam she co-opted from her ex-husband.

"You know how we met?" Phil asked, not waiting for my answer. "Debbie had a stopped-up toilet. A toothbrush she'd been using to clean the grout in her bathroom had been in a bucket. She emptied out the bucket into the toilet, the toothbrush got stuck and, the next thing she knew, she was up to her ankles in water."

Yuck.

"She was so cute. So bubbly and full of life. I never met a woman who could giggle like that." He smiled to himself. "She was wearing a bikini. Polka dots. Said she always wore a swimsuit when she cleaned the shower."

Or was trying to seduce the most successful plumber in town.

"What about her former husband?" I prodded.

Phil rested his chin on his hand. "That guy couldn't find the business end of a wrench. He was useless. Used to fall asleep in front of the TV every night. Guess that's because he was a drug addict, too. Do you know about that?"

I played innocent. "I heard he went to jail for drugs. Don't know what exactly."

"You name it, he did it. Had the whole pharmacy to himself, like an alcoholic owning a bar. Valium. Percoset. I don't know what else. Debbie never put him down, though. She always referred to him in the best light, of course."

"Of course."

"She tried to get him into rehab but he refused to admit that he had a problem. Finally, when she found out he was hurting other people and not just himself, she went to the authorities." Phil looked at me. "It was the right thing to do."

"Absolutely." I thought of Ern's protestations that he was innocent and that Debbie had set him up. She had a lot to gain by getting Ern out of the way. She had a scam to profit from—and a chance at Phil.

"How long after Ern left did you two marry?"

Phil blushed. "The day he was shipped off to the penitentiary, Debbie and I drove to Maryland. She didn't want to. It was my idea. She refused to . . . you know . . . until she had a ring."

Ah, yes. That old trick. Holding out until the ink on the marriage certificate is good and dry. It's surprising more women who want to get married haven't figured out all they have to do is claim a vow of chastity.

"I have to ask you, Bubbles," he said, after an uncomfortable moment of silence had passed. "Was there anything else Debbie said today?"

There was a lot Debbie said, most of it obnoxious bragging, but this was not the appropriate occasion to go into detail. "What do you mean?"

"I mean, I guess . . . " He played with the pom-pom on his hat some more. "When she knew she was . . . uh . . . having an attack. Did she say anything? I wouldn't ask except that I have this burning need to know, for some reason."

"She said something about having a deadly wheat allergy."

Phil shook his head. "She's not allergic to wheat. She's allergic to latex."

Was, I thought. "I know. I must have misunderstood."

"Anything else?"

"She said she felt dizzy. And hot."

"But what were . . . what were her dying words?"

I sat back. In the span of only a few hours, I'd been asked that question twice, first by Ern Bender and now by Debbie's own husband. Though, between both of them, Debbie's husband made the most sense.

"She said she loved you, Phil. Those were her dying words."

"Really?"

"Honest." And it was true, sort of. Okay, so Debbie hadn't specifically croaked, "I love you, Phil," before collapsing, but she'd said as much.

"You don't know how much better that makes me feel. Debbie and I loved each other more than you could imagine. A lot of people doubted that because she travels so often and I'm always making house calls late at night. The thing is, they don't know. They couldn't know how special our relationship was."

"I know," I said, though I didn't. And I never would.

Chapter Ten

The unfortunate thing about Phil Shatsky showing up at my door weepy and flattened with grief was that I couldn't very well launch into the fourth degree about his affair with Marguerite and whether what Ern Bender had told me was true.

I mean, there he was sobbing and sobbing after I lied that Debbie's last words were that she loved him. He used up all my tissues and one roll of toilet paper, which happened to be my last roll. And then he moved on to paper towels. His nose was bright red and raw.

Meanwhile, I was keeping one eye on the clock, picking over what was left of the chicken and cold mashed potatoes on Jane's plate and trying to come up with an easy exit line so I could take a shower to get ready for the fund-raiser.

No matter what I said, Phil wouldn't leave. "I can't go back there. Oh, no," he moaned, wistfully parting the shades to see his house across the street. "I can't be there among her things, alone."

"You won't be among her things alone," I said. "There are twenty women crowding your living room right now."

"Yes. But they're not Debbie. Can't I stay here? It's

so homey and warm. There's so much dusting to do. I promise I won't get in your way. And I'll help around the house."

In the end, I agreed to let him stay until I left for the fund-raiser. Can't say it was the most comfortable arrangement, me taking a shower with Phil clanking pots and pans downstairs in the kitchen, playing the score from *Rent* full-blast. For one thing, I was treated to a jet of cold water whenever he turned on the faucet. For another, he was making a lot of noise.

And crying. Crying. Crying. Crying. It was enough to make a healthy adult woman rethink the virtues of creating more sensitive men.

When I emerged a half hour later in the silver-sequined halter-top dress I'd bought from Almart, my hair in a classic twist, my feet stuffed into black pumps, I found that Phil had dried his tears and completely transformed my kitchen.

It was spotless. Not a dish was in sight, not even a Tupperware container of leftovers. The counters were scrubbed clean. The refrigerator gleamed. Even the decades-old grime ringing the burners was gone. The air smelled of cinnamon and fresh nutmeg.

Phil was rearranging my spice rack. I never even knew I had a spice rack.

"This is incredible." I ran my finger along the banister. "It's totally clean."

He tossed a jar of Mama's Butter Buds into the trash and shuddered. "It's my therapy. Some men have football and beer. Some men get rid of their stress on the links. Others go hunting or fishing. I organize. I can't tell you how much better I feel."

I could have made a crack about my home being in a lot better shape if more people in his life died more often, but decided on second thought that might be tasteless.

"My, my." He put his hands on his aproned hips. It was the blue flowered one Mama used on special occasions; it went nicely with his red Santa pants. "Look who's all dressed up and ready to party."

"I'm going to the Help the Poor Children Fund-raiser."

"Not in those shoes you're not."

I glanced down at my shoes. Basic black pumps. "No?"

"They're just fine . . . if you like looking like the church secretary."

I brought my hand to my mouth. "The church secretary!"

"How about red? You have anything in red?"

Of course. I had *everything* in red.

I ran upstairs, dug out a pair of red sparkled high-heeled stilettos from the back of the closet, blew off the dust and returned. Phil was done organizing the spice rack, and he was frowning at my cluttered refrigerator. He also might have had a batch of Christmas cookies going. Explained the cinnamon.

"I thought you were going to a fund-raiser, not off to see the wizard," he said when he saw my red sparklies.

It took five tries for Phil to be satisfied with a pair of silver slingbacks. I'd forgotten I'd bought them last fall for Mickey Sinkler's wedding.

"Now about those lips . . ."

"Phil. I *have* to go." I gave him a quick hug.

Phil held on to me. "You have saved me tonight, Bubbles. I didn't know how I was going to make it. You're an angel."

"It's okay, Phil." I tried to break away, but he clung on. "Really. No problem."

He gently brushed back my hair and kissed me softly on the cheek. "I will never forget your kindness."

When he bent to kiss me on the lips, I ducked and dashed to the door and ran outside.

Smack into Chinchilla.

She was bundled in her coat, side by side with two other women. They did not look like they were from the

Welcome Wagon. There wasn't a casserole or a pan of brownies among them.

"Funny thing," Chinchilla said, playing with the heart pendant at her neck. "Once Phil read your note, he was worse than he was with Marguerite. Had to see you right away. Like a teenager in love."

"I'm sorry," I said, trying to pass through them to get to my car. "I'm very late."

"Not as late as Debbie." Chinchilla gripped my arm. Before I could wiggle free, I found myself completely encircled by angry housewives in furs, smelling of scalloped potatoes and corned beef hash.

Chinchilla wouldn't let me go.

"Okay, what is it? You want me to get Phil out here?" I asked. "What have I done?"

"Rumor has it you were the one who was doing Debbie's hair when she 'mysteriously' and 'suddenly' collapsed."

"So?"

"So we were talking. You do Debbie's hair, she dies. You come home and Phil can't wait to take you in his arms. It's all coming together. You two are shacking up."

This was crazy. "We are not shacking up. He came over to my house to get away from you harpies."

A vixen in Chinchilla's gang let out a hiss.

"Don't tell me you two weren't in a clutch. We saw you two making out. We saw through the windows."

Damn. Phil had left the shades parted. That's always dangerous in this neighborhood. Cable's too expensive, so most of us have to find other, and cheaper, forms of entertainment. And spying on neighbors across the street doesn't necessitate a subscription to *TV Guide*.

"It was a quick hug! It didn't mean anything. Look, I'm engaged. I'm getting married Saturday."

"Yeah?" Chinchilla grabbed my left hand. "I don't see a ring."

Because I refused to wear it out of protest, though I

didn't see why I should have to tell her that. "Let me go." I kicked and missed. The women laughed.

Chinchilla dropped my arm. "Seems to us you had opportunity, means and motive, Bubbles Yablonsky. Looks to us like you might have murdered Debbie so you could get your hands on Phil."

Her gang nodded and flexed their fingers, which were covered with gold and silver rings studded with diamonds. The suburbs' answer to brass knuckles.

Chinchilla sneered. "Well, it's not going to work, your plan. I have connections in the police department and I informed my husband about everything I saw tonight. Let me tell you, he was very interested. Very interested. Said it wasn't the first time you'd had a run-in with the law. He should be paying you a visit real soon."

"Your husband?" My stomach was twisting into a painful knot.

"Detective Burge. Know him?"

Know him? He was my most ardent enemy, next to Dix Notch. Above all, Detective Burge despised Stiletto. Stiletto went on the lam once when we found a dead body in the park, just to avoid Burge, and since then Burge had never forgiven me.

In Burge's mind, it was just a matter of time before he could pin me with something.

Like Debbie's murder.

I couldn't make sense of my evening with Phil. All the crying and the clutching. I'd been so stupid not to notice the drapes were open so everyone could witness Phil making himself at home in my house.

Then there'd been the pass he'd made at me. I hadn't wanted to be kissed or hugged. But Phil had been so "clingy." It wasn't easy rejecting a distraught widower. You can't very well slap him in the face or dump a glass of water over his head, not with his eyes still red from constant crying over his dead wife.

If only he hadn't opened those damned drapes.

I parked in the Masonic temple lot, yanked the key from the ignition, got out and remembered who was there. Stiletto.

I felt a new anxiety, different from the anxiety of being caught with Phil or being pegged by Burge for murder. It was the kind of quivering I hadn't felt since my first dance in Northeast Junior High when Randy Mahl, the drop-dead cutie from my eighth-grade typing class, asked me to slow shuffle to "Dust in the Wind."

I negotiated the steep steps to the impressive Masonic temple with its grand pillars and felt a surge of excitement. Music spilled out the double front doors along with high-pitched laughter. Stepping into the marble lobby, I was relieved to see I wasn't the only woman in a sparkly dress. In fact . . .

Wait a minute—that's all there were! Women.

Specifically, women between the ages of twenty and sixty whispering and holding fancy pink drinks in martini glasses. Clearly, they had spared no expense because their makeup jobs were professional and their hair . . . well, let me just say that Debbie wasn't the only woman in town with a passion for extreme up dos.

"May I have your name?"

A matronly woman in a blue gown beamed up at me from a registration table. Her name tag read PAULINE.

"I need your name," Pauline said again, "so I can check you off our list and give you a number. For the auction."

Oh, right. The auction. "Um, actually I'm a . . ."

Hold on. I had to be discreet. People were always trying to get their names or their kids' names into "Talk of the Town," Flossie once told me. Sometimes she went incognito. If it got out in this crowd that I was temporarily taking over for Flossie, I might be so swamped I'd never have a moment alone with Stiletto.

"Reporter," I murmured. "For the *News-Times*."

Pauline checked her list. "I'm sorry. We already have a reporter for the *News-Times* here."

"Really?" Uh-oh. Flossie must have slipped out of her hospital bed. I searched the crowd for a fat woman with a walker and a bum left knee.

Keeping the same sour puss, Pauline said caustically, "To tell you the truth, we had to turn her away because she didn't meet the dress code. Oh. Hold on. She's back."

I followed Pauline's gaze to the door, where a dour figure slouched. She was in the most Gawd-awful teal blue dress that was three sizes too big. However, she was neither fat nor with a walker. She was in a bad mood.

She was Lorena Ludwig, our personality-challenged pugnacious photographer, and she looked none too pleased.

"This is all your fault, Yablonsky," she accused, trudging over in what appeared to be snow boots under the flounces of teal. "I had to go home and dig out my sister's bridesmaid dress. Look at me. I'm drowning in this thing."

Lorena's brown hair was pulled into a sloppy ponytail, the better to show off the cigarette wedged behind her ear, I supposed.

"You didn't have to wear *that,*" Pauline said. "Any skirt would have been fine. Just not jeans. Especially, *those* jeans."

"I still got the jeans." Lorena lifted her hem to expose the frayed and dirty cuffs of her standard Levi's. "I don't go no place without two things: my jeans and my Camels."

Pauline pressed her lips together in disapproval and handed us our numbers. I was 115. Lorena was 116. I told Lorena I didn't see the point in getting numbers anyway, as I was there to cover the fund-raiser, not to bid on some painting or priceless antique. But Lorena said I should keep it, so I did.

We entered the main hall, where white folding chairs had been arranged in neat rows in front of a stage. A chamber quartet played classical music that was very upscale. Michael Bolton or John Tesh fancy. Waiters passed around champagne and more pink drinks to the clusters of women.

I scanned the crowd, searching for You Know Who.

"Man. This ain't like any fund-raiser I've ever been to." Lorena pulled out her cigarette and fingered it with longing. "Take a look at that specimen, would ya?"

A tall blond hunk in a tux walked by, a Nordic god with shaggy hair waving as he passed. A bright red #1 was stuck to his back.

"I want to know what conditioner he uses to get hair like that," I said. "My hair never waves."

"There's a lot from that guy I wanna know. The brand of his conditioner's not one of them."

And then it hit me. Number one?

"Are they numbering the waiters here?" I asked, as another hunk, a black man with a shaved head, strolled past, a woman on each arm.

Lorena popped the unlit cigarette into her mouth. "This isn't your usual charity auction, Einstein. They're not bidding on antiques. They're bidding on bachelors."

Synapses fired in my brain, for once leaping the ganglia necessary to induce quick thinking. Men up for bid. Charity. Hunks in tuxes.

Could it be that Stiletto—*my* Stiletto—would be on the auction block so any old woman could buy him?

I coughed, gagging at the very idea.

Lorena smiled. "Ah, yes, and our professor emeritus finally figures it out. The stud muffin you so incomprehensibly rejected is number three. Right over there."

Lorena pointed to a spot by the stage where the largest group of women huddled. I could barely make out his famous blackish wavy hair. I loved that hair. I'd run my fingers through it many a night as he lay sleeping by my side. It was the same hair that had brushed my cheek and neck in bed.

A pathetic longing swept over me. Okay, he was here.

A few feet away. Surrounded by women who wanted him, and now, being a free agent in every sense, he was free to choose any one of them. And they him. For a lifetime of happiness, romance and hot, passionate sex. Oh, to be entwined in Stiletto's sinewy thighs for just one more night.

I teetered a bit.

"You don't look too good," Lorena said. "In fact, pardon my customary bluntness. You look like shit."

I fanned myself with a program. "Nonsense. I'm fine."

"Sure you are. You always are top-notch when you're green."

A bell rang and Pauline marched up the aisle, clapping her hands and ordering everyone to finish their drinks, perhaps make a trip to the ladies' and take their seats. Except for the bachelors, who were to join her backstage.

Reluctantly the women broke away, heading in droves for the bathrooms, the men left standing like seashells tossed on shore by a receding tide of estrogen. There was the blond Nordic hunk. An adorable freckled, freakishly tall bachelor whom I'd seen on the sports pages as a local boy made big playing professional basketball. The chiseled African-American man whom I immediately recognized from my experiences in the St. Luke's emergency center as bone surgeon Dr. Drake, and Stiletto.

He was looking at me. Straight at me. His dark blue eyes teasing and seducing me simultaneously.

With Stiletto, no matter what I was wearing, I always felt naked.

He appraised me from my silver slingbacks on up and returned a verdict of approval. His mouth opened to say something when a lithe woman in a low-cut black dress and incredibly healthy long, thick blond hair suddenly appeared by his side.

She was in her early thirties with an impeccable boob job—not too big, not too perky—and in impressive ath-

letic shape. She slipped one of her toned arms into
Stiletto's and stood on tiptoe to whisper in his ear.
Whatever she said, it must have been hilarious because
he flashed her his widest, most appreciative grin.

The actress from Allentown. That was his new girlfriend. Sabina whatever. And she was gorgeous!

Stiletto gestured casually in my direction. Sabina
nodded eagerly and then the . . . Oh, crap. They were
headed straight toward me.

"I don't know about you, but I gotta piss like a race-
horse and that line's out the door," Lorena was saying.
"There's a bathroom behind the coat closet upstairs
that no one knows about. Follow me."

"Be right there," I murmured, unable to move as
every muscle in my body had apparently ceased to function.

Lorena left and the next I knew Stiletto was in front
of me, so close I could smell his trademark scent of crisp
clean cotton and fresh air.

"Hello, Bubbles. Glad you could make it." He took
my hand and in one smooth movement planted a gen-
tlemanly kiss on my cheek. It was very reserved and it
occurred to me that this was the kind of greeting Euro-
peans did. Quite a contrast to his fresh pass back in the
newsroom.

I, of course, was glamorously tongue-tied. It was all I
could do to hold myself back from bringing my fingers
to the very spot where his lips had quickly grazed my
face.

"This is Sabina." He touched Sabina's back in the
same way that Notch had touched Alison's. An encouraging pat. "Sabina, this is Bubbles."

My God, his eyes were blue. The tux really brought
out how blue they were. And had he been working out?
He seemed tauter, leaner—though that wasn't to say he
was flabby or anything to begin with. Though, again,
maybe it was the tux.

"It is so very, very nice to meet you."

Someone had taken my other hand. I looked down at the long, slim fingers adorned by a few tasteful rings and realized it was Sabina. She was actually talking to me. Purring, really.

"Steve has told me so much about you. It's such an honor to meet you, finally. I mean, to be in your presence . . ." She cleared her throat, as if she'd said too much. "Congratulations, by the way."

I blinked. "Congratulations? For what?" I was thinking that maybe she'd mistakenly assumed I'd taken over Flossie Foreman's beat as the "Talk of the Town" correspondent.

Stiletto grinned. "For getting married to your dynamic ex-husband, remember? Or has he already slipped your mind? Not that that wouldn't be perfectly understandable."

"Oh." I'd been busted and Stiletto knew it. Already my cheeks were hot. "Right."

"It's like a movie, an estranged husband and wife coming together for the sake of their daughter." Sabina sighed. Her gray eyes sparkled in adoration, as though I was somehow the film star, not her. "I mean, my parents were divorced and a part of me always held on to the hope that they would get married again. In the end, I had to accept they didn't love each other."

"There's a concept," Stiletto quipped. "Two people not getting married because they're not in love. What a radical idea."

I set my jaw. "Some people have been engaged for less." I was referring to the time Stiletto plunked a rock on my finger, a Harry Winston three carat, as a ruse so he wouldn't have to go to work in England.

"*Some* people," he retorted, "get engaged because they fear change and stick with what they know even though they know that what they know is bad for them."

What?

Sabina pressed her finger to her temple. "I do think

I'm getting a slight headache. We better go, Steve. You're supposed to be backstage with the others."

"I'll be right there," he said. "First, I need to speak to Bubbles alone, if you don't mind."

Surprisingly, Sabina agreed to this. She didn't seem at all bitchy, which was how I would have acted if the guy I was dating suddenly insisted on being alone with a woman he'd recently asked to marry him.

Sabina bowed her head slightly and went off. She *backed* off.

"She is incredibly nice, even if she does come from Allentown," I said, thinking, *Even if she is dating you and therefore the object of my derision.*

"Whatever." He moved closer, so close I could see the swirls on his pearl-shaped buttons. "Tony tells me a client of Sandy's died at the House of Beauty right in front of you. Something about an allergy."

I was touched that Stiletto cared. "Yup. Except it wasn't an allergy. It was murder."

The muscle in his jaw flinched. "How do you know?"

I ran through my day, about the tips that had been called into the Lehigh Police Department, about Jeffrey Andre's silly French threat, and ended with the shot fired at the Christmas tree lot. "Clearly Debbie's death was more than a simple accident," I concluded. "And though it sounds whacked, I think someone shot at me to scare me off from asking more questions about her."

It might have been my imagination, or maybe Stiletto was too cool to let on, but he didn't seem shocked by any of it. It was as if he knew. As if he'd been brought up to speed.

"The shot was a twenty-two, right?"

I tried to remember if I'd told anyone that. "Supposedly, but . . ."

"That's their signature. Pretty bush league. Then again, you are dealing with old Soviet reissue and that stuff is all degraded." Stiletto looked over my shoulder, thinking, not really focusing. "What are you packing these days?"

"Me?" That was a ridiculous question. "The only thing I pack is makeup. The only gun I know how to fire is Genevieve's musket and I don't know how to fire that too well."

Stiletto was shaking his head. "Genevieve's got other weaponry. She needs to get on top of it."

Wait. This was crazy. "Do you know these people? You said Soviet reissue. Do you know who was shooting at me today?"

"Sure," he said flatly. "The violent wing of the anti-Christmas lobby." And at that moment the lights flickered, a warning that the auction was about to begin.

For the record, I was beginning to doubt there even was a violent wing of the anti-Christmas lobby. I was beginning to doubt whether there was any anti-Christmas lobby, much less a violent wing of one.

"I gotta go." He placed a hand on my shoulder. Gone was all his flirtatiousness. "Take care of yourself, Bubbles. Be careful. Park under streetlights. Don't hang out in parking lots at night and keep your radar up."

"Why?" I said as he took off toward the stage. But Stiletto said nothing. He just jogged to the black curtains, not even bothering to kiss me goodbye.

That was the first time I suspected that whatever was going on, it went way beyond a hair-extension allergy down at the little old House of Beauty.

I had the feeling it had to do with me.

Chapter Eleven

I washed my hands mechanically in the upstairs bathroom while Lorena ranted from her stall, where she was sneaking cigarettes.

In the brief time I'd been there after leaving Stiletto and company downstairs, she had switched from the *News-Times*'s employment policies to a generic tirade about how crappy the newspaper treated all of us when it came to mileage and how come a swanky establishment like the Masonic temple couldn't afford toilet paper that wasn't cheapo one-ply.

I agreed about the one-ply. Mostly, though, I thought about Stiletto and how he made me feel like no other man had. Alive. Electric. Sizzling. I was so dizzy from mentally replaying our blow-by-blow exchange and wondering what he had meant by "Soviet reissue" that at first I didn't notice the two women who joined me at the sinks.

They were women who took care of themselves, from their flawless skin to their genuine French manicures. No acrylic tips for them. Those nails were natural.

I studied the pair in the mirror. If I were more like them, in black Christian Dior instead of a Miss Missy silver lamé halter dress, with expensive foiled hair instead of an overall sunshine blond strip job, would Stiletto not be with Sabina? Would he have decided I was worth fighting Dan for?

Hold on. *Fighting Dan for.* Where had that come from? Is that what I wanted? For Stiletto to fight Dan for me?

"I still can't believe it," the woman nearest me, a tall redhead, was saying. "I was in the middle of getting dressed when it came on the news about her dropping dead like that and I was stunned. I had to lie down on my bed and just try to absorb it all."

Reality poked me in the ribs. They had to be talking about Debbie.

"I can't get over it, either," the other one, a short brunette in winter white, added. "It was stunning."

"Although not entirely unexpected. I mean, I know this sounds horrible to say, but there was a point last year when I could have strangled her with my bare hands, after she set me up on that cruise. What a sham."

Sham cruise? I pondered the similarities between the words "sham" and "scam."

The brunette nodded. "Don't feel bad, Tess. You're not the only one who was pissed. The Love Boat, she billed it. Love Boat, my ass. More like the *Lust* Boat."

"You can say that again. I'm sorry. I know it's wrong to disrespect the dead but that woman was a con artist."

"Of the first order." The brunette twisted a tube of Lancôme's Perfect Plum and carefully lined her lips.

"Damn straight. There wasn't one single guy—make that one *legitimate, marriageable* single guy—on board. Just pervs wanting to get into my panties for free and, heck, I can get that anywhere. I didn't have to pay for the opportunity."

The brunette smacked her lips. (Don't ever do that, by the way. It totally ruins the gloss.) "I heard she hired a couple of ex-cons when she ran out of so-called eligible bachelors."

"Wouldn't have surprised me. There were two guys covered with tattoos on board. Major tattoos."

The women rinsed their hands one last time and ripped out paper towels. I was dying to talk to Tess the redhead. I had to talk to her. *I wanted to murder her myself.* No kidding.

"Excuse me." I tapped her on the shoulder.

Tess gave me a thorough once-over, mentally grading me a C-.

"I couldn't help overhearing. Were you talking about Debbie Shatsky?"

The women shifted uncomfortably, uncertain what I was about. "Yesss," Tess said slowly. "Why? Don't tell me she's a friend of yours."

How to play this. Reporter or beautician? I sided with beautician. It had worked with Debbie's first husband. It might work with her. "As a matter of fact, I was doing Debbie's hair today, when she, you know, had the attack."

This was big news, immediately elevating my status among the glimmer twins. "Get out! You were there?" The brunette upgraded her appraisal of me. "What happened?"

I shrugged, debating how much information to divulge. Enough to keep them interested, not too much to make them paranoid. "We're not sure. An allergic reaction apparently." I paused for effect. "Personally, I think her death could have been murder."

"Didn't I tell you?" Tess nudged the brunette.

The brunette shifted her feet nervously. "Not that anyone we know would have actually gone through with it, of course."

"Not even Zora?" Tess arched a brow.

"Whew!" The brunette rolled her eyes. "I forgot about her. She really was pissed. I mean, Debbie ruined her life, her career. Everything."

"And isn't she a nurse in Debbie's allergist's office? That's how Debbie met her and talked her into going on the Love Boat."

Ca-ching! I bit my lip to hide my glee. This was soooo good. If I just let them talk, they might tell me the whole story. A scam cruise? Ruining someone's career? The police wouldn't have time to pin the blame on Sandy. They'd be too busy investigating this Zora woman or Ern Bender or who knew who else?

From Lorena's stall came the sound of a lighter being flicked and all hope fizzled.

The brunette tossed her towel into the wastepaper basket and sniffed. "Do you smell that?"

"Her allergist's office?" I chimed, trying to distract them. "How interesting."

Tess wrinkled her nose. "Is someone smoking?"

The toilet flushed and Lorena emerged from the stall, a flounce of her teal dress haphazardly stuffed into her jeans. She ignored the women's glares as she went to the sink and washed her hands.

Two more minutes and I could have learned Zora's full name. Or at least the allergist's.

"Were you smoking?" the brunette asked Lorena.

"No," lied Lorena, who practically had a smoke ring dangling over her head.

"Because there's a sign," the brunette persisted, pointing to the NO SMOKING sign on the mirror. "And it's there for a reason. I don't appreciate having my health compromised by inconsiderate people."

Lorena glanced at it and turned away. "A little smoke ain't going to kill you. You get more smoke in your lungs sitting in rush hour on 22."

"I should report you," Tess declared. "If I'd known there were going to be people like *you* here, I'm not so sure I would have come."

Lorena flicked water off her hands. A couple spots landed on the brunette's winter white suit. Horrified, she tried to bat them off with her paper towel.

"What do you mean, 'people like me'?" Lorena asked.

"People who wear cheap, ill-fitting dresses from some Goodwill bin over their dirty jeans."

Oh, hell. This was going to be bad. That cheap, ill-fitting dress had been handpicked by Lorena's sister for her own wedding. I did a swift check of my surroundings for any weapon Lorena could lay her hands on. Thankfully, the women's room was relatively weapon-free. Then again, Lorena was resourceful.

She set her hands on her blue teal hips. "Well, I might consider that an insult. That was, if it weren't coming from a pathetic, love-starved spinster who has to pay for a man."

The women gasped. I shielded my eyes. Note to self: never, ever bring Lorena on an indoor assignment. From now on she must be outdoors, preferably in the dirt, where she does not have to be house-trained.

What followed next was a lot of shouting and makeshift weapon fashioning. Lorena was wielding a hairbrush and Tess an eyelash curler, like that could do any harm. All chances of getting a scoop were blown and so, I feared, was my opportunity of seeing Stiletto auctioned off since Pauline must have been on her way to toss us out on our butts.

I could not imagine things getting worse. Then again, I'm an idiot. Because just as Lorena was about to face off with Tess, the bathroom door was flung open and in walked Wendy.

As in Dan's ex-wife Wendy.

Wendy was superthin and superrich, thanks to the fortune she inherited from her father's cheeseball snack-food empire. Dan had left me for her back in the day, back when he assumed I couldn't advance his career as an ambulance chaser. She'd made him change his name to "Chip" and stop eating halupkies. Under her spell, he believed he had WASP potential.

However, with Wendy's fortune dwindling thanks to the revolt against high-fat, fried snacks (except in Pennsylvania, where they are still rightly glorified), Dan had turned his attention back to me. That was the only reason I could come up with to explain his fierce determination to marry me. Although sometimes I wondered if there was another motivation, a more sinister impetus.

"Bubbles!" Wendy let the door slam behind her. "What are *you* doing here?"

"You know her?" asked the brunette.

"Unfortunately," Wendy said. "This is *the* Bubbles. The one I was telling you about."

Tess dropped her eyelash curler. Guess I was much more of a celebrity than I knew.

"She's even more absurd than you described."

"White trash," Wendy said with a snort. "Dan went back to her because he couldn't help himself. It's in his genes. Some men will always sink to the lowest common denominator."

In case it wasn't obvious, Wendy despised me. She used to hide her disgust when she was married to Dan. Now that they were divorced, however, the gloves were off and her sixty-five-dollar manicured claws were bared.

"But why should I be surprised? Of course Bubbles is here. She's here to bid on Steve Stiletto, the man who bedded and left her." Wendy licked her thin lips. It reminded me of a wolf, ready to pounce on a rabbit in a field. "I could have warned you, Bubbles, that a man of Steve Stiletto's wealth and pedigree wouldn't spare the time of day for a cheap little blue-collar ho like you. You're more fit to change his sheets rather than sleep in them."

"Don't you have an innocent field mouse to kill or something?" Lorena said.

I was glad Lorena was there to defend me because I couldn't. Wendy's words were too true. Stiletto was rich, educated and aristocratic while I was nothing but a widowed cleaning woman's daughter. Wendy had hit my soft spot and she knew it.

"Which one is Steve Stiletto?" Tess opened the program, searching for Stiletto's head shot.

"Number three." Wendy's eyes glinted. "I was thinking I might bid on him, too."

"No!" I said, before I could stop myself.

Tess flashed me a triumphant grin. "Let me bid for him, Wendy. He's gorgeous."

"That's a wonderful idea, Tess," Wendy said. "It is, after all, for a *good cause*."

"Oh, go ahead and bid, Wendy," the brunette suggested, as if this was some fun game. "After all, you are single again."

Eeep!

Registering my reaction of absolute horror, Wendy was all too pleased to agree. "That's true. All the winning couples get a room and private dinner at the Hotel Lehigh tomorrow night. A night with Steve Stiletto might be just what the doctor ordered. Lord knows I could use a good lay after years of sleeping with the human potato."

She laughed so hard I thought for sure her surgically minimized nose would explode.

That knot in my stomach twisted a bit tighter. I had to outbid her, but how? Together or apart, Wendy and Tess had more money than I would ever have. Which, admittedly, wasn't hard. Any industrious teenager with a paper route had more money than I had.

"Hey," Lorena said, her hand behind her ear, "I think I hear your broom calling, Wendy."

But it wasn't Wendy's broom. It was the opening bell. The auction was already under way.

Chapter Twelve

Pauline was onstage introducing the freckled basketball player when Wendy, Tess, and I took our seats. Lorena didn't sit. She crept around the room looking for photo opportunities. Or other places to steal another quick smoke.

"In addition to serving on the board of Big Brother and Big Sister, K. C. donates one week each summer to teaching disadvantaged youth how to play basketball at his private estate in the Poconos," Pauline read, introducing K. C. the basketball player. "K. C. is an avid golfer as well, hitting three under par, and he loves to sail his catamaran each spring from his beachfront home in Avalon, New Jersey, to his waterfront estate in the Caribbean!"

A chorus of "ohhs" rose from the audience. K. C. smiled and flipped back his tuxedo jacket to reveal a pair of slim hips set off by a plaid cummerbund. Several women bent their heads and took copious notes.

"Once voted Sexiest Man in Pennsylvania, K. C. is thirty-five, retired from playing for the Philadelphia '76ers, and—are you ready, ladies?—actively looking for a soul mate to share his dream of raising a family in the brand-new home that he is building in bucolic

Bucks County!" Pauline applauded briefly. "Shall we start the bidding at two hundred dollars?"

This was met with much more applause. K. C. winked and did another spin.

"Gay."

I nearly fell off my seat. Lorena was crouched next to me in the aisle, adjusting the zoom on her camera. I hate when she creeps up on me like that.

"Not every single man above the age of thirty-three is gay," I whispered.

She snapped a photo of a woman bidding two hundred fifty dollars. "He is. Got it from the guys in sports. Even has a life partner of ten years. The head chef of some fancy Philly restaurant. That's why he's retiring so young and quitting basketball, so he and his partner can adopt a baby from China and open a restaurant in Lumberville."

A woman whose bid of four hundred fifty dollars had snagged K. C. jumped up and down applauding herself. The good-natured basketball star climbed off the stage, embraced her and bent down to kiss her warmly on the cheek. Then he went off to plant similar kisses on the losers. For a gay man with a life partner and a baby from China on the way, he was doing a pretty good job faking it.

I needed to get some color before the auction was over. I kept forgetting that I was actually filling in for Flossie and not here merely to hook up with Stiletto.

Jenna Szvakis, who was sitting in the back row next to her mother, was my solution. I'd been doing Jenna's hair since she was six and even then she'd had a weight problem. Now she and her mother were taking up four folding chairs total and no one was sitting next to them, as if their excess weight was contagious.

Lorena slinked off to do her dirty work while I slid down one chair to Jenna. Jenna was in head-to-toe pink. It broke my heart.

"Hi, Jenna," I said. "Don't you look nice."

Jenna looked up from her program where both K. C.'s and Stiletto's faces had been circled in red marker. "Hey, Bubbles. Thanks. You, too."

I had the feeling this compliment wasn't completely sincere, judging from the way she cringed when she saw my purple nails.

"Mom and I were just talking about what happened down at the House of Beauty this afternoon. Is it true Sandy mixed up the wrong chemicals and poisoned that woman?"

"Absolutely not. We don't know what happened, exactly, but it wasn't Sandy's fault." Maybe I should wear a sign: *Debbie's Death Was Not Sandy's Fault*.

"See," Jenna's mom said. "I told you so. What are you doing at a bachelor auction, anyway, Bubbles? I thought you were getting remarried in a few days."

I half sat on my left hand with its missing diamond ring. "I'm here on business." I explained about now working forty hours at the *News-Times* and how I'd been assigned to cover the auction for "Talk of the Town."

"Oooh." Jenna blew out her puffy pink cheeks. " 'Talk of the Town.' Big-time. I'd love to be mentioned there. My sister was when they had that baby shower at the school where she's a teacher."

Perfect. Eager to be in "Talk of the Town." They would fit the bill. I wrote down their cute quotes about searching for the ultimate men, the joys of double dating and possibly double wedding ceremonies. I mean, how often do a mother and daughter hit the town to pick up men together?

The auction was starting up again. I held my breath as Pauline reached into a fishbowl to pull the number of the next bachelor.

"Number three. Steve Stiletto."

I knew it. My face went red as Stiletto walked out, graciously kissed Pauline's hand and bowed his head endearingly. He grinned as if this were a gas, though his eyes were searching the audience. For his new girl-friend, Sabina?

Or me?

Jenna said, "He's hot. He's my first choice."

She wasn't the only one.

As Pauline launched into her spiel about how great Stiletto was—award-winning international photographer, heir to the famous Henry Metzger fortune, blah, blah, blah—a buzz reverberated throughout the room. Several women sat up straight and got their numbers ready, including Tess, who was sitting across the aisle shooting me darting eye barbs.

The auctioneer banged the gavel. "Shall we start the bidding at two hun—"

"Two hundred fifty!" a woman shot up from the front row.

"Three hundred!" cried another.

"Three twenty-five."

The bids were rapid-fire. Pauline didn't have time to announce one before another woman offered fifty bucks more.

"Well, he's out of my budget," Jenna moaned. "I can't afford to go over three hundred."

I patted her knee. "Don't worry. He's overrated, anyway." I glanced at Tess, who was holding her number halfway, summoning the courage to jump in and make a formal bid.

Aww, hell. I guess I'd have to head her off at the pass. I stuck up my number. "Three seventy-five!" I yelled.

Jenna nudged my ribs. "What are you doing?"

"Shh. Trust me. I'm an expert at this."

Silence. Several people turned to stare my way. Stiletto smiled and shook his head ever so slightly.

Uh-oh. Maybe I needed to put up money in advance. I mean, I only had three hundred twenty-five dollars in my checking and savings. And then there was that four thousand dollars or so I owed Visa. I was a goner if Pauline did instant credit checks.

"I'm sorry," Pauline said, "but we passed three seventy-five a while ago. I believe the last bid was four fifty."

Thank heavens. Not that I had four hundred and fifty dollars, but what was the worst that could happen when they found out I didn't have the dough? Sue me? Ha!

I made a point of making eye contact with Tess as I announced, "Five hundred dollars!"

Pauline swallowed. "That's our highest bid yet this evening."

I squinted. Was Stiletto laughing?

"I thought you said he wasn't worth it," Jenna whispered.

Across the room I could see Lorena wagging her finger at me in warning.

"I'm telling you, Jenna, it's not what it appears. I no more want a date with Steve Stiletto than a flat tire on my car outside. I'm bidding for reasons totally unrelated to him."

"Oh. Could have fooled me."

Tess sat rigid, her hands clasping the number firmly in her lap.

"Five hundred," the auctioneer said. "Do I hear five twenty-five?"

More silence. My nails dug into my palms.

"Wow," Jenna said. "Looks like you're gonna get him."

"You don't know Wendy Ritter. Snakes are always still before they strike."

Tess glanced over her shoulder. Slowly, slowly, she lifted her number. "Five twenty-five."

Damn. Five twenty-five. That was serious business. That was way, way more than I had to spend. That was millionaires' money. Well, I supposed there were worse outcomes than Tess getting a night with Stiletto. Just as long as Wendy didn't, I was okay.

"Five twenty-five. Do I hear five fifty?" Pauline held the gavel aloft.

"Going once, going twice . . ."

Tess threw me a victorious smirk. I pouted as if desperately disappointed.

"Five fifty!" a woman with a piercing nasal twang yipped.

Tess and I quit making faces at each other. Quickly, I looked to Stiletto, who was maintaining a stoic demeanor, giving no clue as to whether he was pleased or displeased by whoever had offered the latest bid.

"Excellent!" Pauline declared. "My, this certainly is shaping up to be quite an auction. Then again, with such impressive figures on display . . ."

There was a round of naughty titters. Some women over on the far right side of the room leaned forward to slap the highest bidder on the back. I stood slightly for a closer look and had my worst fears confirmed. Pencil thin. Black hair. White hair band. Cobralike neck. Skeletal bone structure. Two tiny horns sticking out of her head.

The devil incarnate. Wendy.

Wendy turned to high five her evil socialite friends and, in so doing, caught sight of me. She formed those two bloodless lines that passed for lips into a smirk.

I was sunk. I couldn't beat both Tess and Wendy.

"Don't worry," Jenna said, patting my knee. "He was overrated anyway."

Touché.

"I'll bid six hundred!"

A collective gasp. Stiletto raised his hands to his face in mock shame.

Tess was beaming. She had outbid Wendy by an outrageous amount of money.

"Six hundred!" the auctioneer repeated. "I don't think we can top that."

Wendy could. Wendy loved a challenge. More important, she loved rubbing other people's faces in her cold cash. Or, rather, her father's cold cash. Even if she was going head to head against her own friend, Tess.

"Do we have six twenty-five for this devastatingly handsome man?" Pauline raised the gavel.

Wendy's number fluttered. "Six . . ."

There have been many moments in my life when I've longed for a peashooter and this was one of them. Without a peashooter to shoot Wendy in the neck or to knock her number out of her hand (personally, I preferred the neck), Stiletto was toast. He would have to pay yet one more price for my marrying Dan; he would have to go out on a date with Wendy.

Or would he?

For just as Wendy was about to utter the "twenty" in the six twenty-five Pauline was requesting, a blur of brown hair, teal blue toile and jeans streaked across the ballroom. Lorena hurled herself at Wendy with such force that she knocked her off her chair and slammed her to the floor.

On the stage, Pauline kept up appearances. "Going . . . going . . ."

Wendy's muffled cries rose from the corner. I bit a nail and nearly broke my tooth on the purple plastic. The anticipation was killing me.

"GONE!" The auctioneer slammed the gavel. "To number ninety-three. Congratulations."

It was over. Tess had won. Wendy had lost. Lost a couple of teeth, too, if I knew Lorena.

Stiletto made his way off the stage to congratulate Tess. I averted my eyes so I wouldn't have to see him kiss her.

"That was exciting," Jenna said, "though I don't think you were right about this Steve Stiletto not being worth it, what with the way everyone was bidding. How do you know him, anyway?"

"I've heard stories," I said in a faraway voice. "From all accounts, he's a womanizer and a thrill seeker who couldn't settle down for a half an hour if he—"

"Thanks."

Jenna covered her mouth. Stiletto was standing over us, glorious in his authentic British tux.

"I've been in Afghan war camps, Bosnian trenches and once—because of a slight misunderstanding over some property I happened to be carrying—a Mexican jail. But nothing could have prepared me for a date with Wendy."

I smiled. Stiletto did, too.

Then he took my hand and we were off.

Chapter Thirteen

Stiletto led me by the hand, out of the packed ball-room, all eyes watching.

Deep down I knew that this was all I'd wanted, to be alone with him. This is why I had worked my way to "Talk of the Town." This was why Flossie Foreman was hobbling about on one maimed knee.

I don't know if Stiletto was a secret Mason or what, but he seemed familiar with every back hallway as he led me first this way, then that, until we were several flights up, in a small room with a window that looked out onto the Hill-to-Hill Bridge.

Our bridge.

In one swift movement, he shut the door and seized me. His hands stroked my face lovingly and then paus-ing, hesitating, he bent down and kissed me without so much as a "Do you mind?"

His mouth was hot, almost feverish, though it never left mine as he took me by the shoulders and, tripping over carpet, chair, whatever, forced me against the wall. I gave in, wrapping my arms around him, feeling the smoothness of his tux over his broad shoulders, his hair brushing against my fingers.

I opened my mouth more and let his tongue slip in.

His powerful legs gained the upper hand, wedging their way between mine so that I could sense every inch of him. I was dizzy again, dizzier than I'd been downstairs. Dizzier than I'd ever been in my life.

I couldn't take any more of him with his clothes on. I wanted us skin on skin. My fingers began fumbling for his shirt buttons, clumsily, uselessly trying to work. His hands were already up my dress and debating what to do when all of a sudden he pulled back, gasping.

Passion. Torment. Pure old lust. All the primal emotions twisted what I could make of his face in the dim light. He looked away and rubbed his brow. "I'm sorry, Bubbles. It's just that"—he loosened his collar—"ever since I saw you this afternoon, I've had one thought running through my mind almost obsessively. All I knew was that I had to have you alone. That I had to kiss you like that. I'm sorry."

"I'm not sorry. Not one tiny bit. However, I am afraid I'm paralyzed. If I step away from this wall, I might very well collapse."

Stiletto leaned on a desk I hadn't seen was there. The only light came from outside, from the illuminated Christmas tree on the Fritch Fuel sign. We were in shadows and that was good because I didn't think I could take him under full-force fluorescents, undiluted.

I gripped my dress and yanked it down to more ladylike proportions.

"Where's your ring?" he asked.

At first I wasn't sure to what he was referring: the gaudy cubic zirconia Dan had given me, which I'd promptly dropped into my jewelry box next to my collection from Claire's Jewels, or the Harry Winston gem that I'd returned to Stiletto last month.

"Shit. Didn't he even give you a ring?"

"He did," I said. "I don't wear it."

"Why?"

"You know," I said. "You know why I don't wear it."

Silence. Stiletto reached out and I put my hand in his.

He squeezed it gently and said, "I haven't stopped thinking of you for one minute since I left for England."

"I know."

"You know? That's awfully confident of you."

I laughed. "I mean, I know because I haven't stopped thinking of you, either."

He gave my hand another squeeze. "How's Jane?"

Horrible, I wanted to say. *She's an absolute mess. A skittish child in my daughter's body.* "Okay. I think she's getting better."

"And you still are convinced marrying Dan will do the trick, will bring her back to what she was?"

"That's the going theory, according to our expert."

"Who?"

I explained about Dr. Caswell. Stiletto wanted her first and last names. Then he wanted me to spell everything. I had no doubt he'd investigate her thoroughly.

"When's the wedding?" he asked.

"Saturday."

"Then we have almost a week."

I was dumbfounded. "What are you talking about?"

"Don't you understand that's why I came back, Bubbles? I came back for you."

"I thought you came back for the auction."

"Hardly."

In all the months I'd known Stiletto, I had never felt such a surge of complete love toward him as I did at that moment. I pictured him in London, waking up in his Knightsbridge apartment and thinking, *What the hell?* I could see him tossing clothes into a duffel bag, slinging it over his shoulder and racing to the airport on a whim that his eleventh-hour flight to Pennsylvania would somehow prevent my wedding.

"Thank you," I said, unsure what to do or say. "But it's—"

He cut me off. "Listen, Bubbles. There's something I have to tell you, something extremely important." He paused.

"And?" I said.

"And . . ." He let out a self-deprecating chuckle, the kind people do when they're embarrassed or have done something stupid. "The hell of it is, I can't tell you."

I found this slightly aggravating. "Why not?" Was I too dumb to understand?

"It has to do with Dan, why he's so eager to marry you and . . . other stuff. Stuff that goes to the very heart of who you are. Jane, too. If you knew what it was, you'd cancel the wedding immediately."

"Shit, Stiletto." I pulled my hand away. Now I was getting annoyed. "If it's that important, then I have a right to know."

"You're damn right you have a right to know. I'm with you on that one."

"So?"

"So I can't tell. Not now. I . . . uh . . . haven't been *authorized*," he added sheepishly.

"Authorized?" I got up, my anger now full-blown. "Since when have you ever waited for someone to authorize you? And what do you mean by *authorize,* anyway? Is this some new Associated Press rule?"

There was no answer.

I found the light switch and flicked it on. We were in some sort of storeroom full of office supplies and filing cabinets marked with nutty Mason stuff—Order of the Eastern Star, De Molay, Job's Daughters, Daughters of the Nile—along with card tables and boxes and trophies that were nearly a hundred years old.

I clasped my hands together so Stiletto couldn't see they were shaking. He looked guilty. He was frowning at the floor and—I thought, tellingly—unwilling to make eye contact.

"You know what I think? I think this is all bullshit," I said. "I think you're bluffing on the off chance that you can dupe silly, dumb Bubbles into calling off the wedding just so I won't marry Dan, whom you can't stand."

"Goddamn." He got off the desk and put his hands on his hips. "What kind of asshole do you think I am?"

"A pretty big one, if that's the real story."

"You don't mean that."

"Try me." I had to look away. Raspberry lip gloss stains dotted his fine white collar, which was rakishly undone along with several buttons on his tux—the best I'd been able to accomplish under the circumstances. Did he have to be so handsome?

I searched for a mirror so I could get myself in shape and settled for a plaque on the wall. A tribute to the founding of the Northampton County of the Order of the Eastern Star on January 5, 1914. I stared at the meaningless date, focusing on it so I wouldn't start crying.

Stiletto's reflection appeared behind me. "Bubbles," he said softly. "Please . . ."

I shook him off. "I came here tonight because I had an assignment, Stiletto. That's it. I don't want or need anything else from you. And I suggest you get those lip gloss marks off your expensive tux before your new girlfriend sees."

He looked confused and hurt. "Is that what's getting to you? Sabina?"

"Whatever. I don't know her name or care. That's your business, Stiletto, not mine."

His eyes flashed, his hurt quickly turning to fury. "You're something else—you know that?"

"Yes. As a matter of fact, I do."

I reached for the door, but Stiletto grabbed me.

"Any other man would have told you to fuck off long ago. First you dump me for that pathetic excuse of a man on the weak premise that your daughter—who's smart enough to realize otherwise—needs you to get married. Then, after I haul my ass from London, arguing with myself all across the Atlantic about why I'm being a fool for doing so, you won't even extend the courtesy of once, just once, trusting me."

My heart was threatening to leap out of my chest. It wasn't true. All of what he was saying was a lie. I did trust him. But I couldn't take the chance that he was right. I needed more proof to show Jane that remarrying her father was not in her best interests.

We glared at each other, one of us wishing the other would break down, would apologize, would forgive.

"I guess that's it then," I said. "Might as well take that next plane back to London."

"I would," he said, "except that I've got other commitments to women who seem to appreciate me."

I pursed my lips tightly.

"There are other women, you know, Bubbles," he said in a cruel tone.

"There always were, Stiletto."

"Yes, there always were. But not when I was with you." And with that parting shot, he left, mercifully leaving me in peace to cry out my heart—or what was left of it.

Chapter Fourteen

Tuesday mornings Jane met with Dr. Caswell—or Dr. Lori, as she insisted on being called—and then Dr. Caswell met with Dan and me for an analysis. This often turned into Dan making some claim that I was forced to refute and me feeling reprehensible.

I had come to dread Tuesday mornings.

As my alarm clock radio blared "Grandma Got Run Over by a Reindeer" promptly at six thirty a.m., I lay in bed watching a few snowflakes fall from the overcast sky outside my window, wondering where exactly I might find a reindeer who would be game for a Genevieve/Mama twofer.

I was still in a bad mood due to the fight I'd had with Stiletto the night before. It had consumed me all the way through writing up my "Talk of the Town" piece to my twelve-inch phoner on the Mahoken sewage debate. (It had been tabled, in case anyone's interested.)

All the while the same words played over and over in my mind: *Soviet reissue. If you knew what it was, you'd cancel the wedding tonight. No authorization.*

It just wasn't like Stiletto to bow to authority. Nothing made sense.

I slipped into a pair of stretch jeans, a "modest"

midriff shirt of pure white, did up my hair in a demure twist, popped in some fake pearl earrings to match the one on my belly button and topped it off with scrunch boots in fake white leather. There. If that didn't look respectable, I didn't know what did—despite the scuff marks on the boots.

Jane was downstairs waiting for me with her new backpack slung over her shoulder and her new iPod plugged into her ears. Both the backpack and the iPod had been purchased by Dan in recent weeks. He was spoiling her something rotten, and thanks to the iPod, she no longer talked to me during our morning commutes.

Maybe that was his plan all along.

We sat stiffly in the freezing Camaro parked on West Goepp Street, Jane huddled in her wrinkled old peacoat while I ripped apart my starter. The engine was cold and wouldn't turn over, so I pumped the pedal and let it sit for a bit, keeping watch on Phil Shatsky's house as I waited.

I saw the license plate first: BRIKHOUS. The car in front of Phil's house was a black Lincoln Town Car. You didn't see many Lincoln Town Cars on West Goepp, so it was noticeable, along with the fact that sitting behind the wheel was a woman with huge hair, high and blond like Debbie's.

She wasn't moving or putting on makeup or writing out checks or tweezing her brows or balancing her checkbook or cleaning her gun or doing any of the one thousand things women usually do when they're sitting in their cars.

She was spying. Yes, spying. With a pair of binoculars directed right at Phil Shatsky's second-floor bedroom window.

Jane removed one of her iPod buds. "You really need to get a new car, Mom. This one's a pit. It never starts right up."

"Sometimes that's a good thing." I touched the dashboard lovingly, silently thanking my old Camaro for the opportunity to get a glimmer of the woman I assumed was the infamous Marguerite.

There was a kick in the engine, which suddenly sputtered and turned over. The woman in the car parked in front of Phil Shatsky's whipped her head around. I tried to look busy by pretending to curse my car, but she was spooked. Before I got my left front tire off the curb, she was at the end of the block, headed for the spur route. So much for stealth surveillance.

My Camaro *bump, bump, bumped* off the curb, where I had left it the night before, since my driveway had been taken over by Genevieve's Rambler. I cruised slowly past the Shatsky house, searching for signs of life.

"What's going on with him, anyway?" Jane asked. "Arriving in a Santa suit like that and looking like hell. What's up with his wife and all those women outside with casseroles? Looked like a funeral."

"It was nothing. Just a personal problem."

"And there was a big hole cut into the front page of the *News-Times* this morning and Grandma claims our television's on the fritz, but I think Genevieve rigged it so I couldn't watch the news last night. I'm beginning to wonder if something happened to Mrs. Shatsky. You'd tell me if she got killed or committed suicide or something, wouldn't you?"

Cripes. She was putting me on the spot. "Well . . ."

"Because I'm worried. Last night when you were at that fund-raiser, after Genevieve and Grandma had gone to bed, I heard this sound outside my window. I looked out and there was this man walking around the house. I swear he was trying the doorknobs, looking for a way to get in."

Instead of saying, *That's silly, honey. The Hamels would have heard him, too* or *That's silly, honey. Why would someone want to break into our house?* I hysterically shouted, "Man! What man?"

Jane's eyes narrowed as if she'd had something confirmed. "I thought so. I thought something was up. I hate it when you withhold pertinent information." Then she plugged her iPod buds into her ears, closed her eyes and bobbed her head to the Arctic Monkeys.

Our discussion was over. Jane had shut herself off from me—again.

Dr. Caswell's office was, coincidentally, in the same building as Dan's small "law firm." In fact, he often used the good doctor as an expert witness whenever he sued McDonald's or a candy bar company on behalf of clients who claimed post-traumatic stress after finding bits of human fingers in their food, which according to Dan happened more frequently than one would think. (Though, personally, my guess is that was wishful thinking on Dan's part.)

Dr. Caswell's very nice, but she must not do a very good job on the witness stand because Dan had yet to win one of those cases.

While Jane was spilling her secret fears to Dr. Caswell, I drank a cup of tepid coffee in the waiting room and outlined how I was going to tackle the Debbie Shatsky murder while flying under Dix Notch's radar.

Here was the thing: whoever switched the glues at the House of Beauty would have had to have some familiarity with Debbie and Sandy's routine when it came to hair extensions. They would have had to know that Debbie was going to be in the salon at two on Monday, that she was going to bring her own glue, and that there was a way to switch the substances.

I wrote a note to remind myself to ask Sandy to list anyone who might have been in the salon that day and who was such a frequent customer that she could have known Debbie's routine. Then I would cross-reference those names with a list of suspects.

Suspects. Hmm. I sipped more coffee, which tasted vaguely of boiled cardboard, and mindlessly studied Dr. Caswell's painting of a waterfall.

The first suspect was Ern Bender. He had the least to lose and the most to gain from murdering his ex-wife. His hatred toward her was palpable and, one had to ask, possibly justified.

Then there was the strange stalker across the street in the Mercedes, who might or might not have shot off the top of the Christmas tree and who might or might not be a member of the violent wing of the anti-Christmas lobby. I wrote this down in my notebook and drew a line to Ern. *Related?* I scribbled in the margins.

There was Marguerite, of course, the woman after Phil's heart and other private parts. There were the other housewives who lusted after Phil. And then there was Zora, the angry nurse in Debbie's allergist's office, though why she was angry I wasn't certain.

Too bad I'd blown it with Tess. She could have been a great source. Now she was my enemy, thanks to Wendy, and Stiletto's date, again thanks to Wendy.

Thanks, Wendy.

I tried to imagine what would have made one of Debbie's "lust boat" cruises so horrific. I mean, aside from suffering botulism or seasickness, a cruise sounded awfully nice right about now, what with all the stress in my life. Though I wouldn't want to go with Dan.

Before I could stop myself, my mind had wandered to the Caribbean, where Stiletto and I were enjoying an imaginary cruise. Blue skies, tropical breezes. We didn't stay on the boat long. Not us. No way. Stiletto wasn't one to sit around eating six courses a day and playing shuffleboard. He'd spotted a deserted island and we dived overboard.

White sand under our toes. A warm wind blowing the palm trees lining our secluded beach. No one but us.

As the sun set, golden and rose, on the horizon, we'd strip off our clothes and dive into that pretty blue turquoise sea I've only seen in brochures. I licked my lips, tasting the salt of the water that would be in droplets on the sinews of Stiletto's sensuous neck, the same neck I would be kissing as he took me in his arms, slippery and strong and so very, very . . .

"Wet!"

Dan's voice jolted me out of my daydream.

"Wet?" I repeated, blinking.

"Not wet. What?"

"Oh."

It seemed that I was not on a deserted Caribbean island with Stiletto about to make love in turquoise water after all. I was sitting in my family therapist's waiting room in a concrete office park in a steel town in December accompanied only by my dorky, snide, pompous, uncouth husband-to-be. How depressing.

Dan's paunch spread over his belt and he reeked of virulently spicy cologne. The oil on his hair was so thick, it had dripped and discolored his collar. At least when he had been married to Wendy, she'd weaned him off his Clubman's Hair Tonic addiction. Now he was back to his old habits—too much Leather cologne and grease.

"What are you doing?" he demanded.

"I was . . . thinking."

"About what?"

This was how it was going to be when I was married to him, say? I would have to explain every twenty seconds what my every thought was.

"About the . . . the wedding."

Dan relaxed, his bloated face turning the same color as his shirt. Baby pink. "Well, that's a nice change of pace. I was curious if you were ever going to get involved in planning this wedding, or if I would have to do everything. You know, we still have to apply for our marriage license."

I thought about what Stiletto had said last night, his implication that Dan was eager to marry me for reasons that had nothing to do with his concern that Jane be part of a nuclear family. But what other reasons could Dan have? I didn't have money or social status like Wendy. All I had was a job at the local newspaper. And

Dan hated the *News-Times.* Aside from my house on West Goepp, a four-thousand-dollar Visa bill and three hundred dollars in my checking account, I had nothing.

Really, all I possessed that Dan would want was Jane. And it wasn't as if I'd been keeping her from him. Dan had been a lousy husband, but he was an okay father. Jane never suffered in that regard.

"Well? What about it?" Dan was saying. "How about I pick you up after work and we'll do the deed."

Groan. Not today. "How about tomorrow? I've got so much work—"

"Can't wait until tomorrow. We'll miss the deadline. Let's do it tonight and get it over with. There's a county clerk who owes me a favor after I got her boyfriend out of a hot car snafu. She'll stay open late for me if I ask. Afterward, I'll take you out to dinner. My treat."

Chuck E. Cheese.

There was the sound of a door slamming, Dr. Caswell's secret door on the other side of her office so her patients could leave without presenting themselves to the waiting room. In two seconds, on cue, Dr. Caswell opened the other door to us.

"I can see you now."

Dr. Caswell was a petite, mousy thing of a woman. She was a runner and her arms and legs were tight ropes of muscles. A pair of severe dark glasses sat perched on her nose and her face was devoid of makeup. I had to fight the fierce temptation to rip off the glasses, volumize her hair and give her a full makeover. I'd never met a pair of peepers so desperate for liner and mascara.

"After you," Dan said with uncharacteristic graciousness, sweeping an arm to the door.

"Thank you."

Dr. Caswell approved of our civility. She went to her desk, which, as always, was devoid of any personal effects that might distract her clients' attention.

"I'm glad you're both here today," she said, though I couldn't remember a time when Dan and I hadn't both been there. "We have some very serious issues to discuss."

Dang. Just once I'd have appreciated Dr. Caswell cheerfully announcing that she could see the light at the end of the tunnel, that Jane was obviously on the mend.

She pointedly fixed her gaze on me. "Jane is under the impression that some kind of crisis is going on. She's extremely anxious—not to mention frightened—as to why you haven't dialoged with her about it, Bubbles."

Dialog. It's not a verb.

"There's no crisis," Dan answered for me. "Bubbles's friend messed up at the salon and administered the wrong product to one of her clients, who was allergic— fatally allergic. The ditz's license hadn't been renewed. She's so screwed, it's unreal."

I gripped the armrest of my chair, willing myself not to lunge for Dan's throat as I had the day before.

Dr. Caswell lowered her glasses. "Was this the House of Beauty incident I read about in the paper this morning?"

The House of Beauty incident? So that's what it was being called. Shoot. Alison Roach must have done a story after all. Probably skewed all the facts so Debbie's death came off not as a murder, but as an act of negligence on Sandy's part.

Poor Sandy. With all that was going on, I hadn't bothered to call her last night to tell her what I'd learned from Jeffrey Andre and Ern Bender. I'd totally dropped the ball on our friendship.

"I don't read the *News-Times*," Dan was saying. "Why would I read that rag?"

Because your wife-to-be writes for it, I answered mentally.

Dr. Caswell tapped a pencil on the table. "I don't know if the House of Beauty incident is the crisis to which Jane is referring. What she told me was that some crisis is going on and that it has to do with a man in the neighborhood and Bubbles's work."

That Jane. Still smart and perceptive as always.

Dan rushed at the chance to accuse me of wrongdoing. "What did you say to her, Bubbles?"

"Nothing!"

"Come on."

I looked him straight in the eye. "I haven't said a thing."

"She probably hasn't. That's the problem," Dr. Caswell said. "Jane has very keen intuition. And then there was that man who upset her last night, the one peeking in the windows."

Dan was almost out of his chair. "What's this? What man? Bubbles, why didn't you tell me?"

This must have been the man Jane had referred to on the drive over. I tried not to let it bother me that Jane chose to discuss the incident in full with Dr. Caswell and not me. "All she said was that she looked outside last night and saw a man walking around the house. Maybe, just maybe, he was trying the knobs on the doors. She didn't say anything about him peeking in the windows."

"Trying the door? That's worse than looking in the windows, Bubbles." Dan was practically growling. "And where the hell were you?"

"At work," Dr. Caswell said with distinct disapproval, as though I'd been dancing on tables at a bar.

Dan folded his arms. "Some mother you are."

"Oh, for heaven's sake," I said. "It was probably Mr. Hamel from next door coming over for his *TV Guide* after it got mixed up in our mail."

Wrong answer.

Dr. Caswell raised an eyebrow to signal that my cavalier dismissal was not acceptable. "Really? Would your neighbor have tried the doorknob without first knocking or ringing the doorbell?"

No. Mr. Hamel would have shouted for me to open up. And if no one had been home, he would have broken the glass and opened the door himself. Nothing stands in the way of Mr. Hamel and his *TV Guide*. Nothing.

"Would he have looked in the windows?" Dr. Caswell pressed.

"Christ." Dan's hand was working into a fist. "Who the hell was this pervert? I'll kill him."

Dr. Caswell ignored him, choosing to spit her venom at me. "Would this neighbor have gone to the back door and tried that knob, too?"

That was my cue to act contrite so we could get off this topic and move on. "I'm sorry. I didn't mean to dismiss Jane out of hand."

"I wouldn't think so," she said smugly. "Children don't lie. Adults do."

Dr. Caswell didn't like me. I had no idea why. She just didn't. I must emit some hate pheromones, what with Wendy, Mr. Notch and Lori Caswell all scratching me off their Christmas card lists.

"You assured me that Jane would be safe if she stayed with you, Bubbles," Dan said. "I wanted to bring her to my house, which happens to be in a very safe gated community, but you said no."

"Because you're moving out this week and giving the house over to Wendy. How many moves is Jane supposed to make? Stability. Remember that?"

"Please, please. This isn't helping Jane." Dr. Caswell's tone reminded me of a nun from my catechism class, the one who used to routinely toss me out for showing so much of God's creation.

"What I propose," she continued, "is permanently moving in a relative who will stay at home with Jane and assure her that she is safe."

"A babysitter?" I balked. "She's nearly graduated from high school. I was a mother at her age."

"Perhaps you could have used a babysitter back then, too," Dr. Caswell quipped.

I sat back and crossed my legs. How come Dan never got the blame for knocking me up? That's what I wanted to know.

"This will all be a moot point by next week when I

move Bubbles and Jane into the house I'm having re-decorated in Saucon Valley Estates," Dan said.

My jaw dropped. The Saucon Valley move was not settled. I, for one, had no intention of leaving my comfortable home on West Goepp.

Dr. Caswell beamed. "How nice. I understand those new homes by the golf course are lovely. I do hope you'll agree to this, Bubbles. The change would do Jane good. And a gated community would add to her sense of safety. You're very fortunate to be marrying a man who is so responsible, so concerned for his daughter's welfare."

She made goo-goo eyes at Dan. Dan made goo-goo eyes back. Maybe Dr. Caswell should be heading down to the county clerk's office for a marriage license instead of me.

Bad enough that I was being blackmailed into marrying Dan. Now I had to give up my house and my neighborhood. What was next? My job?

"We'll talk about this later," I said. "Alone."

Dr. Caswell took a few threatening notes. It always made me nervous when she took notes. "In the meantime, I'd like to see a *responsible, mature* adult in Bubbles's house. Jane and I discussed her options and we decided that your mother and her friend, Guenivere, should move in, Bubbles."

"You mean Genevieve?" I couldn't believe it. My life was being taken over by Dr. Caswell and Dan and now my daughter and my mother and my mother's gun-happy friend. "Genevieve's hardly responsible. She operates a firing range off her deck."

"She seemed very capable to me, at least during our brief conference call this morning."

I got out of my chair. "Hold on. You called Genevieve already?"

"And your mother. Jane gave me the number. Frankly, I was afraid it might, you know, slip your mind if I didn't take the reins. You do have a reputation for being rather flighty."

Dr. Caswell was a reincarnated ferret. And not one of those cute ferrets. She was the kind of ferret that bit your ankle or suddenly ran up your pants leg.

"Excellent!" Dan declared. "And Lulu will make sure Bubbles gets cracking on those wedding preparations. So far she's done bubkes. I bet she doesn't even have a dress."

"Oh, dear." Dr. Caswell frowned. "And here Jane is so excited about you two getting together and re-forming a nuclear family."

Another shot of maternal guilt, straight-up.

"Do you have a dress, dear?" she pried.

"Of course! I mean I have lots of dresses, just not a wedding dress. Anyway, we're getting married by a judge. What's the big deal?"

"A judge at the Lehigh University chapel, Bubbles," Dan said. "And there will be one hundred of our closest friends and family present."

"You mean one hundred of your sleaziest clients and three members of my family, since your side is refusing to acknowledge me as a human being."

Dr. Caswell checked her watch. "I'm sorry, but our time is up. I do hope to see you on Thursday displaying more love and harmony than you've shown here, Bubbles. I'm afraid that your negativity is the core reason why Jane's not healing faster."

"That's what I've been telling her," Dan added.

I got up, grabbed my purse and marched out, knowing full well that Dan and Dr. Caswell would raise their eyebrows and shake their heads in disgust. I didn't care. I had to find Jane and get her to school.

I had raised Jane by myself. Not Dan. Not Caswell. How dared they accuse me of harming her? Wasn't it bad enough that I'd had to live with the guilt that my job had caused her trauma in the first place? Wasn't it bad enough I was sacrificing everything to make up for that?

I mumbled to myself in the elevator and as I stormed across the marble lobby, where Jane was waiting.

Except she wasn't.

I checked outside the revolving glass doors. There was no one besides a security guard standing languidly next to a trash can.

"Excuse me," I said, "but did you happen to see a teenage girl with a cell phone attached to her ear?"

"Yeah. She was sitting right here." He pointed to a green metal bench.

"Do you know where she went?"

"She left with some guy about five minutes ago."

Her new boyfriend, Jason, I thought with relief. "Was he driving a Dodge Durango? Did he have supershort hair and a gun rack in his truck?"

"No, ma'am." The security guard pulled a walkie-talkie from his belt. "He was in a fancy black late-model BMW and took off doing sixty in zero seconds. I kind of thought it was strange, a nice girl like her going off with him, but I didn't ask. Not my business."

I was hit by a wave of crushing panic as I thought about the man who'd been trying to break into our house the night before and Debbie Shatsky's murder and the stalker across the street from the Christmas tree lot.

Jane had been kidnapped.

Again.

Chapter Fifteen

My knee-jerk reaction was to call my buddy Mickey Sinkler down at the Lehigh Police Department. For once he wasn't in a meeting or out on patrol or dawdling over coffee in the Lehigh Diner with his fellow detectives. He was behind his desk, defying his job description.

"Jane's gone!" I wailed so loudly the receptionist in the lobby looked up from her magazine in concern. "Someone's taken her."

"Calm down, Bubbles. Tell me what happened."

I told him how Jane had been whisked away in a late-model BMW. "I don't even know anyone who drives a BMW."

"How about Stiletto?"

I hesitated. Mickey had never liked Stiletto, partly because he had been harboring a simmering crush on me since grade school. However, with Mickey's beanpole body, his big ears and five kids under five, he didn't wrap up into what you'd call a sexy package.

"Not Stiletto. He drives a beat-up Jeep."

"Okay, I'll have dispatch radio an alert to keep an eye out for a speeding, black, expensive BMW. That's the kind of vehicle they enjoy pulling over anyway. It'll be a fun way for them to kick off their Tuesday."

Thanks heavens for police discrimination.

"Why don't you try the school? Knowing Jane, she took the ride because she didn't want to be late. It is after nine, you know."

I knew and I didn't buy it. Jane was so cautious these days that she'd ask Mama for her mother's maiden name before she'd let her in the door. She wouldn't just up and leave with a strange man in a black BMW.

After Mickey hung up, I called up to Dan's office. But he was already in a meeting, and even though I told his secretary this was a "dire matter" that required his "immediate attention," she refused to interrupt him.

Just as well. I was tired of being lectured.

I was now fully charged on anxiety and Dr. Lori's bad coffee as I headed to my car. I was also extremely stressed. My hand shook as I fumbled for the keys to my Camaro and I was so unsteady behind the wheel I didn't dare drive.

Jane gone again. Kidnapped!

The all too familiar nauseating mixture of adrenaline and helplessness cramped me in pain. There was only one tonic that could soothe my nerves: Stiletto. But as I had nuked that relationship, I turned to the next best thing.

Popping in a tape of Jon Bon Jovi's "Livin' on a Prayer" I sucked strength from his immortal words. Yes, I would have to hold on to what I got. I would have to live for the fight because that's all God wrought.

I exhaled and inhaled deeply. My hands stopped shaking and I turned the ignition. Whatever awaited me in the next few hours, we would survive. This was a promise pledged to me by none other than Mr. Jon Bon Jovi himself. And Mr. Jovi—or Mr. Bon Jovi, I was never sure—was hardly ever wrong, except maybe with *Have a Nice Day*. That album sucked.

I took a left onto Schoenersville and headed up Elizabeth, skipping red lights and doing sixty toward Liberty. Might have been Debbie's ex-con ex-husband, Ern, who took Jane. He was the kind who probably simmered with anger. Anyway, he'd been in the back of my mind as the possible Peeping Tom from the night before, if indeed there'd been a Peeping Tom.

Not that Jane was lying. Just that she was, um, kind of hysterical these days.

Then, before I could move on to other possibilities, the whole crisis was over in a flash.

I could see them from the corner of Elizabeth and Linden. Bright red and blue lights lining the driveway to Liberty—not that this was an unusual sight. Between the drug dealing and gang fights, the cops here think of Liberty High School as their home away from home.

I pulled up behind the last cruiser and said a silent prayer of hope—hope that it was Jane's abductor they'd captured and not Vicki Mercanceti's son for dealing dope down on Pine Street. There was a shiny new BMW and there was Jane in the arms of Mickey, who was stroking her hair and murmuring words of fatherly comfort.

"Jane!"

She raised her face, black mascara streaming down her cheeks as I approached. But she didn't speak. She turned away.

A kid in a knitted cap and long hair pointed in my direction. "That's her crazy mom. The one who called the cops on her."

I wasn't crazy. I was alert. And my alertness had saved my daughter's life, thank you very much. For plastered against the hood of a cruiser was a very suspicious man in a buttery black leather jacket, khakis and expertly styled short, blond hair. Jane's abductor. Aka the Perv.

Mickey held up a hand to stop me from giving the Perv a kick in the ass. "Easy, Bubbles. It's not what you think."

"Yo! Mrs. Y!"

This didn't make any sense. From behind, Jane's abductor was unrecognizable, but the voice belonged to the boy who frequently raided my refrigerator. He who sprayed whipped cream directly into his mouth and then sucked the gas from the Reddi-Wip can. He who knew unequivocally that SpongeBob SquarePants lived in a pineapple under the sea and that SpongeBob was absorbent and yellow and porous. Nautical nonsense was definitely his wish.

"Gerald Thompson Rogers," Mickey said. "Is he known to you?"

"Of course he's known to me. That's Jane's old boyfriend G. I talked to him just yesterday."

"So he's not a threat to Jane?" Mickey asked, dutifully observing police procedure.

"G's a threat only to the springs on my couch. I'm surprised he's up this early. It's against his religion to wake up before noon."

Two detectives gave each other looks that said it all: another morning wasted by a paranoid mother. They unlocked the cuffs around G's wrists and ordered him off the cruiser.

"Here you go." One of the cops ripped off a ticket and handed it to G. "Sixty-three in a school zone."

"Thanks, Officer. I'll add it to my collection." G gave the ticket a kiss and shoved it in his back pocket.

"Watch it, wise guy. We got penalties for sass in this jurisdiction."

This was all my fault. Once again I'd overreacted. "I'm sorry, G. You wouldn't have gotten the ticket if I hadn't called in the posse."

"And humiliated me forever," Jane added, her first words since I'd arrived. "Do you mind if I actually go to class now? Or would you like to cast me in another mini drama?"

I ignored this, which is the only definitive way to deal with snotty teenage daughters. "What was G doing picking you up, anyway? And where did he get that fancy new car?"

"I'm rich!" G declared, rubbing his sore wrists. "I'm

financially secure. I'm moderately well off. I'm comfortable!"

"He is," Jane confirmed. "I ran into him this morning after his meeting with his accountant, who works in Daddy's office park."

"Accountant?" I turned to G. "Accountant?"

"Hey, man. I got assets to protect."

Jane said, "He sold that aloe vera hair gel recipe of his to Jeffrey Andre, who's licensed it in salons all over the country."

Hold on—that was MY hair gel recipe! He couldn't steal it.

I was ready to call him on the carpet when Mickey said in an ominous tone, "Bubbles? Can I see you a minute?"

Mickey was standing by his cruiser, one foot up on the running board. He had that stern look of disapproval, the kind a father gives a daughter when she backs his car into a fire hydrant. Not that I ever had a father, really. Mine died when he was instantly incinerated in the ingot mold.

"Lookit," he said, keeping his voice low. "I don't mind doing favors for you now and then, running plates and looking up sealed records—"

"Hey, speaking of that." I reached in my purse, pulled out my Reporter's Notebook and wrote BRIKHOUS. Then I ripped the page off and handed it to him. "Would you mind tracing this? I think it belongs to a woman named Marguerite. Right before she died, Debbie said Marguerite was after her husband."

Mickey dropped his jaw as he stared at BRIKHOUS. Because he's a congenital mouth breather, this was a frequent look for him.

I pushed his jaw shut and said, "Pretty please?"

He folded the paper and tucked it in his pocket. "Where was I?"

"You were about to scold me for calling you in hysterics because I thought Jane had been snatched."

"Oh, yeah. Right." He got his bearings and resumed his stern tone. "Claiming Jane was kidnapped . . . that was really over the top, Bubbles."

"But—"

"Let me finish! Do you know how bad I'm going to get ribbed over this? What if every parent called in the SWAT team whenever their kid was ten minutes late for school? Jane's a senior, for heaven's sake. She's almost a legal adult!"

I'd never heard Mickey sound so angry.

"I hate to say this, but I feel it's my obligation as a friend to lay it on the line with you." He took a deep breath. "You're loco, Bubbles. Kinked in the head. I don't know if it's the stress of being a reporter or what happened with Jane last month, but you are not thinking straight these days. I mean . . . you're marrying Dan!"

True. That was nuts.

"I'm seriously questioning whether you're suffering from temporary insanity."

No. I was not suffering from temporary insanity. Temporarily insane people forget to bathe and buy new mascara every six weeks. My mascara was fresh and my body was squeaky clean.

I said, "Aside from remarrying Dan and calling you about Jane—which I feel is perfectly understandable in light of recent events—what, exactly, have I done that would lead you to believe I've gone whacko?"

"How about going around town spreading rumors that Debbie Shatsky was murdered, for starters."

"She *was* murdered."

"No, she wasn't. Debbie had a very well-documented allergy of which Sandy was aware. Unfortunately, Sandy was too overworked during the holiday rush and made a tragic mistake."

I was stunned. Usually I could count on Mickey to keep an open mind. He was my one ally in the police department. "Don't tell me you're buying that bogus line?"

"It's not a bogus line. It's the department's. Didn't you read your own newspaper's story this morning?" He reached inside the cruiser and produced a crumpled copy of the *News-Times*. All I had to do was glance over the headline, *Lehigh Woman Dies from Allergy: Coroner,* and the byline, *Alison Roach,* to know the fix was in.

"What about Debbie's ex-husband, Ern Bender?" I said. "He just got out of jail and he's pissed. You should have heard the way he went on about some scam the two of them had going that Debbie took over. Then she conveniently got rid of him by framing him on those drug charges and had him sent to jail. He told me outright that Debbie deserved to die."

Mickey didn't seem to think this was anything special. "Ern has an alibi."

"Yeah?"

"Yeah. He's in a halfway house and under the strict supervision of a very qualified probation officer who tracks his every step. Ern's not free. He's in our steel-tight criminal-rehabilitation system."

"Oh. I forgot how steel-tight our criminal-rehabilitation system is," I said a bit sarcastically.

He motioned me closer. "Listen, you, I'll give you a heads-up that could get me pink-slipped on the spot if it leaked out I was telling you."

Actually, I lived for moments when Mickey told me confidential police stuff that would get him pink-slipped. "Go on."

"You need to drop this murder stuff for your own good. Maybe Sandy's, too. It's in your best interests to support the theory that Debbie's death was an accident."

"Why?"

Mickey turned down his scanner so his snitch wouldn't be picked up by dispatch. "Because Burge thinks it was murder, too, and he's got a suspect. You."

"What?" What dope was Burge smoking now?

"He has a source who claims that you're having an af-

fair with Phil Shatsky and he's going to be all over you
like a pit bull on a pig's ear within forty-eight hours."

I suppose I should have been shocked, worried, concerned, disbelieving and all that. Instead, I couldn't help
but laugh, which only made Mickey madder.

"It's not funny, Bubbles. This is not a joke. This thing
is shifting from a routine negligent-homicide case into a
full-blown murder investigation with not only you but
also Sandy as the persons of interest."

Okay. He was right. I stopped laughing. "The reason I
laughed, Mickey, is because Burge's so-called source is
his wife, who was out of joint last night because Phil
came to see me before he took one bite of her famous
chicken tortilla casserole."

Mickey wasn't getting it. I explained about the housewives and Phil pussyfooting over in a Santa Claus suit.

"That might very well be, but there were other wit-
nesses who saw you and Shatsky together, making out
in your living room just a few hours after you helped
apply the hair extensions that killed his wife. That looks
bad, Bubbles. Real bad."

Hmm. Out of context that did look bad. I had to
agree with him on that one. I let all this sink in, watching as Jane lingered with G a minute longer.

"In my opinion, the best thing you can do for everyone concerned, including Jane, is to get some professional help so you can quit being delusional," Mickey
murmured. "And if Dan loves you, he'll put off the wedding. What you need now is rest, therapy, maybe a stint
in some sort of institution, at least until Christmas and
New Year's are over. That could get Burge to cool off."

"Locking me away isn't going to solve anything,
Mickey."

"Burge is of a different opinion. By the way, the institution he has in mind throws lousy New Year's Eve
parties."

Not to mention, operates under a pretty pitiful dress
code.

Over by the Beemer, G was writing something down and handing it to Jane, who casually took it and slipped it into her pocket. That was one good reason to go through with the wedding right there—so those two could get together during the reception.

After Jane ran up the steps to class, G joined Mickey and me. He was whistling, actually whistling, and rocking on his heels.

"Gee, it's great to be arrested. The feel of the gun in the small of your back. The look of awe on your ex-girlfriend's face when you're frisked. I'm telling you, nothing turns on chicks more than when you're face-down on a cruiser with your legs spread and a lieutenant's hand running up and down between your thighs."

Mickey and I stared at him glumly.

"What's wrong with you two?"

"I'm about to get busted for murder," I said. "And Sandy might be going down with me."

"Shit happens, Mrs. Y. Shit happens." He patted me on the back. "Hey, Sinkler, how come the cops were all over Jeffrey Andre's salon yesterday asking a bunch of questions about that Shatsky dude?"

Well, well, well. What was this?

Mickey gave me a furtive glance. "Don't know. Not my case."

"I saw Phil Shatsky on TV last night. He's down at our salon all the time, goes in the back room with Jeffrey and shit. It's not just fixing the toilet, either. He brings some creepy dude with him. The three of them hang out a lot. They're doing stuff."

"That so?" Mickey fidgeted with his scanner, as if G's tip was inconsequential, which it wasn't. I found what G had to say very interesting, especially considering the number of phone calls Debbie had placed to Jeffrey Andre's home and salon hours before her death. I wondered who Phil's friend was.

"I think they're smoking weed, from the smell of it.

Not that I do that or anything, Mrs. Y. I only know from what I smell on TV."

"Of course," I said. "Never."

"Isn't there a convenience store you need to loiter at?" Mickey asked.

"Watch out. He's got assets now," I said. "He's got an accountant."

"So do some of the wealthiest drug dealers in town."

G threw up his hands. "I'm no drug dealer. I was just being a good citizen trying to do my civic duty, letting you know about Shatsky and Andre. See you around, Mrs. Y. Bye, pig." G huffed off.

"Why were the cops at Jeffrey Andre's?" I asked.

Mickey took back his newspaper and tossed it in the cruiser. "Like I told Gerald, I have no idea. Okay. I gotta go. And do me a favor. Pretend we never spoke."

I watched Mickey back up and zoom off. He didn't even wave.

Odd. Very odd man, that Mickey.

I returned to my own car and hooked a right toward the historic section on my way to the South Side. There was a lot going on behind the scenes with this Debbie Shatsky case, especially now that G had linked her husband with Andre and "some creepy dude."

I suspected Mickey knew more than he was letting on and he was truly worried that Burge would nail me for murder.

Burge was one of those cops who fired off a couple rounds and then checked to see who got hit. He was directionless, but lethal.

Burge was bad news.

The traffic light at Moravian Academy, Lehigh's only prep school, turned red for an extended period so the kids in their plaid skirts and navy blazers could cross between classes. This would take forever, I thought, enviously studying the privileged students talking to their professors as if they were real human beings and not the ~~prison guards~~ high school teachers should be.

I checked out the car next to me and nearly hit a preppie. Sitting with perfectly straight posture behind the wheel of his Dodge Neon, staring like a zombie, was none other than Phil Shatsky.

His expression was like stone, his posture rigid. Probably thinking of his dear wife, dead. Dead and gone.

Wasn't that just the saddest thing?

"Hey, Phil!" I shouted.

Phil didn't turn. He closed his eyes and let his jaw drop, as if emitting an eternal howl of despair.

I leaned on the horn to get his attention.

Beep!

Phil jumped so high his head nearly hit the windshield. That was nothing compared to my own shock when a woman lifted her own face from Phil's lap, having been caught performing an act, I presumed, for which head majorette Kathy Sweeney had earned permanent fame when we were in Liberty—otherwise referred to as the Full Sweeney.

She stared at me and I stared at her and then Phil took off, laying a patch of rubber so thick it produced smoke.

For good reason, too. The woman had been dressed in Debbie's clothes, right down to Debbie's famous mink coat and right up to Debbie's blond—and lethal—hair extensions.

Chapter Sixteen

It would have been pointless following Phil, who'd zoomed off like a bullet despite the thirty-five-mile-per-hour speed limit. As a popular plumber, he could snake his way around town faster than a slimy ball of grease in kitchen pipes.

I pointed my own trusty Camaro in the direction of the South Side, home to the House of Beauty and the *News-Times,* figuring I'd stop at whichever one was higher priority. I was on autopilot trying to process what I'd witnessed. It had definitely been Phil. I knew that green Dodge Neon and the hula dancer on his dashboard.

But that woman dressed in Debbie's clothes. Oh my God. It was just so . . . tasteless. And let's not even start with what she was doing to Debbie's grieving husband. That was taking consolation a bit too far, if you ask me.

Against my better judgment, the Camaro passed the *News-Times*. Already I was breaking the new rule Mr. Salvo had imposed to keep me from investigating stories that weren't mine to investigate.

Rule #1 was that on days when I wasn't scheduled to cover night meetings I was to report to the newsroom promptly at ten a.m. I was to punch out at six thirty with a half hour for lunch. If I needed to go out on assignment, I must file a slip with Veronica specifying where I'd gone, for what purpose, how I could be reached by telephone and when I'd return.

The clock turned ten as I pulled in front of the House of Beauty where an ominous CLOSED sign hung in the doorway, though I could see Sandy's car in back. All the blinds were drawn. The heavy layers of plastic Christmas decorations fluttered in the breeze, forlorn and dirty. Even the ripped Santa Claus seemed to be in desperate need of a Prozac prescription. The yellow police tape draped across his pack didn't help.

This might take hours, getting Sandy to open up. Sigh. So much for Rule #1.

"Sandy! Open this door right now. It's Bubbles and you know it." I turned the cold handle.

"Bubbles?" Sandy was peeking out from her office door, which opens to the parking lot she shares with Uncle Manny. "Come in the side. I don't want anyone to see me from the street."

Oh, for heaven's sake. I marched around and entered the side door to Sandy's office and storeroom. The washer and dryer were churning. Sandy must have overdone it on the Clorox because it smelled like the Lehigh public pool during an E. coli scare. Complete with the haze from Sandy's cigarettes.

She was chain-smoking. Sandy hadn't done that in years.

She was a worn-out, haggard rag of a thing. Her hair was frizzy, out of its neat hair band, and she wasn't in her polyester peach uniform or even the jeans she irons. (Irons! With a crease down the middle. Can you believe it?) What she was wearing was an old zip-up blue housecoat, the same kind her mother used to wear.

"Have you been drinking?" I asked, eyeing the overflowing ashtrays.

"Only coffee black."

"That's good. That'll calm your nerves."

"Hmph." Sandy stubbed out another cigarette. Her fingertips were turning yellow. "Like I'll ever sleep again. I killed a woman, Bubbles. I *murdered*—"

I slapped my hand over her mouth. "Don't you ever say that, Sandy. Don't even think it."

Sandy bit the palm of my hand.

"Ouch!" I waved it in the air, trying to cool the searing pain. Two neat rows of teeth marks, proof of Sandy's obedience to twice-yearly dental visits, were embedded between my heart and life lines.

Sandy checked out my palm and shrugged. "Sorry. I can't stop thinking about murder. Do you know that the police are over at my house right now, doing a search? Martin's there with the lawyer we hired last night. The warrant says that the police have found undisclosed evidence linking me to"—she choked back tears—"to Debbie's murder."

This was stunning. So Mickey had been right. Burge was determined to bust one of us.

The idiot.

Sandy and Martin lived a quiet life above his bakery in a tidy apartment outfitted almost entirely by Sears. Sandy even had Sears shower curtains, a heavy set of green flowered fabric and liner that could double as hazmat protection. The curtain coordinated with the valance in her bathroom window, the green shag toilet-lid liners and rug, even the wallpaper which was done in a Colonial theme of little farmers sawing wood. Sandy was very big on the whole Colonial style. Though I'd never known ye olde Pennsylvania colonists to sport thick green shag toilet-top covers.

For fun, Sandy and Martin clogged. To them it was a hoot. Most of their friends were cloggers and they camped at clogging campsites, where there were nightly clogging contests.

When they weren't stomping their feet hard enough to break the floorboards, their big treat was to hit the all-you-can-eat Sunday brunch (the one morning Martin didn't have to work) at Kunkleman's, where there was a "live jazz band," i.e., an eighty-year-old guy on an electric piano playing the theme from *Sesame Street*. Then, stuffed and groggy from lack of oxygen, they toured the flea markets looking for more Colonial stuff to go with their Sears, before heading home for an afternoon nap on their matching Sears bedspread.

Is this the kind of woman who murders people? I mean, really, Burge. Get a clue.

"What kind of evidence?" I asked.

Sandy shook her head. Hair fell out onto her desk. "The police won't say. Except that . . . they got a tip."

"Another tip!"

"Another anonymous tip."

That was some busy tipster. Boy, he really had a beef with Sandy.

Sandy reached for her pack of Virginia Slims, but I snatched them away. "Enough, Smokey. Besides, I just saw something that might raise your hopes."

I got up and opened the fridge for a bottle of Diet A-Treat cola. Sandy was low on supplies. I flipped open the cap with my acrylic nail and took a swig. It was the first thing I'd consumed all day. Diet cola. Breakfast of champions.

"Prepare yourself."

"Debbie's back from the dead?" Sandy asked.

"Pretty freaking close," I said.

Sandy dropped the unlit cigarette she'd been preparing to inhale. She picked it up and said, "Don't fool with me, Bubbles."

"I'm not fooling with you. At least, not on purpose." I pushed her so she sat on the desk. "Two minutes ago, maybe five, I dunno, I was parked at the light at Broad and Elm, you know, right by Moravian Academy. It was the extended light, so I had time to kill. I looked over to the car next to me and, sure enough, Phil Shatsky."

She shrugged. "So? He's allowed to go out and about."

"Yeah. Except he wasn't going—he was *getting*. The woman sitting next to him had her face in his lap, and when she lifted it, I swear to God"—I crossed myself to show that, indeed, this was a formal swear to God—"she was dressed head to toe in Debbie's clothes, including the hair extensions. And she was . . . you know."

Sandy said, "No. I don't know."

I mimed a few motions.

Sandy's eyes popped out. "She was pulling a Sweeney?"

"A Full Sweeney. You can take it to the bank."

"You're joking."

"She might have been trying to unstick his fly with her teeth, but I don't think so."

Sandy slid off the desk, gaping. "Did Phil see you see him?"

"Uh, yeah. And he flipped out big-time. Took off before the light changed. Could have killed a whole handful of preppies the way he barreled through that red light."

Sandy ran her fingers through her hair so it stood straight on end. "What does this mean?"

"I don't know. I'm even more confused because Phil came over to my house last night playing the grief-stricken husband. Sobbing like a baby who'd lost his balloon. The only way he found to calm down was to organize my spice rack."

"That's nice," Sandy said, "though kind of strange."

"It was helpful. That spice rack was in disarray. When was the last time I used cumin or coriander?"

Sandy rolled her hands. "Let's get back on track, Bubbles. Then what happened after he got rid of your cumin and coriander?"

"He made a pass at me in front of a curtainless window."

"Get out!" Sandy was so riveted she still hadn't lit that cigarette.

"I kid you not. All the housewives who'd brought him

casseroles were standing outside, including Detective Burge's wife. I bet she's the reason your house is getting searched as we speak."

"Wow." Sandy played with the zipper at the top of her ugly blue robe, going over the details in her mind. "Ginger. Ginger Burge. I used to do her hair before her husband got promoted. Now she goes to Jeffrey Andre."

Yes, I thought, *won't they all.*

The phone rang. Sandy ignored it. Instead, she got up, unloaded the dryer and began folding towels.

"Aren't you going to get it?"

She shook out a washcloth. "Nope. Why bother? I'll just get harassed. People have been calling me all night and all morning telling me that if I had any decency I'd come clean and issue a public apology and surrender my license."

I remembered the expired license on the wall. It must have been eating at her something awful, all this controversy. The House of Beauty was everything to Sandy. Well, next to Martin and her clogs.

The phone stopped ringing and Sandy asked casually, "Is that guy across the street still there?"

I felt a dull thud somewhere deep inside me. "There's a guy across the street?"

"He was there last night when I closed up and I just noticed him again when I went to get more Tide. Figured he's an undercover reporter or a cop. Though I didn't figure undercover reporters or cops drive Mercedes."

Holy crap!

I tiptoed to the door that opened from Sandy's office to the salon. It was disturbing to see the House of Beauty so quiet and dark on what should have been a bustling December morning. The red light on Sandy's answering machine blinked madly. The fish in the fishbowl swam. Other than that, there was no movement. Even the Christmas trees had been turned off.

Kneeling on the wicker couch by the plate-glass window, I pried open the venetian blinds with two fingers. Sure enough, there he was. The Mercedes Santa at the wheel.

He saw me.

I hit the floor on instinct, before the glass shattered and the discharge of the shotgun rocked through every fiber of my being. I don't know if I saw the barrel or if I was spooked by his movements. All I remember is being eye to eye with the dust bunnies under Sandy's couch as the glass rained over me and asking myself what the heck I'd done to deserve this kind of shoddy treatment.

"Bubbles!"

"Drop!" I yelled to Sandy, who was standing in her office doorway like a deer on I-80. "Get down!"

Sandy didn't have to be asked twice. She fell to the floor dutifully and covered her head as I was doing, though I didn't realize it.

We held our breath and waited. A second later, maybe less, the Mercedes peeled away with a screech. I needed that guy's license-plate number. Another opportunity missed.

Sandy and I didn't dare move.

"I could have told you this would happen," I said. "He pointed a gun at me yesterday, though I didn't see it. Shot the top off a Christmas tree down at the lot on Broad and Union. There were rumors afoot that he was a member of the violent wing of the anti-Christmas lobby, but I had my doubts."

"See, that's the kind of secret friends shouldn't keep from each other." She got up on one elbow. "You think the coast is clear?"

"I'm not sure the coast will ever be clear."

The phone rang. Sandy lay there, propped up on her elbow.

"Are you going to get that?" I asked.

"I'm never going to answer another phone again."

"I can't stand it," I said, counting the rings. We were up to nine.

"The answering machine should be picking up."

"The answering machine is full." Stiffly I hunched up, glass tinkling around me as I gently wiped off my hands and inched over to the phone.

"Bubbles, don't."

"I have to." I reached up and knocked the phone off the counter. Sandy flinched when it hit the floor. We were both a bit shell-shocked, I suppose. Jumpy.

I was surprised to hear a woman's voice.

"I'm looking for a Bubbles Yablonsky." She sounded like any number of my regular clients.

"This is she. But I'm sorry. The House of Beauty isn't taking appointments. We're closed until next year." I watched as Sandy crawled to her office.

"I'm not interested in making an appointment. I'm calling about Debbie Shatsky."

I didn't say anything. Perhaps this was the infamous tipster who'd been calling in tips all over town.

"You are a reporter, too, right?" she asked.

"Uh-huh."

"Well, you might be interested to learn that Debbie was in real hot water at the travel agency where she worked. Something to do with fraudulent credit card transactions. She was about to get fired and worse."

"How worse?"

"Criminal charges. Talk to Ken." A phone rang in the background. "I gotta go. Just thought you'd wanna know." And she hung up.

I pressed *69. The recording informed me that the number was private and could not be traced.

Sandy came back clutching her cell. She flicked on the light. "The cops are on their way. Who was that?"

"A woman with a tip that Debbie was in hot water at work."

"Oh." Sandy glanced at the plate-glass window. The blast had brought down the blinds and there was a large star-shaped hole in the middle. "Now what?"

"Now you stay here and wait for the police." I shook

off the shards of glass. Under the overhead fluorescents, I was sparkling. "Lock the windows and the doors and don't open them until you get badge numbers. Tell them they need to find out who made that phone call, if possible. It's probably too late."

"Where are you going?" she asked, panic stricken.

"To Get Together Now! Travel to talk to Ken and I don't need the cops delaying me one more minute."

Chapter Seventeen

Rule #2 was, should a situation arise in which I was not able to stop by the newsroom before going on assignment, I must call in and tell either Mr. Salvo or Veronica where I was headed.

This was why I didn't have a cell phone, because if I did, Mr. Salvo could follow me wherever I went. Though, I had to admit, I would have appreciated the cushion of security, knowing that I had backup as I headed to Stefko Boulevard, where Get Together Now! Travel was located in a strip mall.

It was a fairly bright day to be stalked by a gun-toting Santa Claus. The sky had cleared to a brilliant blue and it was much colder. We might actually have a white Christmas, instead of rain. Mama would be thrilled. It would be great for business.

I took comfort in assuring myself that even a Santa Claus who fired shotguns willy-nilly on Tuesday mornings would know better than to keep on stalking in this situation. The police sirens were blaring up Fourth when I pulled out of the House of Beauty/Uncle Manny's parking lot. Surely my would-be assassin was in hiding.

Right?

Even so, I checked my rearview enough to apply a total

makeover as I took the back roads to Stefko. Stefko is the strip of strips. Your one-stop shopping for cars, burgers, canned goods and a deep, relaxing Korean massage.

A big black bow hung over the sign for Get Together Now! Travel, not exactly what the bon vivant world traveler would want to see, in my opinion, but it was thoughtful of management to honor Debbie, nonetheless.

I didn't know if it was the black bow or the fact that Christmas was just days away, but Get Together Now! was markedly cheerless despite the bright posters of Hawaiian beaches and Venetian gondolas. I entered the door, walked past the set of green luggage on sale and went up to the receptionist, who was sorting brochures of Alaska.

"You'll have to wait," she said without looking up. "All the agents are busy and we're down one, so we're kind of strapped."

I checked around. The only agent I could see was typing on her computer. She had frizzy brown hair and wore a blue suit. A travel agent's suit. The nameplate on her desk said FIONA SWYER. She didn't look up when I came in and I wondered if she might have been the woman who called me at the House of Beauty.

"Actually, I'm here to see Ken," I said. "I'm from the *News-Times*. 'Talk of the Town.' "

"Oh." The receptionist looked confused. "Are you Flossie Foreman?"

"No. Bubbles Yablonsky. I'm her temporary replacement while Flossie recovers from knee surgery." Total lie. I should be ashamed.

"Knee surgery? That's too bad. Arthritis?"

"Looped Lithuanian with a baseball bat."

"I hate those. Okay, I'll buzz Ken."

I went over to inspect the luggage, which was touted as a hot deal. What I wanted to know was why they didn't make luggage in colors other than black, navy, dark green or that grandmotherly floral. They all looked the same and you couldn't tell them apart in baggage claim. If I won the lottery, I was going to go into the luggage business and start manufacturing lavender suitcases, bright yellow totes, orange knapsacks.

"Miss Yablonsky?" A round puppy dog of a man in a puppy brown suit stood by an office door. "I'm afraid I can't see you. Our lawyer . . ."

I extended my hand graciously. "So you're the Ken that Debbie raved about. It's so nice to finally meet you in the flesh."

Fiona Swyer, the travel agent in the blue suit, frowned.

"Thank you"—I checked the receptionist's nameplate—"Angela. I'll only be a moment." I took befuddled Ken by the arm and led him into his own office, shutting the door behind me.

Ken must have been the head honcho at Get Together Now! because he was the only one with an office and because he had a big, impressive leather swivelback chair. His walls, too, sported the de rigueur travel posters: ARUBA, JAMAICA, BAHAMAS—taunting reminders of how gorgeous and exotic the world was in places besides steel towns.

"So you know, I mean, *knew* Debbie?" Ken spoke with a flat Midwestern accent.

"Knew her?" I let out a laugh. "I was there when she died. That's how well I knew her."

"Oh, my. I had no idea." He pulled out a chair. "Have a seat. I really don't have much time, what with the holiday crush coming up. So many people like to get away after Christmas. Me? I prefer the weeks right after Thanksgiving. You can get terrific deals on cruises then. Most folks are unaware."

He smiled insipidly, clasping his hands on his desk. A woman had died, an employee, and here he was yapping on about the best time of year to tour the Panama Canal.

I pulled out my notebook. Ken's venetian blinds were

open behind him, giving me a good view of the parking lot. If I so much as spotted a flash of Santa red or the chrome bumper of a Mercedes, I was out of there.

"Is this a piece for 'Talk of the Town'? Angela said you wrote for 'Talk of the Town.'"

"Yes," I said absently. "It's a quick profile on Debbie. We do that, occasionally."

He scratched his ear. "Really? I don't think I've ever read a profile in 'Talk of the Town.' You wouldn't happen to be a regular reporter, would you? Because our lawyer said we shouldn't talk to regular reporters, though for 'Talk of the Town,' I wouldn't mind. Flossie Foreman's a wonderful—"

"Why would your lawyer say a silly thing like that?" I interrupted.

He regarded me skeptically. "I'm not sure I should say."

"Oh, please." I leaned forward and touched his hand, making sure I flashed a bit of this and that. "You don't have to worry about Bubbles. Look at me? Do I look like a *real* reporter?"

He took in my white, off-the-shoulder shirt and my purple acrylic nails still on his own hand. "I guess not."

"I write for the women's pages, Ken, just so I don't have to deal with messy stuff like numbers and money and icky crime. I'm here only because Debbie was a friend of mine, a dear, dear friend, and I'd like her to be remembered for the delightful person she was, not for the not-so-delightful person the police are saying." I batted my eyes.

Ken examined his tie as though looking for stains that might tell him whether to talk to me. "What are the police saying?"

"I don't think I should say." Sometimes I liked to throw it back in their faces.

"I'd really like to know. It might be important for Get Together Now!"

"I have an idea. Why don't you show me yours and I'll

show you mine? I've often found that this is the best
way to stave off negative publicity."

He thought about this. "If the police are saying anything about the money, I want you to make sure in your
'Talk of the Town' story that you note I had no idea
whatsoever and that I stopped her activity as soon as it
was brought to my attention."

I stepped on my left toe to keep my face straight. So
my tipster had handed me the straight skinny. Debbie's
trouble had to do with money. Well, that wasn't a surprise, was it? Money's always at the root of evil.

Ken was on a roll. "Customers get so squeamish when
they read stories in the papers about their money being
mishandled, even if the stories aren't true."

"I know. They're so unreasonable," I agreed, "especially when Debbie didn't mean to take the cash."

"Well, we don't know that, do we? Gee, it's an awfully
bright day. Do you mind if I close the blinds?"

"No! I mean, yes!" I yelled.

Ken turned with alarm.

"I get claustrophobic."

"That's too bad." He sat down again. "Now what was
I saying?"

"The credit card numbers Debbie had used, unknow-
ingly of course, for her own purchases." She reels, she
casts . . .

She hooks a big one! "Right. Those. It was good Visa
found out before too much money was lost."

"Only a few thousand dollars."

Ken blushed. "I don't know if I'd call fifteen thousand
a few dollars."

"Silly me. I told you I was bad with numbers."

He smiled as though I was adorable. There was a
knock at the door and the sourpuss agent Fiona Swyer
in the blue uniform opened it without waiting for an invitation. She glanced at my notebook, clearly not
pleased to see it on my lap. Nor was she delighted by the
amount of cleavage I was showing.

"Mr. Abrams. May I see you a moment?"

Ken pointed to me. "Can't you see I'm in the midst of an interview? If it's the St. Augustine's Girls Choir, tell them the bus tickets to Washington, D.C., are in the pack on Angela's desk."

"It's not the St. Augustine's Girls Choir," Swyer said. "It's important."

"Maybe I should come back later," I offered.

"Or not at all." Swyer had the nasty I-don't-like-you face down.

The face didn't fool me, though it might have fooled Ken. Days from now, soon after my story about Debbie's pilfering hit the newsstands, Ken would first curse himself for inviting me into his office and then transfer his guilt to others in the office. He would wonder if someone in-house had called in a tip. He would remember that Angela the receptionist had been nice, that Fiona Swyer had disapproved of me.

Ipso facto, her chilly demeanor.

I got up and shook Ken's hand heartily. "It really was a pleasure. Thank you so much. This is going to be a great article about Debbie."

"I didn't say anything."

"You said more than you know." I blew him a kiss and wedged my way past Fiona Swyer, the pin on her lapel catching my eye. It was of a star inside a pentagon. I'd seen the same symbol recently, but where?

"I assume you can see yourself to the door," she said.

I couldn't discern if hers was the voice on the other end of the phone call. However, as a woman who worked among women, I could easily understand Fiona Swyer's motivation for calling me about her formerly perky, popular and apparently felonious coworker Debbie Shatsky. There is no deadlier force on the planet than female jealousy. And Swyer was anything but perky.

"Don't knock yourself out," I said.

She pursed her lips.

Outside on the sidewalk, Angela was fixing a garland that had fallen off the NOW!

"Turns out you're not Flossie Foreman's replacement."

This caused me to revamp my theory about Fiona Swyer. Maybe Angela had been the tipster after all. "Aren't you an intrepid secretary."

She pinned the garland and turned. "What did you come here for?"

"I don't know. I'm still trying to find out." Then, thinking that Angela might actually have some brains behind those overtweezed brows of hers, I added, "Maybe I should talk to Zora in Debbie's allergist's office. I hear she has some pretty strong opinions. Her and Tess."

Angela didn't so much as raise a goose bump. "What Debbie did to those women was unforgivable."

"Unforgivable." I had no idea what she was talking about except my assumption that the unforgivable stuff was connected to the fifteen thousand dollars in Visa charges.

"Have you spoken with Zora?"

"Not yet. Don't know how to find her."

She flicked her gaze to the parking lot, trying to decide. "She works for an allergist right here in Lehigh. Should be easy enough to find if you have a phone book. That way you didn't get her name from me."

"Right," I said. "I just like to call allergists randomly from the phone book."

"That's good. Because there are a lot more than you'd think."

The rest of the day might have proceeded uneventfully if I'd just done what Dix Notch wanted me to do—forget Debbie's case and accept that her death was an accident, nothing more. Even Detective Burge seemed to have lost interest, since he didn't try to contact me as I'd been warned.

I had no idea what he was putting Sandy through. My frequent calls to the House of Beauty and Sandy's home were fruitless. She still wasn't answering her phone and here I had so much to tell her about Debbie's shenanigans at Get Together Now!

Of course I couldn't update Mr. Salvo, either. Couldn't even tell him about the guy who shot out Sandy's front window. I was supposed to be off the case, remember? What was it Notch had said? That if he found me asking *one* question, going through *one* file on Debbie Shatsky's death, I would be canned on the spot.

"Where have you been?" Mr. Salvo asked when I tried to hide my late arrival to the newsroom by coming up the back way and going straight for the mailboxes.

He was wearing a baby blue shirt today with short sleeves, even though it was December. And he had a yellow clip-on tie. A clip-on. And he can't understand why he's still single.

I gathered up my mail and started flipping through it casually, tossing out the Mahoken Town Council agendas as I went. They were just so boring. "Sorry, Mr. Salvo. Jane, Dan and I had an appointment with our family therapist. Then there was some stuff I had to do."

"What kind of stuff?"

"Stuff, stuff." I got to my copy of *Cosmopolitan* and kissed the cover. I missed *Cosmo* so much after leaving the salon. I felt so lost not knowing the twelve ways to drive my man wild in bed so he'd beg for more.

"Nice piece on the Help the Poor Children Fund-raiser."

"Thanks." I went over to the watercooler to get a cup of water.

"Kind of bizarre that Flossie would injure her knee on the day Stiletto blows into town so she can't cover an event where he's on the auction block and where you two were spotted sneaking off to suck face."

My hand shook slightly. I emptied out the rest of the water and dumped the cup in the trash. "The universe works in magical ways."

"So do crazed senior citizens with a penchant for swinging baseball bats at random low levels."

"Yes." I started walking over to my desk, wishing Mr. Salvo would just drop it already, when I stopped.

Something was off.

"Well, at least your mind's on Stiletto and off this Shatsky thing. Man, Notch is driving me up the wall. He is so obsessed with making sure our stories don't imply Shatsky was murdered. Like I told him, if the police come out and say it's a murder, fine. Otherwise, we're just printing what we know. Woman dies in a salon. Period."

"Mr. Salvo, why is Alison Roach sitting at my desk?"

Alison's black jacket, the one she'd worn yesterday, was hanging over the back of my chair. Gone was my photo of Jane, the tiny pink-framed mirror I pasted to the side of the computer so I could check my lip gloss 24/7, and the two bottles of nail polish I kept ready to repair keyboard-induced tip damage.

And where was my beautician's license and vase with the pink plastic flower?

I felt a pang of anxiety. Alison could not take over my desk. I LOVED my desk. I loved it partly because it was next to Lawless, the beat-cop reporter, not that I loved Lawless or anything. What I loved was his police scanner, which emitted a regular chatter among dispatchers, cops, firemen and emergency-service types. Every once in a while, the chatter would break and something big would erupt: a fire, a fatal car accident, a shooting. Then the thrills would begin.

"Is Alison taking over my desk?"

Mr. Salvo shuffled the papers on his clipboard, a sure sign of a guilty conscience. "Uh, Notch decided to move her next to Lawless for, you know, training."

"Training for what? Police reporter? Because that's supposed to be my next job, cops or courts, and so far I haven't gotten farther than Mahoken."

Mr. Salvo didn't say anything until he uttered some

diplomatic nonsense about every rookie reporter needing to learn how to cover a fire, blah, blah, blah.

"And where am I to sit?"

He pointed to lifestyle, where a computer in the smallest cubicle sat untouched, waiting for my fingers. Maybe someone was being a smart-ass, placing me in Flossie Foreman's department after Genevieve's thuggery. Or maybe Mr. Notch was sending me a message that I was on my way out. For if I wasn't mistaken, that cubicle belonged to Marty Finkleman, our eighty-year-old obits writer, who worked part-time nights.

"I'm sharing a desk with Marty?"

"Only for a while, until Alison gets her sea legs. So Stiletto came by this morning looking for some clips," he said, trying to distract my attention away from the usurpation of MY DESK! "Too bad you weren't here."

For once—and only once—I cared about something more than Stiletto. I cared about my desk, the symbol of all that I had sacrificed and worked to achieve. Marty Finkleman's corner cubicle was the lowest of the low. It was the dunces' corner and I was the dunce.

Well, I thought, pushing back my white sleeves, I'd been at the bottom before and had crawled my way up. Notch was sadly mistaken if he thought this public demotion would make me toe the line, that I would humbly do as he ordered until he begrudgingly accepted me back into his good graces.

Now I was determined, more determined than before, to investigate Debbie's murder and write it up into a blockbuster page-one thriller. I would show him and the lackadaisical Lehigh PD that they'd been wrong about Sandy or wrong about Debbie's death being an accident.

And I didn't care if by that time Notch had relegated me to the basement.

Chapter Eighteen

I waited until Doris the librarian left work exactly at five oh one to slip out of my dunce's corner and run down the hall to the morgue.

Doris was a dour woman, as yellow as the rubbery mucilage she used to paste her yellowing newspaper clips to yellow paper for preservation. She excelled in Schadenfreude, the exquisite Pennsylvania art of relishing the misfortune of others. Therefore, I could not dig through clips of Ern Bender and Debbie Shatsky under Doris's vulturelike gaze without fully expecting her to run straight to Notch to tattle.

While other newspapers had upgraded to computerized archiving more than a decade ago, the morgue of the *News-Times* was stuck in the Dark Ages thanks to Doris. I wasn't exactly clear on why they couldn't modernize and lay her off as they had the old guys in the newsprint hats who used to run hot type upstairs. Lorena told me once that Doris had naughty photos of Notch she'd whip out as blackmail whenever he broached the possibility of going completely online.

All I knew was that if I were lucky enough to have naughty photos of Notch, I'd a) induce blindness in myself so I wouldn't have to look at them and b) sure as hell use them to do more than keep my job as a lonely librarian in the windowless morgue.

As I had feared, the *Bender, Ern* file was gone. Possibly it had never existed. Doris maintained an arcane filing system, another key to her survival. It always bothered me that she filed animal abuse cases under "Pets," for example. Or that rape cases were under "Sex." I had to put my head into Doris's head for a second before I was rewarded with one clip in "Pharmacies"—a major fire at Save-T Drugs.

I vaguely remembered the blaze, which had taken out the back half of Save-T Drugs about seven years ago. Ern was quoted in the article as being an assistant pharmacist, which meant the fire occurred before he was busted for selling laced Cokes.

According to the article, the fire was of a "suspicious origin" and was located in the pharmacy section of the drugstore. Ern mused to the reporter that perhaps it was faulty electrical wiring, that he'd been hearing mice late at night chewing on the wires.

Mice? Good one, Ern.

"Meth fire."

Lawless was reading over my shoulder. I should have recognized the reek of chocolate and peanut butter. Lately he'd fallen off the candy wagon and had sacrificed his soul to the god of vending machines, provider of Holy Twix. His relaxed-fit Dockers were no longer relaxed; they were downright uptight.

"It came out at his trial that Bender was cooking up methamphetamines in the back room and stealing Sudafed from Save-T to do it." He finished the last of his Reese's. "Some kindly neighborhood druggist, say?"

I quickly slipped the article back into the file. How could I have been so stupid as to just stand here reading this? Now Lawless would surely rat me out to Notch.

"It's the twentieth anniversary of the big Mahoken town hall fire," I lied with false innocence, shoving the file back into the cabinet. "Happened to come across this."

"You were looking for a clip on the Mahoken town hall fire in the pharmacy file?" Lawless grinned. "Come off it, Yablonsky. You and I both know what you were up to. You were digging up background on Ern Bender."

"Never!"

"You could get axed immediately for that. Notch sent out a memo that we weren't to discuss anything Shatsky with you and that included her ex-husband."

I tensed, waiting for Lawless to pick up the phone and interrupt Notch's nightly edit meeting with the glorious revelation that he'd found me snooping. Notch would love nothing more than to fire me in front of all the editors as proof of how willing he was to exert his power. He would have done really, really well in the Crusades.

But Lawless didn't pick up the phone. Nor did he lecture or warn me. He said, "I followed you back here so we could talk. Dix Notch is out of control and we have to stop him."

This made me shut the file drawer much louder than I intended. "What?"

"I know, I know," he said, hitching up his trousers legs and perching at the edge of Doris's desk. "You and I aren't famous for getting along. But in these circumstances I think it's best that we join forces."

"Okay." I pulled out Doris's fancy ergonomic backward chair. "Keep talking."

"He's psycho about this stupid Shatsky case, which seems like a routine accidental poisoning if you ask me. I mean, the woman had an allergy to latex and died. So what? Lots of people have allergies and die. To bees, to penicillin, some to peanuts. Though, if you ask me, I think that one's way overblown."

I swallowed. Where was Lawless going with this?

"I don't have a conflict of interest—unlike you—and I'm the cop reporter. I'm supposed to be writing this, right? It's my fucking job."

"Right." Though Lawless would do one heck of a lazy job.

"I mean this is standard stuff. But not to Notch. Jesus H. You'd think this stupid fatal allergy involved the White House the way he's all over it. He wants total control. Won't let me make one phone call."

"Not one phone call?"

"Can't even discuss it with my standard sources. Threatened to fire me if I did, too."

I leaned back in Doris's goofy ergonomic chair and nearly fell over. Lawless actually saved me by reaching over and catching the back. "This fucking chair cost two grand, you know," he said. "I don't know what Doris has got over Notch but she uses it to acquire some pretty useless shit."

Lawless liked to swear. He was a swearing virtuoso.

I steadied Doris's chair and said, "So who's covering the Shatsky homicide if you're not?" Like I didn't already know the answer.

"That pipsqueak rookie Alison Roach." Lawless snarled. "Notch is calling her into his office every ten minutes and she's reporting on this exactly the way he wants. I swear, she must be giving him hummers because he can't leave her alone."

"Full Sweeneys," I said.

"Pardon?"

"Full Sweeneys. That's our term for hummers."

"What's a partial Sweeney?"

"A very bad Saturday night."

Lawless scratched his ear. "Whatever. The point is that while I'm not one to run with conspiracies, I'm beginning to think with the way he's controlling this story, Notch has something to hide. Now I'm questioning whether this wasn't a freak latex poisoning death, but maybe more. Maybe"—Lawless coughed as though he were choking on his own words—"maybe you're, um, right."

This time I held on to Doris's desk so I didn't tip backward. "Can I have that in writing?"

"Don't be smug. Listen, if you tell me what you've

found out, I might be able to put it together with what I know and we can compare notes to determine if Notch has some connection to this murder."

I couldn't see how. Besides, I didn't trust Lawless. He could be spying on me for Notch, though what Lawless said about Notch and Alison Roach was true. It did raise the possibility that Notch was snuffing a story for his own purposes. Notch had a lot of close ties into Lehigh's business community. He did not operate independently, as newspaper editors should. He was more concerned with greasing his own wheels than the wheels of justice.

Then again, this was coming from *Lawless*.

"I can see you're not sure about my proposal. Fine. I understand. You think I might be a mole for Notch. So, to show I'm on the up and up, I'll share some juice a cop told me this afternoon." Lawless walked over to the library door and shut it. "Ern Bender came to the police station last night looking for protection. Said his life was in danger and he couldn't protect himself because, as a felon, he's not allowed to have a gun."

Lawless scrutinized my reaction carefully. I still wasn't sure if he was on the take, so I tried to keep my expression neutral, even though this validated my hunch that the Christmas tree lot hadn't been shot up by the violent wing of the anti-Christmas lobby. It was good to know Bender was alive and not killed by the .22 caliber one-shot that had killed the blue spruce.

"Here's something else. I got a call this morning from a guy I've written about for five years. Louie Murray, aka Louis Moran aka Lucky Louie aka Lola Lou. That was during his drag years."

"Sounds like a busy man. Except for his drag years."

"That's Louie all right. Busy. Used to run a craps game in Freemansburg. Been in and out of jail a dozen times. Anyway, he read Roach's story this morning about Shatsky being a successful travel agent and all, how she was a fifth-degree queen of the muckety-muck

for the Order of the Eastern Star and such. Fucking
church lady. Seems he had quite a problem with that."

Something in Lawless's statement hit a nerve, trig-
gered a memory I couldn't quite place in context. I hate
when that happens. It's like forgetting what you want to
say. I just knew this was what my senior years were going
to be like if I didn't start eating gingko by the bucket.

"Are you listening to me?"

"I'm listening," I said, still trying to remember.

"Louie claims Shatsky hired him last year, during one
of his brief vacations from the clink, to work on one of
her Love Boat cruises off Atlantic City. Wasn't interested in him serving drinks or swabbing the deck. Louie
claims she wanted him to put his con artist skills to good
use posing as a rising Lehigh steel exec looking for the
perfect wife. Louie said he got laid on that cruise more
times than he could count and still Debbie paid him big
bucks for his services."

That was it! The night before in the women's room,
either Tess or the brunette had mentioned the "lust
boat" cruises being filled with ex-cons. But why would
Debbie use ex-cons to pose as loopers? Why didn't she
use the real thing?

Loopers were men, always men, who ground out suc-
cessive six-month stints at the steel plants in Baltimore,
Williamsport, Johnstown, Lebanon, Pottstown and, if
they were fortunate, San Francisco, before being
deemed worthy of vice president status. They were the
industrial equivalent of circuit riders, lonely and often
single, looking for women willing to pull up roots twice
a year and move on. Either that or settle for a one-night
stand.

For many in Lehigh's working-class community, marrying a looper meant a step up the economic ladder, a
financially secure lifestyle. A looper who survived the
circuit was assured a six-figure salary, a nice house in a
good neighborhood, an automatic membership to the
country club and the permanent title of vice president.

I had to hand it to Debbie. Booking cruises so single women in Lehigh could meet lonely loopers was an inspired idea. That was, if the lonely loopers were really loopers and not ex-cons.

Hold on. "Did you say Louie got laid?" I asked.

"More often than Mohammed's prayer rug. If what he says is true, it's a helluva story, ain't it?"

And how much better a story it would have been if I could interview women who'd been victims of Debbie's scam. Women like Tess and the brunette. Then again, what was I saying? Tess *despised* me. Damn. And she would have been so perfect!

"You're thinking and that scares me," Lawless said. "It's unnatural. You're supposed to put on mascara and lipstick, tease hair, not think."

I carefully slid off Doris's chair. It tottered back and forth. "Could you get Lucky Louie to confirm on the record that he was hired by Debbie to pose as a looper?"

Lawless shoved his hands in his pockets. "I don't know. Louie doesn't want to go back to jail. He wants to keep his name out of the papers for now. He's looking at a job in substitute teaching, should the teachers go on strike next month. Wants to keep a low profile."

That sounded like another page-one blockbuster right there: *Con Subs for Scabs*. Too bad I didn't have the time. "You think he'd be willing to go as background? Maybe he could find other ex-cons. Surely he wasn't the only bachelor on board."

"I'll try it, see if I can entice him. When she died, Debbie owed him five hundred bucks for the last cruise, so he might be inclined. What about you?"

"There are some women I could talk to."

"From the salon?"

"No. But that's not a bad idea."

The phone on Doris's desk rang. Lawless picked it up.

"Uh-huh," he said, eyeing me. "She's here. No . . . no. I won't let her go." He hung up and I flew at him.

"You set me up!" I screeched, feeling his chest for a wire, reaching around to detect if a tape recorder was concealed in the small of his back. "You are a spy for Notch and now he's coming to get me."

Lawless clinched me in a bear hug. "Knock it off, Yablonsky. Get ahold of yourself. It's not Notch who's on his way. It's your nutty mother."

Mama stood frowning in the doorway next to Genevieve, who was holding a large garment bag. "Well, I never. Less than a week before the wedding and still throwing herself at men."

"What can you do? It's the Lithuanian in her," Genevieve said. "We got a sex drive that just won't quit."

Lawless and I snapped apart. He fled that room faster than the hot summer when he was gypped out of a Push Pop and chased the Good Humor truck four blocks.

Mama watched him go. "I know you told us not to show up when you were at work but since it's after five we figured it would be okay. Turns out you were just making hoohaa in the library, anyway."

She was in a new Christmassy outfit of a cranberry-colored flared skirt and a green cardigan decorated with snowmen and snow-covered houses and a lot of snow-related activity. Genevieve, on the other hand, wore a black turtleneck and, *gulp*, Aberdeen plaid trousers. Her thighs were larger than the entire landmass of Scotland. Angrier, too.

"We weren't making hoohaa. Lawless and I were talking business."

"Hmph," Mama hmphed, unconvinced.

"If it was sexual harassment, I got my home castrator in the Rambler," Genevieve suggested. "Might be a bit rusty after the incident at Niagara Falls and whatnot."

"Thanks. I'll keep it in mind. Not for Lawless. I got other rusty home castrator candidates. I could make a list. A long list." I pointed to the garment bag. "What's in there? Your outfit for the Christmas pageant?"

"Hardly," Mama said. "Give it to her, Genny."

Genevieve thrust out the garment bag, which was surprisingly heavy. "It's for you."

"We went to Jersey yesterday to find camels. And we saw it in the window of Loehmann's. We had to buy it."

I sniffed the garment bag. It smelled vaguely of a circus. "They're selling camels at Loehmann's now?"

"Don't be silly. Try it on. Genny and I can't wait."

There was only one bathroom in the library and it was for Doris's personal use. She kept it locked when she was off the clock. Even when it was available, it was more her space than the *News-Times'* space. She stored a coffeemaker in there, a box of tampons, her toothbrush and toothpaste and a collection of makeup that didn't seem to do much good.

"I've got nowhere to change and I'm not going into the newsroom." I handed the dress back to her. "I'll try it on when I get home. Dan's going to be here soon. We're getting our marriage license tonight."

Mama slapped her cheek. "Oh, thank heavens. We were worried you were going to miss the license deadline. That's a load off our mind."

"I got an idea," Genevieve said. "Why don't you and I stand guard out in the hall, Lulu? If we see Dan, we'll run interference. Meanwhile, Bubbles can try on the dress here."

"What's the rush?" I said. "I'll try it on tonight. No biggie."

Mama shifted her feet and looked furtively at Genevieve. "The thing is, tonight might be too late."

"For what?"

"To make closing time at Loehmann's," Genevieve said. "We gotta get the dress back by then."

"Especially if you like it," Mama added, tossing the garment bag back to me. "It's your wedding dress."

I couldn't believe it. She was at it again. Shoplifting—my wedding dress!

Mama had a bit of a problem in the kleptomania department, depending on her medication levels, though Genevieve had promised to keep an eye on her. I didn't think taking the dress outside "to check it in the natural light" would work as an excuse this time, not with the crossing of state lines.

"If this dress is over three thousand dollars, then it's a federal felony which might require investigation by the FBI," I said. "That is, if it's stolen."

Mama blinked, all the color suddenly gone from her rouged cheeks. "It's not worth more than three thousand dollars."

I thought so. And here I was, holding the hot merchandise.

Genevieve waved me on. "Go on, try it. Look at it this way. You're test driving a dress like a car. Don't buy a car until you test-drive it, right?"

This made sense in a distorted, oversexed Lithuanian way. "Okay. But you two have to not budge from the hallway and give me a high sign if anyone comes."

"How about . . . 'Get that stolen wedding dress off, Bubbles. It's your boss!' " Mama said. "Is that a good high sign?"

I told her that would do. My firing was looking more and more imminent, anyway.

They left and I hung the dress up on the handle of a filing cabinet. Carefully, I zipped it open, fully expecting an explosion of toile or chiffon. Mama preferred dresses that resembled the white crocheted canister covers in her kitchen. You know, the ones with the doll sewn in the top. Her bedroom bureau was covered with them.

The bag opened. I peeked inside and was flabbergasted. This was not a crocheted canister cover by any stretch. This was a beautiful V-necked gown with a ruched bodice and faux pearls and silver beaded straps in ivory silk. It was gorgeous!

I pulled off all my clothes and stepped into it. I couldn't wait. The dress slid over my skin like water and fit like a gem, hugging my waist and flattering my hips.

It wouldn't have to be altered at all. The silver beads made the most of my shoulders and the ruched bodice lifted my bust regally. This was too good for Dan. This dress was too good for Cinderella.

There was a knock on the door.

"Just a minute," I called as I struggled with the side zipper.

"Bubbles," Mama croaked from the hallway. "Get that hot dress off. We got trouble."

Oh, crap. Notch. And here this zipper was stuck. I pulled it up, down. Nothing. Finally, I just kicked my clothes and looked for a place to hide. There was scuffling on the other side of the door and a man's voice, low and gruff.

I thought of throwing myself into a file cabinet, but they were all stupidly stuffed with files. Doris's desk wasn't any help and her bathroom was locked, damn it.

There was no out. I watched dumbly as the handle turned and the door opened, covering my eyes so I didn't have to meet Notch's furious gaze. There were footsteps and then the door shut. I waited, counting to ten before I peeked between my fingers and saw that it wasn't Notch.

It was Stiletto.

Chapter Nineteen

Slowly I brought my hands down. Remembering that I was in a wedding gown, a very sexy wedding gown at that, paralyzed me into self-consciousness. I stood frozen against the filing cabinets, submitting myself to Stiletto's inspection, which he insisted on conducting despite my obvious mortification.

He said nothing as he let his dark blue gaze travel over me, from my bare shoulders and exposed cleavage to my relatively narrow waist and the outline of my thighs. I could tell he approved, at least according to the way he smiled knowingly at his favorite parts.

"New career style?" he asked.

"Not exactly." I held out the skirt and let it drop. "Just trying it on before the cops arrest Mama. It's hot."

"You might say that."

I brushed back a strand of hair, remembering our fight from the night before. It helped to dissipate some of my uncharacteristic modesty. "I'd take it off except the zipper's stuck."

"Want some help? I've had some experience with dress zippers, you know."

This could be trouble.

He didn't wait for my permission. Instead, he placed

the files he had borrowed on Doris's desk and took the matter into his own hands. He knew exactly where the zipper was and exactly how to unstick it. I held my breath as his capable fingers swiftly unsnagged the head and he slowly proceeded to unzip.

"That's far enough," I said, pushing his hand away. "Thank you."

I looked down. Stiletto's rough hand was on my bare hip and not showing any signs of budging. He was very close. So close I could feel his breath on my neck, smell the leather of his jacket.

"You better take this off," he murmured. "Your mother says Dan's going to be here any minute to get a marriage license. Don't want him to see you like this before the wedding, do you?"

But I didn't think Stiletto really cared whether or not Dan saw me like this before the wedding. Emily Post wasn't foremost in his thoughts. I had a hunch what was foremost in his thoughts and it had absolutely nothing to do with etiquette.

"Do you mind?" I said.

"What's the matter, Bubbles?" He paused. "Don't you *trust* me?"

Oh, what a bastard he was to throw the trust issue back in my face. "We're done discussing that, Stiletto. I have very good reasons for marrying Dan and you have offered nothing to show me why I shouldn't."

"How about the fact that you can't stop thinking about me?" He grinned, cocky, enjoying the torment he was putting me through.

I wrenched away. In so doing, half of my dress split open and my strap fell off my shoulder. It was Stiletto who gently slid it back. He was hesitating, one hand still on my shoulder, giving me the look of a thousand looks, when the phone rang.

"Could you get it?" I said. "I'm kind of . . . you know."

Reluctantly, he dropped his hand and picked up the phone. I could hear Veronica's voice, high-pitched and hysterical, on the other end. "Is Bubbles there? This is really important. We have an emergency."

"Apparently there's an emergency." He handed it to me.

Veronica was so manic she could barely sputter out the words. "Bubbles! Ohmigod. I'm so glad I tracked you down. I was looking all over the newsroom for you. This guy's been calling for the past hour. He's on the other line and won't hang up. I don't know if he's drunk or drugged or what. He keeps saying he knows you're here. He sees your car in the lot and he insists on talking to you. Sounds like a stalker. Should I tell Mr. Notch?"

"Heavens no. Don't tell Notch. Don't do anything, Veronica. I'll handle the creep."

Stiletto raised an eyebrow.

"Did he give you a name?"

"No. He just said that you'd know who he was. Bubbles, he sounds, uh, really dangerous."

"That's okay. Patch him through. I know how to handle dangerous men." I stuck out my tongue at Stiletto. He laughed halfheartedly, but I could tell he was concerned.

"Hold on," he said. He headed for the other phone by the rear file cabinets. Picking up the receiver he said, "Okay, Veronica. This is Steve Stiletto listening on another line. Send him through. I'll take care of it if there's any trouble."

I cupped the phone under my chin and pounded my chest. "Me, Tarzan. Me, Stiletto."

"Stiletto?" a voice on the other line said. It wasn't Veronica anymore. It was Ern Bender.

I swore silently. Stiletto nodded to show me it was okay to go on. "This is Bubbles Yablonsky. Are you looking for Steve Stiletto?"

There was a pause and then Ern hissed, "You lied to me. I don't like it when people lie to me."

"Pardon?"

"You said you were a hairdresser. Now I find out

you're a reporter. That's not cool, not cool at all. I have half a mind to make you pay for that."

He sounded one hundred percent different from the rather stable, albeit possibly intoxicated, Santa Claus at the Christmas tree lot. I looked over at Stiletto, whose brows were furrowed, and prayed that he wouldn't tell Ern to take a flying leap.

"I am a hairdresser," I said. "I'm both. I didn't lie to you."

"You know too much. Already, you know too much."

I paused, trying to choose the right words, and settled on my favorite tact: stupidity. "I'm sorry. You'll have to excuse me. I don't know what I know. I don't even know who you are."

Stiletto grinned.

"You know who I am. Ern Bender. Debbie's ex-husband. I've been keeping tabs on you. You went straight for it. You couldn't resist."

I hadn't noticed anyone following me. Then again, I often don't check my rearview mirror unless it's to apply makeup. Old habits die hard.

"What couldn't I resist? Mr. Bender, why were you following me? I have no idea what you're talking about."

"Let's quit with the games. What is it you want, money? 'Cause I know the people who will pay for it and pay handsomely if that's what you're after. Name the price."

Okay. This was really getting frustrating. Stiletto gave me a quizzical look. I shrugged. "I swear to God, Mr. Bender. I am totally clueless."

"Oh, you're tough. You think you can drive a hard bargain. Well, let me give you a heads-up, hairdresser. The people who killed Debbie don't bargain. They made her an offer, and when Debbie held out, she ended up dead within twenty-four hours. Isn't that warning enough?"

A dull headache was spreading across my brow as though a steel band were being tightened above my ears.

"Please, I'm begging you. Give me a word, a clue, anything. Because right now I am being totally honest. I have no idea what the hell you're talking about."

"The star file. There's one more copy. You came looking for it from me yesterday, but I didn't have it. By now I know you do. You went right to Debbie's hiding place."

"What do you mean the star file? And who wants it?"

"The people whose names are in it. They have a right to it. It was their information, not Debbie's."

"And they are . . . ?"

"The same people who are coming after you if you don't wise up. Stay tuned, hairdresser. We'll be in touch."

He hung up.

Stiletto gently replaced the receiver. "This dude for real?"

"I think he is."

"Then you've got a problem."

"Or a great story." I tried to hang up, too, but my hand kept insisting on shaking uncontrollably.

Stiletto came over and covered mine with his. His felt solid and warm. Secure. My hand stopped shaking.

"You want me to stick around?"

"Just long enough to do me a favor, if that's okay."

Stiletto smiled. "It's more than okay."

"You say that now because you haven't heard the favor. Once I ask, you may never be willing to speak to me again."

Chapter Twenty

I waited downstairs in advertising with the lights off for Dan to pick me up so we could get our marriage license. I hated to admit it to myself, but after my conversation with Ern Bender, I was scared. I didn't dare stand outside on the corner of Fourth Street in the dark alone. Plus, it was snowing pretty hard and I'd run out of Final Net. Hair today, alive tomorrow, I always say.

With Stiletto's back turned, I had changed into my regular clothes so Mama could return my dress to Loehmann's before the store detectives caught up with her. She was none too pleased to see Stiletto in the library with me and let me know as much by making weird eye movements supposed to convey her displeasure, though, frankly, they came off more as muscle spasms.

It was good to get it off my chest. I mean, the story about Debbie's murder, my suspicions and witnessing Phil Shatsky in a Full Sweeney. As an experienced photojournalist with an ear for news and lips for more than gabbing, Stiletto knew better than to talk.

He sat on the library floor, his arms resting on his bent knees, and listened closely while I rambled about Sandy likely being sent to prison and Detective Burge's wife accusing me and how Jane was absolutely not getting better.

"I don't know, Stiletto," I told him. "I don't know what I'm doing wrong. I mean, I raised Jane to be independent. I had no choice, what with going to night school and working a full-time job. Now she's more clingy and scared than when she was a little girl in kindergarten."

"Yeah, well, getting kidnapped will do that to you. Give her time, Bubbles. One day she'll surprise you. She'll wake up and do something to show that the real Jane is still there." He fetched a tissue from Doris's Kleenex box. I bet Doris had counted all her Kleenex and would be alarmed the next morning when she came to work and found five missing.

I wiped away my tears, hesitating before blurting the one neurosis that had been keeping me up nights. "I'm beginning to think I suck as a mother."

"That's bullshit and you know it. It's not even worth discussing. Unless . . . Hold on. That's what Dan's telling you, isn't it?"

Yes, I wanted to say, *and Dr. Caswell, too,* though I wasn't about to let Stiletto know.

"Guess what. Dan doesn't know anything. Nothing." Stiletto held up his hands as if stopping himself. "Don't get me started. You're getting married to the creep. I don't want to go there."

That's okay, I could have said. *You can go there.*

"Listen, trashing Dan's not going to help Jane, and to tell you the truth, I can't see how I can help, either," he said. "But how about this story you're working on, Debbie Shatsky's murder. Is there any way I can help you with that?"

As soon as he said it, I realized he could.

An hour later, Stiletto and I had fine-tuned our plan to get Tess to spill the details about Debbie's lust boat cruises. On second thought, I'm not sure "fine-tune" was an accurate description. More like thrown-together. A thrown-together, half-assed plan.

As Stiletto said, half-assed plans were the best kind.

"Had to make me get out of the car and come to the door, didn't ya?" Dan said, when we pulled off in his BMW 320i. "Couldn't be out front waiting like I asked. A little consideration would be nice once, Bubbles."

I made myself small in the black leather passenger seat and worked hard not to think of how many nights I'd be in this role. Me, the cowed, verbally abused wife. Dan, the hair-tonic-dripping lord and master.

How was it that a man like Stiletto could only view me as strong and beautiful and resourceful, and another man like Dan could only pass me off as weak and dumb and useless?

Certainly it wasn't me. I was the same old Bubbles Yablonsky.

"Now, when we get to the courthouse, don't say nothing to Vern. She's the clerk who owes me big-time, and if it got out she was pushing through the paperwork 'cause I'd greased a few palms to get her low-life, car-thieving boyfriend off the books, it'd be bad for all three of us."

Dan's car phone rang. It was Jane checking up, reporting that Mama and Genevieve had arrived with a white noise machine, a humidifier, two electric blankets, a box of Christmas decorations, three boxes of multi-colored blinking lights and Robert Goulet's complete yuletide collection.

I motioned to speak with her but Dan didn't let me. After he hung up, he explained. "Every minute on a cell phone is my money wasted. That's why I don't trust you with a cell, because you have no sense with electrical things.

"Back to Vern." He gripped the wheel with his black leather gloves. "She talks a lot. Has a big mouth. Don't pay attention, and whatever you do, don't ask any questions. Just smile and nod like a good wifey-to-be." He patted my knee. "Okay?"

"Okay," I said, since it wasn't as though I was dying to have a chat with Vern, anyway.

"That's good. I like it when you agree with me. You should do that more often, okay?"

"Sure." But I lied. I was just tired of saying okay.

The big stone courthouse was almost dark except for a few lights in the basement and the lobby. It brought back memories of last month when I'd interviewed Julia Simon, a homeless woman charged with murder who collapsed and died while I was interviewing her. There was something wrong with me, I decided, that caused strangers to drop dead when I was around.

I plodded after Dan, who confidently informed the security guard on duty that he was there on business related to his legal profession. The security guard clearly knew him and clearly didn't give a shit. He let Dan and me pass through the metal detector, which was turned off.

Vern's office was in the basement. She was waiting for us, bags under her eyes, limp hair framing her face. She looked as tired and worn-out as I felt. And she looked as though she was thinking the same thing about me.

"This should take fifteen minutes," Dan said. "You got your driver's license, Bubbles?"

I reached for my purse. This was it. This was the moment of truth, making it legal. I couldn't help but think back to that day when I came home early from the House of Beauty and found Jane asleep upstairs in her crib and Dan on the couch with the Avon lady. The naked Avon lady. I could still see her black lace bra flung over Jane's high chair.

Never again, I swore. I'd spent the prior three years putting Dan through law school by shampooing at the House of Beauty nights. After he left me, after he said proudly that the Avon lady was the best lay he'd had in months, I never got a penny of alimony from him. Only insufficient child support and a judicial order that he contribute to my continuing education.

Dan had laughed. The judge had cut him a great deal. Bubbles go to school? Not. But I did go to school and kept my job at the House of Beauty and raised Jane. A million credits later, including a thousand failures, and I won a job writing features on strawberry festivals and flatulent greyhounds for the *News-Times*, thanks in part to Mr. Salvo, my Two Guys journalism professor, later to become my own editor.

Things were looking up. Dan had married Wendy and the two of them took wildly expensive vacations and made fun of me. Fine. I was achieving goals I'd never even dared to dream. I investigated and wrote a blockbuster that the *Philadelphia Inquirer* bought. Then I came on as a real reporter for the *News-Times*.

Along the way I met Stiletto, the most cocky, arrogant, talented and gorgeous man ever. Stiletto taught me about taking chances, whether that was hanging off a bridge to get the perfect shot, or going undercover in Amish country to find a runaway bride. He stood behind me when a judge fined me thousands of dollars for not handing over my interview notes.

He made love to me in his big bed with the soft white sheets while rain pattered on the roof and a fire crackled in the fireplace. We were joined by more than physical passion—though we were pretty joined by that, too. We were joined by the sense that we belonged together for a higher purpose yet to come. We were each other's future and, as corny as it might sound, a team.

And then . . . then it all went to hell. My daughter slipped away from me one night into the wrong hands of the wrong man and I was damned lucky to get her back alive.

At a price.

"This price," Dan was saying, as he finished up the

paperwork. "Forty bucks. You're not going to charge me that, Vern."

Forty dollars. It was nothing! The shindig at the union hall on Saturday was setting him back ten thousand times that.

Vern narrowed her eyes. "I should be charging you an extra fifteen to expedite this before your wedding. You don't even have your divorce decree."

Dan fluttered a paper in her face. "Sure, I do. Whaddya call this?"

"Not notarized."

"What does it matter? I'm remarrying my first wife. She's standing next to me."

"Yes, but what about your second?"

"I told you. That was all taken care of in Guam."

"Guam," Vern repeated disdainfully, pressing her own notary stamp onto the paper.

"I'll call my secretary to see if she's still in. Maybe she can dig up an official copy." Dan went out of the glass doors to the darkened linoleum hallway to call his secretary.

Vern eyed him through the glass. "What's a smart girl like you doing remarrying a bum like that?"

"Pardon?" I asked, violating Dan's order to keep my mouth shut.

"I read your stories in the paper. They're good. Lots of detail. You're one of the few reporters who gets it right. You're too sharp to be hooking your star to him."

This was rare, compliments from a bureaucrat. "Thanks. I, uh, admire your clerking."

Vern smiled wryly. "You do know, don't you, that he's been sleeping with that secretary of his for years."

Silence. I twirled my laminated driver's license on the counter. More pain.

"You must have something to offer—that's all I can say. No one does anything for nothing, especially Ritter."

She was right, of course.

Vern lifted the lid of the photocopier and slid our marriage license application underneath. "Take, for example, his second wife. She had the dough, until he ran through that. Then he couldn't ditch her fast enough. Now he's back after you with a vengeance. You've gotta be asking yourself, what does he want so bad that I've got?"

"His daughter."

"And what do you get?"

The light pulsated as it copied our application. "I get to keep her."

"Ahh."

The doors burst open and Dan returned, regarding both of us with suspicion. He wanted me to verify if I'd been gossiping with Vern. So I took out my compact and refreshed my lipstick like a good little wifey.

"Sorry, Vern. Secretary's gone for the night. I'll have to get you the divorce decree tomorrow, if it's come back from Guam."

"You better," Vern said. "Or else the marriage is null and void."

We left and trod joylessly up the marble stairs, past the security guard and out the door. The snowy night air was refreshing. The star of Lehigh was lit up on South Mountain for Christmas and white lights lit up the trees by the courthouse door. It was very romantic.

Well, it would have been if I'd been with any other man besides Dan.

"You weren't gabbing with Vern, were you? Because I told you to keep your mouth shut as far as she was concerned."

"Vern didn't say anything I hadn't heard already," I said, linking my arm in his. "Where to now?"

Dan was startled by my physical contact. "You don't want me to drop you off at your car?"

"We just applied for a marriage license! Isn't that cause for celebration?"

I could tell he was surprised and pleased. "I just didn't think you'd want to go to dinner with me, that's all. You're usually so uptight about that, going out with me."

"I wasn't talking about going out to dinner."

He quit walking. A snowflake landed on his nose. I went on tiptoe and licked it off.

"Bubbles . . . I . . . I . . ." He ran his hand up my arm and touched my face. "I thought . . ."

"We have our marriage license, why wait? Let's get a suite at the Hotel Lehigh and do it up right. Tonight."

A low growl came from his throat. "A suite?"

"I already made a reservation."

He licked his puffy lower lip. "I didn't think you were going to, you know, be that way with me. I thought that wasn't part of the bargain. What's come over you?"

"Call it a sudden wave of lust." And I kissed him to show him I was sincere and also to shut him up.

Phase I of Stiletto's plan was under way.

Chapter Twenty-one

A fifteen-foot Christmas tree trimmed in red velvet bows and gold balls dominated the grand lobby of the venerable Hotel Lehigh. I was in awe gaping at the garland-festooned banisters and the dramatic flower arrangements. It was everything I imagined the Hotel Lehigh would be and then some.

Women in diamond necklaces leaned on the arms of men in formal wear as they strolled across the thick Oriental carpets. A live jazz band played a mellow version of "Winter Wonderland," barely audible over the tinkling glasses and guests laughing in the ballroom upstairs. The air was thick with wafts of smoke, alcohol and perfume. This was what it was like to be an adult. A *real* adult.

"Must be some soiree upstairs," Dan said, a note of disgust in his voice. "Sounds like a bunch of banshees if you ask me."

They weren't a bunch of banshees. They were the men who had been won at last night's bachelor auction and their dates. I saw no reason to tell Dan this, however. It would be hard enough keeping him from spying Stiletto. Dan had a sixth sense about such things.

"You sure you want to do this tonight? Don't want to wait until the honeymoon?"

"I'm sure." I kissed him again and tried my hardest not to retch. "I don't think I could stand the suspense."

He squeezed me around the waist, too hard and too high, copping a feel to check if my breasts were still worth the hundred-sixty-nine-dollar suite plus tax. "Okay. Why not?"

I stood back as he approached the high marble counter, got out his credit card and took care of business. Carefully, I scoped the lobby, the bar to the left, the stairs to the mezzanine and the ballroom upstairs.

And that was when I saw him. Stiletto in a navy jacket, white shirt and classic gray pants. He was leaning on the banister with his hand in one pocket. In his other he held a drink. He lifted it in a salute.

My heart again. It beat hard. I knew then that for as long as I lived, even when Stiletto got into his eighties and was wrinkled and gray, he'd still be able to do that to me. I'd catch sight of him in his wheelchair and go weak.

That is, if I ever saw him after tonight.

"Done and done." Dan dangled the room key. "Now how about some champagne to loosen our rusted bolts?"

"I couldn't have put it more romantically."

He leaned over and whispered in my ear, "Be prepared for a night that will leave you so spent you won't be able to get out of bed in the morning." Then he slapped my ass for punctuation.

I didn't know how much more of this I could stand. I mean, really. Was Jane's mental health and need for family security worth—dare I say it?—sleeping next to her father? What had I gotten myself into?

Dan went over to the bar to order the champagne, being too cheap to go through room service. He turned and winked. I winked back. It was all very smarmy.

The bartender was swamped and had no time for Dan, who might as well have worn a Tightwad Tipper

Club Member pin on his lapel. Dan waved a hundred-dollar bill to get him snapping.

I felt an arm slip around my waist as I was pulled behind the Christmas tree by Stiletto.

"Having fun?" He brushed back my hair as if about to kiss me.

"Never more so."

"It's written all over your face, you saucy wench." He smelled vaguely of scotch. I kind of liked it. "Tell me, how did the Don Juan of Lehigh, PA, manage to seduce you this time?"

"Told me to be prepared for a night that would leave me sore in the morning."

Stiletto winced. "The Ben-Gay approach. Never tried that."

"And I wouldn't start now."

Impatient to get through this unnecessary conversation, he brought me to him, placing his hand firmly behind my head, and kissed me. For one heady moment, the sounds of cocktail chatter, soft jazz and laughter swirled and mixed with the smell of scotch and pine and perfume as Stiletto's soft mouth hardened against mine, our tongues shyly, playfully searching for a deeper intimacy.

Then I remembered and pushed him away. "Are we crazy? What about Dan?"

"Who's Dan?" He was looking down at me with unabashed lust, completely unconcerned what others might think should we be caught making out behind the Christmas tree. This, I decided, was a male trait, the ability to block out the world when consumed by the overpowering primal urge of procreation.

"We need to focus on what we're doing," I said.

"Absolutely," and he bent down for another go.

"Not that," I said, pulling away. "Tess. Debbie Shatsky's murder. The Santa Clauses who are shooting at me."

"They have nothing to do with Debbie Shatsky."

As soon as he said it, I could tell he realized he'd crossed a line.

"How do you know they have nothing to do with Debbie Shatsky?"

He squared his shoulders, the blood returning to his brain at last. "I don't. It's just a hunch I have from, you know, being experienced in the field and all."

"Right." I scrutinized him. Once again I had the feeling Stiletto was much more aware of what was going on than I was. Like *Soviet issue*. What did that mean?

"So," he said, all businesslike, "are you ready to go through with this?"

I glanced over my shoulder. The bartender was handing Dan an ice bucket. "Is she here?"

"Powdering her nose. She's already sucked down three cosmopolitans like they were water."

"Do you think she'll talk?"

"If she doesn't pass out first. Did you get the room?"

"I reserved 236."

"Right next door. I'll try to be quick."

I didn't know about that. When it came to Stiletto in bed, nothing was quick.

"You know what to do," I said.

He tapped his temple. "Got it all in here."

Then Stiletto slid something cool into my hand. It was a key.

"A copy of mine. In case you change your mind about Dan."

Dan was in the middle of the lobby searching for me like a lost little boy. In his arms was the ice bucket, in which a green bottle leaned at an angle. Even from where I was standing, I could make out the label. Korbel. Nine dollars and fifty cents at the state store.

"Don't I wish."

Dan and I stood stiffly side by side in the elevator as a technical rendition of "Silver Bells" played on the speakers. He punched 14, the top floor, and we went up.

I tensed. "Fourteen? But I reserved 236."

Dan winked again. If he kept this up, he was going to

have to see an optometrist. "It's a surprise, baby cakes. I got us the top floor. The penthouse."

No, no, no! We were supposed to be next door to Stiletto. He had given me an adjoining room key.

"You look shocked." The doors flung open. Dan stepped out holding his sweaty ice bucket and turned. "What are you waiting for?"

"Just a bit nervous."

He held the doors open. "A blushing bride. Cute. Okay, let's move it."

This was all wrong, I thought, following him. The plan was that Stiletto and I would be next door so we could reach each other for quick consultations on interviewing Tess. I had a tape recorder and a mike that I was supposed to extend under the door that adjoined our rooms. It was a perfect, no-fail plan.

Except for the Dan part. Though I was pretty confident I could handle him, too. I'd been married to him long enough to know how.

"Here we are!" He stood before a set of double doors. "Want me to lift you over the threshold?"

"Uh, no, thanks."

"Oh, c'mon."

"We have to be married first."

"We're supposed to be married to have sex and that's not stopping us."

Geesh. "All right already." I put down my purse.

Dan squatted and held out his arms like they were forklifts. "On the count of three. One . . . two . . . three."

I jumped in his arms and heard a loud *craaack*. It reminded me of ice breaking on Lake Wallenpaupack in the spring.

"Oh, oh," Dan moaned, unable to move. "What have you done to me?"

I felt a surge of hope. "Are you hurt?"

"Am I hurt? Cripes. I think you broke my back."

"Does that mean you can't carry me over the threshold? Are you, perchance . . . too old?"

Dan's grasp stiffened. "Like hell I'm too old."

He started to straighten, but couldn't and ended up mincing in a half squat, like an arthritic chimpanzee. With every laborious step, he'd let out a grunt and I did nothing to ease his difficulty.

Finally, after several torturous minutes making his way across the vast set of rooms, he dropped me on the majestic king-sized bed with a "There!"

Then he collapsed himself. He lay curled in a fetal position.

I got up. "Maybe I should get some ice."

"There's ice in the bucket." He grimaced. "Come on. Take your clothes off. I didn't go through all that for nothing."

I wagged my finger. "Absolutely not, mister. You could have done some serious damage. This needs to be taken care of fast. You don't want to show up at our wedding like this, do you?"

And before he could argue, I pulled out the chilled bottle of champagne and shoved it up his shirt against his spine. If Dan hadn't been crippled, I think he would have clobbered me.

"Holy Mary, mother of God, what in the tarnation are you doing?"

"Cold. It's good for you. Then hot. Alternate every five minutes. I'll go dig up a hot-water bottle. Don't move a muscle."

"Like I could."

I grabbed the room key out of his clenched fist and ran to the door. In the hallway I took a deep breath and thanked God for finally throwing me a bone. I needed to find Stiletto and fast, before he made a fool of himself with the people in 236.

The elevator took forever. I had to listen to Karen Carpenter—AGAIN!—as we inched floor by floor to the lobby and when I got there found no sign of Stiletto.

Instead, I ran into Wendy.

Chapter Twenty-two

She wore a plunging black dress that was so tight her emaciated body took on the appearance of an exclamation mark.

"Hello, Bubbles. Fancy meeting you here." Next to her was a man I recognized from the Help the Poor Children brochure as a fitness instructor who was building a gym at the Hellertown exit of I-80. He reminded me of a Jack Russell terrier. My guess was that this was the poor schmuck Wendy had won at the auction.

"Was it my imagination," she said, an evil glint to her eyes, "or did I see Dan at the bar a few minutes ago?"

"Yes. Dan was at the bar," I said. "If you'll excuse me, I have to find—"

"And, of course, Steve Stiletto's here. With Tess. His date."

I smiled to the terrier, who looked confused, hungry and slightly rabid.

"He's in the room with her now," she said. "This is when we couples are supposed to be waited on by room service for a private dinner and"—she cozied up to the terrier—"whatever else happens. Steve left with Tess minutes ago. I can just imagine what they're doing now."

"Flipping through the cable channels is what I'm betting."

Wendy let out a high, wispy laugh. "It must be more than a coincidence that you're here and Stiletto, too. Is this a tête-a-tête?"

"Oh, come on, Wendy." I let out a high, wispy laugh myself.

"Because I could have sworn I saw you two behind the Christmas tree. Tess was very upset."

I frantically searched for an excuse to get away from her. Wendy kept in contact with Dan over the most trivial matters—who would get custody of their Japanese sushi bowls, their latte maker, their organic cotton sheets and customized foot warmers. I could not risk her telling Dan during one of these idiotic conversations that I'd been up to no good with Stiletto.

Finally, the terrier said, "I think our chicken Caesar salad's going to get cold if we don't hurry."

"Silly you." She tapped his nose. "Salad going cold. I *love* it!"

They left in the elevator and I snagged a waiter wielding a silver tray. "Could you get a hot-water bottle? My husband's hurt his back."

"Sure." The waiter took out a pen. "What room?"

I hadn't expected that.

"Can't you just give it to me? That's why I came all the way down."

"Sorry, ma'am. Hotel policy. That way we have a record of what room it's going to."

Damn! I told him it was the suite on the fourteenth floor and he would have to open the door because Dan was incapacitated.

"You could have just called down for it." He tucked the pen in his shirt pocket and promised to have someone run one right up.

Which didn't leave me much time. I turned and ran up the stairs to the ballroom. Finding a fire door, I opened to a fire hallway of cement stairs and metal railings, climbing quickly to the second floor. Room 236 was right down the hall.

Putting my ear to the door of room 238, I could make out a woman's flirtatious laughter followed by a man's baritone. Then there was more conversation. I didn't want to interrupt him too soon, before he'd been able to get Tess to spill about Debbie's cruises. Then again, I didn't want Dan to get suspicious.

I waited for a few minutes—during which there were several disturbing moments of silence—until I heard the *bing!* of the elevator. The same waiter I'd accosted in the lobby stepped out. He was carrying a tray and headed my way.

"You again," he said. "Still looking for that water bottle?"

"Actually, just waiting for a friend."

He stopped at Stiletto's door. I thought he might call hotel security, but he didn't. He knocked. I crossed my fingers that Stiletto would open the door and not Tess because if Tess opened the door and saw me lurking in the hallway, I was cooked.

"Room service," the waiter said.

The door flew open and there stood Stiletto. I mimed crafty hand signals for him to talk to me.

The waiter took the tray inside and I caught a glimpse of Tess sitting in a chair, her hair tousled and her dress askew. She was sipping something. Stiletto put his finger to his lips.

When the waiter returned, Stiletto took out a wad of bills and pressed them into his palm. "One other thing," he said, closing the door behind him.

"Yes?" the waiter said, staring in amazement at the amount of money.

"Would you mind entertaining my date for a few minutes? You know, run through the highlights of the dinner you've brought us."

"But it's chicken Caesar salad."

"The wine then. Uncork it. Rave."

"You didn't order wine. The dinner came with water."

Stiletto ended up pushing the kid inside.

"Okay," he said to me, once the door closed. "What's up? You're not in 236."

I did my best to ignore the definite lipstick stain on his collar. "Dan moved us to the penthouse as a surprise."

"Oh, boy, the penthouse. He's really determined to get some action if he's forking over his precious money for a penthouse."

That old sick-in-the-stomach feeling again. "Please. Don't remind me."

"What are you going to do for the rest of your life? Lie back and think of Lehigh?"

"Not tonight at least. Dan threw out his back carrying me over the threshold."

It was all I could do to stop Stiletto from laughing so hard Tess would burst out, demanding to know what the ruckus was about.

"Shut up!" I hissed. "You'll blow everything."

"I could go there," he said, "but I won't. Damn, that's priceless. Where'd you leave the sad sack?"

"On the bed. I shoved a champagne bottle up his back and now I'm going for a hot-water bottle. Cold. Hot. Cold. Hot."

"Jesus. You don't have to torture him."

"Don't I?"

Stiletto shook his head. "Remind me not to get on your bad side. I always knew that underneath that fabulous body and blond hair hid the soul of a suppressed sadist."

"You wish. Listen, what have you found out from Tess?"

Stiletto checked the door. "Here's what she told me. Debbie Shatsky sent Tess a personal invitation a few months ago. It had a Lehigh Steel logo on it. Looked very official. Same Steel letterhead. The works.

"Anyway, the invitation made it sound as if Get Together Now! Travel and Lehigh Steel were jointly holding a one-night affair on a yacht so that loopers could meet Lehigh's most sought-after single women. A space was reserved for Tess, provided she paid a small fee for, quote, 'incidentals.' "

I sniggered. "Guess my invitation must have gotten lost in the mail, say?"

Stiletto missed the joke. "Exactly. Tess said she called Debbie after getting the invite, to check it out, and Debbie alluded to choosing her name from some blue book or society directory and that Tess had been recommended by so and so who knew so and so."

"In other words, she picked Tess's name out of the phonebook."

"Who the hell knows? Anyway, Tess RSVP'd. Two days later, she receives a packet in the mail with a listing of all the loopers who were to be on board. Every one sounded better than the last. Harvard MBA grads, Heisman Trophy winners, you name it. In addition, all the men claimed they were eager to settle down."

"That old line."

"It also included a form Tess had to fill out, including a space for her credit card number and expiration. Allegedly, to hold her reservation on the cruise."

"Credit card fraud. Maybe that's what Debbie's boss was talking about today. Ken—"

There was a commotion on the other side of the door. Tess's voice was raised and the waiter was sounding frantic. I swore I heard him exclaim that the curtains were hand sewn in Delaware.

Stiletto talked faster. "Bottom line is, if Tess's appetite had been whetted after reading the bios on the loopers, any suspicions she had vanished when she saw M and B and A. She stupidly gave Shatsky her credit card number and wasn't billed until two months later. Not by Get Together Now! but by a nonentity called findamannow.com."

"How much?"

"Four hundred bucks."

Holy crapola!

"She should have gone to the attorney general's office. But she was so embarrassed by having findamannow.com on her credit card bill she couldn't. Of course, she really was trying to find a man, so that made it worse." Stiletto shook his head. "I had to pour a fourth cosmo into her to get that out."

This was fascinating, though I suspected Debbie had more on Tess than Tess was willing to tell Stiletto, no matter how many cosmopolitans she had in her.

Stiletto frowned at me. "What? I didn't do good?"

"You did good. Probably too good." I reached up and tried to wipe off the lipstick.

"Oh, that. Well, a man's gotta do what a man's gotta do."

"You and James Bond."

"Hey. It's a public service I provide, sacrificing my body for the pursuit of truth."

"What a noble ethic."

He grinned. "Ethics have nothing to do with it, I'll have you know."

"Yes," I said, "that doesn't come as a surprise."

He put his hand up against the wall and leered down at me. "Any more sacrifices I can perform on behalf of . . . the cause?"

I took a minute to think. "Three things. The most important is that you convince Tess to talk to me on the record."

"Consider it done."

"And if she won't talk to me . . ." I paused. Man, it sucked to say this. "Ask her if she'll talk to Lawless."

"He of the vending machines?"

"Like you said. A woman's gotta do what a woman's gotta do. We also need the names of more women, especially this nurse in Debbie's allergist's office, Zora."

A phone rang inside. We both jumped. It wasn't a cell phone. It was a hotel phone. I tried to think positively. Maybe it was the front desk looking for the waiter.

Stiletto and I stared at each other, breath held.

The door opened and the waiter came out, discreetly closing it behind him. "I'm guessing that of the two of you, you're Bubbles," he said.

"Oh, no."

"That's right. The phone's for you."

"Who is it?" As if I couldn't guess.

"Your husband. He sounds pretty, um, upset. He wants you to come upstairs right now and to stop making out with what he called the Italian gigolo." And then he gave Stiletto the kind of look that for as long as I live will make me laugh so hard, tears will roll down my cheeks.

Dan was standing.

That in itself described how angry, how furious, how ready to rip my head off he was.

He was also beet red and, possibly, foaming at the mouth.

"So you were with him, like Wendy said."

"Wendy couldn't wait to call you, could she?" I walked past him and got my purse. "Stiletto and I weren't making out. We were talking in the hallway. It was hardly a scandal. I see your back is better."

"What were you doing, then?"

"Work. We were talking about work and I can't discuss it with you because you're representing Phil Shatsky on a related matter"—I paused—"unless he fired you already."

"He didn't fire me. That's not the point." He took a step and grabbed the small of his back. "It's a spasm," he hissed. "I've had them before. They're killers."

"Maybe you should go home and take a nice hot bath, pop a couple of Tylenol and call it a night."

Dan regarded me through pain-filled eyes. "I get what this was about now. The sex. The room here. You had no interest in sleeping with me tonight, did you? You just wanted to be under the same roof as Stiletto."

I slapped my hand to my chest in exaggerated indignation. "Why, Dan Ritter, how could you say such a thing to me? You know I find you the sexiest, studliest man on Earth."

He hesitated, debating whether to allow himself to believe I was sincere. Men can be so gullible that way.

"And I knowww you find me the sexiest woman, too. I also know that after we're married you'll be just as loyal as before we got divorced. Oh, that's right. You cheated on me, just like you cheated on Wendy with your secretary."

He winced again, though I couldn't distinguish whether this was because of his back or because of what I said.

"I knew you and Vern were gossiping in the clerk's office." He twisted as if in agony, as if somewhere Wendy had a voodoo doll of Dan and was poking pins in him, which, now that I thought about it, was not such a bad idea. I would have to look into getting one of those dolls for myself.

"Maybe if you hadn't made the poor clerk stay after hours and if you hadn't stiffed her the mere forty bucks, which will undoubtedly have to come out of her wallet, she wouldn't say such nasty things behind your back."

"All right, all right. I get your point. Now come over here and massage my back. Where's that hot-water bottle?" He tottered to bed and fell with a crash, like a giant redwood.

I walked over and stared down at him as he barked orders.

"Don't just stand there. Get the Tylenol. And some ice. I'm going to need round-the-clock care. This is all your fault, Bubbles. If I could sue you, I would. Now go get a doctor!"

"Okay." I bent over and removed Dan's wallet from his suit jacket, pulling out the hundred-dollar bill I'd seen him waving about earlier.

"What are you doing?"

"You want me to get fast service, don't you?"

He grumbled that fast service would be damned nice for a change.

I stuffed the wallet back in his jacket and slid the hundred neatly in my cleavage. Then I kissed my finger, pressed it on Dan's cheek and went to the door.

"Don't take too long!" he hollered after me.

"I won't. I promise."

I exited our presidential suite and hit the elevator button. It arrived creaking and lurching ominously. I went down, passing Stiletto's floor and trying not to be bothered by the idea of him with his lipstick-stained collar in a room with Tess. I hummed "Silver Bells" to keep my mind off their hot and heavy petting. The tune was stuck in my brain from the earlier elevator ride up. It struck me as oddly romantic.

The lobby was a lot less crowded now that the Help the Poor Children couples were all tucked away in their rooms, getting to know one another. I went to the front desk and politely reminded them of the hot-water bottle.

"Yes. I'm sorry," the man in the dark green jacket said. "It should be on its way up. We're somewhat busy tonight because of a special event we're holding."

The Help the Poor Children event, I assumed.

"Is there anything else I can help you with?"

Yes, I told him. I wondered if he could be so nice as to call me a cab.

Had I been wrong to leave Dan? I halfheartedly asked myself as I looked out the window and admired the star of Lehigh on the top of South Mountain, lit up as it only was during the Christmas season. I rolled down the window and let the brisk night breeze fly into my face as we crossed the Hill-to-Hill Bridge.

Someone had put a lone electric candle in one of the mill's dirty windows, and through the grime and soot, it still shone bright, a testament to the spirit of people like us. People who've grown up under the spewing smokestacks, the clouds of orange sulfur and snow of ashes. We still shine through. We cannot be extinguished.

"Is this okay?" the cab driver asked as we pulled up to the *News-Times.*

"This is fine." I handed him the hundred.

He let it lie in his palm. "I don't know if I got change for this. This is a big bill."

"I don't want change. Merry Christmas." And I got out. There is no satisfaction so sweet as spending the money of a person you truly despise.

It was after nine and there was no point in me returning to the newsroom. All I really wanted was to go home, take the phone off the hook (so Dan couldn't call) and indulge in a long, hot shower.

Then I would pad downstairs in my slippers and robe, where Mama would have dinner waiting for me. Sauerbraten, marinated since Saturday, made with gingersnaps, and German spaetzle with green beans. A baked apple and cranberry crisp topped with vanilla ice cream and a handful of chopped walnuts and raisins for desert. Yum.

The Christmas tree would probably be decorated to ridiculous lengths. Those big, multicolored lights, crazy glass balls and all the ugly ornaments Jane and I had made in elementary school, which Mama had saved carefully. Tinsel, of course, and gold garlands. And how could I forget the angel on top.

The house would be perfumed by the cinnamon of the baked apples and the metallic odor of Genevieve's musket grease, since she never went to bed without oiling her musket. I could see the two of them in my living room, finalizing the last-minute details for their senior citizen Christmas pageant and fair while Jane sat at the kitchen table doing her homework.

I had to admit it was nice having those two crazy broads at my house. I couldn't wait to get home.

I crossed Broadhead Avenue, bending my head to a blast of wind coming off South Mountain. The neighborhood was particularly deserted as it usually is on a cold winter night. Even the Tally Ho across the street seemed dark and subdued.

Mine was one of only two cars in the darkened parking area, which wasn't much more than a gravel pit. As soon as I inserted my key into the Camaro, I knew something was off. The car was already unlocked.

I hesitated, debating whether I'd remembered to lock it that morning. Surely I had, especially with all those Santa Clauses shooting at me. Then again, I had been known to space out and just forget. Moreover, I couldn't call the cops. If I called them in a panic the second time on the same day, Mickey Sinkler really would have me committed.

And then I heard it, an awful gurgle coming from within. It was the unmistakable, desperate sound of an animal in the last throes of life. I reacted to it almost instinctively, throwing open the door and peering inside, not stopping to consider the danger of what I was doing.

I should have. For slumped in my passenger seat was a Santa Claus in bad, bad shape. I could barely make out that his head hung in a grossly distorted way and that a whitish foam bubbled on his lips.

It was Ern Bender, and tonight he was no jolly old elf. He was an unconscious one.

Chapter Twenty-three

"**D**ead."

"Shit!" I got up from the wooden table so fast Detective Vava Wilson reached for the gun in her holster. "He was alive when I found him. Barely, but alive. I got him to the hospital as fast as I could."

Senior Lehigh Police detective Jim Burge closed the heavy steel door and said nothing. I didn't like that. Then again, I didn't like being in this green-painted cinder-block room with the one wooden table and the one-way mirror where who knew was watching.

"Died from a combination of rapid kidney failure and a heart attack. Typical result of a methamphetamine overdose." Burge dropped a file folder on the table as if for emphasis. "When you found him, he was breathing rapidly, choking on his saliva, and his temperature was elevated. Those are standard meth-overdose symptoms. That man was an addict. His parole officer predicted this might happen."

"What?"

"That as soon as Bender got out of the pen he'd go back on the smack."

"Smack's heroin," Vava Wilson corrected.

"The twiz, then. Crizzy. Crotch dope. Yammer bammer. Whatever. The point is, Ern was an incurable junkie who couldn't quit his lethal habit."

Couldn't quit? I wondered. *Or was killed?*

Detective Burge didn't care. His only concern—as always—was how his latest case would elevate or diminish his status in the department.

Tonight, Burge was in an undercover uniform of tweed slacks, red suspenders and a white turtleneck sweater. I didn't know what Ginger, his wife, had in mind, letting him walk out the door like that. With his graying hair and middle-aged paunch, he was looking more like Santa Claus than any number of the Santa Clauses who'd been following me lately.

"So you think Ern Bender's death was an accident, too?" I asked.

"Unless he intentionally overdosed himself. The medical examiner hasn't made a final report, but according to a quick inspection of the body, Ern was found with the needle and syringe still in his pocket, half the meth mixture gone."

"I didn't think you shot up meth," I said.

"Snort it, smoke it, swallow it, sprinkle it on your Wheaties." Burge hitched up his pants, a move intended to emphasize his authority over all matters pertaining to crotch dope. "But for the real rush, the so-called flash, what you want to do is shoot it up. That's what hardcore addicts like Ern craved. Idiot ended up killing himself."

I had serious doubts that Ern had killed himself, but I didn't say anything. Already Mickey thought I had gone loco for running around town claiming that a woman with a well-known allergy had been murdered. No point in adding Burge to my list.

The thing was, I was beginning to seriously question if Debbie's death and now Bender's were about illegal drugs. I thought about his meth lab at Save-T Drugs, which burned half the store, destroying the entire pharmaceutical area, including all medications and, according to the article I'd read, all records, too. And now he was dead of methamphetamine after serving time in jail for lacing cherry Cokes.

You'd think that stint behind bars would have been enough to cure him.

"Okay, Bubbles," Vava said in a soft, understanding voice, placing her well-manicured hand on my thigh, "tell Detective Burge what you described to me a few minutes ago, about when Ern Bender called you at the *News-Times*."

I looked up at Burge, who was still standing, thumbs behind each of his red suspenders. I thought about Ginger peeking through the window to catch a glimpse of Phil Shatsky hugging me and then Mickey's warning that Burge considered me a suspect.

"Shouldn't I call my lawyer or something?"

"What for?" Burge exclaimed. "You're not under arrest. Not yet."

Vava gave Burge a look that said *Shut up*.

"You can get a lawyer, Bubbles," she said. "Heck, if I were you, I might. But let me be honest. The only reason we're interviewing you in this room is that we need privacy. And this case has been a bitch."

"That's the truth," Burge added.

"Was Debbie Shatsky's death an accident? Or was Debbie poisoned intentionally? Who knows? And now this. It's enough to drive us all nuts, especially with these wild tips we're getting every five minutes." She smiled. I liked her lip gloss. It was the kind of lip gloss your favorite teacher wore. I bet it was flavored, like with berries. It made you want to trust her.

I leaned back and repeated what I'd just told her, about visiting Ern at the Christmas tree lot, about the tree being shot and how I was saved by an Iraq War vet, then about Ern's phone call that afternoon and his confusing claim that I had found "the star file."

"Found 'the star file,' " Burge said again, finally sitting. "Damn. What does that mean?"

I shrugged. "I have no idea. But he implied that Debbie had the one remaining copy and that whoever killed her had made her a deal to buy it. She'd held out, and within twenty-four hours, she was dead."

"Why didn't you call us with this?" Burge raised one of his unkempt eyebrows.

"I don't know." I looked at a spot in the table where someone had carved FUCK THIS. "To be honest, I kind of wrote Ern off as a whacko. When we met at the Christmas tree lot, he was obviously drinking from a cough-syrup bottle. Do you know how many drunks call the *News-Times*? We should put an alco-sensor on the phone after happy hour."

Burge snorted.

I said to Vava, "What do you mean you've been getting bizarre tips?"

She was about to answer when Burge pursed his lips in disapproval. "In any given day, the department gets tons of unsubstantiated tips," he interjected. "Detective Wilson's new to the position. She hasn't gotten used to that yet."

Next to me, Vava stiffened. She didn't appreciate being disrespected in front of a civilian, especially a civilian who also worked as a reporter and was the mother of her daughter's friend.

"Was it a so-called *wild* tip that led you to conduct a search of Sandy's apartment?" I asked. "Or was it your wife?"

Burge ran his finger across his jaw. "How'd you find out about the search?"

Thereby confirming that it was a tip, I decided. "Sandy was a mess when I stopped by the House of Beauty on my way to work and found her crying in her back office. She said the cops were all over her apartment. Shortly after that, someone shot out her front window. Nearly blew off my head in the process."

Vava took a few notes on her yellow legal pad. "I responded to that call. You weren't there. Why not?"

"I had to get to work eventually. Besides, put that together with the shooting at the Christmas-tree lot and a girl gets a little jumpy. I wasn't too eager to stick around."

"And neither was your friend," Burge said.

I was confused. "What do you mean? She's the one who called 911."

"I know. We have a tape. We saw the window. We searched the salon and found a casing that has been stored as evidence."

"But we didn't find Sandy," Vava said.

Again, an electric sensation prickled my arms and neck. Sandy. When had I last spoken to her? There'd been so much going on, I'd kind of lost track. I remembered trying to call her at home and at work and there being no answer. I'd assumed she wasn't picking up the phone. Shoot.

"Is she okay?" I blurted.

Vava shook her head slightly. "We don't know. Her husband seems to be very concerned. It's after eleven and she still hasn't come home."

"That's three hours after her bedtime!" I said. Now I knew something was really wrong. Sandy was always in bed by seven forty-five—except on clogging nights.

"She's on the lam," Burge said, brusquely. "We have a warrant out for her arrest. That's why she fled."

This piece of news sent me out of my skin. "A warrant for her arrest? Why? Is she a suspect? I thought the department was ruling this an accident." I was on the border of hysteria. First my best friend was missing. Then an arrest warrant was issued for her. This was madness.

"We need to bring her in for questioning," Burge said. "Nothing more. So if you see her, kiddo, don't think of being a Thelma driving Louise down to Mexico. Then she will be criminally charged, definitely."

"If she comes to you, call us," Vava added. "Promise."

"Sure," I said, though I was thinking, *No freaking way.*

Whoever had done this table's graffiti had had the right idea.

FUCK THIS.

It was after midnight when I finally straggled home, noting, almost casually, that Phil Shatsky's house was dark aside from the second-floor bedroom window, where a rather pornographic red light glowed. I studied it dully. I was just too tired to process what that meant.

Mama had left the Christmas tree on, not a wise move considering the hot lights and the brittle needles. I unplugged it, tossed my purse on the couch and went to the sink to wash my hands. The kitchen phone was off the hook, which meant Dan must have called so often that Mama disconnected. He'd be asleep by now, so I hung it back on.

I was in trouble. He would find a way to get me back for ditching him in the Hotel Lehigh. He would get me back big-time.

Tonight, however, Dan was the least of my problems. Sandy had now won the dubious honor of becoming head trouble doll.

I picked at the sauerbraten Mama had left on a foil-covered plate. I realized that Ern Bender had been my only link to the group that wanted the star file. And now he was gone. That left me feeling strangely vulnerable, as if Ern had been a friend, which he hadn't been. In fact, there was good reason to believe he might have been the one shooting at me.

So why didn't I feel relieved?

"Bubbles?" Mama was standing on the stairs in her pink chenille bathrobe. Her hair was in a mass of foam curlers that no human being could sleep on without suffering permanent brain damage. "When did you get home?"

"Only a few minutes ago. Thanks for saving me dinner." I ate some spaetzel.

"Don't eat standing up. It's not healthy."

"What's unhealthy about it?" What was unhealthy were these green beans. Overcooked beyond recognition.

"It messes up your GI track. Trust me. I know." She pulled out a chair from the kitchen table and pushed me down, slapping the plate in front of me. Then she sat at the other end, grabbed a toothpick out of the toothpick holder Genevieve must have brought and said, "What did you do to Dan?"

"I didn't do anything to Dan."

"He's very angry."

"Yes, I know."

Mama pointed to the beans with her toothpick. "Eat your beans. You need something green in you."

"These aren't green. They're"—I scrunched up my nose, trying to think what they were—"tan."

"Eat them, anyway."

I ate one. It tasted like metal from the can.

"He threatened to call off the wedding."

Hallelujah, I thought. *Thanks be to God.*

Mama picked at a molar as I scooped up a baked gingersnap. "You don't seem too upset by that."

"Should I be?"

"He's the father of your daughter who needs to be part of a family. I thought you were doing this for her."

"I was and now I'm thinking that maybe I made a mistake."

Mama pounded the table so hard the sugar bowl rattled. "That is so selfish of you, Bubbles. Dan is a good man. Okay, he's no Stiletto with the tight jeans and the long hair, but he's a decent, hardworking, honest man who wants what's best for his daughter, even if that means remarrying a woman he never loved in the first place."

I put down my fork and pushed aside my plate, trying to reel in my anger. It was time to lay it on the line with my mother. "For your information, the man you think is so honest happens to be blackmailing me into marriage."

Mama didn't even blink. "Is that what Stiletto told you?"

There have been very few moments in my long and often trying relationship with my mother when I could have slapped her. This was one of them.

"No. That is what Dan told me. That if I didn't re-marry him, he would use a report by our family thera-pist, Dr. Lori Caswell, to discredit me."

"Discredit you how?"

This was the hard part. I stared at my hands, which were dry and in desperate need of lotion. Stress. That's what ruins skin. Stress. Sun. Smoking. The three sins of skin care.

"Dr. Caswell has decided because I did not protect Jane, and therefore set her up to be kidnapped while working on a story that was over my head, this made me an unfit mother."

Mama opened her mouth to object, but I went on. "She also said that I've been a poor mother all the way around. I allowed Jane to pierce herself all over the place and date lowlifes like G and drink A-Treat and eat Tastykakes for breakfast. There's also the issue of my pattern of being away from home at night, either when I was taking courses at Two Guys or working for the *News-Times*.

"In short. I am maternal scum. And Dr. Caswell says she is prepared to deliver this report in court if Dan wants full custody of Jane. Which brings me back to why I'm getting married. That's exactly what he'll do, seek full custody if I don't marry him."

For once, Mama was struck dumb. She sat there, fid-dling with the toothpick, saying nothing.

Finally, I had to ask, "What are you thinking?"

"I'm thinking how did my daughter who's so clueless on the outside and so smart on the inside get so clueless on the inside, too."

I was incensed. Where was the sympathy I was look-ing for? The understanding shoulder? The *there, there, pat, pat, you're doing the right thing*?

"Listen, honey," Mama said, "I've worked this farm of life long enough to know a cow patty and that's what Dan's delivering here. Cow patties."

I was shocked. Mama never swears.

"You're a grown woman. I can't tell you how to lead your life. But if I was you, I'd be thinking long and hard how to undercut this slimy, adulterous ex-husband of yours so you can walk away from this wedding with not only your daughter, but also a signed, sworn IOU from Dan that he will pay for her college education, and grad school if she so chooses."

I was impressed. When Mama gets on her muscle, she is unstoppable.

"What happened to Dan the decent, hardworking blabbity-blah?" I said.

"That's when I figured he was going to be my son-in-law again. Now, after hearing this, he is nothing more than a street cleaner to me, a bum on the sidewalk who picks through cans."

I bit a nail, a nasty, nervous habit of mine. "I'm not sure I can risk it. I mean, Dan is part of the court system. He knows the judges, the cops, the clerks, everyone. He pays them off."

"What you should be asking yourself is if you can *risk* going insane living with that leech. And as for the judges and all that, you might also want to ask yourself how many of them would like nothing more than to see Dan Ritter go down in a hellish ball of flames once and for all."

Memo to self: *Never get on Mama's bad side.*

"And as for Stiletto, do you love him?"

I straightened my posture and said in as sincere a tone as I could manage when speaking to a woman in a pink chenille robe and a head full of curlers, "I do."

"Do you think he loves you?"

"Yes." I paused, making sure in my heart if this was true. "I believe he does."

"Then you better tell him right quick. That man's been jerked around more than a kielbasa at a weenie roast."

She was right. Mama was absolutely right. I'd been living in a fog, the way I was dutifully following Dan's lead and submitting myself to his threats. I loved Stiletto. Stiletto loved me. That was simply the way it was.

We would spend our lives together. Yes. I wanted to shout this out loud from the top of my lungs: WE ARE GOING TO SPEND OUR LIVES TOGETHER, STILETTO AND I. MY DREAM WILL COME TRUE!

It was too late to call him with the wonderful news now since it was after midnight. I would tell him first thing tomorrow. I closed my eyes and pictured us under the Hill-to-Hill Bridge in his Jeep, our favorite spot, and how thrilled and happy he would be when I quietly, lovingly declared that I would be his wife as he'd hoped. That I would be honored to wear his ring for eternity.

And then I'd tell Dan to take a hike.

I opened my eyes to find Mama staring at me, a half smile on her face. "Dear child, you got it bad. How in the world did you think you were going to get through that wedding when you were so in love with someone else?"

"I was going to hold the hand of my daughter and focus on the fact that I was marrying Dan for her."

Mama placed her own wrinkled, veined hand over mine and squeezed it to show she loved me, too. "Don't ever forget how special you are, Bubbles. You're more special than you know."

"Only to a mother."

"No!" She regarded me squarely, her jaw set in a firm lock. "Don't ever think that. When I tell you you're special, I'm not just blowing smoke, Bubbles. You're special. You have and will always be my precious baby, my little pretty Lithuanian princess."

My eyes felt hot as tears bubbled to the surface. Little pretty Lithuanian princess. Mama hadn't called me that in years. That was what she used to say when I was a little girl playing dress up in my pink Disney Cinderella gown and plastic tiara. She'd exclaim, "There's my little pretty Lithuanian princess." And then she'd curtsy.

So very long ago.

Caught in a moment of utter nostalgic sappiness, Mama and I quickly brushed off our tears. Mama blew her nose into a paper napkin and I blinked rapidly. We were not the types to let ourselves get mushy. At least not for long.

Mama changed the subject. "By the way, you should know that Ern Bender's mother is holding a shiva or sitting a shiva or whatever it is at our high-rise."

This showed how fast news spread in my mother's circles. Already they knew that Ern Bender was dead and what funeral preparations were under way and who would be bringing the potato salad and pineapple upside-down cake. "What's a shiva?"

"I'm not sure, exactly. I think it's a Jewish wake that starts the day of the burial and lasts seven days and there's no vodka."

No vodka at a wake? In our circles, that was like not having wine at communion or cake at a birthday.

"Anyway, I thought it would be nice for you to stop by tomorrow and pay your respects. Genevieve and I are going at seven, if you want to come with. It's a habit, to go to wakes at seven. We're bringing a kosher honey cake. Bring a geranium. Should be fun!"

Only Mama and Genevieve would find a wake fun.

The phone rang and Mama and I both jumped.

"Holy hell!" Mama exclaimed, checking the time on her watch. "It's so late. I could have sworn I took that sucker off the hook."

I rushed to answer it, fully prepared to tell Dan now that the wedding was over.

"Don't even start, Dan. I've got something to tell you."

There was silence.

"Bubbles?"

It was Sandy.

Chapter Twenty-four

The whine of Jane's blow-dryer woke me from a deep sleep that had not come easily. I spent most of the night drifting off and then twitching awake remembering Sandy's odd phone call, the way she sounded drugged and dazed.

Drugs. They were everywhere in this story. Though, my understanding of methamphetamines was that they jazzed you, not depressed you. And Sandy sounded very depressed. Understandable, when I thought about it.

My bedside clock read seven oh one a.m. It was still dark outside, a cold dark, though not in the Yablonsky house. Right now it was a tropical eighty degrees. This was what happened when you had Mama and Genevieve as housemates. I should have put a lock on the thermostat. Either that or opened a spa.

I leaned over the edge of the bed, found the Lehigh phone book and looked up the number for Martin's bakery. He answered sounding busy, repeating an order for two crullers, one glazed, one cinnamon, and coffee.

My stomach growled. I would have killed for a bedside delivery of a glazed cruller and coffee.

"Yo!" Martin said.

"Hey, Martin, this is Bubbles—"

"Wait a minute, wait a minute. I ain't Martin. Who's this again?"

"Bubbles . . . I—"

"I'm transferring you upstairs. Hold on."

Upstairs was the Sears-encrusted apartment Martin shared with Sandy. He answered on the first ring with a desperate, "Sandy?"

That was more like Martin.

"No, sorry, Bubbles."

"Oh." He was deflated.

"But I did talk to Sandy last night. That's why I'm calling."

All I heard was Martin's heavy breathing.

"Martin?"

"I don't know. I don't know if we should talk on the phone. I think the cops might have the lines tapped."

"You're kidding?" This investigation into Debbie's death was really getting out of control. Okay, so I was partly to blame for screaming bloody murder, but still.

"I don't know what's going on," he said. "I didn't sleep at all last night. I'm so worried."

"Don't worry. Sandy told me she's fine. She said she's in a safe place and she'll come home when she gets her head together."

"Head together. Why does she have to get her head together? Why can't she come home and be with me? Whatever lie she's too embarrassed to admit, I'll understand. We'll work through it."

Little silver bells—different ones from the ones I'd been listening to Bing Crosby croon for weeks now—went off in my head. Talk about your ring-a-ling.

"Martin? What do you mean by, 'Whatever lie she's too embarrassed to admit'?"

"I wish I knew. It was what she said to me in our last conversation. She kept apologizing and saying stuff like she never meant to lie to me, that she just wasn't ready."

"Ready for what?"

"I have no idea. That's what's driving me mad. I can't

even work. I can't take a shower or eat. All I'm doing is sitting by the phone and waiting for her to call or come home."

"What else did she say?"

"Nothing. There was the sound of a police siren in the background at the end of the call, and then she told me she loved me and always would. I didn't even know her window had been shot out. It was only because Detectives Burge and Wilson were here, going through our apartment, that I found out. They heard it on their scanners. You can imagine how disturbed I was after learning about that."

"Yes." I listened to Jane pounding up and down the hall. "Did the police ever say why they were searching your apartment?"

"Supposedly, though I didn't get it. The lawyer I hired—a guy named Jack Doyle of Doyle, Doyle, Doyle and Lefkowitcz—read the warrant. He said they were looking for evidence of certain prescription drugs Sandy had taken."

Drugs. Again with the drugs. "What kind of drugs?"

"I have no idea. I mean, Sandy has to have a blinding migraine before she'll pop an Advil. You know she doesn't drink alcohol. She doesn't do anything."

Except smoke.

"Anyway, they didn't find anything. I know that much. Took me an hour to get the place back in order. I couldn't get over how they trashed our bedroom and living room. I found a scratch on the underside of the coffee table!"

I rolled my eyes. Neat freaks. Incurable.

Martin made me swear I would call him as soon as I heard from Sandy. I promised I would.

Then I got out of bed and hit the shower, choosing a festive red sweater with a plunging neckline and my favorite hip-hugging black pants. I had to look extra nice today, not only because it was a Wednesday and I had to go to work or because I planned on tracking down

Zora, the nurse in Debbie Shatsky's allergist's office, and then heading off to the shiva with a pink geranium.

But also because this was the day I would tell Stiletto I loved him and that, yes, I would be his wife.

Jane sat primly next to me as I drove her to school. I found myself longing for the mornings when she'd be passed out in the passenger seat, one foot up on the dashboard, exhausted from staying up all night parceling out physics problems with her nerdy friends, like Vava's daughter, Dericia.

While waiting for Burge to return with the preliminary reports on Ern's death, Vava had let it slip that Dericia had been accepted early admission to MIT. I gushed I was thrilled for her, and in a way, the good, saintlike part of me was.

But the not-so-saintlike part of me was jealous. Shortly before she'd been kidnapped, Jane had been informed that her chances of winning early admission to Princeton, her dream school, were essentially nil. Sometimes I wondered if that was what sent her into this Barbie-doll oblivion, that the kidnapping had been simply an excuse.

"Cheerleading tryouts for basketball are tonight, so I'll be late coming home."

Yet one more example of Jane's post-kidnapping pathology. Never before would she have tried to join the squad—except by the wrists, with rope. And then Lord knows what she would have done with those girls then. Dunked them in chocolate pudding, probably.

"You don't want to be a cheerleader, do you?" I asked.

"And what's so wrong with cheerleading? It's a very athletic sport these days. It's not like when you were in school and it was just an opportunity for sluts to flash their thighs."

"Now they flash their *toned* thighs."

Jane punched my shoulder. "Hey, Grandma showed

me the wedding dress she found at Loehmann's. It's beautiful! It's everything a wedding dress should be. Aren't you superexcited to wear it?"

This was the hard part about canceling the wedding: telling Jane. And as much as I loathed Dan, I really felt I should talk to him first before announcing to the world that the wedding was off.

"Hmm," I replied neutrally.

"What? You're not excited?"

Fortunately, we'd arrived at the school. "We need to talk. How about over dinner?"

"I have cheerleading practice until late."

"And I have a shiva. Okay. Tonight, then. I have something important to tell you."

She eyed me suspiciously. "It better not be that you're backing out of the wedding because then I really will lose it. I might even run away. Dr. Caswell says I'm very volatile right now. I could do anything!"

I leaned over her and unlocked the door. "And right now what you have to do is go to class."

It was early when I got to the newsroom. Well, early for journalists. Only Veronica and a couple reporters were at their desks and they weren't working any too hard. They were sitting back reading the papers, checking their e-mail, dawdling over coffee. Even the police scanner seemed extraordinarily quiet, delivering a mellow, chatty buzz about broken-down cars and missing dogs.

I slinked past lifestyle and headed for my corner desk. The "lifestyle ladies," as Mr. Salvo called them, were gathered about the food editor's desk taste-testing an almond Christmas ring, the recipe for which would be featured in the Thursday food section. It looked delicious, buttery dough around an oozing almond filling with little green and red cherry pieces to make it Christmassy.

There were lots of "oohs" and "hmms" and "Let me

have a small piece" emanating from their end of the newsroom. I listened a bit closer and found they were also discussing diets, specifically Weight Watchers and how many pounds they'd lost. All while helping themselves to "just one more slice."

This is why women live longer than men—because we truly are the Queens of Denial.

I plunked down my own coffee and newspaper, turned on the special light that was needed because my computer was in such a dark area and booted up. Marty Finkleman, the obit writer, had left his stuff scattered about, faxes from funeral homes, a coffee cup and an empty packet of gum.

Tossing out the coffee cup and the gum wrapper, I held the faxes in my hand, unsure whether it was okay to throw them away, too. It was too much like discarding lives: FRAYN, CARL, 73, of Lehighton, of lung cancer Monday in St. Luke's Hospital. BUDD, FRANCINE, 88, of natural causes in her Freemansburg home. SHATSKY, DEBORAH, 38, of a sudden illness in Lehigh.

I glanced over Debbie's pathetically short obit. Wife of Philip, daughter of Marie and Pervical, both deceased. Graduate of Liberty High School and Shippensburg University, employee of Get Together Now! Travel, member of St. Dominic's Roman Catholic church, the Northampton County Order of the Eastern Star, chapter #23, and the St. Dominic's altar guild. Private funeral only. Donations sent to St. Dominic's.

I found it even more tragic that Debbie's obit was the rubber stamp of a million other Lehigh women. The schools, the churches, the organizations. Nothing out of the ordinary. I dumped it in the trash.

Then I got out the phone book and flipped to PHYSICIANS—ALLERGISTS in the yellow pages. Who'd have thunk there'd be so many? Must have been the damp Lehigh Valley air. All that mold.

I caught a whiff of old-fashioned rose perfume and turned to find Flossie Foreman in a leg cast, spying on me from her cubicle.

I waved and she ducked back. I think she was scared.

Back to the phonebook. I started with the A's because, heck, where else was I going to start? The first office I called was Abramovitz, Abram; I got a receptionist named Marie. No Zora. The next, Arkin, Alan, was closed for the holidays already. Baum, Regina had a receptionist named Antonio, who had never heard of a receptionist named Zora. And so it went until Kuchner, Ralph.

"Excuse, me," I said robotically, having repeated this line ten times already, "but I'm looking for a receptionist named Zora. I wonder—"

"This is Zora," she said perkily.

I sat up. *The* Zora? The could've-murdered-Debbie Zora? But she sounded so . . . young! And so innocent. "Uhm."

"Can I help you?"

I really hadn't been prepared to find her so easily. "My name is Bubbles Yablonsky. I'm a reporter at the *News-Times*."

"Oh, geesh," she said. "The doctor is booked with patients today and—"

"I'm calling about Get Together Now! Travel and Debbie Shatsky's so-called lust boat cruises. I just want to talk to you."

There was a frozen silence.

"How did you find me?"

"Some well-meaning people said you'd had a bad experience." I hesitated. People who've been scammed are reluctant to come forward out of fear that people will mark them as stupid for having been such suckers. I needed to assure Zora that she was not alone.

"There are other women," I said. "Smart, successful, beautiful women who also suffered."

"If I talk to you," she said, "can it be off the record? That's *if* I talk to you. I'm not saying I will."

I hate when people ask this. There's no way to answer them honestly without first knowing what they're prepared to say. "How about we just meet first?" And then I zinged her with my clincher. "You don't know how many lives you could save by coming forward."

A second pause. I heard another phone ring in her office. I envisioned some whiny patient with a sinus infection seeking emergency assistance or a case of Christmas-stress hives.

Then Zora said, "You know the Laundromat on Third? Meet me there at noon. I'm picking up some dry cleaning on my lunch hour." And she disconnected.

Dry cleaning. That was a commitment. If she'd suggested meeting at a restaurant or a park, I'd have doubted her. But with dry cleaning there's a ticket. She'd have to show.

Feeling victorious, I hung up and summoned the confidence to call Stiletto at his home. His housekeeper answered and seemed awfully surprised to hear me.

"Why, Bubbles, how are you? I never thought we'd see you again."

I stifled the impulse to blurt that she'd be seeing a lot of me very, very soon.

"Is Steve there?"

"He's almost out the door. Let me catch him."

I twirled my hair, listening to his footsteps stomping across the hardwood floor, coming to the phone. I was so excited, I didn't know how I was going to get through the hours until I saw him.

"Bubbles?" He said this sounding more confused than overjoyed. "Why are you calling me *here*?"

Here? Was there some reason I couldn't call him at home?

"If you want to discuss last night, there's not much more to tell you. Tess didn't talk about the Debbie Shatsky situation after that. She kind of, um, fell asleep."

"I see." And did that mean he stayed by her side the whole night?

"Listen, I'm sorry to bother you," I said, suddenly feeling very awkward, "but I hoped we could meet this evening."

"Actually, I have a prior—"

"Oh, stupid me." I reflexively slapped my head, even though I was on the phone. "I forgot. I have a shiva to go to at seven. How about before that? Sixish?"

He hesitated. Why was he hesitating?

"You can just tell me now."

"No. I really can't."

"Okay." He sighed. This was a far cry from the flirtatious Stiletto who'd ambushed me behind the Christmas tree and lustfully attacked me in the storage room of the Masonic temple. "I've got some last-minute Christmas shopping to do. Meet me in front of the Moravian Bookstore at five thirty. If I'm late I'll find you."

Gee. Didn't mean to put you out, buddy.

And then he added, "It's probably good for us to get together, now that I think of it. I should clarify a few things before I go."

My throat tightened. "Go?"

"We'll talk about it this afternoon. See you then. I gotta run."

And he was off.

Chapter Twenty-five

I tried not to obsess about Stiletto, but it was hard. He'd sounded so different from last night, changed, somewhat cold. I found myself replaying the evening. Had he been mad that I went back to Dan? Or was it something else? Perhaps he'd fallen in love with the soused Tess. It was all so perplexing that I got absolutely no work done on my Mahoken budget story.

No shock there. Anything or anyone can distract me from a Mahoken budget story. A squirrel eating a nut on the telephone wires outside my window can demand my full attention when the only other option is comparing fiscal-year increases for road maintenance and repair as outlined on a helpful diskette Gloria, the Mahoken clerk, had sent me.

The only positive thing to come out of the Mahoken budget story was the CD Gloria included with the budget proposal and minutes: the five best songs from *Styx Greatest Hits*. Gloria was a big Styx fan, as am I, natch. How could you not be when they were the authors of the incomparable "Show Me the Way."

Back to Stiletto. What was it with this "go" business? He hadn't mentioned going anywhere. On the contrary.

At the Masonic temple he'd explained that he'd come *back* for me. He never said anything about *going*.

On reflex, I reached for the phone and automatically dialed the House of Beauty to run all this by Sandy. Then a recording came on, Martin's voice stating somberly that the House of Beauty would be closed until further notice and would Sandy please call him. He was worried.

That was when I remembered. There were other, more pressing issues than the hidden meaning behind my conversation with Stiletto.

My best friend had disappeared.

I was grateful when noon rolled around so I could get out of the newsroom to meet Zora. How wise of her to pick the lunch hour. That way I didn't have to justify to Mr. Salvo where I was going—nor was I obligated to lie that my travels had nothing to do with the Debbie Shatsky case. All I had to do was sign out with Veronica.

"And you're going where?" she asked, holding a pen over the pink WHILE YOU WERE OUT tablet.

"Um, to get my dry cleaning."

"*You* have dry cleaning?" She emphasized the "you" as if, in living in a moss-lined cave with trolls, I would have no need of well-starched, perfectly pressed formal wear.

"Of course."

"But everything you wear is polyester."

"It's the kind of polyester you have to dry clean." What the heck did I know from dry cleaning and how come Veronica cared, anyway?

"Okay." She made a prudish tick on the pad. "But Mr. Notch is going to be suspicious. If you said you had to go out and get your nails done or your brows waxed or stock up on the Wednesday night Lotto tickets, that he might have bought."

"Yeah, well, it's dry cleaning." I left debating what kind of bleached-blond bimbo Veronica took me for.

It wasn't hard to spot Zora when I arrived at the Tip

Top Laundromat. For one thing she was in a nurse's out-fit and in her hand were a bunch of other plastic-covered nurse's outfits. She must have been picking up cleaning for the whole staff. Either that or she had a very limited view of her wardrobe potential.

Zora was a tiny woman with the unfortunate body of my Eastern European ancestors. Heavy on the bottom, heavy on the top with a smallish waist between. She made the most of the waist by choosing an A-line navy blue peacoat. Still, there was little she could do about that bottom aside from an ass transplant. Suffer through swimsuit season was all. Vow to find a man who was driven wild by the women in Gdansk.

"Zora?"

She smiled, fully expecting a chance run-in with a friend. When she saw it was me, however, her smile turned upside down. "You're the reporter, aren't you?"

"Yes. But I'm very nice. Honest."

My weak attempt to appear harmless didn't sway her. "I've been thinking about why you called and I'm not sure I have anything to say."

"Maybe you don't. All I'm asking for is five minutes of conversation." I reached out and took the dry clean-ing from her hand. It would be hard for her to run away when I had two hundred dollars' worth of uniforms.

She flexed her arm. "Thanks. Those were heavy. I was going to hang them in my car, but I was afraid I'd miss you if I did. You know how it is. You wait for someone and wait for them and then as soon as you leave for just a minute they come and assume you stood them up."

I slapped her shoulder in a friendly way. "That is so true. Come on. I'll carry. You talk."

She shoved her hands in her pockets as we shoul-dered our way down the sidewalk, against the flow of workers on their lunch break. It was a tough crowd. Everyone was laden with red-and-green bags of Christ-mas gifts and no one was full of merry cheer. I swear a kindly old lady tried to trip the Salvation Army Santa

Claus standing by his little pot, ringing his bell. No, really.

This was the last minute "I have to get something for my pickle-puss boss" shopping. This was the kind of shopping that broke your budget. There were no sales, only desperate parents fearful of failing their beloved ones on Christmas morning. Husbands who felt guilty for waiting until the eleventh hour. Wives who felt guilty for running out the credit cards, tired from staying up to all hours wrapping and baking. Even the clerks were snappy as they snatched your cash.

This was the brutal, bitter end, and I was glad to have Zora's story to keep my mind off my own shortcomings in buying everything on my family's Christmas lists. This year I was woefully behind. I was also woefully broke. Coincidence? I think not.

Zora's own woes began last summer when she received a thick invitation from what she had assumed was Lehigh Steel inviting her aboard a "Meet and Greet Cruise" off Atlantic City. The invitation specified that it was a way for the latest batch of "loopers" to become acquainted with Lehigh's most desirable single women.

Okay, Zora might be nice and smart and funny and maybe for all I knew she was a tigress in bed. But she was hardly among Lehigh's most desirable single women.

She read my thoughts. "I know. It struck me as odd, too. So I called Debbie at Get Together Now! Travel. Hers was the only number listed on the invitation."

"And Debbie told you she'd picked your name from a social directory or that you'd been referred by a friend of a friend."

"Right." Zora stopped in her tracks. "How did you know?"

"I've been asking around. Go on."

Like Tess, Zora had been intrigued by the impressive listing of impressive loopers. "I never knew they were of that caliber. All those degrees and income-earning potential, and they were gorgeous, too. To think they were looking for wives. Well, I was so curious, I had to go on that cruise."

I was dying to get my hands on one of those invitations. We could run a photo of it next to the story. Though what was I talking about? Notch would never print a story about Debbie Shatsky suckering single women onto her "lust boat" cruises. I wasn't even supposed to be asking questions. If he found out what I was up to, I'd be spending the afternoon clearing out my desk. Whichever desk that was.

We arrived at Zora's car, a baby blue Saturn parked at the corner of Third and Monocacy. She opened it and I handed her the dry cleaning and she hung it up on the hook by the backseat.

"So I sent in my credit card number to hold my place on the cruise." She slapped her forehead. "Stupid, stupid, stupid me. Then I went to the cruise."

"And?"

"It was a bust. There were like three guys there and I wouldn't let them so much as wash my windshield, much less spend an evening with me." She folded her arms and leaned against the Saturn. "Debbie claimed that most of the loopers couldn't make it because of work obligations and she was really, really sorry. But the men on board were clearly not loopers. I swear one of them was an ex-con, though that didn't stop a few women from trying to hop his bones."

I thought of the call Lawless received from one of his criminal sources. Louie. Lucky Louie. "Probably."

"I told Debbie I wanted my money back and that I was going to call my credit card company and have them stop payment. She warned me not to. She said if I did, my life could get very complicated. That was the word she used: 'complicated.' "

"What was she talking about?"

Zora dragged her foot across a crack in the sidewalk, where a bottle cap was stuck in the dirt.

"If it's confidential, I won't put it in the story," I said, kicking myself as I did so. *Don't offer to take someone off the record, you nincompoop.*

"Promise?"

I begrudgingly promised. It was too late now to back down.

She let out a heavy sigh. "I don't know where Debbie got this information, but she knew something about me, a secret I foolishly assumed only my doctor and I shared."

I swallowed, rapidly running through the possibilities. An illicit affair rife with venereal disease? An abortion? Halitosis? Psoriasis? Incontinence? Irritable bowel syndrome? Restless leg syndrome? Overactive bladder? Poor credit rating?

"You mean medical information, right?"

"Obviously."

"What kind of medical information, exactly?"

She lifted her gaze from the sidewalk. "Lookit, I'm sure you're nice like you claim. You seem very down to earth. But if I was too embarrassed to tell the cops about this, no way am I telling you."

I felt stung. "Okay. I respect that." Though, honestly, how could she lump me in with cops? "What happened then?"

"After I called her bluff and had my credit card company retract the charge, an anonymous call was made to my boss at Central Valley Hospital concerning this medical fact. The next day I was suspended without pay. It was fortunate I wasn't sued. They'd have won."

"What for?"

"Lying on my employment application," she said crisply. "I'd lied because I wanted to keep this particular problem of mine private. But Big Brother is everywhere now, especially in the medical professions, and Debbie could have been his sister. Knows all, sees all. I don't know how she got her juicy tidbit, but it destroyed me."

"Enough to make you want to kill her?"

A December wind kicked up, blowing street grime and trash down Third Street. Zora and I had to close our eyes. When it was safe to open them again, she said, "No. I couldn't kill anyone. I'm a nurse. I'm trained to promote and nurture life, not extinguish it."

That wasn't true for all nurses in the Lehigh Valley. One monster came to mind: a guy who ended up killing patients here and in New Jersey. I shuddered, thinking about him.

Zora reached in her pocket and took out her car keys. "I better go. I've said more than I wanted to."

She was walking around the front of the car when I asked her one last question.

"By any chance, do you fill your prescriptions at Save-T Drugs?"

She inserted the key in her door and paused. "Years ago. Why?"

"Because Debbie was married to a pharmacist there, a guy who later went to jail, Ern Bender."

Zora nodded, as if this thought had already occurred to her. "But all my records there were destroyed in the fire like the rest of my family's. After that, I went to CVS. It's closer to my house and Save-T Drugs was shut down for like two months, anyway."

Right, I thought, watching Zora get into her car and pull away from the curb, *unless those records had been somehow saved—like in the star file.*

Oh my God. The pieces fell together and a picture formed. The star file contained Save-T Drugs prescription records, I thought, turning around and heading up Third to the *News-Times*. That was what Ern meant when he told me he'd been the one with the information and the idea for the scam, but Debbie took over both.

Holy crap. Goose bumps broke out all over my body. Prescriptions revealed so much about a person's most private and personal concerns. Concerns that none of us would want our employers to know, not to mention our neighbors and friends.

I considered all the possibilities that could be damning: drugs to treat depression or alcoholism, drugs to reduce the severity of mental illnesses like schizophrenia and frightening diseases such as cancer and AIDS. There were drugs to treat impotence, embarrassing foot odor, uncontrollable flatulence, kleptomania, rampant swearing, homicidal and suicidal tendencies, menopausal hot flashes and ravenous food cravings.

Pharmacists had so much information at their fingertips. So much power. Too much, if you asked me. Which explained what Ern meant when he said Debbie could turn the town upside down with her scam.

I was willing to bet that if I could find Tess and confront her, she'd admit that the reason *she* never called the attorney general's office wasn't because she'd been so mortified by having findamannow.com on her credit card bill, as she'd explained to Stiletto. She hadn't gone to the authorities because, like Zora, she'd been threatened by Debbie who must have had access to damning medical information on Tess, too.

Information held in the star file.

But why "star"? What did it mean? It was impossible to understand without context.

I was back to where I started. I had bubkes.

"Yablinko!"

Dix Notch's voice rattled me from my deep thoughts. He was right in front of me in his black Brooks Brothers wool coat holding his dry cleaning and staring at me intently. "I saw you interviewing that nurse back there. What were you talking about?"

What was he doing, stalking me, too? "Nothing, Mr. Notch. We're just friends."

He slung the dry cleaning over his shoulder and moved closer. "Really? That didn't seem like a friendly chat. That seemed more like an interview. You were talking about the Shatsky death, weren't you?"

"We were talking about medical privacy."

Notch flinched as if he'd been socked on the jaw.

"What do you mean by medical privacy? Is this for a story?"

I was about to answer with some equally vague mush of lies when I caught sight of a very familiar Mercedes with an all too familiar Santa Claus behind the wheel. He was parked illegally at the corner. He was watching us.

"Mr. Notch," I said calmly, keeping my body still so as not to alert jolly old St. Nick with the .22. "I think what you want to do without looking is to step sideways into the doorway of Tip Top Laundromat right now."

Notch started to turn his evil bald head and I grabbed his face. "I said, don't look."

"What's wrong with you?" Mr. Notch said, appalled. "Are you sick?"

"Just do as I say. Step off or your head's going to get blown off any minute."

"You're psycho—you know that?"

That was when I caught the slightest glimmer of gunmetal gray offset by the red of the Santa suit. The Salvation Army Santa Claus. He had a gun. He was going to shoot us. He was going to shoot Mr. Notch.

I am ashamed to say that it took a precious second or so for me to decide whether that was a bad thing.

I decided it was.

"Nooo!" I bellowed, moving forward like a bull and head butting Mr. Notch so hard in the gut that he teetered backward and fell flat on his ass, his dry cleaning, thankfully, buffering the blow between his cranium and the hard, cold sidewalk.

I fell on top of him, just like the Iraq war vet had fallen on top of me in the Christmas tree lot, thereby possibly saving me from at worst death or, at the very least, a bunch of uncomfortable pine tree splinters.

"What are you doing?" Notch hollered, his face becoming its traditional bright crimson. He squirmed beneath me. "You dingbat. You crazy idiot."

He tried to get up but I pushed him down. This was

not easy. Notch might have been a jerk, but he was in excellent shape.

I covered my head with my arms, waiting for the gunfire. It didn't come. Curious, I opened one eye and found that we were surrounded by multiple pairs of legs.

"Honestly, old man, she's young enough to be your daughter," I heard one man say.

And then a woman in disapproval: "Oversexed. That's what these middle-aged men are. It's all that Viagra. Think they're eighteen again, fornicating on the sidewalk in the cold light of day."

Notch was now beyond crimson. He was fire engine red. Plus, he was still prone and I was straddling him. Thank heavens, I'd decided not to wear a skirt. Being a lady in this business can get you killed.

"Get off me. Get off me right now."

I rolled off and Notch crawled to standing. He batted at his dry cleaning. Little stones were clinging to it. There were scuff marks from the shoes of those who'd been standing near us and someone had spilled coffee on his neatly starched white collars.

"Look at this. Look at this." He spun the shirts around and pointed to dirt on a sleeve. "Twenty-five dollars' worth of cleaning ruined."

But I wasn't looking at his stupid dry cleaning. I was looking past him, past the crowd to the spot where the Mercedes had been parked. It was empty. And all that remained of the Salvation Army Santa Claus was his pot, abandoned even though it was stuffed with dollar bills.

I didn't have one Santa Claus after me, I had two, and with Ern Bender dead, I had no idea who they were.

Or, worse, why they were so very desperate to have me dead.

Chapter Twenty-six

"You're gonna need more corroboration than two unnamed, hard-up broads," Lawless said, reading over my shoulder, sucking on a candy cane. This prompted me to run my hand along the back of my neck to check for candy cane juice. I have a serious phobia about sticky stuff on my neck.

"Do you mind?" I typed the last of what I could remember from my interview with Zora and hit SAVE. The good news about being stuck in a corner by lifestyle was that no one in the newsroom cared what I was doing. As long as I had my Mahoken story ready for tomorrow, I was off everyone's radar.

Alison, on the other hand, was the center of attention. She had more electrical gadgets on her desk than the entire showroom of Circuit City. Tape recorders. Headphones. Cell phones. An iPod. Her personal laptop. And a PDA, whatever that was.

Yet, oddly enough, I had never actually witnessed her leaving the newsroom or my old desk.

I'd thrown caution to the sulfurous wind of the South Side and brought Lawless into my confidence. Maybe that was stupid. I didn't know. I needed another brain besides mine to help me find Sandy and the star file. Okay, I'll admit it. I needed support.

Lawless's reaction was to listen and take a few notes himself. He was working on Louie to go on the record. And he had a few calls into a source in the attorney general's office to find out if any women had filed complaints about Debbie's lust boat cruises.

We were reviewing my notes when Mr. Salvo approached, his yellow legal pad under his arm. Before the five thirty edit meeting, Mr. Salvo dashed around the newsroom asking each reporter what she or he had for the next day's paper. Every night he was in a lather, as if he'd never put out a newspaper before. Usually, I found it quaint.

Today I found it nerve-racking.

"How's that Mahoken budget story going?" he asked.

"Quick," Lawless hissed. "Switch screens like I taught you."

Nervously, I fumbled with the buttons on the keyboard, afraid of deleting what I had already written, not sure what to do. Finally, Lawless leaned over and with one gooey finger pressed something that made it appear as if I'd been diligently working on the end-of-year budget workshop for the upcoming Mahoken fiscal year that began January 1.

Mr. Salvo beamed at us. "Well, that's a refreshing change of pace, I must say, to see you two working together so amiably."

Lawless and I pasted on insipid smiles.

"Just passing on some writing tips, Tony."

I nudged him with my pen. As if!

"That's terrific. No more poking around in that Shatsky homicide, right, Bubbles?"

"So, it's a homicide now, is it?" I said.

"Homicide is merely the Latin term. 'Homo' meaning human. 'Cide' meaning kill. No murder implied," said Mr. Salvo, ever the professor.

"Hot damn," said Lawless. "I could have sworn 'homo' meant something else entirely."

"Alison's doing a bang-up job on that story, I'm proud to report." Mr. Salvo said this with about as much sincerity as a Florida swamp developer. "She's got a lot of talent for such a young woman."

Lawless next to me fumed. "She doesn't know shit and you know it."

"Read tomorrow's page-one story and be the judge."

"What's it about?" I asked innocently, hoping and praying it wasn't about Sandy flying the coop. That could really paint her in the worst light.

"Now don't distract me. I'm not supposed to be talking about this with you. Let's discuss Mahoken."

"Mahoken. That's the magic word," said Lawless. "I'm out of here."

I gave Mr. Salvo a two-sentence description of my budget story: proposed Mahoken budget to increase spending by five percent over last year. Millage could be raised by as much as .02 cents per one hundred dollars of real-estate value.

He was practically salivating. What is it with city editors that the words "millage" and "increased spending" can turn them into drooling idiots? I wanted to explain to him that back when I was a civilian, way before I ever became a reporter, a story like that would have been a reason *not* to buy a paper.

Then again, back then all I read was "Dear Abby" and weddings and, maybe, the personals. Then I skipped straight to the coupons.

Then again, that's all I read now.

"That's definitely a page B1 above the fold, though it could work as a front-page below the fold."

"Oh, joy."

Mr. Salvo took a note on his pad. "You got anything in the hopper we can use while you're on your honeymoon? It's death, this week between Christmas and New Years, you know. There are just so many end-of-year wrap-ups we can do."

The hopper was his word for storage. It was my duty

as a beat reporter to manufacture stories—in my abundant free time—that could be culled at any moment and run on slow news days.

"I'm not going on my honeymoon," I said.

"No?" Mr. Salvo stuck his pen behind his ear. "Going to take it later, are you?"

I observed the two wet spots under his armpits. I was really going to have to buy that man a couple of arm shields. Maybe I could sneak them into his stocking.

"No. I'm not getting married."

His pen dropped.

I leaned over and picked it up.

"Does Stiletto know that?" he asked.

Mr. Salvo and Stiletto were old friends. Their relationship went wayyy back and once nearly got me killed. "I'm telling him in an hour."

He checked his watch. "You better make it fast."

"Why?"

"You don't know?"

"No. Do you?"

Those armpit stains spread some more. "I gotta go. I'm late for the meeting." And he ran away like a little kid running from a bully on the playground.

This was really beginning to annoy me, all the secrecy about what Stiletto was up to. I wished these men would stop being so babyish and come right out and tell me what was going on.

The phone rang. It was Dan. Speaking of babies.

"How the hell are you, toots?" His voice was slightly slurred. He sounded as if he'd had a few. Clearly, the men in my life were collapsing around me.

"Dan? Are you okay?"

"Sure, I'm okay."

"You're not . . . mad?"

"Oh, I'm mad, all right. I'm downright furious." He slurped, as if from a straw.

This was very weird. In fact, now that I thought about it, this whole day was shaping up to be something out of the Twilight Zone. Multiple Santa Clauses stalking me like zombies after human flesh. Lawless helping me. Stiletto's coldness on the phone and then Mr. Salvo's cryptic remarks about Stiletto.

"I've had four Tylenol with codeine and so I one hundred percent forgive you," Dan said. He slurped some more. "They're for my back. The Tylenol."

"I hope you're not drinking alcohol with those meds. That could kill you."

"I'm not drinking alcohol. I'm sucking on a milk shake. It's damn tasty. Strawberry, I think. Or maybe chocolate. I can't tell. Whatever it is, I'm going to drink one every day for the rest of my life. I LOVE these."

"Dan," I said, not even stopping to think about what I was about to say, "I can't marry you."

There. Done.

This was answered with a loud, long slurp. "Whaddya mean, you can't marry you?"

"No. It's *I* who can't marry *you*. I'm sorry. It wouldn't be right. I don't love you. I don't even like you."

Dan burped. "Okay."

"Okay?"

"Sure, whatever."

This was stunning. I couldn't believe my good fortune. "Are you for real?"

"Of course, I'm for real. Hey, what're you doing for Christmas?"

I hadn't thought about it. My entire future had stopped with the prospect of saying, "I do." Everything after that was blank.

"I don't know. The usual." Frankly, I was still trying to absorb his acceptance of my rejection.

"Great. I'll come for Christmas dinner at four. I'll bring my present for Jane and a date, if I can scrounge one up at the last minute."

Were my ears playing tricks? Was this Dan's idea of a joke? It was all too easy. Then again, maybe not. Dan had never professed to love me, either. It could have been that he was just as relieved to be rid of me as I was of him.

"What about the wedding arrangements?" I asked.

"Don't worry. I'll take care of everything. Hey!"

"Yeah?"

"We still have our appointment tomorrow morning with Dr. Caswell, right?"

"Do you want me to pick you up? Can you drive?"

"Don't worry about me, toots. I'll be there with bells on." He yawned loudly. "Man, I'm bushed. See you tomorrow in the a.m." He was actually very pleasant.

"Nighty night," I said.

I looked at the clock on my computer screen. It was almost five thirty. Then I heard a thud followed by a snore. Dan had just passed out with the phone off the hook.

Chapter Twenty-seven

I hadn't felt so light and free in months!

I couldn't stop from grinning in the *News-Times* green tiled women's room as I carefully applied my face, lining my lids with fawn eye shadow, adding a deeper mink in the creases, highlighting under my brows with stardust. Every once in a while I'd stop and smile at myself in the mirror. It was like having the test results come back negative or the final exam being canceled. Breaking up with Dan was better than winning the Lottery. I know—sacrilege.

I hadn't appreciated how tight I'd been lately. Now I could actually sense the knots in my back muscles unraveling. My lungs inhaled and exhaled with new elasticity. I must have been holding my breath ever since I'd accepted Dan's marriage proposal. So that explained why my skin had turned so yucky and pale.

Best of all, this wasn't the best part. The best part was yet to come when I surprised Stiletto with the news that I was once again a free woman.

Wait. I didn't want to imagine how he'd look, how he'd swing me around and wrap me in his arms and kiss me until we fell down, breathless. I erased all images in my mind. I wanted a fresh slate. Tabula rasa, it was called, according to what I could remember from my Lockean Empiricism for Dummies course at Two Guys.

I blew Veronica a kiss and didn't bother to complete her stupid sign-out sheet as I wooshed past her, leaving a trail of Chloe perfume. She was predictably shocked and immediately reached for her WHILE YOU WERE OUT slips to jot down my exact exit time and how I'd completely disobeyed management's orders by flagrantly refusing to punch out.

I was free. I was in love. And I was going to marry Steve Stiletto. Not even Dix Notch could dampen my mood.

Stiletto was not in front of the Moravian Bookshop when I arrived ten minutes late. That was okay, I told myself. He'd warned me that he might be running behind.

A light snow fell on Main Street as shoppers rushed past the eighteenth-century stone buildings, where Advent candles had been placed in the multipaned windows. It was a scene out of Currier & Ives, the Victorian gaslamps, the cobblestone street, the funny, narrow German architecture. The majestic Moravian church that sat above us on a hill at the corner of Church and Main glowing white.

It was the most romantic evening ever to become engaged.

I ducked into the bookstore, thinking maybe Stiletto had started without me. The wooden floors creaked under the weight of so many people buying beeswax candles and Moravian stars, from tiny little paper ones to huge leaded crystal. I searched past the candy counter and the deli, trying not to be persuaded by the fresh, hot cinnamon cookies or the paper-thin sugar wafers.

A recording of the Bach Choir singing "Silent Night" played softly as I searched the bookstore and then the gift room. But my search was fruitless until I went outside and spied Stiletto nicking into Musselman's Jewelers.

The naughty devil.

"Yoo-hoo!" I shouted.

Stiletto turned. He was dressed more formally than usual in a black wool coat like Mr. Notch's. His stubble was gone, and the white silk scarf draped casually across his lapel gave him the appearance of being the multi-millionaire I tended to forget he was.

"Where were you?" he asked when I caught up to him. "I was waiting."

"I looked for you inside the bookstore. I thought maybe that's where you were." I couldn't help smiling. I so wanted to tell him everything right away. "Can we grab a few minutes?"

He checked his watch. "I have to pick up this gift before they close. Come on."

This was not exactly what I had in mind. He took big strides ahead of me as if I didn't exist, though he held open the door like a gentleman. Inside, Musselman's was as hushed as the blue velvet-lined cases displaying diamond tennis bracelets, Rolex watches and the most stunning pair of emerald earrings I'd ever seen.

Sniffing obscene wealth, a salesman rushed to assist. "May I help you, sir?"

I thought Stiletto might laugh at being called sir, but it didn't faze him. Apparently people called him sir quite frequently. "I'm here to pick up a piece of jewelry I ordered."

"Ah, yes. The reset sapphire. Absolutely lovely."

As if just remembering I was by his side, Stiletto shot me a stricken look and pulled the salesman out of my earshot.

Sapphire! How did Stiletto know that sapphires were my favorite precious jewels? It made me blush, his thoughtfulness. A final Christmas present to remember him by. A wedding gift. Oh, if he only knew that he wouldn't be saying goodbye. He'd be saying, "I do!"

I could barely stand the suspense. It was *killing* me.

The salesman slipped off and Stiletto returned.

"Sorry about that," he said gruffly. "Didn't mean for you to hear the gory details."

"That's okay." I was still grinning like an idiot. "Listen, Stiletto, there's so much I have to tell you, so much I have to explain about how I came to accept Dan's proposal in the first place and how I was pressured—"

He placed his finger over my lips. "No, don't, Bubbles. I'm the one who owes you an apology."

"An apology? What for?"

"For making light of your situation. I hadn't stopped to really consider Jane's fragile state of mind and that, of course, you'd put her first. You're her mother and a damned good one at that."

If he only knew what the professionals had to say.

"Stiletto, I don't think you understand."

"I do. It hit home last night at the Hotel Lehigh when you and Dan reserved the penthouse, when he called you and you went as a fiancée should."

"I knew you were mad about that."

"I wasn't mad. Sad, maybe, but not mad. The good news is that I finally realized what kind of obligations you have. I'm an independent guy, but you . . . you have a whole family already, Bubbles."

"Would you like to see it before I gift wrap it, sir?" The salesman was back with incredibly lousy timing.

Stiletto excused himself and the two went off for more consultation. I could make out a small black velvet box and something glittering. In fact, I was being so nosy that I didn't at first notice *her* walking through the front door.

Even though she was encased in a full-length mink, it was hard to miss her toned legs, the slim ankles and the way she carried herself with physical confidence. Every aspect about her was healthy. Her body was healthy. Her superwhite teeth as she smiled were healthy. And there wasn't a split end on her thick, buoyant mane of silky blond hair.

I was a squishy, tawdry, sickly bitch in comparison. My

hair was all of a sudden way too bright. My skin too covered in foundation. My clothes were, well, from the Westgate Outlet. Need I say more?

I was not Sabina Towne, the actress from swanky Allentown. I had not jetted in from California to help organize the Help the Poor Children fund-raiser. I was not dating Stiletto.

She saw me and cocked her head in a questioning way, as if trying to figure out if she should acknowledge my presence. But I wasn't the issue. I wasn't why she was here. She was here for Stiletto and I watched in perverse fascination as she tiptoed behind him and slapped her hands over his eyes.

Playful. I'd heard that some women were. But I'd never actually observed a playful member of my species in action.

Stiletto jumped in flirtatious exaggeration and the salesman, being an expert in the business of expensive love tokens, quickly hid the velvet case, smiling at Stiletto and Sabina as if they were the most adorable couple on the planet.

So the sapphire had not been for me after all. It had been for Sabina.

A rush of nausea came over me. My knees cramped and I reached out to the glass counter to steady myself as my spinning head tried to comprehend exactly what was going on. Whereas I hadn't been able to stop grinning before, now I couldn't stop from feeling as if I was about to throw up.

"Bubbles?" Stiletto's voice came from far away. "What was it you wanted to talk about?"

Sabina was there. "Nice to see you again," she said. "Too bad you didn't win Steve the other night."

I must have looked like the biggest dolt in the universe the way I was gripping the counter and baring my teeth with such insincerity that I could have been an embalmed corpse at Kowalski's Funeral Home. *It's all over,* I kept thinking. *You're too late. You missed your opportunity.*

"It was just to get them bidding," I said as casually as I could. "You know how Stiletto and his ego are, all bummed out if no one bids over four hundred. And, of course, Help the Poor Children is a cause that's near to my heart."

Stiletto made a doubtful face.

"But the bids for Steve were the highest that evening." She leaned against him, comfortable and secure in their physicality.

"Yes, but, for him, not so good. Quite disappointing, when you think about it. A few years back and he would have brought in a thousand at least. I'm afraid the old guy's slipping."

Stiletto narrowed his eyes. "Like hell I'm slipping. I could have easily gone over a thousand if some crazed maniac hadn't thrown herself on the high bidder, thanks to you . . . know . . . who."

"Gotcha," I said, my senses slowly returning.

"Well, I for one am grateful for your support," Sabina said graciously. "I mean, with all that's going on in your life, your daughter, your upcoming wedding, it was so thoughtful of you to think of my charity. It's always a pleasure to meet another person who puts philanthropy first."

"That's Bubbles," Stiletto said, his blue gaze boring into me as intently as ever. "Always philanthropic."

Okay. What the heck did that mean? Would somebody please hand me a copy of the codebook? Mine must have gotten lost in the mail.

"Have you told her?" Sabina asked.

Stiletto cleared his throat. "Sabina has invited me to join her in Greece over the holidays."

"Oh." I couldn't think. All brain activity ceased.

"I have a house there," Sabina prattled. "I did a film a few years back, *Helen of Troy*. Maybe you saw it. I know. There are a million *Helens of Troy*. Anyway, I absolutely fell in love with Greece and the Aegean Sea. It's so blue. Have you ever been there?"

Sabina might as well have been conversing in Martian. I had no idea what she was saying.

"No," I said. "I've never been out of Pennsylvania."

"Really?" She batted her eyes. "Anyway, we're making a sequel, *Helen of Greece,* and start shooting next month with George Clooney. In the meantime, Steve and I will have my little house on Lesbos all to ourselves. Just the two of us."

Did she just say Lesbos?

Stiletto said, "Don't look so shocked, Bubbles. By that time you'll be settling into your new role as Mrs. Dan Ritter. Or will it be Mrs. 'Chip' Ritter?"

I had to pull myself together, here. I couldn't just let this woman walk off with him. I couldn't let her kidnap him to an island of lesbians as if he were cast in some low-budget porn movie.

"I don't know if it's Dan or Chip. I don't care. Listen, Stiletto. . . ."

The salesman returned with the wrapped package that Stiletto clearly was attempting to hide from Sabina, as if she had no idea. As for the salesman, I was going to have to sic Genevieve on him when I was done with this crisis. Either that or give him a speed lesson in tact.

When the two men went off to finish the transaction, Sabina reached out and touched my arm. This was probably some Californian gesture meant to convey a secret. "I know Steve feels so bad about not being here for your wedding. After all, he did come all the way back from England for it."

"He won't be here?" Not that I had invited him. I just didn't know what else to say.

"I'm afraid we're leaving on Friday night. The production company chartered a private plane for me and"—she shrugged—"it's not like you can turn down a private plane. Or, rather, that you'd want to." She giggled again.

I envisioned Stiletto and Sabina sitting on leather couches thirty-eight thousand feet above the ground, sipping champagne and playing footsie on their way to her bleached house on the bleached beach of the turquoise Aegean.

This gave me a splitting headache.

"We better go," Stiletto said, his coat pocket now bulging with Sabina's sapphire.

"Steve's whisking me off to New York to see some show on Broadway. I have no idea what it is. Was he always so full of surprises?"

"Yes," I said, though I hadn't really considered him to be a Broadway musical kind of guy. "And the thing about it is, the surprises never stop."

"Funny," Stiletto said dryly, "I could have said the same about you."

Sabina wrinkled her nose. "I can see now why it didn't work out between you two. People so alike rarely stay together for very long."

Shut up, Sabina, I wanted to say. *Just, please, shut up.*

Chapter Twenty-eight

I could not afford to waste one minute being depressed. I had exactly forty-eight hours to somehow win Stiletto back before he hopped a private jet to Greece with twinkle toes. This got me to thinking bad thoughts, about how desperate times called for desperate Lithuanians.

Yes, I was referring to Genevieve.

No, I scolded myself, remembering poor Flossie in her leg cast. *Never again.*

"What's wrong with you? Why the long face?" Mama said when I showed up at her door to attend the shiva for Ernie Bender.

"She's going to sit shiva! She should be dancing, maybe?" Genevieve barked from the living room, where she was polishing some kind of machete.

I pushed past Mama and plunked my geranium on her tiny kitchen counter. My mother's apartment in the senior citizen high-rise was a miniaturized version of a real house. The stove had only two burners. The refrigerator was half the size of a standard Amana and the counter was about the length of my arm.

Unfortunately, she'd brought along all the furniture from her prior home, giving the place a crowded,

Keebler-elf feel. And it smelled of pot roast simmering in a Crock-Pot. Wherever my mother is, there is pot roast in a Crock-Pot.

"I got problems," I said. "I talked to Dan and Stiletto."

Genevieve lowered her machete. "And?"

"And it was exactly the reverse of what I expected. Dan took the news like a trouper, put up absolutely no fuss when I dropped the bomb that I didn't want to get married."

Mama crossed herself. "The god of Loehmann's has smiled down upon me. I can still return the dress."

"You mean you haven't bought it yet?"

"I told them you were trying it on and hadn't decided. Let's just say I had my doubts." She placed her hand over her heart. "A mother knows, Bubbles. A mother knows."

I gave her a look. The only thing this mother knew was how to pilfer three thousand dollars' worth of toile and satin under her plus-sized muumuu.

"That's not the problem," I continued. "The problem is Stiletto. He's going off to Greece Friday night on a private jet with Sabina, the actress from Allentown. She's taking him to the island of Lesbos."

"My people," Genevieve mused whimsically.

Mama waved both her hands in disgust. "You're through. You blew it, Bubbles. Come on, let's go sit shiva and mourn your lost life. We gotta get to your house and be there when Jane gets back from cheerleading." She grabbed her honey cake.

"Hold on!" I placed my hand on her wrinkled little arm. "Aren't you going to help me?"

"You didn't need my help getting his attention. You didn't need my help getting him into bed. You don't need my help now. At this stage of the game, kiddo, Steve Stiletto, the gigolo, either loves you and is willing to do what it takes to win you or he's a wimp who wants to give up and go to Greece with boop-boop-boopie-do. Hurry up, Genny."

Boop-boop-boopie-do?

Genevieve put down the machete and waddled to the door. "You know I got a standing offer. It may be rusty, but it works."

"Thanks, but no, thanks, Genevieve," I said, closing the door behind us. "I think I'll pass on the home castrator today."

Mrs. Bender lived three floors up in apartment 1705. Miraculously, it too smelled of pot roast.

"Okay, now we'll knock but no one will come to the door," Genevieve said, taking a tissue out of her purse and wiping off her lipstick.

"What are you doing?" I asked in horror.

"Removing my makeup. I forgot to tell you. You shouldn't wear makeup at a shiva."

Mama and Genevieve busily set to rubbing off their rouge and coral lip color. I didn't know what kind of strange ritual this was, but I refused to comply. I do not go out in public without makeup.

As Genevieve patted her cheeks, she went on to explain shiva protocol. "The mirrors will be covered so the mourners don't have to look at themselves in grief. Also, that way people concentrate on what's important, the deceased, not about their appearance."

No mirrors. No makeup. Not concentrating on appearance. This was getting worse and worse.

"And it's best not to talk about anything but the dearly departed. Then only in moderated, respectful terms."

"How do you know so much about sitting shiva?" I asked.

Genevieve counted on her fingers. "My fourth. No, my fifth husband, Abe, was Jewish. We were married only six months before he dropped dead."

"What happened to him?"

"Victim of bad timing. Made the mistake of walking in front of my bullet." She crumpled her tissue. "I buried them all, you know, my husbands."

"I'd keep your trap shut about that. It could be taken the wrong way by the wrong people," Mama said.

Like the police, I thought.

Genevieve knocked. She was right. No one came to the door. We just let ourselves in.

Mrs. Bender's apartment was identical to Mama's, only darker, if that was possible. The curtains were drawn, and as Genevieve had predicted, the mirrors were covered with scarves. Mrs. Bender must have been hard up for furniture because she and two other people were sitting on little, short children's stools.

"Why don't I go down to Mama's apartment and get her kitchen chairs?" I whispered to Genevieve.

"They're supposed to be low to the ground," Genevieve said. "It's symbolic."

Symbolic for what? Bad knees?

Mama stood awkwardly with her honey cake, unsure what to do since Mrs. Bender and her offspring hadn't even so much as looked up to greet us. They were awfully haggard, hunched over in their low chairs. There was a big box of Kleenex on the floor near them and a woman who appeared to be in her early forties kept sniffling.

If Detective Burge could have seen them, maybe he wouldn't have been so cavalier about Ern being a drug addict. People are people, no matter how they live their lives or how they die. Most have someone somewhere who grieves for them when they go. It's easy to forget that when drugs and alcohol and crime are involved.

Mama found a spot for her honey cake on the kitchen table, where other people had brought casseroles and fruit. Then we sat on folding metal chairs. Genevieve's bent slightly, I noticed, when she put her full weight on it.

I crossed my legs, uncertain what to do next. No one was talking. No one was drinking. No one was punching someone out in the parking lot. It was unlike all the Polish/Lithuanian wakes I was used to.

Genevieve broke the ice. "Shoot, Arlene, that was a

bummer of a thing to have happened to Ernie, OD'ing on crystal meth like that."

Mama kicked her.

Arlene dabbed at her eyes. "He was a good son. A good son I had to bury today."

"It would never have happened," the younger woman next to her mumbled, "if he hadn't married that slut."

"She's the one who caused all his trouble," Mrs. Bender added. "She was the one who made up those lies and sent him to jail."

Now we were getting somewhere. That was more like the Polish/Lithuanian wakes I knew. As Grandmother Saladunas used to say, it's not until the accusations are thrown and the fists follow that the healing begins. There was also a line about slugging back shots of vodka, but seeing as this was a nonalcoholic affair, I figured it didn't apply.

There was another knock on the door. I resisted the natural instinct to hop up and get it. A woman opened and entered. She was dressed entirely in black with a sheer black veil.

She was familiar. And not in a good way.

She passed slowly behind me, the edge of her large leather purse brushing my hair as she found a seat next to Mama. Saying nothing, she crossed her hefty ankles, folded her hands in her lap and proceeded to stare straight at me.

It gave me the willies.

"Who's the angel of death?" Genevieve asked out the side of her mouth.

"I have no idea."

"She can't take her eyes off you."

Indeed, the more I shifted in my seat and tried to focus on the covered mirrors, the one candle lit on the table in the center of the room and the bowl of pickled eggs, the more her eyes followed me behind her black veil.

Who was she? Why was she here?

"This is my daughter, Bubbles," blurted Mama, who was incapable of enduring pauses in conversation. "She knew Ernie, too—say, Bubbles?"

Oh, crap. I wished she hadn't brought that up.

Arlene turned to me with a questioning expression. "How?"

"I, um, interviewed him twice and, uh, well, there was that bit in the end when he was found comatose in my car last night."

Arlene burst out in a fresh round of tears.

Thanks, Mom.

Ern's sister said, "I didn't know you were her. Thanks for getting him to the hospital so fast."

There was no way to respond to that. Any half-witted human would have gotten him to the hospital. "No problem," I replied, wincing as I said it.

Arlene kept crying. This was the worst. I had to get out of here. I was breaking out into a full-body sweat. Possibly because the apartment was no cooler than a hot sauna in an Arizona desert in July.

Finally, Mama said, "Does anyone watch *Survivor*? I love that show. Except for the nights when they eat bugs. It's the slugs that make me wanna barf."

That was when I decided I couldn't take another second.

I got up and felt the woman in the veil following me with her eyes. Then there was Arlene acting expectant. I knew I was supposed to say something good about Ern, but all I could think of was to tell Arlene that he made a "terrific Santa Claus."

"What?" she asked in a pained voice.

"Selling Christmas trees," I explained, confused as to why this compliment had prompted Arlene to sob even more. "Dressed up as Santa Claus on the corner of Union. He made a great Santa Claus."

Arlene's daughter smiled wryly. It was the universal signal that perhaps it was best that I leave.

Genevieve rolled her eyes.

"Bye! Thanks for the, um, chair," I said as I almost sprinted to the door, glad to be out of that hot, stuffy living room and in the hot, stuffy hallway of the senior high-rise.

I couldn't imagine being a close relative and having to sit shiva for seven days. Talk about your grief counseling. Geesh. After seven days of shitting shiva, I'd never want to think about the deceased again.

I proceeded down the carpeted hallway to the elevator and punched the DOWN button. I waited, listening to the televisions playing in other apartments, the *bing bing* and muffled applause of game shows and the sound of Arlene's door opening and closing and the woman with the veil exiting quietly into the hallway.

Damn.

I pushed the DOWN button again, as if that would do any good.

She approached me with even, purposeful steps, as if she were familiar with this particular elevator and harbored no concerns it would whisk me away before she could.

I found the illuminated red EXIT sign over a door to a stairway, calculated the possibility of the woman in the veil with the ridiculously high heels keeping up with me and decided to go for it.

Without checking, I quickstepped to the stairs, taking them two at a time. Every once in a while I'd pause and listen. Then I'd keep going. It wasn't until I hopped onto my sixth landing that I realized no one was following me.

"I have got to get a grip," I said out loud to no one. "I am getting paranoid."

It was true. Though, to be honest, I had reason to be paranoid. Even if the Iraq vet who saved me in the Christmas tree lot was right, that his blue spruce had been decapitated by a violent wing of the anti-Christmas lobby, there was still the Santa Claus who shot out Sandy's window. And what about that Santa in the exact same Mercedes staring at me near Tip Top

Laundry? Or, worse, the one posing as a volunteer for the Salvation Army? How creepy was that?

I pushed open the door and buzzed the elevator on the twelfth floor. No way was I running down all those steps if I didn't have to. It came right away. I got in and thought of how I'd reacted in Arlene's hallway, how I now felt extremely foolish. The woman in the veil, whoever she'd been, must have pegged me for crazy, running off like that.

But I wasn't safe. For waiting for me when the elevator doors opened in the lobby was none other than the woman in the black veil. And now I remembered why she looked familiar.

Fiona Swyer. The agent from Get Together Now! Travel, the one who'd tipped me off that Debbie was a common thief.

Chapter Twenty-nine

"**H**i, Fiona," I said, stepping off the elevator. "How did you know Ern?"

Fiona kept her veil down. "You're not supposed to know who I am. And I didn't know Ern except through Debbie. Those two together were bad news."

"So I understand." I pointed to her oversized purse where the corner of a large orange envelope was sticking out. "Is that for me?"

"Maybe. It depends." She nodded for us to move aside to a corner under a bulletin board about EXCITING HAPPENINGS AT LEHIGH'S SENIOR CENTER: LET'S GET MOVING! There were pictures of seniors exercising, touching their toes and walking in their sweats. Underneath were names and cute, inspirational quips: THERE GOES CHARLIE! LOOK OUT NEW YORK MARATHON! IS THAT ISABEL? HURRY UP, BOYS. SHE'S A FAST ONE.

"What's happening with the story? I heard you got in touch with Zora."

"Yup." I was really curious about that envelope. "That wouldn't happen to be the star file, would it?"

"I don't know what it is." She fingered the envelope. "None of this will get back to me, right?"

"I don't even know who you are or that you called me at the House of Beauty."

"Shit. Haven't you heard about Deep Throat?"

"This is a senior center, not a parking garage, and no matter how heinous Debbie's murder, it doesn't compare to bringing down the White House."

"That's true." She fingered it again. "Inside this envelope is a CD. I found it stuck to the under side of Debbie's drawer when I was cleaning out her desk at work."

"Just happened to be cleaning it out, eh?"

"I was a friend. It's what friends do."

"I'll buy that."

"Anyway, I tried to open it on my computer and couldn't. I needed Excel. Do you have Excel?"

"I like to think I excel, but, no, I have no idea what Excel is."

She handed me the envelope. "Get Excel. This might help your story. I don't know. It seemed meaningful, that Debbie went to such lengths to hide it."

I slipped the envelope into my own purse. "Thanks."

Fiona said, "You might think I'm a crummy friend for ratting on Debbie like this, especially since she's dead and all. I just want you to know that Debbie was more than a coworker. She was a *sister*. Do you understand? A *sister*."

I suspected there was some hidden meaning in how she was stressing the word "sister." Was that code? "I'm not sure I do."

Then she did the weirdest thing. She stuck out her hand as if to shake. Reluctantly, I shook it. She shook back in an odd way, kind of pinching the flesh between my thumb and forefinger.

"Understand now?"

"I . . . I don't know."

"You will." She dropped my hand.

There was a loud *beep* behind me and the elevator doors flew open. Mama and Genevieve tumbled out in midargument. Genevieve was holding the Crock-Pot of pot roast. Mama had a brown paper grocery bag.

"I told you and told you not to bring up nothing but Ernie," Genevieve was saying. "And there you were flapping your gums, going on and on about your toe fungus."

Mama bent down and scratched her foot, nearly emptying the contents of her bag onto the lobby floor in the process. "Well, excuse me, Miss Manners. I couldn't help it that the fungus was on my mind. My toes were itching something awful."

"Class," I said. "That's what you two are, class."

Genevieve thrust the warm Crock-Pot into my arms. "Don't talk to me about class, Sally. I wasn't the one who told a grieving Jewish mother that her son made an excellent Santa Claus."

I turned to introduce them to Fiona, but Fiona was gone. I had the feeling I'd never see her again.

Maybe it was the shiva or perhaps it was my epiphany that while Mama, Genevieve, Jane and I sat around my tiny wooden table in my cramped kitchen eating pot roast and noodles at "the ungodly late hour of eight p.m.," as Mama declared, somewhere in the magical metropolis of New York, Stiletto was wining and dining Sabina over white linen table cloths and crystal, the sapphire burning a hole in his pocket.

I had little appetite for the dinner I loved more than any other. My mother's pot roast. There was no meal more warming on a cold winter's night like tonight, which happened to be the longest night of the year, than this slightly spicy, hearty dish. Her secret ingredients were cloves, ginger snaps and sour cream whipped into the gravy. Served over broad Pennsylvania Dutch egg noodles and a side dish of peas and I was in heaven. Yum, yum.

And yet I couldn't eat a bite. Nor could I get my mind off the image of Stiletto impulsively grabbing Sabina and kissing her at the fountain in Rockefeller Center, like they were always doing in the movies. Actually, I wasn't sure if it was Rockefeller Center, only that during Christmas there was a big tree and ice skaters.

Oh, God. Maybe he took her ice skating and *then* kissed her. *Really?* I asked myself. Was Stiletto the ice skating type?

"What's the matter with you now?" Mama asked.

I looked up from my plate. All eyes were on me, including Jane's young, honest ones. "Nothing," I said.

"She's lovesick—that's her problem," Genevieve said.

Jane quickly said, "With Dad, right?"

I kicked Genevieve under the table to tell her *Good going.* All of us had black-and-blue shins from the frequent, surreptitious kicking we did in this family.

"Of course with Dad," I lied.

The thing is, I wasn't ready to break the news to Jane. Not yet. Not here. Maybe during our counseling session with Dr. Caswell tomorrow morning. Yes, that would be the perfect opportunity, with Dr. Caswell right on hand to offer professional support.

"By the way," I said, changing the subject, "do you know how to run Excel, Jane?"

"Uh-huh. We use it in school. Though I don't have it on my computer. I know a couple of kids who do, though."

"Do you think you could get that program tomorrow? I was handed a really important file today and I'd love to see what's in it."

"How do you know it's important if you don't know what's in it?" Jane asked, biting into a raw carrot. I wondered where it had come from since Mama was a firm disbeliever in raw vegetables. She didn't trust them. She didn't trust anything that produced gas or vitamins.

Then I noticed Jane hadn't touched her pot roast, either. Could it be that she was returning to her vegetarian diet?

"Why aren't you eating your pot roast?"

Jane glanced over my shoulder and said, "Forget

that. How come Santa Claus is back to peeking in our window?"

I spun around fast enough to catch a flash of red. I was now primed to feel terror at the mere hint that Santa Claus was near.

"He ducked down," Jane said, getting up slowly, her fingers gripping the table edge in alarm. "I saw him. He was spying on us."

I fought back a surge of panic and fear for my daughter's mental stability. Jane mustn't be distressed. However, I also needed to make my family safe. "Don't worry," I cooed, repeating the calming words Dr. Caswell had taught me. "You are in a safe and secure home environment—"

"Would you cut that out, Mom? I am soooo sick of Caswell's crap. I'm not a nutcase."

"You're not?" I said, before I caught myself.

Jane gave me a dismissive look. "Hey, Genevieve. You bring that musket?"

Genevieve patted her side. "Got Brown Bess tamped and ready."

Jane said, "You go around the back. Grandma, grab the baseball bat and go out the kitchen door with me. Mom . . . I don't know. Sit there and look stupid."

"You mean, I'm the decoy?"

"Something like that," she said.

I watched her and Mama tiptoeing out the kitchen door while Genevieve galumphed out the back. I sat playing with the food on my plate, waiting to be shot at or ambushed by Santa and being deliriously happy for the first time in weeks.

The old Jane was coming back. My maternal instincts sensed it.

That was when I heard the *squeak* upstairs. I knew that squeak. It had awakened me once before when Brouse had tried to strangle me in my sleep. It was the sound of someone breaking into my bedroom from the fire escape.

And me here without my musket or a three-hundred-pound, gun-happy Lithuanian to fire it.

I glanced around the kitchen searching for some sort of weapon that couldn't be yanked out of my hand and used on me with lethal force. Any of my knives might do. They were all as dull as overprocessed hair. I needed to buy a sharpener or something. I couldn't cut so much as a tomato with what I had on hand.

Grabbing the dullest I could find, I climbed the stairs, my heart pounding so loudly in my chest, the burglar probably heard it, too. To steady myself, I thought about how good it would be to finally get this sucker behind bars so I could go out and about, Christmas shopping, for example, without having to worry about Santa taking a potshot at the bread maker I planned on buying for Mama from Hess's.

Because, let's face it, you really can't return a bullet-ridden bread maker. At least, not at Hess's. Even with a gift receipt. Believe me, I've tried.

The door to my bedroom was closed. I could hear him inside. He was opening my drawers, rifling through them. Maybe he was looking for the orange envelope Fiona Swyer had given to me this evening. Maybe he was here for the star file.

Carefully, I pushed the door open ever so slightly. Santa was in my closet, flipping through my clothes. Okay, this was it. Now or never. Either I ambushed him first, relying on the element of surprise as my ally, or he made toast out of me later.

"Hold it!" I yelled. "Stop what you're doing."

I had expected him to spin around and fire, so I flattened myself against the wall. Instead, Santa threw up his hands.

"Don't shoot," she said.

She? Wait a minute. I knew that voice. And those curls, too.

I lowered the knife. "Sandy?"

Slowly she turned. Her face was a mess, dirty and tear

streaked, and so was her Santa outfit. She also smelled kind of, well, rank. Like she'd been swimming in a sewer.

That was so not Sandy.

"What are you doing dressed as Santa Claus?"

"I bought it off a homeless guy. I think it has fleas." She scratched her chest. "I needed to borrow some fresh clothes and couldn't come up with any other place to go. Please don't yell at me."

"I wouldn't yell at you. I'm glad you came to me." Though, personally, I was thinking it might have been better if she'd stayed on the fire escape and hollered for help. Fleas were darn hard to get rid of.

I said, "Let's get you into the shower for a deep scrub. There's pot roast and I'll make coffee. Then we can talk."

She shook her head. "I can't talk. I'll never be able to talk. This is a secret I'll have to keep for the rest of my life. I'll just have to live on the run, is all."

I discreetly brought my hand to my nose, to cut the stench. "It's a secret that has to do with a prescription you had at Save-T Drugs, right?"

Sandy widened her bleary red eyes. "How did you know? Did the police tell you that?"

"No," I said. "But it's only a matter of time before they find out." And then I quickly unbuttoned her Santa outfit before I had an even bigger problem than a woman wanted by the law stinking up my bedroom.

Genevieve gladly took Sandy's flea-ridden Santa outfit outside, doused it with gasoline, dumped it in an old oil bin that had been rolling around the back of her Rambler and set it on fire in the garden. Aside from killing husbands and firing off rounds, Genevieve is never more content than when she's given an opportunity to burn trash.

Meanwhile, Mama, Jane and I pulled down all the shades while Sandy steamed up my bathroom, scrubbing off the dirt and garbage she'd picked up from sleeping on the couches in the Trailway's bus station.

An hour later, donned in my white terry cloth robe, having been sated with pot roast, warmed noodles, peas and a leftover cinnamon-walnut apple crisp with raisins and vanilla ice cream, she sat on the corner of my couch cupping a mug of decaf coffee and confessed her sins between yawns.

"It started a few years ago, when Martin and I decided to have a baby. He was all gung-ho and I, you know, wasn't."

I'd always suspected this, but hadn't said as much. It was the neat freak in her. Anyone who had a nervous breakdown over the unavoidable dust bunny wasn't ready to procreate.

"Women are miserable when they're pregnant, and unhappy when they're not," Mama said from the sewing machine, where she was adding the final trim on a shepherd's outfit for her senior citizen Christmas pageant Friday.

"I thought you wanted to get pregnant," Jane said. She was supposed to be studying calculus, but I noticed she kept putting down her pencil and listening. I considered this another sign of recovery, the fact that she was back to hanging out with us and being part of the family, so I didn't nudge her to get back to work. Jason had called twice and she'd made a lame excuse each time to call him back.

"Don't get me wrong. I'm dying to be a mother now." Sandy's eyes welled up. "And I'd probably be one, too, if I hadn't put it off so long."

I handed her a tissue and she blew her nose loudly. "You're not that old, Sandy. You'll get pregnant. Look at Mama. She was something like fifty when she had me."

Mama tossed a pin cushion at my head.

Sandy wiped her eyes. "No, I won't become pregnant because Martin will never sleep with me again."

Mama leaned over and slapped her hands over Jane's ears. Jane batted her off.

"Yes, he will. He'll understand," I said.

"But I took birth control pills secretly for years. For *years*, Bubbles."

"So what? It's your body, isn't it? If you weren't ready to have children, that was that. Okay, so maybe you should have discussed it with him first, but for some reason you didn't. Martin will deal."

"I sprinkled arsenic in my second husband's morning coffee for three years and he never blamed me," Genevieve said.

Mama finished off a hem. "He didn't have a chance since it killed him."

"I was trying to build up his immunity for when the commies came and poisoned us all, thank you very much." Genevieve huffed and went back to sticking price tags on the commemorative snow globes featuring miniature senior citizens dressed as Mary and Joseph.

"What I don't get," Jane said, "is why you had to run away. Why do the police even care that you took birth control pills? It's not like it's any of their business."

Sandy and I regarded each other. Well, this was the moment of truth, wasn't it? Did Debbie know that Sandy had been taking birth control pills? Had she threatened to blackmail Sandy by threatening to tell Martin?

"Actually, Jane, it is the police's business." Sandy put down her coffee and sighed. "Someone had called in a tip to the police—likely the same SOB who tipped them off that Debbie had been poisoned—and told them that I had murdered Debbie because she'd threatened to tell my husband that I was taking birth control."

"Murdered over birth control pills?" Jane tossed her pencil into the air. "That is so bogus."

I held my breath, dying to know what Sandy thought of *that*.

Unfortunately, the phone rang, right when we were getting to the good part.

"I'll get it," Jane announced, hopping up from the kitchen table. "Probably Jason again. Oh, I have really got to break up with him. He is such a pest."

I crossed my fingers.

"I didn't kill her," Sandy whispered to me, when Jane got on the phone. "I would never have killed Debbie, even if she had been blackmailing me, which she hadn't been."

"I know *that*," I whispered back. "The question is, who did? And who is calling in these bogus tips?"

"Mom, it's for you." Jane covered the receiver and mouthed, *It's the cops!*

Sandy went rigid. "Don't tell them I'm here. Please. I want to go to your bachelorette party tomorrow. I don't want to spend the night in jail."

Bachelorette party. The farthest thing from my mind. I took a minute to compose myself and then got on. "Hello?"

"Seems like you're having quite a shindig over there." It was Mickey Sinkler, a poor excuse for a cop if there ever was one.

"What makes you say that?"

"Lots of commotion in the background."

I motioned for Mama to step on the pedal of her sewing machine. "Getting ready for the big senior citizen Christmas pageant."

"Right. I forgot about that."

Excellent defense, I thought. *Man, you're good, Bubbles.* "You calling for a particular reason?"

"Yeah. Wanted to know if you'd had a surprise visit lately from anyone we know?"

I glanced over at Sandy, who was scraping the last bit of ice cream off her plate. "If you're talking about that one-hundred-dollar Waterford goblet on my wedding registry you're supposed to be sending me, no. It hasn't arrived."

"That's because my money's on you bailing out of your upcoming nuptials. There's a pool going on down at the station. The odds happen to be in my favor."

"I'll tell Dan." I paused. "Anything else?"

"You remember that license plate you wanted me to

trace on the Lincoln, the one belonging to an alleged Marguerite who allegedly was after Debbie Shatsky's husband?"

Finally, I get a break. "And?"

"Nothing. The license is held by a Mark Knoffler. And because I am a detective with a well-honed budinsky streak in me, I checked him out thoroughly. He's unmarried, and as far as I can tell, there is no Marguerite at that address. He's thirty-two and an architect, which might explain why his license plate spells out brick house."

I weighed my options. "I'll be needing the address anyway."

"What for?"

"Let's pretend there was a for-sale sign on his car. Let's pretend I'm interested."

Mickey grumbled. "Goddamn it, Bubbles. You are such a pain. Okay, I'll give it to you against my better judgment and only because you'll spare me no relief if I don't. Though I'll tell you this much. You're wasting your time. Plus, you might piss this guy off."

"Yeah," I said, "but it's a really nice car. And you know me, Mickey. I'm always looking to upgrade."

Chapter Thirty

I arrived at Dr. Caswell's office the next morning tired and slightly put out. Jane and I had had a fight. A huge fight over whether she should keep her standing Thursday-morning appointment. She didn't want to. I wanted her to. She refused to see it my way. These were the joys of raising a teenager.

"This is not optional," I told her as she massaged blue gel into her hair. "Dr. Caswell insists that missing even one session could set you back."

"Dr. Caswell is a moneygrubbing fraud who is stoking my fears instead of encouraging me to find my inner courage."

"Who told you that?"

"I figured it out for myself."

"How?"

"Because, despite the low opinion with which you and Dad regard me these days, I do happen to have a brain, you know. A pretty good brain. And when an absolute moron like Dr. Caswell says to me in a baby voice that I should try out for cheerleading because it's quote unquote wholesome and it will build my confidence, I'm smart enough to know it's time to blow."

So that was what had happened. The cheerleading. "Guess tryouts didn't go so hot, say?"

She slammed the brush down and stared at herself in the mirror. "They sucked. Lissy Clarke and her ilk are nasty, stupid sluts and I can't believe I let myself humiliate myself in front of them. Cheerleading is pure bullshit."

"I'm sorry." I tried to be sincere, but it was hard subduing my absolute delight.

"And that athletic argument is a crock, too. You're in a short skirt. You're upside down. You do the math. Sure, right, it's a sport. A sport for pervs who get off seeing teenage girls flash their butts."

I said nothing. Better to let her rant.

Her cell phone blared "Girls Just Want to Have Fun." Jane snatched it up and read the number. "Ugh, Jason. We are sooo over. I wish he'd stop calling and give me my space!"

Yes, I decided, there would be no need for further sessions with Dr. Caswell.

As for being tired, that was purely Sandy's fault. You really don't know someone, even a best friend, until you lie awake at night listening to them grind their teeth, snore, flail as if they're on fire and moan about inventory.

"More blue rinse. More bleach. Is the shampoo low?" The words replayed in my brain like a bad Billy Joel song.

Of course, it didn't help that I had my own love inventory—or lack thereof—to toss and turn over. Whenever I closed my eyes, I saw Sabina tiptoeing behind Stiletto and him spinning her around and kissing her. I saw them together in his bed, warm and breathless from passionate lovemaking. I saw Stiletto presenting her with the sapphire ring on a brilliant white Grecian beach.

My life. I really needed to take out a low-interest loan and buy a new one.

To top it off, there was my bachelorette party tonight.

As Sandy rightly observed, Lorena had gone to a lot of trouble making the arrangements, and backing out now would have been just plain rude.

This might explain why I'd chosen to wear all black today: a black wool dress with a gold belt. Black knee-high leather boots and onyxish earrings. I was in a funereal mood.

Dr. Caswell's door was open when I arrived. There was no sign of Dan in the waiting room, and for a minute there, I was hopeful his bad back had kept him in bed.

But I was wrong. As is my fate, I am wrong about a lot.

They were waiting for me, Dr. Caswell and Dan. Caswell looked exceptionally prudish, even for her, in a high-necked military green sweater and similarly colored corduroy slacks. She had on her dark, mean glasses and her hair was in a sloppy bun.

Dan was in his standard business suit. He was holding a set of white papers. Unfortunately, it appeared that the Tylenol with codeine had worn off. He was slightly bent and scowling. Man, I missed that Tylenol with codeine.

"Where's Jane?" he asked.

"And good morning to you, too," I said. "Hello, Dr. Caswell."

Dr. Caswell didn't say hello.

Okay, there were plenty of reasons for Dan to be upset with me. But what had I done to Dr. Caswell, aside from acquiesce to her every admonition and agree with her every instruction?

I told them that Jane could not make it and that, for the record, she wouldn't be attending any further sessions.

Dan flashed Dr. Caswell an unveiled I-told-you-so look.

"Jane can't be done with me," Caswell said sharply. "I'm not through with her."

I shrugged. "Too bad. She's through with you."

Dan launched the accusations. "How long did it take you and your whacky mother to work on her? What did you threaten her with? No food? No TV? No phone?"

I pressed my lips together. Clearly, I'd walked into some sort of trap. "I don't have to put up with this. Jane is doing just fine. So you know what? I guess I'm done with Dr. Caswell, too."

"Show her," Dr. Caswell hissed.

Dan thrust out the papers he'd been clutching in his fat, sweaty hands. "You're not done. This is only the beginning. Consider yourself served."

The papers had been typed and prepared impeccably by Dan's secretary, the bimbo he was sleeping with. It made me curious. I wondered if she'd bothered to ask herself why she was sleeping with a man who was demanding TEMPORARY AND EMERGENCY CUSTODY OF A MINOR CHILD from his ex-wife, the same woman he was supposed to remarry in two days.

"Give it up, Dan," I said, handing the papers back to him.

He backed away. "Those aren't mine. Those are yours. And there's another set I'm filing when the court opens in an hour."

"You're not serious."

"The hell I'm not. You have proven repeatedly to be a neglectful mother, Bubbles, and this latest development of Jane dropping out of counseling is just further evidence."

"You didn't even bother to read my affidavit," Dr. Caswell said, "did you?" She snorted in disgust.

Okay, maybe *that* was a rhetorical question. Still working on that.

"When the judge reads Lori's affidavit and your track record, let me assure you, my dear ex-wife, that Jane will not be spending Christmas in the Yablonsky household. By the way, the only judge on the bench in family court this week is Judge Roy Hopkinton. Everyone else is already on Christmas vacation."

Hopkinton. No way! Hopkinton was as corrupt as they came. Plus, he was Dan's best friend, a regular golf partner and investor in some shady real-estate dealings.

"Don't forget," Dan added, "that Roy is a silent partner in that Pocono resort I bought last year. The last thing he wants is a coinvestor who's so distraught over his daughter's mental health that he pulls out all his equity. Especially a coinvestor who contributed thousands of dollars under the table to his reelection campaign."

I gave the papers another look. I was screwed and my fresh understanding of this was clear to Dan. I could sense him gloating, smirking. I wanted to cry, but that would only have added to his pleasure.

"Is this all because I canceled the wedding?"

"Put it this way. Had you not called me at home yesterday and taken advantage of the fact that I was loopy on pain medication, we'd be having a nice chat about wrapping up these counseling sessions."

I looked at Dr. Caswell, who quickly checked her desk as if she just realized that perhaps she'd gone too far. Maybe it was what Dan had said about Hopkinton. Judges and lawyers investing in real estate together can add up to some hefty jail time. Throw in a psychologist who testifies often on behalf of said lawyer and you've got yourself a tidy federal investigation.

Too bad Dan was the father of my child. I'd have loved nothing more than to spit and roast him on page one.

"And if I say I'll marry you now?"

Dan clasped his hands behind his back and rocked on his heels. "Then there will be no need to remove Jane from your household because it will be *our* household."

My hands were shaking. I couldn't stop them. *It's only for a few months, less than a year. Then Jane will be eighteen and can choose for herself. Say no!*

But it was such an important year. It was the year she would graduate from high school, pick a college. I couldn't miss that. Not after all we'd worked so hard to achieve. We were a pair, Jane and I. She was my family and I, hers.

"There's something I don't understand," I said. "Why do you want to marry me, anyway? I mean, we don't get along. We don't even like each other."

Dan rubbed his brows as if we'd been over this and over this. "I thought that was clear. We're getting married for Jane's sake." He waved to Dr. Caswell for back up. "Right, doctor?"

This time, Dr. Caswell did not share in his conspiracy, but kept riffling through her papers in a rather annoying way. What was she getting out of this? Like Vern, the clerk in the courthouse said, people look out for themselves. Which brought me back to Dan. Why was he so determined to be legally wed to me, a woman he often publicly introduced as Queen of the Dumb?

I knew this much about my slime ball of an ex-husband. He wouldn't be exerting all this effort—roping in Dr. Caswell and paying full boat for this wedding—if money weren't involved. Big money, too.

"Next year," I said, tossing the papers onto Dr. Caswell's desk. "We'll get married in January when I'm not so rushed by the holidays."

Dan balked. "You can't do that! I've got everything paid for. The caterer, the wedding planner, the band, the—"

"Judge."

We faced each other for several minutes, neither of us willing to speak or give in.

I was startled when Dr. Caswell said in a quiet tone, "I'm sorry, Bubbles. I've searched through various remedies and there's no easy out for you. He holds all the cards."

She was tortured. She understood that she had made a very, very bad mistake aligning her star with Dan. "I'm sorry," she said again. "I didn't know it would turn out like this. I'm afraid that for everyone's sake the best choice is to marry him until Jane turns eighteen."

She was right. I knew it. And Dan, smirking like the brute who'd sucker punched the math geek, knew I knew it, too.

"Fine," I said, getting my purse. "We'll be married for a year. And then Jane will turn eighteen and I'll go to that Guam you're so fond of and divorce you like that!"

Dan bowed, far from perturbed as I would have predicted. "As you will" was all he said. Then he picked up the papers I'd tossed and ripped them into shreds.

Whatever scheme he had going, surely it was motivated by pure evil.

I was deflated, as if I were merely going through the motions as I headed to the swanky north side to track down Mark Knoffler. Stiletto would be off to Greece, Dan had me cornered and Marguerite didn't exist.

If only I hadn't gotten my hopes up about Stiletto and me. I mean, what had I expected? Stiletto's not the kind of doormat to lie around, allowing women to walk over him. I'd turned down his marriage proposal for a man I clearly despised. That's gotta drain the testosterone out of a guy.

Unless he bounces right back and starts sleeping with the Lehigh Valley's most beautiful celebrity, who jets off with him to Lesbos for the holidays.

Hot damn.

I took Illick's Mill Road to the Main Street extension and followed the tree-lined street as it narrowed, dipping into the valley of the Monocacy Creek. The bare branches of the large oaks bent so low they practically touched the roof of my Camaro. This was my favorite part of town. Quiet. Stately. Private.

Mark Knoffler's house was of the old Pennsylvania stone variety. It was up a slight driveway to the left, perched at the edge of a ravine. A Lincoln was in the driveway. I bet he was one of those architects who worked from home. Lucky stiff.

As I got out, I smelled wood smoke wafting from one

of four chimneys. Four chimneys. I could see him now. He probably wore black turtlenecks and played classical music full-blast as he sat before a roaring fireplace, drawing on his draft table.

Girlfriend? Something thin and chic. An artist, perhaps. Lived in New York or Philly and joined Mark on the weekends. Name? Suzanne.

Dog? Purebred Weimaraner. Answered to Max.

Activities? Anything requiring athleticism and daring. Extreme kayaking in the Irish Sea. Mountain climbing in Colorado. It went without saying that Mark ran five miles each morning at the crack of dawn, his breath blowing white, Max the Weimaraner by his side. Suzanne at home curled on the couch sipping her hand-brewed Italian espresso coffee, glancing over the *New York Times*.

I was a moron. I'd been standing in Mark Knoffler's driveway inventing Mark's ultrapreppy fantasy world for him, staring at nothing but the trees. He'd probably already called the fuzz. Or maybe Suzanne had.

Max the Weimaraner did not bark when I rang the doorbell. Nor did Suzanne the artistic girlfriend answer the door. Mark did. He was wearing gray sweats and a brown-and-white Lehigh University T-shirt. He was balding.

He seemed a bit groggy, as if he'd just rolled out of bed and yanked on the sweats. The sweats were TV sweats, not tight running sweats. It was fair to say after assessing his small, middle-aged gut that Mark's treadmill had been gathering dust in the basement for a while now. What was left of his brown hair was lopsided. He had bed head.

"I don't do Avon," he said, closing the door before I had a chance to put my foot in.

"I'm not an Avon lady. My name is Bubbles Yablonsky. I'm a neighbor of Phil Shatsky's and a reporter at the *News-Times*."

Mark arched his eyebrows as if this visit might be

more interesting than a year's supply of Skin So Soft. (Though, really, what could be more thrilling than that?)

"I'm looking for a Marguerite," I said, taking a chance.

Mark didn't move. He didn't say, *I'm awfully sorry, but you have been mistaken. There is no Marguerite.*

Instead he said, "I'll go get her, though it might take some time. She likes to sleep in."

Then he closed the door. I hadn't been invited in, either.

I often try to put myself in the places of the subjects I'm interviewing so I can get a better sense of what they're feeling. If some poor woman whose husband had recently blackmailed her into marriage had shown up at my doorstep asking for a Marguerite, I'd like to think I'd have invited her in.

Ten minutes later, during which I cleaned out the receipts from my purse, organized my pens, paid my phone bill and removed a suspicious candy stuck to my checkbook, the door opened and there stood Marguerite.

At least, I'd assumed it was Marguerite. She was dressed in a luxurious Japanese blue silk kimono and her rather large feet were stuffed into matching slippers. Nails were long and red, the kind you find on women who don't do dishes. Yet her hands were rough and callused.

But there was that hair. It was the same hair I'd seen profiled in the Lincoln parked in front of Phil Shatsky's house. It was big, big blond hair. And that's coming from a woman who knows a thing or two about follicle volume.

"I'm so sorry to keep you waiting," she singsonged in an absurdly high falsetto. "Won't you come in?"

I entered a foyer that opened to a step-down living room, the opposite wall of which was nothing but windows looking out to the ravine below.

"Can I get you some coffee?" she asked.

There was something off about Marguerite.

It might have been the chest hairs.

"No, thank you." I bit my lip, thinking about how to phrase this. "You're Mark Knoffler, aren't you?"

He grabbed my arm. "It's the makeup. It's too much, isn't it?"

My skilled eye took in the penciled brows, the blue lids and kohl-rimmed eyes framed by thick false eyelashes. "Actually, I think your makeup's perfect. And I work as a hairdresser, so I should know."

He brought his red-nailed hands to his lips. "That's it. That's how I know your name. Phil told me about you. You're the one who found Debbie."

"I was the one who was working on her hair when she died." I pointed to the living room. "Do you mind if we sit down and talk? I'm beat."

He apologized profusely for being so rude and sat me in a pink floral chair. Then he ran off to make tea and returned with a complete silver service and poured me a cup, asking me if I'd like sugar or cream. Every once in a while, I'd catch a glimpse of his black socks under his robe, his white calves with little black hairs.

When the elaborate tea preparations were done, he said, "You're probably wondering about this." He picked at the lapel of his robe.

"Not really." I put down my cup. "To tell the truth, I was wondering how you got hold of Debbie's clothes when I saw you in Phil Shatsky's car giving him a Full Sweeney."

Mark nodded. "That's easy enough to explain. Debbie gave them to me. Actually, I'm extremely proud of how well I pull off this other persona. I'm not a transvestite by nature. It's a stretch for me."

"Pardon?"

"You see, every time Debbie went shopping and bought a dress on sale, she'd pick up one for me, too, provided she could get it in my size." He held out a plate of cookies. "Cutouts? Or are you sick of them already?"

"Never." I chose a Santa Claus and bit the head off. It was his just deserts for shooting me up all over town. "Why would Debbie buy clothes for you when you go around giving her husband Full Sweeneys?"

"Have you ever been married?"

"Funny you should ask. I'm about to get remarried on Saturday."

"Then you have my sympathies."

"Thanks."

He dipped a candy cane cookie in his tea. "So you should understand what I mean when I say that no one can judge a marriage unless one's in it."

"Amen to that"—I was going to add "sister" and stopped—"brother."

"I probably shouldn't be telling you this, but I really don't care who knows now. I don't think Phil does, either, after all that's happened." He took a deep breath. "Debbie and Phil's marriage was arranged. Arranged by me." He added this juicy addendum with pride.

I regarded my Santa Claus with the red sugar and picked off his foot, trying hard not to convey the shock I felt. "I see." Though I didn't. "How did that happen?"

"Debbie used to be my travel agent. She knew I was gay and I knew she was having problems with her ex-husband, Ernie. Do you know about him?"

"Kind of. He practically died in my car last night."

"That's too bad," Mark said without emotion. "Anyway, I had just met Phil and we were hitting it off and looking forward to a long-term relationship. One problem. Ninety percent of Phil's business is centered on housewife referrals. Women choose him above others because he turns them on. He is a stud among plumbers. He'd get three offers of marriage a week before he married Debbie. I kid you not."

"Which is how Debbie came in."

"Right. She needed an excuse to get away from Ernie, as well as a house and companionship and a man who could protect her if Ernie came back for revenge. While

Phil, who was afraid of losing business if it got out he was gay, needed a—"

"Beard," I said.

Mark frowned. "I really hate that term. It's wrong on so many levels."

"Sorry. But didn't Debbie mind Phil going off with you, especially when you were disguised as her?"

He stirred his tea, thinking. "It was beginning to bother her, yes. Lately, she'd been making overtures to Phil. I think she was buying the right-wing who-ha that gay men can be set straight. Hello? Like, didn't she ever hear of biology?"

I didn't think he'd win with the biology argument, but decided to hold my tongue. Instead, I remained focused on whether this bizarre configuration might have led to Debbie's murder.

"What do you mean by overtures?"

"Of the sexual kind."

"She must have been lonely." I recalled Debbie's constant, loud boasting about how great her marriage was, how hot the sex. It was just as Mama had taught me growing up. The only reason people brag is to draw your attention away from those failings they hope you won't see.

"If you ask me," he continued, though I hadn't, "Debbie got the better end of the stick. Phil kept that house in immaculate order. He did all the laundry, all the cooking and even cleaned her cat's smelly litter box. All Debbie did was pay the bills."

Ding! Money. That was Debbie's thing.

"She paid the bills?"

"Why else would Phil agree to this arrangement? He lived rent- and board-free. The only bill he ever paid was the insurance on his car."

A kept man. And he didn't even have to sleep with her. He was like a nongigolo gigolo.

"Still, how does a woman who works as a travel agent afford to pay for all that?" I asked.

Mark scooted to the edge of the couch. "Now, if

you've been able to track down little old me, Bubbles
Yablonsky, hairdresser and reporter, I'm sure it comes
as no surprise to learn that Debbie always had a scam
going."

I finished off the Santa Claus. "She had more than
one?"

"Whatever worked."

"Like the Lust Boat cruises."

He held up his hands. "You'll get nothing from me
about Debbie's dealings. And Phil doesn't know, either.
We operated on a need-to-know basis with Debbie, and
our position was the less we knew, the better."

I picked up my cup and finished off the tea. It was delicious, perfectly brewed, flavorful and comforting. Why
didn't I drink tea more often? It was so much more tol-
erable than coffee. A much better way to start the day
than with Diet A-Treat.

"One last thing," I said. "Before she died, Debbie was
in the salon loudly telling of a Marguerite calling her
house at three a.m. and of being in love with Phil. But if
you're Marguerite, then that doesn't make sense."

"Then maybe the story wasn't meant for you," he
said. "Maybe the story was meant for someone else in
the salon to overhear. Did you ever think about that?"

"The only other people in the salon were Sissy Dolan
and Tula Kramer, two grandmothers who've been
Sandy's clients since she opened the House of Beauty
about twenty years ago."

Mark shrugged. "Then you never know. For some
women, the only reason to be married is to have a husband to show off. It's kind of sad, when you think about
it. But that was Debbie. She had no inner life, just an ex-
ternal one. She was like a Christmas ornament, shiny
and fragile and completely hollow inside."

Chapter Thirty-one

It turned out that my Thursday was to be a day of surprises. First, Jane declared her independence from Dr. Caswell. Then Dan forced me into marrying him once and for all. Marguerite turned out to be Phil Shatsky's gay lover. And when I walked into the newsroom I discovered that, lo and behold, I no longer existed.

"I'm sorry, Miss Yablonsky," Veronica said in perfect innocence, "but unless you have an appointment, I can't buzz you in."

I regarded the swinging half door that separated the reporters at the *News-Times* from the people they were supposed to be writing about. I could leap that sucker, even wearing this black knit dress.

"Cut it out, Veronica, and let me in."

"Honestly, Dix Notch has declared you don't exist. We're supposed to pretend like you never worked here. All your stuff has been packed in boxes and has been sent to your house, except for your extensive nail-polish collection. That I threw out."

"Threw out!" Okay, *that* was over the line. I had over twenty bucks' worth of Sally Hansen in my upper-right-hand drawer.

"By the way, you never did do my nails for free like you promised."

Oh, brother. As though I hadn't had more pressing issues. "If you're not going to let me in, then at least let me talk to Mr. Salvo. He'll take care of it."

"Mr. Salvo and Mr. Notch are out with the other editors at the Union Club for their annual holiday lunch. They won't be back for hours and I'm to call security if you so much as touch that door."

This was nuts. Not Notch banning me from the newsroom. There was nothing new about that. He was always finding one way or another to get me canned. And I'd assumed my days were numbered when he exiled me to the corner of lifestyle. But throwing out my nail-polish collection? That smacked of pure vindictiveness.

I searched the newsroom for an ally, someone to rescue me from this manicure-craving Cerberus, and spied Lawless crossing to his desk from the cafeteria. I waved to him.

He completely ignored me.

"Lawless!" I shouted.

He sat down, opened his brown paper bag, pulled out a sandwich and popped open a Coke.

"LAWLESS!"

Nothing. He was pretending not to hear me, the scum.

I watched as Alison carried over a salad in a tidy Tupperware container. She sat next to him at her—my—desk, stirred the salad with a fork and took a long draft from a water bottle. And then, much to my horror, she leaned over and offered Lawless something. He smiled, nodded and took a bite of her tomato.

Lawless eating a vegetable. I felt the Earth move. It was clear they were now much, much more than simple coworkers.

He was in love. He and Alison had been conducting an affair behind my back.

Without waiting for Veronica's meaningless approval, I snatched up her phone and dialed 215, Lawless's extension.

"Lawless," he answered.

"So," I began, "Alison is an untalented rookie, is she? Taking your spot and stealing the stories that are rightfully yours, eh? Looks like you two are cozier than you let on."

Lawless turned his back to Alison and covered the phone. "Will you chill out?"

"No, I will not chill out. What happened to all my notes I took yesterday? Where are my computer files?"

"Shhh. You're going to ruin everything."

"I don't give a rat's ass." Suddenly, I was furious and only part of my anger had to do with Lawless. It was Notch who'd had me exterminated. It was Dan who was forcing me into marriage. They were the ones I wanted to throttle.

But Dan and Notch weren't on the other end of my line. Lawless was, and like it or not, he was going to have to bear the brunt of my fury.

"I knew I couldn't trust you. I just knew it. I confided in you and you've been running into Notch's office and feeding him everything I've said. Then you've been canoodling with Alison, the young and pretty college grad."

Lawless glanced at me and turned away. "Did Veronica hear you say that?"

I did a quick check of Veronica, who was playing at sorting the afternoon's mail, her ear tuned for maximum information retrieval.

"I don't care."

"She's the one you've got to watch out for. She's his snitch."

"Bull. You're the one who finked to Notch, Lawless."

He let out an exasperated sigh. "She's going to repeat everything to Notch when he comes back, so shut your pie hole. Now let me explain something to you and then you can go."

Go? I hadn't planned on going anywhere.

"You know that so-called star file you're so eager to

get? I think Notch is in it somewhere. That's why he wants this story off page one. That's why he fired you today. He's got something to hide."

"But—"

"No buts, Bubbles. He's also got a rock-solid case for firing you. You knew that Sandy had gone on the lam and yet you didn't tell anyone here."

"I told *you*."

"Which should prove that I haven't been snitching to Notch. The point is, you didn't tell Alison, who was writing a story that made us look like idiots when it said Sandy was not a suspect. Turns out, there's a goddamn warrant out for her arrest."

Only for questioning, I thought.

"And there's something else. Notch received a call today from a woman named Tess Montague."

Oh, no, I thought, *Tess*.

"Apparently you interviewed her extensively in the bathroom of the Masonic temple about Debbie Shatsky and you never identified yourself as a reporter. You told her you were a beautician, nothing more. That's grounds for immediate termination and you know it."

"Bull. Tess is friends with Dan's ex-wife, Wendy. She knew full well I was a reporter."

"Not until after she'd answered your questions did she find that out. That's what she told Notch."

He was right. I hadn't been up-front with Tess and that was grounds for immediate termination. It was in the ethics handbook. Thou shalt not misrepresent. Though I'd had my reasons and they'd been valid ones.

"I have to say, Bubbles, as much as I'm on your side, misrepresenting yourself was really dumb. What were you thinking?"

"I don't know," I said glumly, massaging my temple. "It's so much easier sometimes. Whenever I say I'm a reporter, people either tense up and shut their doors or they burst out laughing."

Lawless was silent.

Suddenly, I was overcome with exhaustion. Stupid Debbie Shatsky and her big boasts. Things would have been so different if I hadn't volunteered to help Sandy in the salon on Monday, or if Debbie hadn't been desperate for superhigh hair.

To think my career at the *News-Times* had been done in by hair extensions. Not by all the bigwig steel lawyers who had tried to cut me at the knees, but by latex and hair, the death knell rung in the women's room of a Masonic temple.

Ironic? Uh, yeah.

"It's over this time," Lawless said softly. "I'm afraid you've run out of second chances."

"I know," I said, and thanked him for his kindness. One more touché to irony that, in the end, Lawless would be my only remaining friend.

Yes, it was over. My career at the *News-Times* was done. I hung up the phone and managed a forgiving smile at Veronica. Then I took one long, last sweeping glance of the newsroom, the cubicles, the papers piled high and the reporters hunched over their keyboards.

I'd invested so much hope, so much of my time trying to be an award-winning reporter. I'd written about strawberry-picking festivals and Fourth of July parades and finally worked my way to exposing corruption at every level, especially at the Steel.

But in the end, I had lost the brass ring on a technicality. Yet it was an important technicality. If reporters demanded reality from their subjects, they must demand it from themselves.

Then I saw Alison, her fork stuck in her salad, her phone tucked under her jaw, her fingers tapping wildly on the keyboard. So confident in her prospective success and yet so unwilling to leave the isolation of her desk and the security of this newsroom.

I voted her most likely to start fabricating her sources.

Enough. No more. It was not as fun as it was before.

The *News-Times* and I were through. Forever.

Chapter Thirty-two

Jane was bent over her laptop when I got home carrying whatever my Visa had room for. That was the one benefit of getting fired right before Christmas, a two-week severance check and a self-destructive impulse to spend oneself into a mad spiral of bankruptcy.

For Mama, I'd bought the bread maker she requested. For Genevieve, a new pair of night-vision goggles, as her old ones had been run over by the ATV she'd been riding at the time. (Long story. Let me just say that it involved a survivalist named Lebron, the FEMA mission statement and a townie bottle of Mad Dog 40/40.)

Jane had been much harder to buy for because I wasn't sure what personality I was dealing with. I mean, should I have bought her the complete series of *The O.C.*? Or a complete set of Jane Austen? Or were they one and the same and I hadn't been swift enough to pick up on that?

In the end, I broke the bank on a Red Hot Chili Peppers CD and stereo hookup for her iPod. Then I threw in a copy of Betty Smith's *A Tree Grows in Brooklyn*, because Jane likes trees. Dan calls her a tree hugger.

I plunked the groceries on the counter and tried to

hide my other shopping bags as I tiptoed upstairs to shove them under the bed. Being curious and greedy like most teenagers, Jane should have been trotting after me or jumping around asking nosy questions.

She wasn't. Instead, she was intently poring over a book, an old encyclopedia she used to love to read before she got kidnapped.

"What're you doing?"

Jane flinched. "Ohmigod, Mom, you scared the shit out of me."

"Aren't you supposed to be hanging out with friends at the mall or whatever it is you and Jason do?"

Jane gave me a look. "Jason and I are split. As a matter of fact, I'm killing time waiting for G to pick me up. Says he's taking me someplace special, whatever that means. Most likely a bowling alley."

It took all the muscles in my mouth not to smile.

She gestured to her laptop. "I opened that file on Excel. I'm not sure it's worth anything. It looks like maybe the person who gave it to you copied the wrong thing."

Damn. I knew it was too good to be true. I reached into the refrigerator and pulled out a Diet A-Treat, popped it open, grabbed a bag of Christmas Doritos from my groceries and went to the table. Lunch as I knew it.

"What's it say?"

"Not much." Jane dug her hand in to the Doritos and pulled out a fistful of chips. She was wearing a supertight BEATLES T-shirt and tight, ripped jeans. There were at least three earrings in every ear and we were engaged in an actual conversation that didn't involve weight, the state of that day's complexion or how little to eat.

It was a miracle.

"The file is called STAR, like you predicted. But then when I open it, there's just a listing of four names. Ada, Esther, Ruth and Martha."

"Sounds like the entire blue-hair client list at the House of Beauty," I said.

Jane half laughed. "Right. Well, they also could be some kind of code or combination. Computer passwords, I'm thinking. Other than that, the only thing they have in common is that they're from the Bible. That's why I'm looking up their origins."

I tried to think if I'd come across any Adas, Esthers, Ruths or Marthas during my investigation. Nope. A Tess and a Zora. A Vern. A Marguerite and a Fiona. Debbie was Debbie. I didn't know if that came from the Bible.

"Do you know if those are the names of Debbie's mother? Her sister? Maybe Phil Shatsky can help us?" Jane asked.

Good idea. While Jane continued to read up on the women in the Old Testament, I went to the phone, my favorite source of all knowledge, and called Phil. The phone rang and rang.

"Where's Sandy?" I asked, waiting for Phil to pick up.

"Getting ready for your big bachelorette party." Jane ate another Dorito. "You are still getting married, aren't you?"

"Of course. Why would you ask?"

Jane shrugged. "I don't know. There are some evil rumors going around."

"Hello?" It was Phil, sounding rushed.

I told him who I was and apologized for this being a bad time. "Hey, listen, you don't happen to know if in Debbie's family Esther and Ruth, Martha and Ada are significant, do you?"

There was a frosty silence. "Bubbles, I'm using all the restraint I can muster not to light into you."

I froze. This was the part of reporting I hated, when people got mad at me. "What have I done now?"

"Digging into my personal life. What business is it of anyone's if I happen to be gay and in a long-term, committed relationship with another man?"

He really was superticked. And, honestly, now that I thought about it, I didn't blame him. No one likes to be spied on. No one likes their private affairs to be aired.

Mark probably called him as soon as I left and told him everything.

"I'm sorry," I said.

"Sorry is not enough," he snapped. "All I can tell you is that I better not see this in the newspaper tomorrow. I shouldn't have to explain how this could affect my livelihood. Isn't it enough that I've had to bury my wife today? Do you need to treat me like a pathetic celebrity, too?"

Now I was feeling awful. Like true sewer muck. There was nothing to say.

"It's not going to be in the newspaper. You don't have to worry about that. I no longer work for the *News-Times*."

Jane snapped up from her encyclopedia.

"Why?" Phil asked.

"I've been fired."

"For what?"

"Personal stuff." I winced.

"Yeah? Well, note how I am decent enough to be polite and not ask what kind of personal stuff," he shot back, though his voice had softened somewhat. "Why do you need to know if Esther, Ruth, Ada and Martha were significant to Debbie's life anyway?"

"It was on a CD that belonged to her."

"To Debbie?"

"Right."

"Where did you get it?"

Gee, I wished he hadn't asked that.

"It kind of slipped into my purse. Well, I better be going. I have a bachelorette party tonight and—"

"Wait. You can't leave it like that. What else is on that CD?"

Thankfully the doorbell rang loud enough, I was certain, for Phil to hear.

"Nothing. Forget about it." And hung up. Man, did I feel crummy.

The doorbell rang again. Jane got up to get it. "It's

probably G. Did you get fired fired? Or is this another one of Dix Notch's temper tantrums?"

"Fired fired," I said, my hand still on the phone. What had I done to poor Phil?

Jane answered the door and said, "Mom?"

It wasn't G at the door. It was Stiletto.

He was wearing a white T-shirt under a gray sweater under his leather jacket and those killer tight jeans. He hadn't shaved and his hair, never neat, was tousled as if he'd been pulling his hands through it. It made me want to tousle it some more. The whole package, frankly, made me crazy.

Especially since I knew, finally knew, he was out of my grasp.

"Hi, Jane," he said. "You look great, much better than when we last met."

Jane twitched her lips with disapproval. "What are you doing here?"

"Thought I might say goodbye to your mother." He looked over at me and cocked his head as if to ask if that was fine by me.

"I suppose that's okay." She opened the door wider to let him in.

"Actually," I said, nervously, "it's not okay. I've got to run down to the city center to help Mama and Genevieve with the Christmas pageant and—" God. I was so afraid, I could hear the panic in my own voice.

Even Jane could sense my reluctance. "Why don't you talk to him, Mom? You two should have a few moments together. I'll wait outside for G. You know how he hates to come to the door, anyway."

I watched her—anything to keep from making eye contact with Stiletto—as she got her purse and shut down her laptop and then went outside just as G's slick black BMW pulled up.

"That kid's all right," Stiletto said, watching her through the window. "Who's the spiv in the Beemer?"

"G, if you can believe it. He's hit pay dirt as a stylist hawking aloe vera."

Stiletto snorted and shook his head, as if that weren't the darnedest thing. "Doesn't Dan drive a black BMW?"

Lead in my gut. Stiletto was right. "Ugh. Don't say that. I'd hate to see Jane end up with a future Dan."

Stiletto turned back to me. "And yet you're marrying him."

"Yes," I said.

"Why, Bubbles?"

This was my cue to explain. This was it. Tomorrow night he'd be off to Greece and he'd never know. "Because I have to."

"No, you don't."

"Yes, I do."

He came over to me and took my hands in his. I could feel the electricity between us as if we'd never been apart. I tried to pull away, but he wouldn't let me go.

"Tell me what's going on. What's Dan holding over you? I know he's got some sleazy scheme."

Tell him, my stupid brain screamed. "I . . . It's that . . ." And then I thought of Dr. Caswell's affidavit, that I was an unfit mother, a selfish, conniving disgrace to women everywhere, and how embarrassed that made me feel. I couldn't go on.

The back door was flung open and a blond head popped around the corner from the kitchen. At first I guessed it was G, coming to fetch something for Jane. Then I saw it wasn't him at all.

It was Sandy. Sandy as a blonde. And she was wearing my clothes. A pair of leopard-print tights under a zebra-patterned skirt, a scoop-necked red top and a black belt.

She looked awesome.

"Oh!" she said, startled. She was holding a shopping bag and in her hands was a pair of sunglasses, part of her disguise. "Oh," she said again.

"Sandy?" Stiletto said. "What's with the getup?"

Sandy darted a curious glance at me.

"She's dressing up for my bachelorette party," I fibbed. "It's tonight. In fact, we're supposed to leave in twenty minutes."

Stiletto's shoulders slumped in disappointment. "Then, this is it. This will be the last I see of you. This is goodbye."

"You know what?" Sandy said. "I need to drop off these Christmas presents and go to the little girl's room." She slipped past us to the stairs. "So you two take all the time you need. I'll be running the water and I won't be able to hear a thing!"

She dashed up the stairs. I was impressed because those were two-inch heels and I knew Sandy was only used to flats.

"I better go," Stiletto said.

"Yes."

We stood there for a few minutes, the tension building between us. He wouldn't let go of my hands. He kept staring at me. I couldn't comprehend that this was the last time we'd see each other. It didn't seem possible.

And then, before I could help myself, I threw my arms around him and sank my fingers into that hair, pulling him to me. It was wrong. I knew it. It would only make our parting harder. I didn't care. I didn't care about Sabina. I didn't care about Dan. And, being the lousy mother I am, I didn't at that moment care about Jane.

Stiletto's lips returned the passion. It was still there. It hadn't left. He pushed me against the banister and kissed me hungrily. I ran my hands across his broad shoulders and could feel his heart beating through his sweater. I inhaled the smell of wool and implanted it into my memory. Whenever I was near wool, I would think of Stiletto. This would be my secret.

Finally, he broke away and nuzzled my neck. "Do you love me?" he whispered in my ear.

I fought back tears. "Yes. I love you with everything I have."

"Then don't marry him."

"I have to."

He planted a kiss on my cheek, then held me at arm's length. "Bubbles, this is a very short life and you and I took a long time to find each other. Don't ditch it on a dare."

I couldn't speak. I was all choked up.

"Meet me tomorrow evening under the Hill-to-Hill. I don't have to be at JFK until nine when my flight takes off. If you have any last qualms, if you need to get away, I'll help you. I'll take care of everything, okay?"

I nodded, though I knew I wouldn't. I couldn't.

"Whatever he claims he's after," Stiletto said seriously, "it's a lie. You have to trust me."

I looked up at him, blinking through tears. "How do you know he's lying?"

"Why the hell do you think I flew all the way back from England?"

Well, I didn't know why, did I? "I thought because you wanted to have some fun with me before I got married."

He kissed me again, softly. "You never really did get me, did you? I'll wait until seven. It's your decision."

Then he turned and went out the door. He hadn't even driven off when I felt Sandy's hand on my shoulder.

"So you weren't in the bathroom running the water after all?" I said, wiping my tears on my sleeve.

Sandy took me in her arms, not saying a word, just soothing me.

She was so much lighter and smaller than Stiletto and she didn't smell a thing like wool. She smelled like cigarettes and perfume. And I was so glad she was my very best friend in the world because with her quiet touch she could shoo away all the boogeymen who were out to get me.

I could live without Stiletto, I supposed. Not easily, but I could.

However, I would die without Sandy. Best friends are not optional.

Chapter Thirty-three

Phil Shatsky was watching us from his living room when we left for the bachelorette party. I saw him part the curtain. I saw him standing in the window, his hands on his hips. I think I even saw him grimace. I told this to Sandy, who was driving, and she told me I was imagining things.

"You're under so much stress, Bubbles. What with Stiletto leaving, getting married, losing your job. I'm impressed you're holding up as well as you are. If I were you, I'd get blotto tonight—that's what I'd do. I'm your designated driver. Go for it."

I didn't feel like getting blotto. I felt edgy. Taut. My senses were heightened, as though I could hear better, see more clearly. Something was going on. Something was happening in the universe. And I needed to be as sober as a judge when it all came down.

Okay, maybe not a Pennsylvania judge. Bad example. A Utah judge. Yes, they were all sober, right?

"Where are we going anyway?" I said, when Sandy crossed the bridge into Allentown.

"Hubba, Hubba. It was Lorena's idea."

I didn't know what Hubba, Hubba was. But I did know that if it was Lorena's idea, it was bad.

"It's an all-male review," she said, sitting a bit straighter. "I'm glad Martin hasn't a clue. He'd be horrified to know I was spending the evening throwing myself at seminaked men, though I don't plan on doing that. I see my role as your escort. That's it."

"Naked men?" I cocked an eyebrow. "You know my mother and Genevieve are coming?"

"Who do you think made sure we each have a stack of dollar bills?"

Oh . . . my . . . God. I slid down in the seat as we pulled to the door of a low, all-black building to find Lorena, Mama, Genevieve and Tiffany, a hippyish former House of Beauty hairdresser, bouncing in line like schoolgirls waiting for the sock hop.

"You're serious, aren't you?" I said.

Sandy killed the engine. "Like I said, you better get blotto."

As soon as Sandy and I got out, Mama hollered at the top of her lungs, "There's the bride. There she is." She was holding something in her hand. Something white. It was waving in the breeze.

Oh, super. It was a gag veil.

"Just go with the flow," Sandy murmured. "Play along."

"I'm glad you haven't turned yourself into the police yet. If you hadn't been here, I don't think I could have stomached it.

"A strip club!" I squealed, faking shock and awe. "You girls are wild."

They whooped with delight.

Mama stood on tiptoes and plunked the veil on my head, marking me for the evening as the world's biggest doofus. I smiled weakly at the bouncer by the door. He smiled back. Seen one fake bride, seen 'em all, was his attitude. He had adopted the patient, mature demeanor of someone who is accustomed to handling lightweight middle-aged women who've tipped back a few too many strawberry daiquiris.

Genevieve was teetering already, a dipsy smile on her face. If I didn't know her better, I'd say she'd already gotten into the kitchen sherry.

"We had a few drinks before we came over," Genevieve confided. "You know how expensive cocktails are when you buy them at restaurants."

"That's okay. I'm buying, drinks and cab rides all the way around," Lorena declared. She wore electric earrings that blinked S-E-X on one ear and H-O-T on the other. "Our only goal tonight is to let loose and give Bubbles the send-off she deserves. After all, this is the closest she's going to get to hard bodies for a longggg time. She's marrying Dan, don't forget."

Everyone buckled over in hysterics, as though my misfortune of being bedded by a pompous, fat jerk was a sitcom. Sandy patted my shoulder.

The bouncer gave us the lowdown on the rules. No climbing on the stage uninvited. No baring of breasts or other bodily parts. We were allowed to touch the men, not lick them. (This made us go "Ewww.") We were not allowed to stick our hands down their privates or pinch their derrieres.

"Oh," Genevieve moaned, "I was looking forward to that."

Think of it this way, I reminded myself as our party followed him through the darkened hallway illuminated by black lights, down the stairs and toward the rising sound of pounding base beats: in two hours it will be over. All I had to do was pretend to have a good time and then we could all go home and I could go to bed.

I would think about tomorrow, about the wedding rehearsal and dinner to follow, later. I would not think about it tonight.

And I definitely would not think about Stiletto.

A waiter who wore only black pants and a neat white bow tie walked by with a platter as if we were invisible. That was some set of pecs, I had to admit, as Lorena hurled herself at him with a flying leap, tackled him to the ground and ordered, "Shots, stat!"

When he left with her credit card, I said discreetly to Lorena, "If you don't mind, I'd just like a Coke or something."

"Nothing doing, bride." She lit a cigarette and exhaled right in my face. "And put your veil back on. Someone's got to be the virgin around here."

More hysterics. They were out-of-control giddy, even Sandy, who was getting lots of compliments on her new Bubblesish look. It was beginning to have an effect on her, too. She wasn't acting quite herself.

"Hey, ladies," Genevieve shouted. "Pay attention to the first act. It's a good one. They come on as construction workers and then strip down to Speedos."

Sandy and I exchanged looks.

"By any chance have you been here before?" I asked Genevieve.

"Me? Here? Of course not." She patted back her silver hair. "The only reason I'm here is for you, Sally, for support. I consider these establishments to be the downfall of America. It's bad enough that men come to places like this, but women? It's the end times, I tell you. The end times."

"Hey there, Annie. Looks like you're itching for a bigger gun." A simply gorgeous man with smooth black skin wearing not much more than stirrups and a cowboy hat sat himself on Genevieve's lap. Then he proceeded to rustle up one of her hefty earlobes.

She squealed and produced a wad of bills for his G-string. "I was hoping you'd be working tonight, Tex."

Like an arcade game that had just been fed quarters, he proceeded to move his body up and down over Genevieve's massive frame. If I'd been management, I'd have been concerned. That was a lot of Lithuanian mass times cowboy energy for a couch that didn't look all that sturdy.

"Tex?" I said, as he walked off to lasso up some more cashola.

"It's a coincidence. He bags at the ShopRite."

"Looked like he wanted to bag you."

Genevieve turned red.

The shots arrived as an emcee performed introductions. All the women lifted their glasses to their lips, except for Sandy and me. She stared at hers with suspicion.

"Go on, Sandy," I said. "Just do it. I'll drive home."

Sandy sniffed the shot. "It smells kind of sweet. Like peppermint."

Yes. That would be Lorena. She was a Lehigh Valley girl, born and raised. If it's sickening sweet and alcoholic, it's down her throat.

"On the count of three," Lorena ordered. "One . . . two . . . three." They knocked them back.

Sandy took a stingy sip, smacked her lips and regarded the shot glass with new appreciation. "Oh, my. That's strong, isn't it? It burns." Then she finished it and squinted in pain.

I'd never seen Sandy drunk before. I doubted it would take much.

"Another round!" Lorena demanded. Apparently not wishing to be pretzeled into one of Lorena's famous head locks, the waiter reappeared like magic.

"Take mine," I said to Sandy.

"Should I?" She frowned, as if she really, really shouldn't.

Mama, who was now sitting on top of the couch, not on the seat, raised her shot and declared, "To Bubbles!"

"To Bubbles!" everyone agreed.

This time Sandy downed the shot in one gulp and even licked the rim of her glass.

"Here they come!" announced Genevieve, who had assumed the role as our one-woman guide to Hubba, Hubba.

Indeed, there they were. Four construction workers, dirty from a hard—and I mean "hard"—day on the job, manly and sweating, strutted onto the catwalk. What was this? Why, they were ripping off their pants. Who knew you could just rip off Carhartts? And look what they were wearing underneath? Jockstraps!

Drawn by estrogen-fueled madness, two women rushed to the stage, waving dollar bills. I turned to make a crack to Sandy and noticed that she wasn't sitting next to me anymore.

No. In fact, she was front and center on Genevieve's massive shoulders.

"Take it off!" came Sandy's distinct voice. "Take it *all* off!"

"Yeah," Genevieve echoed. "We want to see your package." Then she stuffed a wad of bills in the rugged driller's G-string (because, let's face it, a G-string is as necessary on the construction site as a hard hat) and was rewarded with a red bandanna that seconds before had been carefully positioned in a strategic place.

I was beginning to see the practicality in that no licking rule.

The construction workers went backstage to take showers or whatever it is construction workers do after working all day and coming home to rip off their clothes and prance around in bikinis. Delirious to have handsome, built, naked men all to themselves, the members of my bachelorette party ran back for another refill of peppermint schnapps before the next act came on.

"Okay," said Sandy cautiously, "but I can only have one more round."

Though it would be two, as she was also sucking down mine.

This time, no one even bothered to stage the pretense that this party was for me. There was no countdown. No salute to the bride. They just downed the shots and rushed off to secure a good spot by the stage to catch the next act.

Public servants. A cop. A fireman. And . . . I think the last one was supposed to be a doctor. Wasn't quite sure. He was in his greens and wore a stethoscope. Correction, he *twirled* a stethoscope while removing his pants. Yes, that did require seven years of schooling, not to mention residency.

"And the poor bride-to-be is left all alone."

I stood up, nearly knocking over the table of shot glasses. It was Phil Shatsky, a menacing gleam in his eye.

"What are you doing here?" I asked.

"I'm still pissed," he said. "You owe me, Bubbles."

Frankly, I didn't owe him a thing. If anything, he owed me for giving him that opportunity to put on the public display of heterosexuality for the benefit of Ginger Burge and all his groupies, who'd been staring in my window the night he kissed me in my living room. What a phony.

"Ada, Esther, Ruth and Martha. Where did you get that?" He blocked me so I couldn't leave.

"I don't know. It was something someone said."

"I want that CD."

"I'll make you a copy."

He grabbed my sleeve, threateningly. "No. I want it now."

"But I'm at—"

"Now!"

I'd never seen Phil this way before. Usually he was so docile and accommodating, not threatening and scary like tonight.

"Let go," I said evenly.

"Come with me. We'll go to your house."

"No!" Geesh. Wasn't anyone going to help me out here?

I looked at the stage, where a cop was just a few feet away. Okay, he wasn't a real cop and he was wearing only a hat, a pair of Ray-Bans and a holster. Still, a cop was a cop, no?

"Why is it so important?"

"Because it is. Stop stalling."

At that moment, he gripped both my arms and I knew I was really in trouble. If I didn't do something drastic, this was going to end badly.

"Let go of me!" I threw my body toward him, off the couch, disrupting his equilibrium. It was enough for me to break free and hop onto the stage.

It was against the rules, getting on stage. I knew it.

That's why I did it.

"No way, lady," the stripping cop said. "You gotta get down. Get off and take a cold shower, sober up."

I grabbed him and was nearly overpowered by his misuse of Old Spice. "Listen, I'm not drunk. You've got to help me. There's a man over there who's after me."

"Bubbles! What the hell do you think you're doing?" Genevieve bellowed.

The cop took off his Ray-Bans. His face was instantly familiar, though I couldn't place the name.

"Bubbles?" he asked. "From the salon?"

People started booing. "It's me, Eric," he said, cheerfully. "From the medical examiner's office. I was in the House of Beauty the other day."

Oh, great. Sissy Dolan's grandson. Once Sissy found out I was here, the whole world would know and my rep would be dirt.

"You work here?" I said, to keep up the conversation. Of course he worked here. He was prancing around in his skivvies.

"Moonlighting." Keeping a protective arm around me, he shielded his eyes and looked out to the crowd. "What's this about some guy being after you?"

"Save her! Save her!" the crowd yelled, apparently thinking a cop checking the horizon while saving a virginal bride was part of the act.

A bouncer approached the stage, ready to haul me off. I saw Genevieve say something that caused him to reflexively cover his testicles.

"Do you know who it was?" Eric asked.

"It's Phil Shatsky." I pointed a shaking hand toward the couches. There was no sign of Phil. "I'm sorry. I didn't mean to ruin your act. It's just that I was so scared. I didn't know what else to do."

"It's okay. It's okay," he said calmly. "I'll take you backstage. And then we'll get the bouncer to do something."

He signaled to the deejay, who wound up the exit music. Swinging his baton as he exited, Eric guided me, the frightened, virginal bride, into the wings. A bouncer was waiting for us or, rather, waiting for an explanation. When Eric told him what had happened and I gave him Phil's description, he went off to see if Phil was still around and to find out how he'd gotten into the club in the first place.

In the absence of adrenaline, my body started shaking. "I shouldn't have jumped onstage. I didn't know what I was doing."

Eric gave me a quick hug. "Are you kidding? That was so good, we should write it into the act."

It was not until we were under normal lights that I could appreciate Eric's fine physique. He wasn't that tall, but he was built. Sissy Dolan was often going on and on about what a great kid he was, how he was putting himself through Drexel's medical school by working as a tech in the medical examiner's office. No wonder his nails were bitten to the quick. The guy was stressed and overworked.

"Does your grandmother know you do this on the side?"

"No, and if you tell her I'll never hear the end of it. She thinks I'm a good Catholic boy who's waiting for a good Catholic girl to come along and make me six babies." He went to the watercooler and poured me a cup of water into a white plastic cup. "Drink up."

As I drank, I also came to my senses and immediately felt foolish. Poor Phil. Once again I'd overreacted. I needed to get a prescription for valium or something. Mickey Sinkler was right: I was a mess.

"I'm thinking about it now," I told Eric. "I completely overreacted."

"You wouldn't be the first bride-to-be to flip out

here," he said. "It can be a little intense. And it's not like you had an easy week. I remember your expression when I told Sandy that I'd found the glue in her toilet. Both of you were freaked. I felt kinda bad. Maybe I should have waited until the salon was empty."

"So you think Sandy's innocent?"

"Well, they weren't her prints on the container, were they?"

I nearly dropped my cup of water. "What?"

"The prints on the Tupperware that was found in the bathroom. My understanding was the prints didn't match hers. They matched Debbie Shatsky's and someone else's. I don't know whose. They don't let me in on that level of the investigation."

Fingerprints. Why hadn't I thought to ask the cops? This totally cleared Sandy. She could come out of hiding now and go to my wedding and be my matron of honor and . . .

"Thank you, thank you, thank you." I planted a huge kiss on Eric's cheek just as the bouncer returned, followed by Genevieve, Mama and Lorena, looking concerned.

"No sign of that guy you described," the bouncer said. "And Harry at the door says he didn't see him come in. How many of those schnapps you have?"

Lorena rushed to my rescue. "Buzz off, fat boy. If you'd done your job like you were supposed to, this wouldn't have happened." She put an arm around me and helped me off the chair. "Come on, Bubbles. I think we better cut the night short."

"Thanks, Eric," I said.

Eric winked. "Anytime, hot stuff."

Boy. I should have hung out at the coroner's office more often. Who knew med techs were so cute? And helpful, too!

The bouncer directed us to a back door that led to the parking lot so I wouldn't have to face the embarrassment of going into the club. It felt great to be out of the hot club and in the brisk December night air.

Lorena took out her cell and dialed for a cab. Mama and Genevieve leaned against the wall, fanning themselves. Tiffany had found a friend and was staying. They were having a heck of a time.

"Me? I'm ready to pass out," Mama said. "Where's Sandy? She staying, too?"

I hoped not because I did not want to have to stick around to drive her home.

"Her car's gone," Lorena said, pointing to an empty parking space. "That's not good. She had three shots."

Six, I thought, those horrible prickles of alarm spreading over my body. Lorena was right. Sandy's car was gone. "Something's wrong. Sandy would never have driven drunk."

Lorena shook her head. "That's the problem after you've had a few. You think you're invincible. I bet she just got in the car and left."

"Without me?" I said. "Never."

Chapter Thirty-four

That night I found it was impossible to report a missing woman who had already been reported missing.

Martin would move out if he knew that Sandy had not only lied to him about taking birth control pills while they were trying to get pregnant, but had also hid in my house without calling to let him know she was safe. There was no way I could explain that Sandy so loved him and was so scared of losing him that she'd dropped out of his life. It was too illogical.

And if I told the cops that I'd harbored a fugitive, I'd really be in hot water, Lorena pointed out in the cab on the way home.

"Look at it this way. If you were on the lam from your husband and the law, would you want your best friend to call the police?" she asked, point blank. "*Especially* if you were driving around with six shots of peppermint schnapps in your system?"

No, I had to agree, I would not.

For the rest of the night I sat by my front window with the house lights off, drinking coffee by the gallon, waiting for Phil Shatsky to return to his house on the good chance he'd come knocking at my door.

He didn't. His car never pulled into the driveway.

Ada. Esther. Ruth. Martha.

What did it mean?

At six a.m. on the dot, I called Martin's bakery. He was working again, sounding as bleary and depressed as I felt.

"Oh, hi, Bubbles. Is this the big day?"

"Tomorrow." I rubbed my eyes, trying to stay awake. "You hear anything from Sandy?" *Please say yes!*

"You'd be the first to know if I had," he said.

Damn. Now what?

"How about you?" he asked.

"Ditto, though, listen Martin. Tell Sandy I ran into the medical technician who found the glue in her private toilet. Apparently, her prints aren't on any of the stuff."

"I know," he said.

"You know?"

The bell in his store tinkled. "Yeah. Found out the other day. If Sandy had been here, I could have told her. Shoot. I got a customer. I gotta go. Do you think she's okay?"

"Sure," I lied. "Just scared. But you know Sandy, always responsible."

Wheeling around town on six peppermint schnapps.

"Promise you'll call if you hear anything."

I promised and hung up. I should have made Sandy phone him last night. It might have been the last time they spoke.

Okay, I had a whole day ahead of me and no sleep to keep me going. Tonight I had to walk down the aisle in Lehigh University's chapel in preparation for the Big Walk on Saturday. I had to sit next to Dan at the rehearsal dinner and pretend all was hunky-dory.

As for Stiletto?

Cripes. I couldn't think about it. I was barely functioning as I was. Plus, I was about to throw up from all the coffee.

I went upstairs, took a long, hot shower, went in to my room and promptly passed out on my bed. I woke to a muffled knock at my door and drool puddling at the corner of my mouth. I had no idea where I was or the date or why my hair had dried into a tangled mass or why I wasn't at work.

All I knew was that it was snowing pretty heavily and it was almost a quarter after noon and that I was half naked, wrapped in a towel.

"Mom?"

The door opened a crack. I got up and gathered the towel around me. And then I remembered. It was Friday. I wasn't at work because I'd been fired. So why was Jane home?

"Why aren't you at school?" I roared.

"Because I don't have school," Jane said, coming in quietly, carrying what looked to be a newspaper. She was wearing a black T-shirt that said in gold letters CALIBAN that at first glance I misread as TALIBAN. "It's the Friday before Christmas. We have vacation."

I slapped my forehead. I was a bad, bad mother. Dr. Caswell had been right. I couldn't keep track of my kid's vacation. I even let her wear T-shirts advertising terrorist groups.

Jane sat on the corner of my bed and eyed me with alarm. "Were you passed out?"

"Yes! I was so tired."

"You mean, you got wasted on shots like Grandma?"

It took me a while to figure out what she was saying. "No, no. I stayed up all night spying on Phil Shatsky. I didn't have anything to drink, well, except for a couple of pots of coffee. I had to stay awake to see if he came home."

"Oh." Jane seemed confused, though I couldn't imagine why.

"Have you heard from Sandy?"

"No. Where is she?"

"Good question." I pointed to the newspaper. "Is that today's?"

"Wednesday's. I wanted to read Debbie Shatsky's

obituary." She folded it to the obituary section and pointed to a paragraph. "What does this mean, Order of the Eastern Star?"

I took the paper. "Hah! This is why Mr. Salvo taught us in Two Guys journalism class never to abbreviate on the assumption the reader always knows. For example, you shouldn't write ACLU on first reference. It's the American Civil—"

"Mom. What *is* the Order of the Eastern Star?"

"It's one of those secretive Masonic women's organizations. Genevieve knows all about it, being a dyed-in-the-wool conspiracy theorist. Don't get her started. She's got this map of Washington, D.C., that shows how the Pentagon, the Lincoln Memorial, the Capitol and the White House make a Pentagram and the Masonic sign."

Jane stared at me. "How much coffee did you say you had?"

"A lot. What do you care about the OES?"

"I don't know. Those four biblical names kept me up all night. G and I were working on them."

"G?"

"He knows a lot about codes, actually. From playing video games. They're all about codes."

Of course. I knew there had to be some value to playing Super Monkey Ball for twelve hours straight.

"Hold on. I want to get that encyclopedia." Jane left the room.

I took the opportunity to slip on a pair of jeans and a royal blue turtleneck sweater. I grabbed the pump bottle from my dresser and wetted my hair, pulling it back into a bun. Then I did my eyes in blue with blue mascara and plunked in a pair of blue earrings Stiletto had given me.

I was very blue, in more ways than one.

When I was done, Jane was back, reading furiously. "This is it, Mom, though I have no idea what it means. The star in the Order of the Eastern Star is upside down. The points all mean something: Ada, Ruth, Martha, Esther and Electa."

"Electa?" I made a face. "Who names their kid Electa?"

"Not to pun but you're missing the point. Rearrange them. Ada, Esther, Ruth and Martha. Those are the names in the computer file. 1–5–19–14. Those are the numerical equivalents."

I'd seen that number before, though not in that way. Split up. But where?

"You know what this means, don't you?" I asked rhetorically, having finally grasped that concept. "It means we have to go to Genevieve. Genevieve will know what this means."

"That's okay. I love Genevieve."

"She'll be dressed as the Virgin Mary and riding a donkey while selling snow globes."

Jane swallowed hard. "No one said investigating a crime was pretty. Let's go."

Chapter Thirty-five

"**O**h, sure. Ada, Esther, Ruth, Martha and Electa. Should've come to me right off. I'm your go-to gal for that bunch of no-goodniks." Genevieve pushed back her Virgin Mary blue headdress, exposing her white wimple. "I ain't gonna mince words, ladies. It's common knowledge among us who keep track of such that the Order of the Eastern Star is a Satanic cult that entices innocent women through the devious attraction of bake sales."

"Bake sales?" Jane asked.

Genevieve shot her with her finger. "Watch it, you. You're too young to appreciate the allure of a well-crafted Bundt cake. They don't call it devil's food for nothing."

Jane snapped her mouth shut.

"Okay. So what is it you want to know, Sally?"

At that moment, there was a lot I wanted to know.

Right off, I wanted to know how Mama and Genevieve had managed to convince seven busloads of senior citizens in the tricounty area that Lehigh could steal Bethlehem's Christmas business by offering deep, deep discounts on snow globes.

I wanted to know how they managed to turn the

courtyard between the library and city hall into a manger with stables, several camels, three wise men, a bunch of arthritic shepherds, eight angels in Depends, a couple sheep and, inexplicably, a Jersey cow.

Mostly, I wanted to know where Genevieve got off portraying herself as a teenage virgin appointed by God to be the Blessed Mother of Our Savior.

But, as time was limited, I asked her the significance of the four names.

"Question numero uno. Where'd you get this info, Sally?" Genevieve asked. "Where'd you find out about them?"

I reminded her of the woman in the veil at Ern's shiva, the woman who had followed me out into the hallway. The woman who turned out to be Fiona Swyer from Get Together Now! Travel, where Debbie had worked. I told her about how Fiona kept emphasizing that she'd been more than a friend of Debbie's—she'd been a *sister*.

"Did she use any hootchie-cootchie code?"

I tried to think back. "No hootchie-cootchie code that I can remember. She asked me if I had Excel. Then she shook my hand."

"*How* did she shake your hand?"

"She shook it. That's all."

A shepherd went by wearing striped robes over his winter coat. He told Genevieve to go long and then he threw a doll. Genevieve caught his pass like the football receiver she should have been.

"The new baby Jesus," she said. "We lost the original. Think some kid stole it out of the crèche. Either that or it was drop-kicked by those teenagers on skateboards."

Jane covered her eyes.

Genevieve tucked the baby Jesus under her arm. "Listen, no one just shakes a hand, not if they're with the OES. Try me." She stuck out her mitt.

I put my hand in hers and did my best to re-create the

way the woman had pinched the fleshy part between my thumb and forefinger.

"Oh, yeah. There's some serious OES stuff going on there." Genevieve checked over her shoulder and led Jane and me around the side of the library to the Japanese garden, placing the baby by a miniature bridge. "You know what the secret phrase of the OES is, don't you?"

"Fairest Among Thousands, Altogether Lovely," Jane said. "I read it online."

Genevieve said, "Read that another way and it spells FATAL."

I felt a chill and it was not the wind coming up from the Lehigh or the snow that was falling in big flakes. FATAL. That had significance. That *meant* something.

"Fatal," I repeated, things clicking.

"That's right. FATAL. Like I told you, it ain't just bake sales at the OES. Also, the Eastern Star, a direct reference to the star of Bethlehem, is upside down. How's that for blasphemy? And each of the points represents something. For example, Esther is white. Wheat is for Ruth."

I grabbed Jane to steady myself.

"Mom?" Jane was staring at me, aghast. "What's going on?"

"Wheat," I said. "Fatal."

Genevieve nodded with approval. "Good girl, Sally. Now you're catching on."

"No," I said. "Debbie's last words were 'wheat' and 'fatal.' I'd asked her if she was having an allergic reaction and that's what she answered. I thought she was saying she had a fatal wheat allergy."

Genevieve emitted a high whistle. "See, that's what happens when we let you civilians dabble in matters of which you know not. You're ignorant, is all. Now, if I'd been there, with my knowledge of the Masons and their ilk—"

Bingo! I realized where I'd seen the numbers 1–5–19–14. "The Masonic temple. I have to go there. Jane, you stay with Genevieve."

Jane looked pleadingly. "Mom. Please?"

"Now don't be down, little Sally. I got plenty of funnel cake to keep you happy, just like they make at the Allentown Fair with powdered sugar and everything."

"Mom!" Jane called again.

I couldn't stop to listen or worry. Jane would be safe with Genevieve. About ten pounds fatter when I returned, but safe.

It didn't take much to enter the Masonic temple, where Stiletto and I had made out in the storage room. All I had to tell the housekeeper, a broad woman in a gray dress with poorly dyed red hair and a deep Irish brogue, was that I'd lost an earring there the other night and ask if I could look for it. She held out her hand. I shook it and she instantly warmed.

The secret handshake of the Order of the Eastern Star. How many other doors would it open?

I went up the stairs, trying to remember where Stiletto had taken me. The temple was empty, aside from the housekeeper, who seemed more interested in salting the front steps than what I was up to.

Was it four doors? Five doors? Definitely past the coat closet. I found it at the end of the hall. I put my hand on the doorknob and opened slowly. It was the storage room, all right. File cabinets, easels, folding chairs, card tables, the awards.

Instantly, I was overcome with memories of Stiletto's kisses, the insistent way he'd forced me in here, the fabulous passion and unquenchable hunger we had for each other.

Mustn't go there now, I thought, running my hand along the filing cabinets, looking for the plaque I'd seen the night I was here. There it was. Hanging in the same spot, untouched.

It was in commemoration of the OES Northampton County Chapter's inception on January 5, 1914. 1–5–19–14. Ada. Esther. Ruth. Martha. It was a long shot. Then again, it was too much of a coincidence not to be.

Carefully, I removed the plaque from the wall and turned it over. Nothing but green felt. Disappointing. I shook it. There was no rattle. Damn.

And then I saw it. The thinnest slip of plastic sticking out from the green felt backing. With my superb acrylic nails, I pinched the felt and pulled it slowly to reveal a CD in a thin plastic case affixed underneath.

This, I was certain, was the star file and I bet it opened with Excel.

There were footsteps in the hallway. Most likely the housekeeper coming to check on me. I had to act as if I'd been searching for an earring.

I tossed my purse aside and went on my hands and knees. She would come in and ask if I'd found the earring. I would have to look disappointed and tell her no, but that it was okay. It hadn't been worth anything and then she'd leave and I'd follow. I couldn't wait to get back home and see what was on this CD.

The linoleum tiled floor was incredibly dusty. My nose itched and I felt the pressure of an oncoming sneeze.

Ah-choo!

"God bless you," a man's voice said right as I felt the hard, unmistakable pressure of a gun on my vertebrae. This was not good.

I glanced over my shoulder and was surprised to find Santa Claus in full costume, the white beard, the bushy white eyebrows, the apple cheeks, red suit and black boots, holding not only the gun, but also my purse.

"Let's go," he said gruffly. "And hurry up. We don't have much time."

Well, I guess that made sense. I mean, he sees me when I'm sleeping. He's sees when I'm awake. He sees

if I've been bad or good, so I better be good for good-
ness' sake.

I wasn't about to pout or cry. I did as I was told. Santa
Claus had come to town and he was looking for the star
file.

Chapter Thirty-six

It was a sad sign that my initial reaction upon seeing the gun and then being forced to the basement of the temple was one of relief. *Thank, God,* I thought. *I won't have to go through that idiotic rehearsal dinner. I had nothing to wear, anyway.*

And then an even more promising concept: *Maybe he'll kill me so I won't have to marry Dan!* Talk about your lucky loophole. Death was the ultimate excuse, was it not?

But . . . what about Stiletto? He'd asked me to meet him by seven under the Hill-to-Hill Bridge and already it was around one and I had the feeling jolly old St. Nick didn't plan on letting me go, well, ever.

"Keep moving," he ordered, shoving the gun into the back of my neck as we descended a dark, mustysmelling cinder-block staircase. That was the problem with Lehigh basements: rot. Really, the Masonic temple should look into getting a dehumidifier before they contracted a bad case of black mold.

We were in definite centipede territory now. I stepped carefully as we passed a roaring furnace and a dripping pump room.

"It's haunted, you know," my captor said. "This mansion was built by Elisha Wilbur so he could keep an eye on the train track, make sure it was on time. Others have said they still see him at night, watching from the windows."

"And yet the trains are still late. How's that for irony?" Irony and a rhetorical question in one. I was getting these down.

We came to a padlocked door. It was superdank and cold. I rubbed my arms as he inserted the key and pushed me inside a pitch-black windowless room.

The door shut. I heard him set the padlock.

Well, this was pleasant. Cold. Wet. Disgusting.

Flick! A flame lit and over it a horrendously made-up face glowed. Holy crap! It was Elisha Wilbur himself.

"Hey, Bubbles." Sandy leaned over and lit her cigarette. "Nice accommodations, say?"

Sandy! She was alive. I impulsively hugged her and nearly got my hair singed in the process. "You're okay! You're not dead!"

"Not yet." She exhaled, coughed and pushed me off her. "They plan to kill us, you know."

"So I assumed." I motioned for a drag, sucking in the scratchy smoke, which immediately made me light-headed and slightly nauseous. Only true addicts crave drugs that will make them light-headed and slightly nauseous.

"Thanks." I handed it back to her. "You're calm, for someone who's about to be killed."

She waved the cigarette, her lit tip making a glowing curlicue in the dark. "The way I look at it, at least I won't have to face Martin."

This was true. "The way I look at it, at least I won't have to get married."

"Two white chicks who would rather die in a Masonic temple basement than put up with their husbands. What does that say about the state of feminism today?"

I thought about this. "Was *that* one of those rhetorical questions?"

"You know," she said, "I think it was."

"Yes!" I pumped my fist. Two in a row. "Though, Dan aside, I do worry about what my getting killed will do to Jane." I didn't mention Stiletto. I didn't want to open that can of worms. (Honestly, what company cans worms?)

Sandy finished her cigarette. "Jane will be fine. Someday she'll write a book about you being murdered in the Masonic temple and she'll be on *Oprah*. It's the best thing you can do for her future, getting murdered. I bet Princeton accepts her right away."

Another excellent point. "What happened to you last night?"

"I was in the club looking for you. Everyone just kind of left me. I went down some hallway and then I was grabbed."

"By whom?"

"I don't know. He wouldn't let me look at him. He threw a hood over my face and tied my hands behind my back."

I tried to picture that. "Odd that you can walk around Hubba, Hubba with a hood on your head and your hands tied behind your back but you're not allowed to get onstage and lick the dancers."

"Yes," she said.

"Where were the bouncers?"

"Beats me. I was wearing a pillowcase, so I couldn't see." Sandy said this as though I were a moron for not remembering the hood. "Probably they thought I was a celebrity and wanted to leave incognito."

"Was it Phil Shatsky?"

"I don't think so. Phil's kind of short. This guy was about my height."

"Like the Santa Claus who stuck the gun in my back and brought me down here," I said.

"Like Phil's lover maybe?" she asked.

I mulled this over. "No. It wasn't Mark Knoffler. Mark's nails were impressive. This Santa Claus had short, bitten, stubby nails."

"Ick."

Sandy and I sat on the damp, cold cement floor and shot the breeze for an indeterminable amount of time. We talked about babies. I told her about Stiletto and Dan's threat to have Jane and me separated if I didn't marry him.

Sandy revealed that she'd been of the opinion that Dan was operating on an ulterior motive, though she hadn't thought it was her place to say so. Like Vern the county clerk, she noted that Dan rarely, if ever, did anything for love. What he wanted was status and money, and he would go to any lengths to secure both.

I told her about Dr. Caswell's report and was surprised when Sandy laughed.

"Dan paid her off. It's obvious, Bubbles."

"But she's a psychologist. She has a code of ethics."

"She also has bills to pay like the rest of us. Wasn't Dan the one who found her in the first place?"

"Right." I thought about how Dr. Caswell served as Dan's expert witness in those crazy I-found-a-finger-in-my-Big-Mac cases that he never won. "You mean . . . I'm not a bad mother?"

"No. However, you are a schmuck for trusting your ex." She put her arm around my shoulders. "Why didn't you tell me all this before?"

That was when I burst out crying about how embarrassed I'd been, how the report had filled me with shame.

"I'm gathering Stiletto doesn't know, either."

"Of course not."

Sandy exhaled. "Oh, brother."

After that, we took turns putting our heads on each other's laps, napping.

Finally, to keep our rising anxiety at bay we played the game Worst Song Ever. Sandy voted for Foreigner's "Hot Blooded," which just so happened to be one of my secret favorites, ever. I voted for the Four Seasons' "Who Loves You, Pretty Baby?" and Sandy hit me.

I'd forgotten that it had been her first dance song with Martin at their wedding.

We were so wrapped up in debating the virtues of Bad Company versus Frampton in his *Frampton Comes Alive* glory days that it took us a while to realize people were outside. There were voices above us.

And, more ominous, a strange hissing sound.

"Oh, shit. It's started," Sandy said, leaping to her feet.

I got up too, my muscles tight and sore from the dampness. "What's started?"

"The Christmas party upstairs. He said that was when they were going to kill us. His plan was to fill up our cell with undiluted oxygen. No one would hear our screams, the party would be so loud. And there'd be no evidence afterward."

That was ridiculous. "You can't die from too much oxygen."

"Yes, you can. I read it in a divers' magazine they sent to the House of Beauty. You need carbon dioxide to trigger lung function. Too much oxygen and your lungs stop working."

"What about Michael Jackson and his little oxygen tent he sleeps in?"

Sandy's hand was on my shoulder. "I like you, Bubbles. You're my best friend and a lovely person. But sometimes you get so distracted."

I wasn't sure, but I suspected this was her polite way of calling me dumb. Well, she could call me dumb all she wanted. She wasn't the one who had just determined the identity of our captor.

I had.

The voices were coming closer. They did not sound like party voices. They sounded like Genevieve. And another woman whose voice I recognized.

Vava Wilson, the cop.

"Scream!" I ordered to Sandy. "Bang on the door."

We screamed our hearts out and made our fists and

toes sore as we pounded mercilessly. Yet no one seemed to hear us.

"The furnace is on. It's drowning us out," Sandy said, alarmed. "They're turning away. They're going up the stairs. Please, people, don't do that. Come back, come back!"

What to do? Quick. Think, Bubbles. What resources were at hand? I didn't have my purse, so any hair-spray mechanism was out. My earrings were useless on the padlock outside our door.

And then it dawned on me. What gets people's attention more than anything else these days?

"Sandy. Light a cigarette."

"I only have one left. And it will burn really fast in this oxygen. We might even explode!"

"Just do it."

"You do it. I'm too scared." She handed me the cigarette and lighter, fumbling so badly she dropped them on the floor.

Ignoring all centipede concern, I felt around the dirty, wet concrete until I found them. Okay, this was the moment of truth. Now or never.

I put the cigarette in my mouth and flicked my Bic. A flame shot up.

"Wow." Sandy backed off.

I brought the cigarette to the door and exhaled. If I knew Genevieve—and, unfortunately, I did all too well—she'd smell smoke and put up a racket. Genevieve was a rabid antismoker. Or just plain rabid.

"It's not working. They can't smell it," Sandy whined.

"Just wait. It takes a while." I knew this from my days sneaking butts in my bedroom. As I recalled, it took Mama exactly four minutes from cigarette ignition to detect the smoke downstairs. And by then I had out my Lysol.

The furnace took a break from its incessant roaring. It was silent, except for the murmur of partygoers upstairs. I finished the cigarette to the bitter end and tried to push the butt under the door, taking solace that my vice had not been wasted.

That was when we heard it: *stomp, stomp, stomp*.

"They're coming back!" Sandy said.

"Don't say it. Scream it." We set to pounding and kicking and wouldn't give up even when we heard the commotion of people trying to break the lock on the other side.

Finally, the lock clanked to the floor and the door whooshed open. Sandy and I fell out, right onto Vava Wilson, Martin and Genevieve. Detective Burge was noticeably absent.

Martin shoved me aside and gathered up Sandy, who collapsed into hysterics, a far cry from her stoic presence in our cell. He was crying, too. They looked as one, two heads buried in each other's neck, sobbing and hugging. I had the feeling that Sandy could tell him she hired a spaceship to sleep with multiple aliens and Martin wouldn't have minded.

They'd be fine.

"I knew you were here," Genevieve said proudly. She was still in her Virgin Mary blue. "The folks upstairs said they hadn't seen hide nor hair of you. Your car wasn't in the parking lot or nothing, but I had faith. I knew you was in here even if your Camaro wasn't."

My car. He'd taken it. I was really beginning to dislike Santa Claus.

And then I remembered. "What time is it?"

Genevieve checked her watch. "Eight twenty."

Crap. I'd missed him. Unlike Genevieve, Stiletto had probably lost the faith and was off to Greece with Sabina.

"You okay?" Vava asked.

"As okay as can be expected." I felt dull, as if all energy had leached out of my body and into the basement drain of the Masonic temple.

I turned to Genevieve. "Thanks. If it hadn't been for your neurotic, paranoid delusions, Sandy and I would be dead."

"No thanks necessary or deserved." Genevieve put her hands on her broad hips. "I thought I knew the layout of this Masonic temple like the foxholes around Camp David. Turns out I was missing a few details. Damn those online maps."

Vava said, "Who locked you two in here?"

"Eric Wachowski," I said. I'd recognized his poor manicure from the night before at Hubba, Hubba. Also that cologne. It was unmistakable. Like they used to say in the commercials, an Old Spice man was unforgettable.

Vava's eyes widened. "You mean Eric the tech over in the medical examiner's office?"

"Exactly."

Vava reached for her radio. I held out my hand and stopped her. "But he didn't kill Debbie Shatsky. If you give me a chance, I'll prove to you who did."

Chapter Thirty-seven

It took less than twenty minutes of a conference call between Vava Wilson, Detective Burge, me and—oh, brother—Judge Hopkinton, for Hopkinton to grant us an emergency warrant so I could wear a wire. I had to hand it to the corrupt history of the Pennsylvania judicial system—sometimes crooked and lazy judges came in handy. Hopkinton didn't think twice.

Vava snaked a wire into my bra. "Nice bra," she said.

"JCPenney, two for eighteen bucks. Excellent support."

"I need support."

"Don't we all."

She clipped the wire to a recording device strapped on my back. It was nice to know I didn't have to worry about those ethical violations anymore, that I could go around being wired and kind of misrepresenting myself and I wouldn't have to face the wrath of Dix Notch.

Those *News-Times* days were sooo over.

It was well past nine when we pulled out of the station. I'd called Dan at the restaurant where the rehearsal dinner was under way without me and apologized for missing everything.

Get this. He didn't buy that I'd been locked up in the

Masonic temple until I explained about Hopkinton and that the police were about to arrest Debbie's real murderer. Then his mood improved because an arrested murder suspect meant a solid defendant to sue in Phil Shatsky's civil case, a defendant who wasn't Sandy.

He couldn't wait to hang up and call Phil right away, offering his services in the legal representation area. Money, that was all Dan really cared about.

With Vava's permission, I used her cell phone to call Stiletto. I got his housekeeper. He was gone. He'd left for JFK an hour ago.

I clicked the cell shut and told myself there would be plenty of time to cry when this was over.

"Man trouble?" Vava kept her eyes steady on the road, carefully negotiating the blinding snowstorm.

"Yup."

"Aren't you getting married tomorrow?"

I looked out the window, at the snow clouding up my view. I didn't answer her. I couldn't.

Eric Wachowski's car was in the driveway when Vava pulled to the curb, her lights off. We sat watching the kabuki play silhouetted in the plate-glass window.

"I'll be right behind you. There are already four officers stationed around the house." She gestured with her chin to a pine tree, where, sure enough, a man in a Windbreaker sat hunched.

The radio truck was parked a block away. All I had to do was turn on the transmitter and they'd be listening to my every word. It was go time.

I opened the door and got out, fumbling under my turtleneck to click on the transmitter as Vava had shown me. I adjusted my faux-rabbit-fur coat and marched up the front walk, doing my best to ignore the pair of eyes in the bush by the front door.

Sissy Dolan answered wearing a Christmassy bathrobe of green chenille. I bet she had a whole set of Christmas items—Christmas table runners, one of those crochet

Christmas toilet-paper covers. She even had a red Santa
Claus suit tossed over her wingback chair.

"Bubbles? What on earth are you doing here?"

"May I come in?"

"No!" Eric leaped up from the couch, flicking off the
television. He was dressed in a navy sweatshirt and
jeans. No Santa outfit for him tonight.

It was too late. I was in. And Sissy Dolan, though a
murderer, was too polite to let her hairdresser stand out
in a snowstorm during the Christmas season. She did,
however, draw the drapes over the sheer panels. Crafty
little thing.

"I'm sorry to bother you at home," I said, walking
over to Eric, for better reception. "It's just that I think
you may have picked up the wrong CD today. I was
hoping, maybe for a price, we could exchange."

"What?" He tried to smile and was so nervous he
couldn't lift the corners of his mouth. "What CD?"

"The one you took when you took my purse. It's the
Mahoken Town Budget and some really awesome Styx
tunes. I think you were after something different, unless
you, like me, can't get enough of 'Too Much Time on My
Hands,' though, I'm partial to 'Lady' myself."

He didn't answer. He went to a bedroom, opened a
drawer and came back with the CD, shoving it into the
laptop that was on a dining room table. While he did the
computer stuff, I said to Sissy, who was glaring, positively glaring, at me with hatred, "You should come in
for a wash and set. We're running a postholiday twenty-
percent discount now that the House of Beauty is re-
opening."

Sissy pressed her lips together.

On cue, "Fooling Yourself (The Angry Young Man)"
blared from the speakers.

"I LOVE that one," I trilled. "Crank it!"

"Shit." Eric flicked it off. "This isn't what I wanted."

"Good going!" Sissy said, eyeing my coat.

I bet she had a hunch I was wired. I had to get her talking, fast.

"What do you care about the CD, Sissy?" I said. "It's Eric who's going to jail if he gets caught. He's the one who killed Ern Bender with an overdose of methamphetamine and then tried to murder Sandy and me with oxygen. Those medical supplies really come in handy, say? Does the med school know you're using their equipment?"

Eric got up from the laptop and approached me. Those guys in prison were going to love him in the yard. Such a bod.

"What do you want?"

"What do I want?" I pressed my hand to my chest. "I think the question is, what do *you* want? And why?"

"I need Debbie's list."

I was keeping an eye on Sissy, who had slipped into the kitchen. "You mean the old Save-T Drug prescriptions?"

"Right. There was one more copy. There are names on it. People's lives could be ruined if it got out what they were taking."

"For example, in your case it was"—I took a wild guess—"steroids?"

"Steroids? Hah!" Sissy was back. And, darn it, if she wasn't holding the most adorable little pearl-handled pistol.

"Grandma, don't!" Eric ran to her and she motioned him away.

"Get over there, Eric. You were the one who got me in all this trouble. Put your hands up, Bubbles, where I can see them."

I looked at Eric and shook my head. What grandmothers will do for their grandsons.

"He's going to make an excellent heart surgeon someday. I've scrimped and saved to help him through college and med school. I'll be hog-tied if he can't do what he was born to do because of some brain-rotting disease."

Say it, you old bat. *Say the magic word so the posse outside can rescue me.*

"I know," I said, trying to egg her on. "I hate that disease, which is—"

She waved her hands. "Bah!"

Eric, meanwhile, was inching closer to her. He hadn't seemed so concerned with killing me earlier. I guessed he didn't want to make a mess on Grandma's rug.

"Get back, Eric." She was fast. "If I took care of that blackmailing Debbie Shatsky, you better be sure I can handle this dim bulb and make it look like an accident, too. I just gotta think, is all."

"Now, Sissy," I said, restraining my jubilation, "you're not saying Debbie's death wasn't accidental. It was just a misfortunate allergic reaction to latex. That's what the police said."

"The police don't know boo. They're too lazy to do the footwork, is their problem."

Did you hear that, Detective Burge?

"Everyone at the House of Beauty knew of Debbie's allergy. Christ, she told us often enough." Sissy clucked her tongue. "Everyone knew she come in on Mondays for her hair, too, boasting about her hoity-toity husband. I didn't have no beef with her until she called up Eric and threatened to expose his drug-abuse history to the whole med school board. Methadone. So what that he took methadone? Got him off heroin, didn't it?"

Eric's gaze was fixated on the part of my coat that had opened when I lifted my arms. "Shut up, Grandma. She's wired." He lunged for me. Grandma fired and I fell back, toppling a china figurine from an end table. It hit the floor with a resounding *crash!*

The front door was flung open. I heard the shouts: "Police! Put down your weapon." And I saw Eric stand, his hands up in the air, his body weak with resignation.

It was over. He'd killed Ern Bender and tried to kill Sandy and me to cover up an overprotective old lady's crime. And she'd killed Debbie so her star grandson, the first generation to go to college, wouldn't have his career ruined.

It was kind of sweet, when you thought about it, in a screwed-up steel-town kind of way. It made me cry.

Styx should write a song about it. It could be their comeback tune.

Chapter Thirty-eight

The star file was password protected, unfortunately. After retrieving the CD from the Order of the Eastern Star plaque, where I had left it, Vava Wilson took it to headquarters and fiddled around with some possible combinations. FATAL turned out to be the user name. WHEAT, the password.

What it opened was a treasure trove of personal information that, as Ern Bender had indicated, could bring down the entire town. I wasn't allowed to see the whole list. However, I did learn that a certain hairdresser who had just opened up a swanky salon in the warehouse district was HIV positive, a fact that could have completely shut down Jeffrey Andre's salon if his immunity status had been made public—as Debbie had threatened.

Debbie had managed to suck out over ten grand from Jeffrey Andre, who was a good friend of Phil and Mark's, the two men G saw socializing in Andre's back room. This went far to explain why Phil was so concerned about the list. He knew Debbie had been blackmailing his buddy and he was trying to help.

The only other name Vava divulged was Dix Notch's. All I can say is I hoped he owned stock in Merck, what with all the Viagra he'd consumed over the years. And the antibaldness medication? No wonder his scalp was so red. Rogaine overdose.

I did not bother to read the papers on Saturday morning to find out how they'd covered Eric Wachowski's arrest and the booking of his grandmother for murder. Sissy Dolan admitted to switching the glues; her grandson admitted to dumping the evidence in the toilet so Sandy would appear guilty and then calling in various tips to keep the investigation off his granny.

Anyway, I had more pressing concerns on Saturday morning.

Like getting married.

The House of Beauty was closed. Again. This time, not for murder or negligence or an expired license, but because Sandy was getting everyone ready for my wedding. Already a black limousine was parked outside, waiting. Periodically a chauffeur in a driver's coat and cap would get out and brush off the lightly falling snow from the car's hood. I'd never ridden in a limo before—well, not by choice. Anyway, my car was still missing, so I was, um, stuck with the limo.

"This is it." Sandy stood over me. We exchanged glances in the mirror. "You look fabulous, if that's any consolation."

I did look fabulous. Sandy had done up my hair in a classic twist and stuck in sprigs of baby's breath. I was like a snow queen in the gown Mama had bought from Loehmann's, with the halo of tiny white flowers and the real pearl earrings from my grandmother Saladunas.

Mama and Genevieve were already at Asa Packer Chapel at Lehigh University. Dan had arranged for them to arrive in a separate limousine. Jane was waiting outside in the limo. Now it was just Sandy and me, Sandy in a deep green satin dress that looked beautiful with her pale coloring and hair.

"I . . . I want to say . . ." Tears choked her voice. She put her hand on my shoulder and I put my hand on hers.

She didn't have to say the words out loud. I knew what she was thinking. "It's okay. You don't have to thank me."

"No, it's not that." She wiped her nose with the back of her arm and untied the apron from around her neck. "I want you to know that if you ever need to get away from him, I'm here for you. Any time of day or night. You can count on me, Bubbles."

I spun around in my chair. Sandy's eyes were red rimmed. It was a hell of a thing for her to say minutes before I was supposed to get married.

"That bad, say?"

She nodded. I could tell she was trying hard not to cry so her mascara wouldn't run. "That bad."

"I don't want to marry a man I'll have to run away from."

Sandy shook her head.

The doorbell tinkled and Jane walked in, outrageously underdressed for this kind of weather. She was in a strapless red satin dress and her hair was streaked to match. "Are you coming, or what? I've been out in that limo waiting for hours."

Minutes, but who's counting?

I checked with Sandy who nodded in encouragement.

"Jane," I said, sliding out of the chair with a rustle, "I have something to tell you."

She sucked in a breath.

"I can't marry your father."

Sandy reached out and gripped my hand while I waited for Jane's reaction.

"I don't love him, Jane. I don't even . . . *like* him. I was only doing it for you and that's wrong. That's no role model. You need a mother who follows her own heart and listens to her conscience."

Jane stood stock-still, rigid. Then she let out a breath and exclaimed, "Oh . . . my . . . God!" She collapsed onto

Sandy's wicker couch in front of the window, still boarded and taped from the shooting. "I can't believe it."

I rushed over to her. "Don't be mad—"

She sat up. "Mad? I'm not mad. I'm fucking relieved."

"Relieved?" I was so relieved myself that I didn't admonish her for swearing—another bad-mother moment for me.

"Living in Saucon Valley? Hello? It was going to be hell. I'd be trapped out there without my friends or my hood and with you two biting and snapping at each other." She arched her back and unzipped her dress. "Can I get out of this now? It totally pinches."

I looked at Sandy in astonishment. She was smiling. "Isn't that what your mother always told you? To thine own self be true."

"You mean it?" I said to Jane. "You're not just being nice?"

"I'm a little old for wanting Mommy and Daddy to live together. I'm pretty much an adult, in case you hadn't noticed."

I'd noticed. With a burst of exuberance, I wrapped my arms around her and squeezed her so tightly she gasped for air. "I love, love, love you."

She broke free and held me by the shoulders. "Ditto, Mom. I love you, too. Big-time. I'm proud of you for having the guts to say no."

With this, Sandy began bawling openly. I joined her even though all this crying was going to wreak havoc on our makeup.

Jane said, "You two really are out of control—you know that? By the way, the wedding starts in five minutes. FYI."

Sandy handed me a box of Kleenex. "You better get over there, quick. You want me to go with you?"

"That's okay." I grabbed a handful of tissues. "I don't need the support."

"I meant to redo your makeup in the car."

Of course. Sandy had her priorities. "Not that, either. Dan will have to see me as I am."

"That's crazy talk." She tossed me her makeup bag. It weighed, like, five pounds. "If you're gonna break up with Dan, you gotta look killer good."

No truer words had ever been spoken.

The limo let me off out front of Asa Packer Chapel. G was outside waiting for Jane. He was dressed in a bright purple tux with a pink frilled shirt and spats. It was my only regret in canceling this wedding, that I could not see him walk her down the aisle wearing that getup.

"Can you get Dan?" I said.

"Calling it off are we?"

I nodded. G checked his watch. "Damn. An hour ago and I would have hit pay dirt. I think Sinkler's gold, though. He had you bagging out right before it started."

It was encouraging to know someone had profited from my misfortune. I waited in the foyer for Dan, nervously twisting and untwisting the folds of my dress.

He burst in from the double doors.

"What is it now? Last-minute jitters?" His hands were on his hips. He was wearing a very nice, very expensive tux with a red rose in his lapel.

"I think you know," I said, resolving not to fold. "I can't go through with this."

"Back. Forth. Back. Forth. Ding. Dong. Ding. Dong," he mocked me. "Just say okay, and we'll start."

"No. I can't say okay. This is it, Dan. I'll suffer whatever consequence I have to. I'm not getting married. You paid off Dr. Caswell to write up that bogus report on me. You threatened to take Jane. You have pulled every trick possible and I'm through playing your games."

He took stock of me. Whatever could be said about Dan, no one disputed his courtroom abilities. His strengths were being able to recognize defeat and calculating his next move to his next win. "All right. So you're not gonna marry me. Not today."

"Not ever."

"I'd think about it if I were you. This could get ugly."

I inhaled deeply. "You mean about custody over Jane."

"I mean what I mean. Just know you've had fair warning." He shot his cuffs, flashing his diamond cuff links. "You're in for the fight of your life, toots. You'll lose everything you've got."

I knew he was right. Dan was just that weirdly obsessive and vengeful.

"The thing is, Dan, I don't have anything except Jane and my house. I don't even have a job. Can't get blood from a stone."

He smirked. "Christ. You have no idea, do you?"

"Idea about what?"

Behind us the organ played "Morning Has Broken" once more. I could hear rustling in the pews and murmuring. Guests were getting restless.

Dan regarded me, calculating, always calculating, his next move. "You'll find out soon enough, so I might as well tell you—"

The door opened and G peeked out. "You gotta say something, man. Folks are talking. Everyone wants to know how they made out in the pool."

"Bye, Dan," I said. "I'll leave this to you."

Dan hesitated. "We'll talk."

"Sure," I said, though I was thinking, *No way.*

With one last, longing look, Dan turned and followed G inside.

It was over. I didn't have to marry Dan. I was free.

I breathed in and out, opened the heavy wooden doors to the new world awaiting me. Snow blanketed Lehigh's campus, covering the large oak trees and sloping lawns with a new white coating. The air was fresh and clean.

I walked slowly down the stone steps. With each step, I thought, *I am free. I am free. I am free.*

The driver of the limo stepped out of the car and rushed around the front. I was about to tell him he didn't need to open the rear door for me when I noticed there was something small and gray in his hand. Keys?

Then I watched as if in slow motion as he lifted his hand and pointed the gray thing straight at me. For some reason, I couldn't move. I was mesmerized, wondering what he'd do next. And then I saw the yellow flash, right before I heard the clap of a gunshot and felt the searing heat, followed by the unfathomable sensation of overwhelming pain.

I'd been shot.

Chapter Thirty-nine

"She's down!"

His voice came from right by my ear, so loud it hurt. My face was hard against the stone, my lips tasting snow and salt, my body racked with the force of being thrown onto rock-hard slate. I'd like to know what it was with men shoving me to the ground lately. Must have been repressed hostility toward blond hairdressers or something.

Nearby, a tire screeched, spraying snow and grime over both of us.

I thought, *This is a ruined dress and Mama probably hasn't even paid for it yet.* I could see the headline now: *Runaway Bride Shot in Stolen Dress: Mother Pleads Poor Eyesight.*

"He's gone," Stiletto said. He happened to be lying on me, shielding me with his body. "Are you okay?"

That, I decided, was the kind of stupid question people asked when they had nothing else to say. I mean, I was eating gravel—literally—and snowy gravel at that. Plus, I'd just been shot.

"I think I've been hit," I said. "Right below my shoulder."

Stiletto touched my arm and I could feel warm stickiness. I knew without looking that it was blood.

"Let's get you inside." He called over to someone named Barry and told him to have the church evacuated except for "the family" because "they'll need protection, too."

The family? But why would my family need protection and from whom? It was as if I'd suddenly stepped into a *Godfather* movie, what with all the shooting and talk about protecting the family. It wouldn't have shocked me to see Al Pacino walk by in a shiny suit.

There was lots of commotion, lots of people running out of the chapel and shouting. Everyone was quickly ushered past me. This was going to take a lot of explaining back at the House of Beauty, how I ended up underneath another man—Stiletto, no less—in plain daylight two seconds after I was supposed to marry Dan. I wasn't sure the blue hairs would buy the old I'd-been-shot-at excuse, seeing as it had been used by every scared bride in Lehigh before.

A man with very short hair and black Ray-Bans knelt beside me. I recognized him right off as the Iraq war vet who'd saved me at the Christmas-tree lot, the anti-Christmas lobby conspiracy theorist. But why would he be at my wedding? Maybe I'd suffered a head wound as well. Nothing made sense.

"All clear," he said to Stiletto. Then, nodding to me, he said, "It's an honor to serve you again, your—"

"Not yet, Barry." Stiletto rolled off me. "We need to get her inside first. Don't know how many others there are."

"Good point. I'll cover."

Barry and Stiletto helped me up. As soon as I stood, my arm started throbbing. It was killing me. Seeing my wound, Stiletto slid out of his jacket and pulled off his black T-shirt. I curiously noted that when I saw his bronzed chest bared in the cold December air my pain temporarily subsided. Perhaps this was a medical technique hospitals could use instead of dosing patients with Advil: parading men with six-pack abs past women in, well, *need*.

Holding one end of his shirt in his teeth, Stiletto tore it in two. He took one half and wrapped it tightly around my wound. The other half he used as a tourniquet.

"Here," he said, taking my arm and laying it across his broad, naked shoulder. "You'll need to keep it elevated."

Wasn't going to argue with that.

He grasped me firmly about the waist, pulling me tightly to his warm body, and led me into the church. Barry kept his hand on the gun hidden beneath his coat as he scanned the perimeter with expert eyes.

Barry might have been an Iraq war vet. I'd buy that. But I had doubts that he made a living selling Christmas trees. Most Christmas-tree salesmen didn't have FBI badges on their belts.

I said, "FBI?"

Barry shrugged. "It'll all be clear soon enough."

Once we were inside the chapel foyer, Barry slammed shut and bolted the door. It seemed absurdly festive in the chapel in contrast to the violence that had broken out minutes before. The pews were still adorned with white bows and clusters of white roses. The altar was draped in white and there were flowers everywhere. With Dan's money, Mama had heeded no expense. I'd never seen—or smelled—so many irises, sweet peas, peonies, orchids and, my favorite, lilies of the valley, all in white.

Frosted glass Christmas balls hung from a large, full green pine, which was also decorated with silver ribbons and the teeniest white lights. The church was aglow with lights and dozens of lit white candles. With the white runner up the aisle, the dark chapel had transformed into a romantic winter fairy land. It was magical.

Mama and Jane were in the front row, gaping at me. Jane screamed, "Mom!"

"I'm okay, honey. Nothing but a graze." I eyed the two men in suits at either end of the pews, guns holstered across their buttoned-down white shirts. They each had white things stuck in their ears like they worked for the Secret Service.

Dan was nowhere to be found.

Okay, this was weird. What the hell was going on? It was as if we were in a militarized zone.

"All secure there, Butch?" Genevieve appeared out of nowhere in a crazily flowered dress holding not a musket, but what I was pretty sure was one of those Russian AK-47s. Now that was what you called a mistake. "I've got the perimeter deloused except for the windows. Tiny Nuts is still at large."

"Who's Tiny Nuts?" I asked. "And where'd you get that gun?"

Genevieve looked not to Stiletto or me, but to Barry. "Has the unit been apprised?"

"Not yet," Stiletto said, grinning. "Tiny Nuts. That code name still cracks me up, Genevieve."

"Call 'em as I see 'em."

Stiletto escorted me to the altar steps. I sat down next to him and faced Mama and Jane. Mama was also in a flowered dress with a black plastic purse in her lap. I could spy the tops of her knee-highs below her hem. I was slightly insulted that for my wedding she hadn't sprung for the fancy whole-leg kind of stockings, though maybe they didn't make them in her size—square.

"This is it, Bubbles," she said, sniffling. "The day I've waited my whole life for."

"I'm not getting married, Mama. Didn't you hear?"

With this, she burst into tears. Jane took her hand, giving it a little pat.

"Do you know what this is about?" I asked her.

Jane said, "Kind of. It's not bad. Well, it might be bad now, but it could be good. It could be really cool if, uh, you survive."

Teenagers.

I turned to Stiletto. "Do you know?"

"I've known for quite some time."

"You wanna tell me?"

Stiletto looked up at Barry. "Do I finally have the goddamn authorization?"

"Go ahead. I'll back you up if Washington bitches," Barry said.

"Washington!" I screeched. "What's Washington got to do with my wedding? Or the Debbie Shatsky homicide or whatever's going on?"

Stiletto slowly took my arm from around his shoulder. "The guys in Santa Claus disguises who've been shooting you have nothing to do with Debbie Shatsky or your wedding or any newspaper article you've ever written, Bubbles."

Mama's whole body was heaving with tears. Genevieve, meanwhile, was slinking from window to window with the ease of a trained assassin.

"Does this have something to do with the stolen dress at Loehmann's? Because I might be able to scrounge up enough money to at least pay half. They don't have to shoot me."

Stiletto smiled. "This has nothing to do with Loehmann's. The men who've been shooting at you are from the Lithuanian Liberty Union."

At first I thought he was talking about my high school, Liberty. "I don't remember many Lithuanians there. At least not anyone who was organized."

"Kazys Grimzakas," Mama said. "He is the most evil, the most ruthless bastard on Earth. Heads the Lithuanian Liberty Union." Then she made a gesture otherwise known as "flipping the bird," but when I was growing up, we'd call it the "Polish Hello."

"Kazys Grimzakas is based in Lithuania," Stiletto said patiently. "And the Lithuanian Liberty Union is an extreme-right-wing, superviolent organization, which, among other outrageous things, claims the Holocaust never existed."

"Creeps," Jane said, folding her arms.

"Oh, it existed, all right," I said. "I saw *Schindler's List* on cable. There was original footage. How could you not believe it existed?"

"Because they're fascist, Mom."

"Okay, so they have a fetish. But what does that have to do with me?"

Stiletto and Jane exchanged glances of disbelief. Then he said, "Even more than Jews or democracy or fairness, there's something else Kazys Grimzakas and his band of criminals in the LLU hate."

A greasy black head popped up in the window to our right. Dan was hopping up and down outside, trying to peek in the chapel. "Dan!" I exclaimed.

"Tiny Nuts!" Genevieve sited her gun. "Jump higher so I can get you where it counts. Those are awful small targets." She was about to pull the trigger when Barry ambushed her from behind, not an easy feat when you considered Barry weighed half of what she did and Genevieve had an awful hankering to blow away something with that machine gun.

After the commotion settled down, Stiletto continued. "What Kazys Grimzakas fears is the rise of the Lithuanian aristocracy. There's nothing the Lithuanian people love and revere more than their King Mindaugas. Even though he reigned as far back as the thirteenth century, for them he is their leader of mythical proportions. Almost like their King Arthur. And if a person could claim to be a direct descendant of King Mindaugas, he'd be put on a throne today.

"Kazys Grimzakas will go to any length to make sure that doesn't happen. He has publicly vowed to assassinate anyone with legitimate claims to the throne."

"So?"

"So, Bubbles," Mama said, "your father was related to King Mindaugas. So am I."

I swallowed hard. This was my worst nightmare come true. "You mean I'm . . . inbred?"

Jane said, "Isn't it evident?"

"No, you're not inbred. Not much, anyway." Mama moved forward in her seat. "Listen, Bubbles, let me cut to the bone. You know how you get down on yourself, how you think you're a bad mother, how you figured you'd never be anything more than a high school dropout, a graduate of Two Guys Community College and a hairdresser at a small salon. Remember that?"

"Uh-huh." That was my life all right.

"And remember how I kept telling you that you were special and you shouldn't think of yourself that way? I used to call you my little Lithuanian princess, right?"

The pieces were beginning to fall into place. I couldn't believe it was true. "Yes."

"Well, I wasn't lying. You *are* a Lithuanian princess." Mama's lower lip quivered as she fought back tears. "Not just mine, everyone's. You are the only rightful living heir to the Lithuanian throne. You and you alone."

I was stunned. I didn't know what to say as I watched Genevieve carry her AK-47 from window to window, as the Secret Service men talked to one another through their microscopic mouthpieces.

It was true. I was a princess.

"And you?" I said to Stiletto.

Stiletto shrugged. "Interpol."

"All along?"

He nodded slightly, a bittersweet half smile on his lips. "All along, Bubbles. I never was a photojournalist. That was just a cover."

"But?" I searched his face, trying to find if he loved me or if our nights together and his marriage proposal had been him just doing his job. Part of the cover.

"Well, let's not just sit here, people," Genevieve hollered, throwing down her gun. "We have to hail our rightful monarch. We are in a place of worship, after all. Better crown her now while her head's still on her shoulders."

And before I could protest, Stiletto lifted me up so I

was standing before a line of my first subjects—Mama, Genevieve and Jane—each in a curtsy.

Next to me, Stiletto opened a black velvet box, revealing a magnificent platinum tiara of sapphires and diamonds, which formed into a cross and an upside down M at the center. It was the jewelry I'd seen Stiletto pick up the other night for Sabina, though I never saw anything quite that magnificent in Musselman's glass cases.

"The royal crest of King Mindaugas," Stiletto said, placing the tiara on my head. "It is seven hundred years old and the one remaining piece of the missing crown jewels, worth an estimated seventy million dollars. It can be worn only by the one true heir to the Lithuanian throne."

"It's where it belongs," Mama said quietly.

The tiara was so heavy on my head it was giving me a headache. Not anything like the plastic tiaras we used for dress up as kids.

"To Princess Bubbles!" Genevieve shouted. "All bow to Princess Bubbles!"

And so they did, even the Secret Service agents, even Stiletto, still naked from the waist up. That would be a royal decree when I took the throne, I decided, to insist that Stiletto—all good-looking men, for that matter—walk around naked from the waist up.

Oh, and that the official Lithuanian national anthem should be changed from *"Tautos Himnas"* to "Too Much Time on My Hands" by Styx and that hot pink would be the national color. Maybe funnel cake could be the national food. Either that or pierogies, though the Polish had stolen that one right off.

This was going to be fun!

As long as Kazys Grimzakas didn't get to me first.

Read the award-winning
Bubbles Yablonsky
series by
Sarah Strohmeyer

It doesn't help that her name's Bubbles.
Or that she's a gum-snapping hairdresser.
Or that she's saddled with a sleazy
ex-hubby, a precocious daughter and a
shoplifting mother. What can a beautician
do to add new highlights to her image?
Now, with a well-muscled photographer by
her side, Bubbles is playing star sleuth.

BUBBLES UNBOUND
0-451-20844-8

BUBBLES IN TROUBLE
0-451-20850-1

BUBBLES ABLAZE
0-451-21217-7

BUBBLES A BROAD
0-451-41177-3

BUBBLES BETROTHED
0-451-21568-0

Available wherever books are sold or at
penguin.com